CASCADE

For Lucy,
With best wishes
for the future
Pete
30.09.2021

By

PETER HARPER

Copyright © Peter Harper 2021
This book is sold subject to the condition that it shall not, by way of trade or otherwise, be lent, resold, hired out, or otherwise circulated without the publisher's prior consent in any form of binding or cover other than that in which it is published and without a similar condition including this condition being imposed on the subsequent publisher.
The moral right of Peter Harper has been asserted.
ISBN-13: 978-1540460264
ISBN-10: 1540460266

In memory of my Father
'…who opened my eyes.'

Daylight Thrillers
www.ricochet-universal.com

CONTENTS

PROLOGUE 1
PART 1 IDENTITY TRAUMA 6
    CHAPTER 1 6
    CHAPTER 2 18
    CHAPTER 3 24
    CHAPTER 4 40
    CHAPTER 5 55
PART 2 AND THEN CAME REVENGE 83
    CHAPTER 6 83
    CHAPTER 7 93
    CHAPTER 8 112
    CHAPTER 9 124
    CHAPTER 10 145
    CHAPTER 11 153
    CHAPTER 12 176
    CHAPTER 13 189
    CHAPTER 14 197
    CHAPTER 15 206
    CHAPTER 16 235
    CHAPTER 17 250
    CHAPTER 18 271
    CHAPTER 19 282
    CHAPTER 20 298
    CHAPTER 21 308
    CHAPTER 22 330
    CHAPTER 23 337

CHAPTER 24	356
CHAPTER 25	367
CHAPTER 26	392
CHAPTER 27	401
CHAPTER 28	421

Special thanks to those dear people who generously gave up their time to tackle each draft. To say that I am indebted to them for their invaluable comments can only remain forever an understatement.

This is a work of fiction. Names, characters, businesses, organizations, places, events and incidents either are the product of the author's imagination or are used fictitiously. Any resemblance to actual persons, living or dead, events, or locales is entirely coincidental.

Take every chance
Drop every fear
– Theodor Seuss Geisel

PROLOGUE

…thirty-eight years ago…

Kabérou, People's Democratic Republic of Séroulé, West Africa

Mama always seemed to call her at a difficult moment. Always! Well, today Mama was going to have to wait. The local boys had told her she couldn't climb as high as them. So climbing trees had now become an important business, because she was going to watch each of their shiny faces drop to the ground in defeat in front of all the girls.

'Zinsa! Zinsa! Come quickly.'

Zinsa dug her fingertips even harder into the bark, crisscrossed and knobbly like the skin of a crocodile, and hauled herself further up the tree, inching ever closer into the shea's tangled and secretive canopy. The second bough would take her above the mound of excavated earth and rock, but it was the third bough she wanted to reach, extending her view of the savannah woodland that brought perfect joy to her. A living dreamscape, vibrant with wildlife she was anxious to befriend.

'Zinsa! Zinsa! Zinsa!...'

While a curious trail of dust lay across the horizon, Zinsa concerned herself more with her siblings as she sat astride the second bough to catch her breath. They were huddled together on the retreat's whitewashed terrace, her mother still calling her, her voice fading as the rotor-blades on the helicopter between the mound and the retreat began to whine and turn. And Papa now, arms splayed, ushering them like chicks towards the giant red insect.

Could it be…? In a flash, it came to Zinsa. A party! Hadn't it been mentioned? But in the sky? Mama always said that when they came to Kabérou for their vacation, the President of Séroulé would act as crazy as a coconut. She wasn't entirely sure how a coconut could act crazy, but everyone laughed whenever Mama said that, so just to be 'normal' she'd laugh too. Papa *was* crazy, though. And today, something brilliantly different!

Zinsa set her feet on the bough below, and the skinny branch below that, hearing quite suddenly a different noise beyond the mound to that of the helicopter – like lots of popping. A sort of *tat-a-tat-tat-*

tat, amidst shouting and the occasional scream that made her spine tingle. Was everyone *drunk*, or what?

A quick jump down from the tree, and Zinsa hurried up the mound, careful in her haste of the spear grass, razor sharp and just waiting to scratch her legs. *A party in the sky!* The roof of the timber retreat edged into view, but why…why had the helicopter's blades stopped? And now soldiers, everywhere. One of them was dragging the pilot she knew as Uncle Tommy towards the terrace, his body writhing in the dust until another man wielding a rifle came over and smashed it against his face.

Bewilderment fused with panic, and Zinsa felt her chest tighten, catching her breath. She feverishly scanned for her family amid the jumble of soldiers. Papa and everyone seemed to have disappeared. Then a frightful shriek made her turn her head. Two maids were being shoved out of the house. One of the soldiers on the terrace raised a gun, a tall man with a green cap. He let the maids tremble a moment longer, and then he shot them – in the face, both of them. They dropped straight to the ground, what was left of their screams nothing but an ethereal echo over the savannah.

Zinsa found herself edging away, when one of the men noticed her, his steady glare making her mouth drier than the desert sand. She watched him shout something over to the tall man and point in her direction. The man left the terrace, his sinewy physique advancing towards her with the ferocity of a panther tearing in on its prey. Zinsa spun round and hurled herself down the back of the mound, gaining such momentum as to unbalance her. When her foot caught a rodent's burrow it flung her to the ground, alongside her favourite tree. The man's feet pounded ever closer. She wriggled into some long grass, where she lay without a sound, her heartbeat thudding agonizingly in her throat…

He seemed to have stopped. A moment of hope – until his menacing breath hovered above her. Zinsa kept herself 'lifeless', face-down. A hand seized her dress, ripping the neckline. He shouldn't be doing that. He was a *bad* man! Her fingertips brushed against a stick. She seized it and whipped round with no specific aim, but felt a squish as the stick speared the man's left eye-socket. His head snapped backed from her, the reflex tossing aside his cap. Squealing like a snared hyena, he threw the stick away from himself, a dribble of watery blood skating across his cheek.

Zinsa scrabbled to her feet, and ran. In her sights she had the beginnings of a valley, and a forest with the tallest of trees bordering a river she knew as the

Tégine. The forest and its animals scared her, but the man was still screaming, and in-between his screams he was shouting: '*Get her!*' Zinsa didn't look back. Hidden from view by the mound, she just kept running, harder and faster, down into the forest, tripping and falling as she went, cutting her hands and knees.

PART 1

IDENTITY TRAUMA

Oxford
…present day…

CHAPTER 1

The taxi swung right at the lights at the bottom of The High and into Longwall Street. Just outside the medieval city wall stood the post-graduate college of St Thomas Aquinas, with its numerous – and for the most part overly grotesque – gargoyles that jeered down at passersby from an overcast February sky.

Instead of the gargoyles, Shani Bălcescu wanted to visualise her parents. They should be here with her on this special day. But lately it had become something of an ordeal to visualise them, because she was now older than them – four years older, in fact, than her mother. That's when the photographs ended, a couple of months after her mother had turned twenty. There were no more after that, of either of them.

Shani glanced at the girl who had befriended her when they were 'freshers' at Corpus Christi. 'Thanks for coming with me, Christina. Feels life-changing, you know?'

'We're just down the road,' said Christina. 'Don't forget, I'm heading out to Yale for six months. It'll just be Jenny and Angie left at the house after that.'

The cab driver made a U-turn opposite the octagonal bell tower, and the larger than life-sized statue of the Dominican priest the college had been named after, arms spread – Christ-like – as he judiciously surveyed the cityscape.

'Bit scary,' remarked Christina, following Shani's gaze from the cab window. 'The size of it.'

'St Aquinas was one of the good guys,' said Shani. 'Influential when it came to both theology and philosophy.'

The driver dealt with the cases himself, carrying them through the wicket gate set in a pair of Gothic-styled oaken doors some fifteen feet in height.

'What about keys?' asked Christina. 'Do you need

to get any from the lodge?'

Shani paid the driver, adding a tip for the extra toil. 'The Home Bursar handed me a set last week.'

Acknowledging the porter in the lodge with a cheery wave, Shani led Christina away from the vaulted porch, under a grandiose Tudor arch and into the front quad with its symmetrical pathways and stained-glass chapel.

'I must be crazy,' said Christina, looking around herself, blonde hair swirling. 'Three years I've been in Oxford and I've never visited this college. It's beautiful.'

They veered from a colonnade, the pillars of which supported a gnarled vine, and climbed a narrow staircase of quarried stone to the second floor. Shani opened the envelope she'd been given and fished out her study key.

Christina followed Shani into the room, before putting a hand to her mouth. 'Oh, Shani, *look* at the view.'

Shani joined Christina at the quartet of mullioned windows. She'd seen the view before, when shown the room by the Home Bursar. And yes, it felt as breathtaking now as it did then: the Cecil Brampton Library at the far end of the Priory Quadrangle, complemented by a sundial in gold and azure set between sculpted pinnacles.

Christina pointed. 'Can you imagine a clear sky at night, stars twinkling and a crescent moon, little goblins running along the parapet, peeping over the crenulations – or whatever the gaps are called. It would be like something out of a Disney film.' Turning excitedly to Shani: 'Who's your supervisor?'

'Harry Rothwell,' said Shani. 'I only went to a couple of his lectures last term. He'll probably kill me for it.'

'I've heard the name. Canadian, isn't he?'

'I think he's lived much of his life over here.' Shani put her shoulder bag on the swivel chair beside the desk and checked the time on her phone. 'I've a meeting with him in half an hour. But you know...' And then she sighed, already sensing the anticipated change in her mood. 'I just want to be invisible when it comes to the Fellows. For a while, at least.'

'Invisible?' Christina left the window, a slight frown on her brow. 'What are you saying?'

'When we rolled up at the college in the taxi, I thought of my parents. They should be here to see this, my first day as a Fellow of St Thomas Aquinas. I don't want to say it, but I might be building up to an episode. I haven't had one for ages, have I?'

Christina reached out to her. 'Shani – you'll have

me in tears.'

Shani welcomed Christina's embrace. 'I'm trying to be brave,' she said, 'but it's hard. Ever since I found those images on that idiot's laptop it's brought up a load of stuff that I thought I'd dealt with, or buried.'

'Shani, don't do this to yourself.'

'I know I have Andrei as my adoptive father, and I should be grateful, but there's still a massive hole. And it seems to have got a whole lot bigger these past few weeks. Why should that happen? I don't get it.'

'Shani, listen to me.' Christina put her hands on Shani's shoulders and met her eyes directly. 'Don't beat yourself up, not today of all days. You're meeting Rothwell. I'm going now over to Merton to collect my DPhil papers. Give you time to gather your thoughts – positive thoughts, that is. I'll call you later.'

Shani walked with Christina over to the door and gave her a parting hug. 'Just me being me. I'm fine, really.'

'Promise?'

'Promise. Now go. Speak later.'

Closing the door, Shani went to take a look at the adjoining bedroom. The bare walls made her feel she was in a hostel. Of course, it was far from that. She was reminded of the people living on the streets, and how fortunate she was. And yet, such awareness did little to quash her rising sense of aloneness. She turned back a corner on the duvet to make the bed more welcoming, and looked again at the heap of luggage in the centre of her study, trying her utmost not to give in to floods of tears.

*　*　*

Drawing her Barbour jacket around her shoulders, Shani dashed through a light rain shower back along the West Quadrangle and into Staircase VI. On the fourth and uppermost floor she remembered to turn left, into a corridor with a low ceiling.

Professor Harry Rothwell, said the sign above the door.

The corridor smelt musty. Like an old leather shoe left to dry from the rain. She tidied her hair, and knocked on the door. While waiting for a response, she caught some of Oxford's skyline from an arched window, seeing St Edmund Hall and the neoclassical quadrangles of Queen's, the sedate toll of a bell floating across from somewhere in that direction.

A creak of a floorboard, and the door swung open. Shani faced an immediate shock of white hair and a green sweater with a gaping hole, before Professor Rothwell stood back.

'Enter.'

Shani did so, having hoped for a more cordial

greeting rather than a terse 'instruction'. Perhaps he saw her as a nuisance. Something the college had saddled him with for the next four years – regrettably, of course.

'Your jacket.'

Shani handed it over and stepped hesitantly into the centre of the study, the musty smell of the corridor replaced by a whiff of pipe tobacco – or that of a cigar, she supposed. Virtually encompassing her, uneven stacks of books sought to touch the ceiling, as though each was in competition with the other.

Her eyes quickly came to rest on a faded poster, emblazoned with the words:

ALCOHOL,
TOBACCO,
FIREARMS,
WHO'S BRINGING THE CHIPS?

Shani found herself smiling at the poster's off-the-wall candour. Maybe Rothwell was just being Rothwell. That she would get used to his gruffness, if that's what it was. From her experience, you either clicked or you didn't with these people. And if you didn't... *God, help me*, she thought, and felt her mouth dry up.

'When did you arrive?' asked Harry Rothwell, rummaging in a drawer next to his desk.

'About half an hour ago,' said Shani. His accent was still very much Canadian. She'd read somewhere he was born and educated in Montreal, before making the switch to Oxford.

Harry came back to her with two silver Christmas crackers, both with red bows. 'We'll pull them simultaneously. You get a louder bang that way.'

Shani stared at him, speechless, seeing a lined face disrupted by a youthful glint that gave warmth to his steel-grey eyes. Was Rothwell *really* this idiosyncratic? She'd heard stories, of course, and now regarded herself as perhaps being privileged to be essentially witnessing it.

A couple of strident snaps, and the contents of the crackers became visible.

'A screwdriver,' announced Harry. 'I'd better give that to Sabine. She's in charge of DIY, after my attempt to install a letterbox to accommodate A4-sized envelopes resulted in the front door having to be replaced. A rather gratifying miscalculation on my part, I've since realised. And you?'

Shani held up a bottle opener.

'Could be useful.' Harry tossed the remnants of his cracker onto his desk. 'Here's my gag: Why can't a bicycle stand up by itself?'

'I'm not sure,' said Shani, wishing to God she knew the answer. Was he testing her? Like the breadth of her wit, or something? 'I mean it can't, anyway.'

'Because it's two tired. Now yours.'

Shani glanced down at the slip of paper in her hand, and wondered whether they were going to make themselves look completely ridiculous by wearing the paper hats. 'What do these words have in common?' she asked. 'Eye, civic, level, madam?'

'Madam, or madman? My hearing's not what it used to be.'

'Madam.'

Harry paced his study. 'What do these words have in common…? An obvious catch here somewhere, wouldn't you say?'

'I'm not allowed to give you any clues,' dared Shani, finding herself actually wanting to thank Harry for welcoming her with such cheer.

Harry threw up his hands. 'Answer, please.'

'Read backwards, they make the same word.'

'Dismal.' Harry shook his head. 'I should have pounced on that,' he said, waving Shani to an armchair, the armrests of which virtually threadbare. 'You were at Corpus Christi, I recall.'

'That's where I graduated.'

'Yes, very good. Delightful college.' Harry continued to pace back and forth. 'The Pelican Sundial, most striking. I would even venture better than our own. Although, had ours not been moved from the West Quadrangle it would have remained accurate to within a kitten's whisker – so I've been told.' Harry briefly halted his pacing to peer out of a leaded light window. 'I understand you're from the Czech Republic?'

'Yes. Prague, itself,' said Shani.

'But not wishing to be overly personal, the tone of your skin suggests…?'

'My mother was adopted,' interrupted Shani, saving her supervisor from being curious. 'She was born in Rwanda.'

'Ah, I see.' Harry left the window. 'Well, I have to say I've never supervised a Czech before. A first for me. That aside, I can tell you my peers were rather keen for you to be a Fellow of St Aquinas, and so now it's down to us both to prove them right.' Harry lifted her Barbour jacket from the hook on the door. 'My dear, I have to dash to Oriel. A lecture, of sorts.'

Shani took the jacket, hoping to have stayed longer.

'We'll discuss your thesis another day,' reassured

Harry, as if sensing his supervisee's disappointment. 'You've sketched it out?'

'I'm just at that stage,' said Shani, trying to sound enthusiastic against the failed attempts she'd disposed of earlier in the day before the move.

'Then let's pencil in an hour at four on Friday,' said Harry. 'What do you say?'

'Perfect.' Shani shook her supervisor's hand, feeling the skin to be quite dry. 'I want to thank you for taking me on. I feel fortunate, to say the least.'

Harry opened the door. 'We'll undoubtedly have our disagreements, while applying the art of cerebral jousting. Just remember, structure. It's all to do with structure, my dear.'

* * *

Shani closed the door to her study, knowing beyond doubt she was heading for a manic episode – the first inside a year. The pornographic images of amputees she'd found by chance on her ex-boyfriend's laptop, the move itself and leaving behind her friends – and, very shortly, somewhere in the month of March, it would be twenty-three years since her birth parents died. She'd asked her adoptive father way before she became a teenager never to mention the actual date.

To distract herself from the intolerable darkness closing in on her, Shani made an attempt at unpacking, but only managed to organize her toiletries. Sitting on the bed, she realised she hadn't any tea bags. And no honey to stir in. Neither had she a cup, come to that. The three essential items she needed to see her through the next couple of days. The college had supplied her with a kettle and a mini fridge-freezer, and that was about it.

She put her face in her hands, the rush of tears spilling between her fingers. Was this self-pity? she asked herself for the umpteenth time in her life. It seemed to her self-pity and self-loathing were in league with one another. The blessing was that she was too young to remember the car accident on the outskirts of Prague which had killed her parents. It was unfair, that's all she really knew. *Wretchedly* unfair.

Pulling off her jumper, she started on her jeans, only to find herself gazing at her left foot – the foot that wasn't her foot but a prosthesis.

I thought I'd finally dealt with the way I feel about you. That I'd started to accept you. She clenched her hands and pressed them into the mattress. *But really you will never allow me to live my life in peace. Never!*

Shani fell back onto the bed, wrapped the duvet around her body and eventually cried herself to sleep, though not before wishing she was in Christina's arms.

CHAPTER 2

Before the manic episode fully took hold, Shani visited the Covered Market in the centre of town and bought bread, fruit, tea bags, coffee, honey, a plate, some cutlery, and a turquoise mug because she loved anything 'turquoise'. Turquoise sea. Turquoise sky. Turquoise gemstones, as on her favourite necklace. The colour had a calming effect on her.

Then she locked herself away in her study and tried to immerse herself in her thesis, recalling Harry Rothwell's final words to her. *Just remember, structure. It's all to do with structure, my dear.* Night-times were worse than daytimes by far. The previous evening she'd so nearly set off to visit Divinity Road, in East Oxford. But that wouldn't do, of course. Her ex-housemates would mollycoddle her, and she would accuse herself of being a whinging failure. She hadn't eaten much. Episodes always affected her diet, made her stomach (or was it her solar plexus?) feel wobbly. Her mind went round and round at night-time. Her parents, Lucian and Shema; Christina and the girls and what they might be doing; pervert of an ex-boyfriend, and because of him her prosthesis, and how once again she hated the thing because it was lifelike and personal and *dead*, and this *dead* thing was attached to her, and when she took this *dead* thing off there was just a scarred stump. She'd never owned a doll in her childhood, because dolls were *dead*, too, like ventriloquists' dummies. Horrible things!

Shani shivered involuntary, and then berated herself while reaching across the desk for her phone. *You can walk, you silly creature. Isn't that a gift in itself? And now you've won a scholarship to study at St Aquinas. It may not be All Souls over in The High, but it* does *convey prestige.*

It was 10:25. She realised she was quite hungry, confirmation that the episode had started to recede. She considered lunching in college when an altogether better idea came to her. Adding another note to the outline of her thesis, she saved the material on the screen and scrolled through *contacts* on her phone.

'Hi Tim,' she said when the call was eventually answered. 'It's Shani.'

'Shani,' came a cheery response. 'Was thinking of you only yesterday. I've a new Ducati. A Ten-Nine-

Eight.'

'*Oh là là!*' Shani leaned back into a shaft of sunlight. Rather symbolic, she thought. 'But when I get my MV Agusta, I'll thrash you. You do realise that, Tim, don't you?'

'Theoretical bullshit.'

Shani laughed, and felt something lift and tighten in her face. It had been days since she'd smiled properly. 'Aside from needing to get the cobwebs off the Kawasaki, I'm in desperate need of fresh air. Can we meet? I'll buy you a pub lunch in the countryside.'

'The Three Bells?'

'Yes, let's. Midday?' asked Shani.

'Make it half past. Stuff to do.'

Shani felt her phone vibrate and glanced at the screen, seeing the name *Dusana Košata*. 'I'll meet you at the garage, Tim. Have to go, my father's housekeeper's trying to reach me.'

She switched calls, finding herself to be mystified since Dusana invariably called her in the evening. Unless… *Oh, God, don't say!*

'Hi, Dusana,' she said, speaking in Czech. 'I was going to call you at the weekend—'

'Shani, he's had another attack. I had to get the ambulance.'

Shani squeezed her eyes shut in a frantic attempt to

block the words she was hearing. *This can't be happening!*

'I thought we'd lost him—'

'What hospital, Dusana?' Shani asked. 'Na Homolce?'

'I insisted. They know him here.' A pause. 'Shani, something's bothering me.'

'Like what?'

'I've never heard him mention it before, but does the word or name "Zinsa" happen to mean anything to you?'

'"Zinsa"?' Shani frowned and found herself to be as perplexed as Dusana's tone. 'No, not at all. Why?'

'Andrei kept repeating it in the ambulance, and saying, "I should have told her". He was quite agitated. *Very* agitated, in fact. And then he kept repeating the word "safe". Safe, safe, safe… That's when they decided to sedate him.'

'And now?'

'Less anxious. That'll be the sedative, I imagine. But he is asking for you.'

'Dusana, call me if there's any change,' said Shani, sitting at her desk and firing-up her PC. 'I'll get the first available flight and get back to you.' While looking for flights to Prague she called Tim Lewis and explained she was going to have to bail.

'I was going to mention at the pub we're going

down to the coast in a couple of weeks,' said Tim. 'Six bikes. With you, it would have made seven.'

'Text me when you fix a date, Tim,' said Shani, finally locating a direct flight. 'I might be able to make it.'

Shani printed off the Lufthansa boarding pass, and as she did so fear took hold of her. Her stomach pitched at the thought of her adoptive father dying. She couldn't deny that she hadn't been particularly close to Andrei in recent years, but without him she doubted she would have made it to Oxford. Besides, he was her family, there simply wasn't anyone else. No relatives that she was aware of. Nothing at all.

Shani leaned forward and massaged her temples. *Get a grip, girl*, roused her inner voice. *Where's your grit? This day was always going to happen. You've been expecting it!*

Harry, she realised, gazing at the shortcut to her thesis on the screen in front of her. She needed to call him as a matter of courtesy. She folded the boarding pass and reached for the landline, grateful for the distraction. But there was no response.

She stood from her desk and put her phone and tablet into her jhola shoulder bag, followed by the book she was currently reading, a translation of *Le Grand Meaulnes*. She decided to make use of whatever clothes she had in Prague to eliminate having to hang around at the carousel at the other end.

She tried her supervisor again. Still no response. She checked her phone, seeing she had twenty minutes to catch the next coach to Heathrow.

'Andrei, God's sake don't die on me,' she breathed before locking her study door.

CHAPTER 3

They came into Václan Havel, Prague's international airport, on schedule at five to midnight. While the cab swept along the intensely lit Pražský Highway towards Na Homolce District Hospital, Shani likened herself to a benumbed soul sitting in the middle of a desolate landscape, detached from her surroundings and quite alone – her father, having now suffered two heart attacks in as many months, perhaps closer to death than she wanted to believe.

Andrei Bălcescu had lived his life quietly. She could never understand why, since he was a gifted linguistic anthropologist who never complained or said a cruel word to anyone. But apart from the people he played bridge with, he kept to himself and occupied much of his time by reading and taking strolls in the local park. On rare occasions, he would join her when the Bohemians 1905 Football Club were playing at home at the Ďolíček Stadium, a stone's throw from the apartment. But there were times, more so recently, when she'd wondered whether the fatal car accident had dealt Andrei such a blow that he'd never managed to quite recover from it. And perhaps that was why he was so reluctant to talk about her parents. Offsetting this reluctance, and the sombre atmosphere that invariably accompanied it, was Dusana. For the past fourteen years, she had in the domestic sense taken over from when Andrei's wife, Rodica, died of pneumonia after a brain haemorrhage had left her cruelly paralysed.

The driver swung into a broad street named Roentgenova, negotiated a near hairpin-turn and swept past a row of parked cars before arriving at the hospital's main entrance. Shani added a tip to the fare and left the cab, her stomach starting to pitch again as she stepped past the foyer's automatic doors and straight into Dusana Košata's arms.

'Dusana…' Shani kissed her on both cheeks, and immediately sought another hug from her. Despite Dusana's brisk demeanour, combined with her iron grey hair drawn tightly back into a bun, giving the impression of a stern matronly soul, Shani adored her – although, their relationship hadn't always been so cordial; her tomboy teens a catalogue of disapproving glances until her first boyfriend came along.

'Take me to him,' said Shani.

She followed Dusana through a maze of corridors marked *KARDIOLOGIE* with blue arrows alongside, like points on a compass.

'I'll wait outside,' said Dusana.

'I need you with me, Dusana. I don't know quite what to expect.'

They crossed into another corridor with a downward slope. 'You should be alone together,' Dusana said firmly, keeping a steady pace. 'For a while, at least. Andrei would want it.'

They entered a ward with a total of eight beds. Behind the desk directly opposite them, two nurses, male and female, stood to greet her.

Dusana squeezed her hand. 'I'm just in the corridor,' she whispered.

The male nurse took Shani over to the farthest bed and partially drew the curtain around it for privacy.

Andrei Bălcescu lay prostrate, covered with wires connected to monitors, drips on stands, and a catheter. Shani put her hand to her mouth. He looked so frail, like a little child. She sat numbly on the chair beside the bed and found herself clasping her father's fingers, the anaemic skin on the back of his hand like papier-mâché.

'Andrei?' she said, unable to see how he could possibly resume his day-to-day pursuits, sensing they were going to need carers if he ever made it out of Na Homolce.

His eyes remained closed, but she sensed a slight pressure on her fingertips.

'Andrei,' she repeated at once. 'It's me, Shani. Speak to me.'

Andrei moved his lips, and then finally a sound – inaudible.

'I'm here—'

'Child. Forgive me, child.'

Shani felt tears on her cheeks and brushed them away. 'I love you.'

His eyelids quivered and opened a fraction, just grey slits. 'Child, you must forgive me. Zinsa... Séroulé. All gone.'

'Zinsa? What is this "Zinsa"?' asked Shani, feeling frustration rise up in her, annoyed she couldn't simply wave a wand and get Andrei out of the place and back home. 'You said this word to Dusana earlier. What does it mean? Is it the name of a person?'

Andrei gave a little sigh, and closed his eyes. 'Zinsa,' he repeated. 'The little one... Forgive me.'

Shani stroked his hand, and decided to let "Zinsa" go – Andrei's mind presumably stumbling around a distant recollection. 'We've been through some trials together, Andrei,' she said. 'You more so than me, I suppose. You had to deal with the accident, deal with the amputation. That must have been hard for you, especially when I would refuse to wear the prosthesis. I gave you hell. I'm so sorry for that. Then Rodica leaving us. But through it all, you never gave up on me. You sacrificed your time and finances to give me the best education possible.' Shani quickly wiped her cheeks again. 'So why are you asking me to forgive you? There were times when I showed you disrespect. Times when I ignored your advice out of sheer obstinacy. No, you are the one who has to forgive me. We both know that.'

As if exhausted by life itself, Andrei seemed to shrink further into the mattress. 'My child…try not to curse my mistakes.'

Shani instinctively tightened her grip on his fingers. 'Andrei, will you stop talking this way. I'm upset enough as it is. Can't you see that?'

A monitor unexpectedly sounded, followed by another alarm, louder and continuous.

Shani stood up, confused. *It's his heart*, she told herself. *My God, his heart's stopped!*

The curtain behind her was swept back, and before she realised what was happening she saw herself ushered out of the room and into Dusana's arms.

'He's dying,' Shani cried. 'He's going to leave me.' She tried to press her way back into the room.

Dusana hastily drew her away from the door. 'Shani, they need to assist him.'

Shani buried her face in Dusana's shoulder. 'This can't happen. I know we've had our problems, but I still love him. I have to get him to understand that.'

Dusana relaxed her grip. 'He knows that, Shani. Of course, he does.'

Shani began to pace the corridor, Dusana's words barely registering. 'I want him back home. Everything to be as it was. I'll give up Oxford to care for him.'

'Darling, he wouldn't want that. To throw away your academic career?'

Shani turned on her heel. 'Postpone, that's all.'

'And St Aquinas will allow that? I doubt it.'

'I don't care about St Aquinas. I care about Andrei.' Shani clenched her hands. 'This is intolerable.'

Dusana started to speak. 'Andrei couldn't be in safer hands. They know what to do. We have to be patient—'

The door opened and Shani swung round. It was the male nurse. She hadn't noticed before that he had a cleft lip.

'We're managing to stabilise Andrei,' he said.

'What do you mean by "stabilise"?' demanded Shani. 'Is he conscious?'

'Semi-conscious.' The nurse put a hand on Shani's arm. 'He's very weak. It was a severe attack. If we can carry him through the next twelve hours, the prognosis will be far more reassuring.'

Twelve hours felt an age to Shani. Too much time for hope to spiral into sheer despair. 'I want to stay.' She looked at Dusana. 'We can, can't we?'

Dusana spoke to the nurse. 'Is there a seating area nearby we can use?'

The nurse pointed to their right. 'Along the next corridor. There's a water dispenser if you need a drink.'

'But will it be all right to sit with him later on?' asked Shani.

'We're running more checks,' explained the nurse, 'and we need space around the bed to do that. You can come in afterwards.'

Shani walked down the corridor with Dusana, reality starting to take its toll on her. 'I don't want to say it,' she conceded aloud, 'but I'm fearful that Andrei might not make it out of this place.'

The waiting room looked as if it had been recently tidied, several magazines precisely displayed like the blades of a fan on top of a low-slung table. The abstract print on the wall resembled white lilies in a vase. Shani disliked it at the first glance, and even more at the second. She'd always associated lilies with funerals, from as far back as she could remember.

'Did he speak to you?' asked Dusana.

'Yes.' Shani went to the water dispenser and filled a plastic beaker. 'My mouth's so dry.' She slumped into a chair opposite Dusana. 'Just a few barely decipherable words. He looks dreadful. I couldn't understand him. He mentioned this word, or name, "Zinsa" – the one he said to you. What can it mean?'

'It sounds like an African name, doesn't it?' said Dusana.

'And Séroulé, quite distinctly.' Shani took a sip of water. 'That's definitely an African country. West Africa, I think. Did he mention Séroulé to you?'

'No.'

'Some of his anthropological work was conducted in West Africa, but that was years ago.'

'Obviously his mind's wandering.' Dusana drew her handbag closer to herself. 'Probably the sedative they gave him earlier, and what with the heart attack as well—'

'And then he asked me to forgive him,' said Shani, as if Dusana hadn't spoken. 'But for what? Unless it's finally dawned on him that he's given me little support whenever I've tried to research my birth parents.'

'Shall we go back?' suggested Dusana. 'Maybe we can sit with him now.'

'All right.' Shani stood up. 'Thank heavens you're with me, Dusana.'

The moment they returned to the ward, Shani saw what amounted to frenetic activity around Andrei's bed. 'What's going on?' she called out.

A different male nurse to the one she'd seen earlier came towards them, over six foot tall and with hands literally the size of dinner plates when he held them up in a 'no-go' gesture.

'You need to wait outside,' he said. 'Both of you.'

'But what's going on?' challenged Shani. 'He's my father.'

Dusana put her arm around Shani, and the nurse closed the door, leaving them in the corridor.

'He's not going make it,' Shani heard herself say. 'I *know* it.' She angrily crushed the empty plastic cup in her hand, frustrated by her inability to help Andrei. 'His body can't survive this amount of trauma, can it? He'll hate it if he can't go for his walks in the park.'

'We mustn't give up hope.'

'Why did he apologise to me? I should be the one apologising to him. I told him that. He wouldn't listen. Just wanted *me* to forgive him.' Shani put the plastic cup in a bin and felt her throat tighten up. 'I've got to go back in. I'm scared, Dusana. I can't stand this waiting around.'

But then the door opened, and the original nurse with the cleft lip came to speak to them. The quiet shake of his head was enough, and Shani didn't wait to listen to whatever it was he was about to say. She forced her way past him and ran across the ward to Andrei's bed. She was shocked because his waxen skin made him look incredibly unfamiliar, like he'd been embalmed in some kind of laboratory experiment.

The resuscitation team tactfully retreated when Shani fell to her knees. She held the crumpled hand lying on the sheet. 'I love you... I wish I could be with you.'

Just as she tightened her grip on the hand, not wanting to ever let go of him, an unexpected memory flashed across her inner mind: the morning of her eighth birthday, when she awoke to find Objetí, her pet hamster, had died. Andrei found a cardboard box, and she watched herself decorate it with hearts, before walking with Andrei to the park opposite with a trowel to bury her little companion.

Lifting the lifeless hand to the tears on her cheek: 'Oh, Andrei, you know I can't bear being left alone.

Not in this way!'

His lips slightly apart, Andrei Bălcescu's leaden eyes stared indifferently back at her – before a hand settled on her shoulder, startling her. It was Dusana.

'I thought I would be prepared for this day, Dusana,' said Shani, looking up at her. 'I'm not sure what I'm supposed to think, or believe. And I feel cold, all through my body.'

'Then the time has come for us to leave Andrei and go home,' said Dusana quietly.

* * *

They held hands in the back of the cab and hardly spoke as they travelled through the centre of Prague and over the River Vltava, via the Jiráskův Bridge, at the end of which stood a drunken-looking building on stilts called the Dancing House. In her opinion, its concave edifice made it look as though King Kong had struck it with his fist, and that such abstract architecture against the baroque was entirely inappropriate. She glanced at Dusana, her lined face impassive while streetlights flickered across the cab's interior.

'You're so strong,' Shani said.

'I'm in a daze. Heaven knows what I'll feel tomorrow.' Dusana squeezed her hand. 'A good man.'

'I know.'

The cab turned into Sportovní in Vršovice, District 10, a middle-class suburb spoiled only by the graffiti on some of the buildings which Shani thought had got worse. They swept past the Bohemians football stadium to the pale green apartment block at the far end. Without Andrei, it would never look or feel the same to her again. In the months to come, she supposed decisions would have to be reached. She doubted she could afford to keep it.

Shani glanced at the time on her phone while Dusana paid the fare. Just turned two. Her intended pub lunch with Tim Lewis seemed an age ago, and yet little more than twelve hours had passed.

'I'll be all right, Dusana,' she said as the cab pulled away. 'You need to rest. It's been a long and difficult day for us both. I just need a key.'

'I'll see you in,' said Dusana. 'I'm only in the next block, remember.'

Once inside the lobby, they took to the elevator – which started off with an unnerving judder. Shani felt herself tense up. 'I thought they were going to sort this lift out,' she said. 'I'm sure it's dangerous.'

'Andrei complained to the management,' sighed Dusana, gripping her handbag as if it were a fixture to hold onto. 'I complained. Mrs Havranek on the floor below has complained. And the money they charge each month…'

'I feel I should be crying, Dusana,' said Shani.

Dusana took a set of keys from her handbag. 'You will, my dear. One minute, you'll believe yourself to be in control – the next, tears will pour from you. But Andrei's at peace with his Maker. Let us thank God the Father for that.' Dusana had the door open. 'A brandy to settle you.'

Shani followed Dusana into the spacious apartment, with its Goma tribal mask over on the antique bureau. The mask's deadpan slit eyes had frightened when she was growing up and Andrei, seeing how it upset her, shifted it to his bedroom, where it had remained until she left for Oxford. She noted the opened magazine on a coffee table, a paperback alongside – and now, a catastrophic, indelible interruption. Andrei would have had his boiled egg as normal, his black coffee…

'When did it happen?' she asked, falling into an armchair, but not Andrei's.

'Five past eleven.' Dusana poured brandy into glasses. 'I hadn't been here five minutes. Brought his paper. He fell to his knees, holding his chest. I didn't have time to be shocked. The paramedics arrived within minutes.' She crossed the room with Shani's glass.

'I don't know if I can.'

'It might help you to sleep.'

Shani took the brandy. 'Dusana, if my school geography serves me correctly, Séroulé's somewhere down near Benin, or Ghana. But why should Andrei mention it?'

'He spent a lot of time in Africa.'

'But it was mainly East Africa where he conducted his research.' Shani glanced at the mask. 'Rwanda, and what used to be Zaire. That's how he came across my mother, Shema.'

'Who knows, Shani? Poor soul. The state he was in, West and East Africa was probably all the same to him. Drink your brandy.'

Shani did so, pulling a face as the liquor struck the back of her throat like a fireball. 'Oh, my! That's strong.'

'Napoleon.' Dusana followed suit, but without a trace of a grimace.

Shani unbuttoned her woollen jacket. 'I can't get over why he seemed so anxious for me to forgive him. Bizarre, to say the least.'

Dusana finished her brandy and stood up. 'Darling, as I said at the hospital, because he was sedated he was probably quite confused.' Smoothing her coat, Dusana checked her hair in the ornamental mirror. 'Try not to dwell on it. Remember Andrei as Andrei, and not the person we saw this evening.' She gathered her handbag. 'I should go. The cats will think I've deserted them. You need to call Father Prochazka, first thing.'

'I will.' Shani walked Dusana to the elevator and gave her a hug. 'Andrei loved you, Dusana,' she said. 'Always spoke so highly of you.'

Dusana looked back as she stepped into the elevator, and heaved a sigh. 'He was a treasure, Shani. I'll miss him.' The doors started to close. 'Now call me, if you need me.'

'I'll probably go straight to bed. Goodnight, Dusana. Love you.'

The elevator began its downward journey, and Shani retraced her steps along the corridor and closed the door to the apartment. Moments later, she found herself sitting in Andrei's chair with her face in her hands, her tears taking her by surprise. She took a tissue from her pocket. As she dried her eyes, she realised that she hadn't thanked Andrei for bringing her mother out of Rwanda, and giving them both an education and a secure home life. In fact, there was so much she seemed to have left unsaid.

* * *

Lying in bed, memories floated to the surface. Her

childhood, mainly. If it hadn't been for her prosthesis then she imagined Andrei would have had an easier time with her. He'd seen too many physically and mentally damaged people in Africa to understand her plight – or so she thought. In a way, he left her to work it out for herself. Defeatism was what it amounted to, and he wasn't going to play a part in it. A tough lesson.

Shani rolled onto her side. She sensed the brandy was doing its job. She wondered whether the Bohemians had a home game at the weekend. If she felt up to it, she might walk over to the stadium and watch the match. At all costs, she needed to avoid a manic episode, because she knew it would likely be a whole lot nastier than the one she'd just emerged from at St Aquinas.

CHAPTER 4

Her eyes flicked open in terror, cold moisture on her brow.

'God Almighty!' she muttered, and sat upright in the bed.

Shani looked around herself. She was in Prague. Andrei was dead. She recalled the scene at the hospital. The fluttery sensation at the point of her solar plexus that she went to sleep with didn't waste time in re-emerging. She quietly leaned back into the pillows and wiped a hand across her clammy brow.

She could remember the dream in absolute detail. On her desk in her study at St Aquinas was the safe Andrei kept in the living room. She was kneeling on the floor, trying to open it, when the door flew open of its own accord and a horrible goblin with pointed ears leapt from the safe and into her face, throwing her backwards – at which point she'd woken up.

Christina was obviously the culprit as regards to the appearance of the goblin, thanks to the Walt Disney comment she happened to come out with when she saw the view across the Priory Quadrangle.

Shani wiped her brow again, and wanted to check under the bed, just to be sure, but told herself not to be childish. Goblins resided within the boundaries of folklore, whereas the safe… She fumbled for her mobile phone on the bedside cabinet. 05:12. She settled herself back down. What was it Dusana had mentioned over the phone?… *Safe, safe, safe.* Andrei's words to her in the ambulance – or was it at the hospital?

Shani secured her prosthesis under her PJ's, perfectly aware she hadn't a hope of going back to sleep until the question had been resolved. She knew Andrei kept the key in a porcelain vase in the spare bedroom, having come across it while dusting. Out of curiosity she did open the safe at the time, to see if the key fitted. At least, that was her excuse. Her conscience was eased further by the fact that all she found inside was a brown envelope with documents relating to ownership of the apartment.

The key hadn't been moved. Shani shook it out of the vase and went into the living room, where she emptied a bookshelf beside the gas fire. The safe was quite ineffective by her reckoning, made from thin gauged sheet-metal and not even secured to the wall. As she turned the key, she tried to put out of her mind the possibility that she was about to unleash a demented goblin with pointed ears.

In reality, three brown envelopes of equal size stared inanimately back at her. She left the one she was familiar with and went to the recently modernised kitchen, with its harsh lighting and needless expanse of brushed stainless steel.

Shani sat at the English oak table, over which she'd put her foot down and told Andrei he had to keep it. Apart from adding warmth to the kitchen, it held memories of Rodica kneading dough. She examined both envelopes, A4 in size. Outwardly, neither gave a clue as to the contents, no writing or labelling whatsoever apart from what she took to be a reference number of some description: BCB1634. Shani suspected it to be an obsolete envelope from Andrei's anthropological cataloguing system – which she'd always regarded as totally weird and *un*systematic. She opened the envelope. A video. Again, no suitable labelling. *Must be years old*, she told herself. Putting the video to one side, Shani opened the second envelope and took out newspaper cuttings and several black and white photographs. The cuttings were in what she thought to be Romanian, although she couldn't be certain. The heading *Curierul Naţional* rang bells as being a daily newspaper. The article mentioned Séroulé. Mystified, she sifted through the photographs until arriving at a coloured one showing two adults and nine children. Their vibrant, informal clothes gave the impression they were well-to-do folk, with easy-going smiles – like they were on vacation. The people in all the photographs, whether children or adults, were black. Not a white Caucasian amongst them. She returned to the cuttings, a name appearing in front of her eyes that up until Dusana's phone call she'd never heard of before.

Shani left the kitchen for the cloakroom and extended the ladder so that it reached the panel in the ceiling in the spare bedroom. She prayed it was still there, that Andrei hadn't turfed it out. She climbed the ladder and lifted the panel to one side. In the borrowed light from the bedroom she managed to make out a variety of shapes – in particular, a Samsung cardboard box. Shani struggled to draw it closer to herself and started down the ladder, trying to keep the layer of dust off her PJ's. The TV in her bedroom had originally come from the living room, so she took the recorder out of the box, carried it across the corridor and busied herself disconnecting the DVD player. She then checked the remote control for batteries. Empty. She went to a drawer in the kitchen, snipped open a packet of triple A's and reloaded the remote.

The recorder lit up promisingly. Everything seemed in order. Shani inserted the video, sat on the bed and fast-forwarded. Some shades of light and she immediately stopped. Then a moment of fuzz before thousands – or so it seemed – of people dressed as if it were winter were marching towards a police barricade. The person holding the camera had an aerial view, perhaps from an apartment block. The picture was slightly grainy, and the grey weather didn't help. Nevertheless, she could clearly see red, yellow, and blue flags being held aloft – which she instantly recognised as being the Romanian national flag. The parked-up cars looked dated, and she imagined the footage to be at least twenty years old. In the background, two – possibly three – ominous columns of smoke merged into the skyline. A bridge, which suddenly came into view, showed other protesters attempting to join those on the other side of the barricade, in effect sandwiching the police. Despite speaking in a language she couldn't understand, Shani thought the commentator sounded agitated. And she had the impression that Andrei, or whoever, had recorded the footage from a state news program. As she watched, fascinated and wondering why Andrei had kept the tape all these years, the camera suddenly focused on a green car at the barricade, the police manning it wearing riot-gear. The driver of the car emerged and started gesticulating, but the police stood firm. The man threw up his hands in evident despair and returned to the car – and did an unbelievable thing, he drove into the barricade. One of the policemen raised a weapon and opened fire. The car came to a crooked standstill as the protesters on the bridge surged forward.

Shani instinctively put a hand on her chest, and as if she was watching it 'live' wondered whether the poor driver of the car was now injured – or worse. The footage ended abruptly moments later, just as an ambulance came into view on the right of the picture. She rewound the footage. Was it a town, or a city – or perhaps even Bucharest? She leaned forward to search for clues, freezing the footage when she thought she'd found something. And then she did, the name of a boulevard attached to a traffic light to the right of the barricade.

B-dul Vasile Pârvan

Shani left her bedroom for the living room and

took her tablet from her shoulder bag. There were two such boulevards in Romania, one of them in the city of Bacău, which didn't show a bridge crossing a river. She switched her attention to the other Vasile Pârvan boulevard in the city of Timişoara, north-west of Bucharest, and found it to be a perfect match, the bridge in question crossing a river by the name of Beja. She tried various searches, settling for: *green car, riot, Timisoara, Nicolae Ceausescu,* resorting to an approximate translation via a separate site. She suspected that what she had seen on the video related to the revolution which overthrew the president. She ran her finger down the screen on the second article she came to. As she did so, she locked onto three names in the report – and gasped. She couldn't understand a word of Romanian. She didn't need to.

Zinsa. Lucian. Bălcescu.

Then the car manufacturer, *Volkswagen*.

Shani tossed the tablet onto the settee. Not in '89, but without question four years later. In need of steadying herself, she sat on the arm of the nearest chair. This was preposterous. She put her face in her hands. All this time, and she had not the slightest idea – thanks to Andrei and the falsehoods he appeared to have inexplicably and yet so cleverly woven. *Why*, though? To protect her?

Inside the kitchen, Shani picked up a cutting to check the spelling of another name. Tuma Dangbo. Bringing his name up on the tablet, the final pieces of the mystery began to slide unnervingly into place. Tuma Dangbo, President of Séroulé before he was brutally murdered in a coup d'état thirty-eight years ago. She read on, and with a mournful ache in her heart drifted onto other sites.

Zinsa. The little one… Forgive me.

Before she knew it, it had turned eight o'clock. Not too early to call Dusana. And how she needed to! Shani closed the tablet and went to the landline phone in the living room, and the moment Dusana answered:

'Dusana, something terrible has happened. Please come over. I'm not the person I thought I was!'

'Shani, for heaven's sake—'

'I'll tell you when you get here. How long?'

'I'm not sure… Twenty minutes. I need to load the washing machine. Have you called Father Prochazka?'

'No. I can't think straight, Dusana. I'm getting over a massive shock.'

'We'll call him when I get there. He has to be told.'

'I'll see you in twenty minutes. Please hurry.' Shani cradled the receiver. A quick shower. Anything to suppress the chaos inside her head! She didn't feel hungry. A black coffee would suffice. After the shower. That was it, shower first, coffee later!

* * *

Shani waited anxiously outside the apartment, pacing up and down the corridor – which reminded her of Harry Rothwell. She would send him an email, mentioning the mind-blowing discovery unfolding in her life and that she wouldn't be returning to St Aquinas for at least a fortnight, if not a whole month.

Dusana stepped from the elevator, and without a word spoken Shani instinctively wrapped her arms around her.

'I can't believe it, Dusana. I had this dream – nightmare. Horrible goblin inside it. That's how I realised the safe was important. It's all to do with Séroulé. The whole thing is crazy—'

'Child, child, calm down,' cried Dusana. 'Goblins? You're not making sense!' She prised Shani from her. 'Now, you're going to make me a cup of strong tea, and I'm going to call Father Prochazka. Then I will listen to whatever it is you have to say—'

'The stuff I'm going to tell you, Dusana, you're not going to believe.'

They went into the apartment, and while Dusana made the phone call, Shani dropped a tea bag into a cup, stirring it vigorously, desperate to share all that she'd uncovered with Dusana. But she *did* need to calm down in order to organise herself. Dusana was right about that. Before the day was out, she wanted to be in Timișoara, Romania. There was now a possibility her parents 'existed', albeit in a cemetery. That thought alone excited her. Something tangible after all these years. She made another coffee for herself and went into the living room.

Dusana cradled the handset. 'He's coming at midday,' she said. 'As I thought, he's very busy. A wedding's been cancelled for next week and Father Prochazka reckons he can use that slot for Andrei's funeral.'

'Good. Thanks for speaking to him, Dusana.' Shani handed over the cup. 'Take a seat. There's so much to tell you.'

'What's all this about goblins?' Dusana put her handbag and gloves on the dining room table and took off her tweed coat with its oversized green buttons. 'If I didn't know you better, I'd say you're away with the fairies.'

'Forget the goblin-thing. It was just a dream, but it led me to the safe.' Shani perched herself on the edge of the settee. Leaving her coffee on a side table, she said: 'As you know, Séroulé is a West African country. From the eleventh century the region was occupied by various tribes, until the beginning of the slave trade in the sixteenth century. More recently, thirty-eight years ago to be precise, there was a massive coup in which a lot of people died. Tuma Dangbo was the president at the time, and from accounts I've seen so far, a little corrupt. But the coup leader, General Odion Kuetey, seems to have turned out even worse. The West, claims the author of one article, puts up with him probably because of the substantial oil trench in the Gulf of Séroulé.'

'And…?'

'Tuma Dangbo was my grandfather.'

Dusana jerked her head up from her tea, her expression akin to that as if she'd seen a vision of the Blessed Virgin Mary. 'No… Are you sure?'

'Positive. Tuma Dangbo had nine children. The family was at their retreat in northern Séroulé when General Kuetey struck. The youngest child was six years old, and managed to escape. She was called Zinsa—'

'The name Andrei mentioned to us both?'

'Exactly. Andrei must have brought her out of Africa, because we next hear of Zinsa in Romania – Timișoara, to be exact.' Shani tried to control her breathing amidst what felt like palpitations pounding her ribcage. 'This is the worst part. Zinsa married a man called Lucian. They were both killed during a protest march four years after the revolution, on November the seventeenth, twenty-four years ago.'

'Your birthday…'

'Quite. Apparently, Lucian was driving Zinsa to a hospital. She was heavily pregnant – with me. It *has* to be me.'

'Mother of sweet Jesus!' Dusana exhaled a hefty gasp and quietly shook her head.

'Lucian pleaded with the police to open the barrier, but they refused. So he drove into it, and a policeman opened fire. Presumably, they managed to keep Zinsa alive until she had given birth.'

'And you found all this information in the safe?'

'Not all. I used my tablet. What I found in the safe were cuttings and photographs, and a video showing my father and mother at the barricade.' Shani reached for her coffee. It was barely lukewarm. She took a sip and abandoned the remainder. 'A lot to take in, yes?'

'An understatement,' said Dusana. She shook her head again. 'Heaven's sake, I can't believe it, Shani.'

'Had the protest never happened and my parents remained alive, I believe Zinsa would never have been traced to Romania.'

'Why such secrecy on Andrei's part?'

'To protect me from the regime in Séroulé. One

article states that General Kuetey is obsessed with getting rid of anyone related to Tuma Dangbo. I suspect, because of Zinsa's death being world news, I was spirited out of the country by Andrei and Rodica.'

'So your foot wasn't the result of a car accident?'

'Apparently not. I've no idea why it was amputated. That's why I'm leaving for Timișoara later today.'

'Romania?'

'I want to go to the hospital where they took Zinsa. There might still be someone there who can remember that day, or know of someone who does.' Shani noticed the uncertainty on Dusana's face. 'I *have* to go, Dusana. I can't rest, I can't think of anything else. It's totally taken over my mind.'

Dusana's expression softened. 'Darling, you have my support. You know that. Always.'

'Thank you.'

'What a complete shock. Andrei never once hinted about any of this to me.'

'He should have told me, Dusana. He led me to believe my mother was called Shema and that she came from Rwanda.' And then, in the same breath, Shani asked: 'Is it because I can be impetuous at times? Meaning, I would likely have ignored his protests and gone to Séroulé to see what I could find out about

Zinsa?'

'Quite possibly. If all this is as you say it to be, it's clear Andrei made sacrifices, leaving his native land and, so it appears, academia.'

'And the day when Zinsa and Lucian died must have been awful for him and Rodica.'

'Devastating. The little girl they had rescued from Séroulé, only to have her life taken from her in a country they assumed would be a safe haven in comparison.'

'My mind's still in a state of disbelief, Dusana.'

'Hardly surprising…'

'I mean, Andrei maintained they were cremated, here in the Czech Republic. We now know that's extremely doubtful. This is why I have to go to Timişoara, to find answers to such questions as to what actually happened to them.'

* * *

When Dusana left in the afternoon to feed her cats, Shani found the courage to watch the video again. As gruesome as it was, she wanted to see her father – at least, *presumably* her father. And there he actually was, gesticulating at the police. Perhaps there had been complications with the birth and her father had felt compelled to drive Zinsa to the hospital. And now he was trapped between the surging crowd and the barricade, unable to go back, unable to move forward. She stopped the video at the point when he started to drive into the barricade, hardly wanting to see the policeman firing at the car.

Switching off the TV, Shani sensed an excitement within her that she had never felt before. A feeling of warmth, of being truly connected to her birth parents – to Lucian and Zinsa. She realised that calling her mother Zinsa and not Shema was going to take some getting used to, but she quite liked the name Zinsa. Had character about it, and complemented the photographs Andrei had given her of her mother. And yes, she could see a definite resemblance to the smallest child in the coloured photograph she'd taken from the safe, the impish smile equally vibrant as she stood alongside her siblings.

While she packed for the journey, she wondered how old she had been when she was spirited across the Romanian border. And *why* had her left foot been amputated? What could have happened to her to require such life-changing surgery at such a young age? Had she been born with a severely deformed foot? The inflow of questions seemed to rise by the minute when it came to her upbringing's 'darker' side – for that's what it now felt to be.

CHAPTER 5

The Air Berlin Boeing 737 with its distinctive red and white livery rolled up to the hub at Traian Vuia, Timișoara's international airport, as night was falling. A blanket of sleet was blowing in from the east. Shani shivered when the icy air hit her the moment she left the concourse. Welcome to Romania, she thought.

She found a cab straightaway. The driver could speak a little English, and after a couple of attempts she made him understand that she needed to find a room close to the city's main hospital. The sleet turned to rain as they travelled into the city. Shani discreetly glanced down into the footwell to find out what it was that kept rolling around her feet. A bottle of something. Vodka, she surmised, going by the smell in the cab.

From looking at maps, she'd judged the journey would take around thirty minutes, which it did, but cost ninety-five lei, which seemed excessive. Had she been in a different frame of mind, she might have challenged the fare, but felt done in from being on what amounted to an emotional rollercoaster nonstop since five o'clock that morning.

They parked up in a quiet street, the driver pointing across his shoulder. 'Strada Mureşan, hospital,' he said. And to the left of the windscreen: 'Krina Central. Nice. Cheap.'

'*Mulţumesc*,' said Shani, closing the door. 'Thank you,' she repeated in English, in case she'd botched the translation she'd picked up at the airport.

The cab driver drove away, tooting his horn as he did so – perhaps in glee, Shani imagined, at being ninety-five lei richer for half an hour's work. She crossed the unlit street to the house with a green neon sign in its front window: *Krina Central*. She wondered how close she was to where Zinsa and Lucian had lived. Maybe just a couple of kilometres. Whatever, the possibility made her smile and her heart glow with wellbeing.

The door was opened by a little woman wearing a chequered apron, her grey hair painstakingly plaited. Because of the language barrier they relied on hand gestures and facial expressions, although sometimes these seemed to fall out of sequence. The room for one night was cheaper than the cab fare, which seemed to confirm she had been over-charged.

Shani followed the woman up the stairs to the second floor. The ceiling in the room she was shown slanted downwards at a fierce angle above the single bed. Apparently, the bathroom was further down the corridor. Shani looked at her phone. At least she had an adequate signal. Struggling to keep herself awake, she accepted the offer rather than pursue comfier lodgings. When the woman left, Shani went to see if she could draw more heat from the radiator, only to find the knob had been removed. She looked in more detail around room, the kitschy nature scenes of mainly deer in chunky fake gilded frames doing little to lift her spirits, as with the cardboard cut-out of the Virgin Mary propped up against a plastic crucifix over on the dresser.

Shani sat on the bed and called Dusana. At least the mattress wasn't lumpy.

'You had a good flight, darling?'

'It was on time. I'm going to go to the hospital tomorrow, Dusana. It's quite late now. How are the cats?'

'Perfect nuisance,' sighed Dusana. 'I'm boiling the ham for the sandwiches and they're around my feet all the time.'

'I don't think we'll see many people at the funeral. Just his bridge partners, presumably.'

'And Mrs Havranek, on the floor below. Perhaps others from the block will come. You never quite know who might turn up at a funeral.'

'Good point,' said Shani. A chance, she realised, of someone attending who might have met – or could give her background information, on her parents. 'I'll call you tomorrow, Dusana, and let you know how I got on.' She put her phone away and ventured down the corridor, the distant hum of a television or radio below.

The bathroom was hideously cold, if not actually freezing, the window above the stained toilet bowl partially covered by a net curtain that dangled from a single hook. She brushed her teeth, using the bottled water she'd bought while making the connection in Vienna. Back inside the bedroom, she quickly ran a couple of tea tree wipes over herself and decided that if she was going to spend another night in Timișoara, she would have to splash out and find somewhere less depressing and much, much warmer.

* * *

There was a pâtisserie around the corner from Krina Central, in the shadow of the hospital. Shani took her espresso over to the window. She hadn't slept very well. If it hadn't been for the blanket she'd discovered in the wardrobe, she imagined her teeth would still be chattering.

She gazed out across the street. Behind the petrol station in the immediate foreground stood a green façade with hundreds of windows. Was this where they'd brought Zinsa? More than that, was this where Zinsa had died, after giving birth to her? Zinsa from Séroulé, that is, not Shema from Rwanda. And Lucian, what exactly was *his* background? Yes, Andrei had told her that the first twelve years of Lucian's life was spent in an orphanage, before he was adopted by Andrei and Rodica. After college, Lucian had then apparently worked as a draftsman for an architect in Prague. Of course, half of that was untrue. He might well have been a draftsman, but more likely here, in Romania.

It was odd, in some ways she felt closer to Lucian and Zinsa, but in other ways she'd never felt so far apart from them. She could almost touch them, but in reality this could never be the case.

Shani felt her eyes well up and knocked back her coffee. Leaving the garbled chitchat of the pâtisserie's customers for the snow-dusted pavement, she passed some waste ground and a helipad, before arriving at a large sign above a set of glazed doors.

SPITALUL CLINIC JUDETEAN DE URGENTA TIMISOARA

Shani climbed a row of steps, ramps on both her right and left. Once through the automatic doors, she expected to find a reception desk, but instead found herself joining a small queue at a kiosk. The area bustled with activity, children crying for whatever reason, and those who weren't simply running about as individuals of all shapes and sizes moved across the foyer. The man directly in front of her was on crutches, his right leg in plaster up to his thigh. Shani waited until he'd been dealt with, and then spoke to the lady in the cramped-looking kiosk, who welcomed her with a quiet smile. Her shiny blonde hair was flawlessly tied back into a ponytail, her faintly lined Nordic appearance hinting how Christina might look ten years down the line.

Shani smiled back at her. 'Do you speak English – or Czech, by chance?'

'A little English,' replied the receptionist, toying with a biro. 'How will I help you?'

'My mother might have been brought to this hospital, twenty-four years ago.'

The receptionist's puzzled gaze exaggerated the crow's feet that trailed from her eyes. 'Twenty-four years ago? Your mother?'

'Yes. She was black, and pregnant. There was a protest march in the city, and she was caught up in it.'

The receptionist cocked her head, as if hard of hearing. 'And…and she was pregnant?'

'Yes. Nine months pregnant, I imagine.'

The receptionist put the biro down on the shelf in front of her with a smack. 'I see.' She got up, her demeanour at once authoritarian. 'Wait here, please,' she said, and disappeared through a door at the back of the kiosk.

Shani did as she was told, mildly curious as to why the apparent change in the receptionist's attitude towards her. A couple of minutes passed before a man came around the side of the kiosk and pointed directly at Shani to leave the queue. She followed him into a quiet corner. He wore a suit and tie, middle-aged and balding. She couldn't quite gauge his expression, but the way he had 'ordered' her to leave the queue and the red flush on his cheeks implied he wasn't particularly pleased to see her.

'What are these questions you are asking?' His English was surprisingly fluent, though his tone overly brusque.

'There was a protest march twenty-four years ago,' said Shani. 'My father was killed. My mother, also. But she was pregnant, with me—'

'What do you mean your father was killed? How did this happen?'

Shani felt intimidated. She couldn't fathom why first the receptionist had become aggressive towards her, and now this man – who had yet to introduce himself. 'He was shot at a barricade that had been erected by the police. My father was trying to get my mother to a hospital. Perhaps this hospital—'

'Now look, we don't want any trouble,' interrupted the man, his face reddening all the more.

'I'm not—'

'What do you do? You are a journalist, yes?'

'Oh, no. Not at all.' Shani wondered whether a certain amount of fear – the residue of the Ceausescu regime, still reigned over parts of Romania and in the people themselves over a certain age. It's all she could think of in way of an explanation for such blatant animosity. 'I work in Oxford, in England.'

'At the University?'

'As a matter of fact, I do. St Thomas Aquinas—'

'So you are a historian. You have come here to investigate, like the others. I can see it, only you're quite clever, you're using your skin.'

Shani dismissed the man's rudeness. *Using my skin...* Was this confirmation Zinsa had been brought to this hospital? 'Please,' she reacted, 'I think you can help me. I've just discovered that my biological father was Romanian, and that my mother originally came from Séroulé in Africa. Her name was Zinsa Bălcescu. I think she gave birth to me in this hospital, then died from her injuries. I can't prove this to you because I have no documents bearing her name.'

The man nodded. 'Well, you can offer me proof,' he said, his smile sickly-sweet. 'A whole lot of proof, actually.'

'What?'

'Shouldn't be too difficult.'

'Then by all means, ask away,' Shani agreed, wondering who she could possibly report this horrible man to. 'Whatever is necessary.'

The man looked casually across at the reception kiosk, as though he was more interested in the receptionist. 'Do you have any distinguishing features?' he asked, turning to her. 'Any…injuries, shall we say?'

Shani stared at him, trembling with expectation. Was he saying what she thought he was? She managed to nod. 'I do. My foot and ankle on my left side were amputated. I have a prosthesis.' In the same breath, she asked: 'What happened? Do you know?'

The man looked at her with unblinking eyes, before puffing out his cheeks with a protracted sigh.

'Oh, my God…it is true.' He slowly shook his head, and held out his hand. 'I'm Horia Amanar. The head administrator of this hospital.'

'Shani Bălcescu.' Despite her unease over the man's rudeness, Shani shook his hand. Dazed as she was, she realised this person in front of her *knew* something.

'This was a big story,' said Horia. 'Your mother was the sole survivor of Séroulé's ruling family before the coup. You know that, don't you?'

'Yes, but only since yesterday. It was mentioned in an article I happened to discover.'

'I suggest you keep this to yourself. I apologise for my initial discourtesy, but to this day we get people trying to find a lead – trying to find you.'

'After all these years?'

'People like mysteries, and Zinsa is still a mystery and a heroine in the eyes of the Romanian people. Maybe it has been exaggerated by the media. Though her beauty was certainly iconic. You have pictures of her, I presume?'

'Yes, I do. Not that many, though. Perhaps now I'll be able to find more.'

'Well, the good news,' said Horia, 'is that we still have several people who were present that day. The one I have in mind used to be a theatre porter, but is now semi-retired. Follow me.'

Shani tried to keep up with Horia's stride as they crossed over into another corridor, an orderly row of empty wheelchairs parked up on their right. Soon enough, they arrived at a door with a sign on it reading *Camera de Poștă*. Shani followed Horia inside, where two elderly gentlemen were sorting through parcels and letters over on their left. Horia told her to wait by the door. She watched him go and speak to the shorter one of the two. He looked to be quite dapper for his age, with a full head of grey hair and a trim figure. Shani found it hard to believe he was old enough to be semi-retired. While Horia spoke to him, the man straightened his spectacles and looked at her with his mouth open in apparent astonishment. Horia came back over, the man he'd spoken to following.

'There's an empty staff rest-room nearby,' Horia said. 'We'll use that.'

Further down the corridor they entered a room furnished with a row of lockers, plastic bucket chairs and several Formica-topped tables. Shani pulled out a chair and sat next to Horia, who started to speak.

'This is Radu Nemcsik. He was here that day, twenty-four years ago. He speaks some English, but it is better that I translate.'

Shani put her shoulder bag on the table and

crossed her legs, hands cupped around her right knee. 'I want to thank you both.'

Horia spoke to Radu, who nodded and reached past Horia to shake Shani's hand.

Shani took a deep breath, a vague feeling that what she was about to hear wasn't going to sit comfortably with her, the disturbing video she'd watched in Prague uppermost in her mind. 'I would like Radu to explain to me what he saw that day.'

After listening, Radu began to speak, Horia nodding along. 'Radu is saying: *We were busy, people arriving with bloodied faces and broken limbs. The military and the police were brutal…*'

Shani recalled the columns of smoke; the flags being waved by the protesters and the fever-pitched voice of the commentator.

'*…Then suddenly there was news that two people had been shot, and that the woman was pregnant. I was stationed in theatre number three. The woman was brought in, and seemed semi-conscious. I hadn't expected her to be black. She had been shot in the neck and in the left shoulder, and also in the abdomen. I remember the surgeon saying that he thought it must have been a ricochet, the angle being inconsistent with the other wounds…*' Radu tailed off, and so did Horia.

Shani pictured the human carnage now arriving at the hospital, and in particular the frenzied scene in theatre number three as they desperately tried to save Zinsa and her unborn child. She swallowed, and bravely gestured for Radu to continue.

'The surgeon set about his business and he delivered you,' translated Horia. *'The ricochet had damaged your foot, either the bullet itself or a fragment of bone from your mother—'*

'A bullet?' interrupted Shani, her hand moving to her chest. 'You're saying the likely cause of my foot being amputated was a bullet?'

After Horia had spoken, Radu nodded. Horia cleared his throat and continued. *'They managed to stop the bleeding. They tried to save it, there was much debate. Later that day, a specialist surgeon was brought in and he removed it above the ankle. A nurse had been found with the same blood group. But your brother, he had passed away. Still-born. The ricochet had...had killed him outright.'*

Shani gasped as the shock all but swept her off the chair. She stared at Horia, and then at Radu. 'My brother?'

Radu straightened his glasses again, and via Horia, *'You did not know this, that you had a brother?'*

Shani couldn't believe her ears. *A twin brother.* It was too appallingly surreal by far. 'Are you sure, Radu?' she asked. 'I haven't had time to research this, but in the handful of reports I've read there was no mention that I had a brother.'

Radu nodded, and in broken English he said: 'It is true, what I tell you. A baby boy.'

Shani leaned on the table and put her face in her hands as the tears came. She recalled Andrei's dying words to her. *The little one... Forgive me.* She'd presumed he had meant Zinsa, but had the horror of that day affected him so ruthlessly that he had spent the rest of his life trying to blot it out – including her brother? That would further explain why he was so reluctant to talk to her about her parents. She lifted her face out of her hands to see Radu take off his spectacles and wipe the corner of his eye with a finger. Horia's hands, she noticed, were tightly clasped, his previously flushed face considerably pale.

Shani fumbled for a tissue in her bag. 'What happened to the policeman who fired the gun?' she asked.

Horia didn't translate her question to Radu, but answered her directly. 'He...he committed suicide, a week or so later. Not long after. People went against him over what had happened. Before he died, he claimed the gun had developed a fault.'

Shani nodded. It didn't feel like poetic justice to know this fact, since after watching the video the policeman had likely panicked. The officer in charge was, in her view, to blame for not allowing her father through the barricade. She had no idea who this person might be, and had already decided she wouldn't make enquiries. Besides, she doubted she would get very far – ranks would surely close, shutting her out.

'I have another question for Radu,' she told Horia, dabbing her eyes with the tissue. 'I understand if he can't remember, but I would like to know whether my mother ever saw me before she died?'

Radu rocked his shoulders slightly as if in a state of anxiety while replying to Horia. The administrator gave a final nod and turned to Shani. 'Radu vividly remembers the moment you were born, and that she did not open her eyes to see you, but that she touched you before they cut the cord. And you made a lot of noise, so she would have heard you.'

It was ridiculous, almost irreverent. All Shani could think of doing was to jump up and shout *Halleluiah!* because this was joy. Zinsa had managed to endure her injuries until she knew she had given birth. And then she had acknowledged that birth. She had *communicated* with her. *Oh, Zinsa*, she heard her inner voice sing, *you adorable angel, you have given me a light to follow, one of courage and insight!* She looked at Radu, and almost smiled because she wanted to hug him, to thank him – but then another question, and of equal importance. 'Does Radu recall what happened to my parents, my twin brother?' she barely dared to ask. 'Were they…cremated?'

Again, Horia didn't bother to translate. 'They are buried in the Cemetery of Heroes. About thirty minutes by bus, on the other side of town.'

Radu interrupted, and Horia spoke quickly with him. Horia gave a brisk nod and turned to Shani.

'It is a very large cemetery,' he said. 'Apparently, the grave has no name on it. Radu will need to show you where it is.'

'How does he know this?' asked Shani. 'I mean, where the grave is after all this time?'

Horia listened to Radu's reply. 'He puts flowers on the grave every year, on the day it happened. On your birthday, if you like.'

Without a moment's thought, Shani clasped Radu's hand. 'What a kind man. Thank you.'

Horia translated, and Radu nodded and shrugged his slender shoulders.

Horia stood up. 'I've given Radu the rest of the day off. He will take you to the cemetery now. He only needs to get his coat.'

'I was wondering,' asked Shani, 'do you know anything of my father's background – Lucian Bălcescu?'

'They grew up more or less together, Lucian and Zinsa. I believe Lucian, himself, was an orphan. They attended the same school. That's about all I know. A few years ago, there was talk of a film being made for *Televiziunea Română* about them – a tragic love story.' Horia spread his hands. 'It was perhaps just a rumour. Indeed, you will hear many rumours when it comes to your parents. For a while there was talk of government snipers in the area at the time of the protest march, and that they were involved. But it's all nonsense. A policeman fired a semi-automatic weapon. It was captured on film.'

'I've seen it,' said Shani, walking with Horia over to the door. 'For the first time, yesterday.'

* * *

Shani left the mauve and white bus with Radu and followed him along the busy highway. Without Horia's assistance, conversation was limited. But she was happy to soak up the sights around her, watching the people – imagining her mother and father taking similar bus rides to the one she had just taken. Already she could see a huge monument in the distance with black and white horizontal layers, rising above an ornamental wall that – according to Radu's sweeping gesture – surrounded the cemetery. She ran her fingertips along the wall, feeling its roughness, every step she took inching closer to Zinsa and Lucian. They passed by several people selling posies and wreathes from the pavement before turning into the entrance, where Shani found herself taken by surprise by the sheer scale of the cemetery - seemingly an ocean of gravestones as far as she could see in all directions. The black and white monument she'd noticed after stepping from the bus was curved around an 'eternal flame', a large crucifix protruding from the marble edifice above the date *DECEMBRIE 1989*. It was, she knew, the time when President Nicolae Ceausescu was ousted from power in Bucharest and summarily executed with his wife, ending years of repression.

Shani followed Radu as he crisscrossed between the graves, some adorned with colourful flowers, others without any decoration at all. It wasn't particularly peaceful, the constant hum of traffic punctuated by the frequent hoot of a horn. It was, though, interesting. There were trees throughout, mingling with elaborate monuments and buildings, the latter housing administrative offices, she assumed.

Eventually, they came to an open space, and Radu took a path opposite a domed chapel. *A twin brother.* It felt beyond belief, as did the knowledge that he had died beside her in her mother's womb. Murdered, more or less. She'd heard or read somewhere that the loss of a twin impacted potentially in some form or another on the surviving twin. It was the oddest thing, but on occasion when severely depressed she did feel a presence – on her left side, never her right – and wanted it to be her parents. But was it? Could the possible presence be her brother, coming to comfort and reassure her? Or was she herself subconsciously experiencing the *loss* of her brother?

A drop of rain on her hand and Shani glanced at the sky, ominously grey and still very cold. More sleet or snow on the way, she thought.

Radu stopped abruptly, and with his hands clasped in front of himself looked down at a bare wooden cross, before turning to Shani. 'Your family, Shani.'

Shani stared at the cross, approximately four feet in height. She saw that it was slightly crooked and no longer in good condition, although had probably looked perfectly respectable twenty-four years ago. Below it, the remnants of a bouquet, presumably placed there by Radu himself a couple of months ago on her birthday. Shani turned to him, making a gesture with her hands to ask him if he was certain this was the right place, since there was nothing to say so on the grave itself.

'You're sure?'

Radu squatted and cleared some pebbles away to reveal a brass tag anchored to the ground and bearing the number B138. He pointed to a red-bricked building nearby, and beckoned Shani to follow him.

Shani turned from the grave, and as she did so she realised she could only see one other wooden cross amongst the multitude of granite headstones. While following Radu, she suspected Andrei and Rodica were more focused at the time on getting her out of the country, out of reach of the President of Séroulé, General Odion Kuetey – a man according to one report obsessed with erasing her grandfather's bloodline. Maybe, she reflected, her adoptive parents intended to mark the grave with a more substantial headstone, but found the tragedy too overwhelming to return to Romania and deal with such a process.

The building Radu took her to housed row upon row of files on shelves. Radu spoke to a bearded man sitting behind a PC, who appeared to be working alone. He stood and greeted Radu with a courteous handshake, submitting a near bow as he did so. A ledger was found and opened, and Shani followed Radu's finger as he traced over the words alongside the number B138.

Lucian și Zinsa Bălcescu, cu copil mic (băiat), născut mort (fără nume)

The words *fără nume* made her doubt whether the male infant had been given a name. She took her phone from her pocket and indicated that she would like to photograph the document. Radu chewed his lower lip and looked uncomfortable, but the official gave a hasty nod, implying she could do so, but quickly.

Outside, Shani shook Radu's hand. She took a pen from her bag and wrote down her email address and mobile phone number and offered the scrap of paper to him. Radu took the pen from her and did exactly what Shani had hoped he would do by giving her his phone number. She smiled, and held out her arms.

As they embraced, Radu spoke quietly. 'A journey for you. Yes?'

'Yes.' Shani held Radu tightly as tears coursed her cheeks. Here was a person who had witnessed her birth, and the passing of Zinsa. 'She was beautiful, wasn't she, Radu?'

'Yes. A beautiful… How do I say it? I think "spirit". Yes?'

Shani nodded against his shoulder. 'Yes. A beautiful spirit.'

'The journey, Shani. He is a bad man in Séroulé. This I have heard.'

'I'll be careful.'

'After the journey, you will come to me? To my family?'

Shani stepped back, wiped her tears away and smiled. She held his hand between hers, surprised by Radu's prediction that she would go to Séroulé. Was it that obvious? 'I'm honoured, Radu, that you should invite me,' she said. 'I look forward to that precious day.'

'"Preshos"?'

'Special. Hmmm…' Shani patted her chest.

'Ah! You bring your heart with you?'

Shani laughed quietly with Radu. 'And my gratitude,' she added.

They parted with a final embrace and Shani impatiently made her way back to the grave. She needed to give her brother a name. That was of utmost importance. Tuma was an obvious choice, but if her grandfather had been corrupt, she didn't want to taint her brother by using his name. She could call him Lucian, after their father, but wanted the name to have its origins in Africa. She trusted she wasn't being disrespectful towards her father, or Romania, come to that, she just felt closer to Africa more than ever before. Perhaps it was simply an innate motherly-thing.

Shani reached the grave, picked up a pebble and rolled it over in the palm of her hand. She decided to keep it and slipped it into her pocket. The rain had started to come down steadily, but she barely noticed as she knelt on the ground.

'I love you,' she whispered, fresh tears on her cheeks. 'Please help me through this time. Truth is I feel so wounded, so horribly broken. I want to be with you.'

She put her face in her hands and hunched forward. She was missing three people, who should never have died. Three contactable names on her phone. To be able to hug her twin brother, to share her proudest moments with him, to plan Christmas and birthday gifts together for Lucian and Zinsa.

Shani left the graveside, terrified that she might now spiral into a depression – and never withdraw from it, suspended for eternity in a state of purgatory. She turned briefly to look at the desolate wooden cross. 'I'll be back tomorrow. Or later today, perhaps…'

Through the rain, she spotted the man who had opened the ledger watching her from the doorway of the building. Unnerved, and rather embarrassed that she had been talking aloud even though the distance was too great for him to have heard her, Shani nevertheless pulled her coat around herself and hurried from the cemetery.

**

Around the back of the cemetery which, Shani realised, was surrounded by a busy highway, she happened to encounter a quiet, tree-lined street called Răsăritului. There were a couple of guest houses, one of them with a tidy front garden – which swayed her decision. The room she was shown on the second floor was perfect, and even had a shower cubicle in the corner. Wi-Fi was also available, she was told by the man in broken English. She handed over a hundred and twenty lei; happy, this time, to part with the cash.

The manager left the room and Shani started to organise herself. There was just the one radiator, which happened to be roaring with heat. She took off her soaked cotton jacket and jeans and laid them across the radiator. Drawing the curtains, she sat on the bed and pressed the button on the side of her prosthesis to unlock it from the silicone sock. Stripping off completely, she rolled the sock down from above her knee and tossed it onto the bed. Despite all the counselling she'd received over the years, the prosthetic foot itself still felt *alien* to her; something she didn't like to hold, or even touch – let alone look at. The knockbacks hadn't helped, particularly when it came to relationships, especially the pervert of a boyfriend who was actually 'turned on' by her disability going by the images she'd found on his laptop. Well, she had better things to think about now. She'd found her family, her true identity. And yes, it felt like a reawakening, a vibrant initiation that perhaps only orphans meeting their birth parents for the first time could appreciate. Could it even mean, she wondered, closure when it came to her manic episodes?

The stump ached a little so she gently massaged it to increase the blood-flow, and hopped over to the shower cubicle. Her consultant had warned her about hopping, and damaging as a consequence her right hip. But she'd left her telescopic crutch in Prague. She was always leaving the wretched thing somewhere!

Drying herself off, she put on clean underwear and lay on the bed, her mind recapturing the day's dramatic events, before once again settling on Tuma Dangbo, whom she now regarded as a somewhat enigmatic figure. She sat up and reached for her tablet. She'd had little time to research her biological grandfather over the past twenty-four hours, and so began to flick through a few sites. Most seemed to confirm that he was feeding weapons to rebels in Ghana in the hope of triggering a coup. The reason why he wanted to do seemed unclear to her. She examined several more reports, but they were barely consistent, laced with ambiguity. What she found to be conflicting more than anything was that the president of Ghana at that time – thirty-eight years ago – regarded himself as a libertarian, as did by all accounts her grandfather. So why would Tuma Dangbo feed weapons to rebels whose aim it was to overthrow a likeminded soul?

Then she came to an article written in English by a French journalist calling himself Nicolas Dubois. He completely dismissed all claims of corruption against Tuma Dangbo, more or less painting him as an iconic figure who opposed what he saw as the plundering of the African Continent for its oil and minerals by the superpowers and their multinational corporations. Dubois went on to discuss the actual coup. Zinsa Dangbo was the youngest child and managed to escape. Shani skipped down the article, having read much of what was being said elsewhere.

…Zinsa surfaced in Romania, where she had a child in tragic circumstances. After that, the trail went cold and no trace of the child has been found since.

And a son, too, added Shani, wondering why Dubois had omitted that fact. There was an email contact address.

Shani straightened herself against the pillows and considered whether to respond. What would she say?

She scanned other articles by Nicolas Dubois. From what she could gather, he seemed to have focused more on Ghana and Togo than Séroulé, but West Africa was clearly his chosen subject. She started to type in the available box.

I am Zinsa's 'lost child'. If you wish to contact me, you may do so at the address below. But I ask you to regard this communication as being strictly confidential.

She gave him her private email address as opposed to her St Aquinas address, and sent it. Out of curiosity, she typed his name into *images*, adding that he was a journalist.

There was just the one picture of him, a little blurred and quite small. He was blondish and had some designer stubble, which never appealed to her. Nice teeth, though – and smile, come to that. She wondered when the photograph had been taken and what he might look like now. She tried enlarging the picture, but he became little more than a reddish, pixelated blur.

She yawned, closed the case around the tablet and settled herself on the bed. It had been a long day – a day she was hardly likely to forget, steeped with emotion.

* * *

Towards the end, she knew she was dreaming, but it

was a golden dream and she wanted to hold on to it. She was sitting at a Formica-topped table, cradling her twin brother. On her right sat her father, and on her left her mother, only the three of them were skeletons. Despite this, her brother looked beautiful, his toes and fingers moving delicately. She thought it might be her pulse making his little bones twitch, so she carefully laid him on the table. But he still moved. She remembered thinking that this had to be the most magical moment in her life. What could possibly compare with it? She quickly cradled her brother again. Then her mother and father came and put their arms around her, and they became 'a family'…

Shani rubbed the sleep from her eyes while gazing at her jeans on the radiator, the dream's serenity and sense of refuge continuing to occupy her mind. She left the bed and hopped over to the window. Parting the curtains, she'd hoped to catch a glimpse of the cemetery. But the view wasn't broad enough, and all she could see was a section of the highway between the treetops. She sat on the bed and gazed at the stump on her left leg. She tried to hold on to the residual glow from the dream, and tried even harder not to cry. Her mother and father and baby brother wouldn't want to see her crying.

PART 2

AND THEN CAME REVENGE

CHAPTER 6

Porto Sansudou, People's Democratic Republic of Séroulé
General Odion Kuetey sat behind the new console with its three monitors inside his office-suite at the Presidential Palace. The palace's exterior – according to detractors at the time of its completion – was a crude replica of the Hanoi Opera House, built during the French colonial period. Apart from lacking the craftsmanship of the original, they claimed, the 'eyesore' differed in that its façade was entirely pale-blue and had a single broad entrance between aesthetically misplaced Doric columns. Kuetey

immediately hit back, saying it wasn't *supposed* to be a replica of *any* structure. And the detail, under his watchful eye, was nothing short of dazzling. In what other palace in the entire world would you find mother-of-pearl toilet seats throughout? Not even the Royal Family in England lived in – or sat on – such splendour! Jealousy, there was no other word for it. And mostly, he'd often suspected, whipped up by disgruntled residents in the capital city of Thekari, sixty kilometres away. There, the Presidential Palace was smaller, its interior positively drab in comparison and a place he visited only when ceremonial occasions demanded his presence. Porto Sansudou, under his leadership, had become the *de facto* capital of Séroulé. The people here were less belligerent than in Thekari. In point of fact, so far as he was concerned, the inhabitants of Thekari could go and take a hike. (He'd picked up the turn of phrase from an American ambassador who had hunted with him in the late 'nineties.)

Kuetey adjusted his eye-patch and fiddled with switches on the console. Glancing at the National Guardsman standing at attention over by the padded door: 'I can't get this thing to work,' he declared. 'The screens are still blank. I should have three pictures of three cages.'

The brawny guard gave barely a flicker of an eyelid as he stood with hands clasped behind his back, the stiff stance dictated by protocol in contrast to the guard's mandatory tilt of his crimson beret – which could be mistaken for being 'jaunty'.

Frustrated, Kuetey slammed a fist onto the desk. Seizing the yellow phone on his right, he punched in three numbers. 'Ikemba?'

'Speaking, President Kuetey,' responded a servile voice promptly. 'How may I assist you?'

Kuetey shifted his bulk in the made-to-measure swivel chair. 'These screens, there's nothing on them.'

'Are there lights showing on the console?'

'No.'

'It must be the plug, President Kuetey.'

'Where's that?'

'To the right of your computer screen, you will discover a row of plugs. They should all be switched on, otherwise the signal will not reach the router—'

'Yes, yes, spare me the details.'

Kuetey spun his chair and found the offending plug. This should have been prepared for him! He flicked the switch, and a series of lights flashed up on the console, the screens above them revealing the newly installed cages in the basement area under the palace. 'It's working,' he announced. 'Have you got someone?'

'He's being brought over as we speak from the state prison, President Kuetey. A matter of minutes.'

'What did he do?'

'He...he was caught defacing your portrait, President Kuetey, in Tojou. A most wicked individual.'

Kuetey put down the phone. He wasn't going to ask what the wretch had scrawled. It would undoubtedly have been the usual cock and balls! He'd thought the trend had ended, but apparently not. Why couldn't these people praise him? See the good he was doing the country and the relations he had built with the West?

He adjusted the air-conditioning using the keypad on his desk and patted his glistening brow with a tissue. An involuntary burp brought up some acid from his full-English breakfast, prompting him to pour a glass of water. His team of physicians had warned him his weight would further increase his blood pressure, and might well lead to other health issues. Half of what they said was utter nonsense, in his opinion. He loved his food. His dear Mama had always said: 'If it's there, Odion, eat it, because there might be nothing tomorrow'.

Finally. Ikemba, scrawny man that he was,

appeared on the middle screen pushing the half-naked reprobate into the cage, two by two metres square. The gate was locked and Ikemba disappeared from view.

The prisoner stood with his hands on the bars, puzzled perhaps as to why he had been transferred from the state prison.

The yellow phone began to ring. Kuetey snatched the handset. 'Yes?'

'Can you see him, President Kuetey?' asked Ikemba.

'Yes.'

'If you remember, when we discussed the design, President Kuetey, you asked for four squares. The green switches relate—'

'Yes, yes, I know.' Kuetey cradled the handset, straightened his eye-patch and inserted a set of earphones. He flicked down two of the green switches and turned the dial a couple of centimetres. The prisoner started to hop and yelp as the electrical current pulsated into the base of the cage. Then the prisoner thought he had found an insulated corner, until Kuetey flicked the remaining third and fourth switches. He increased the flow, and as the prisoner thrashed about the cage like a madman Kuetey felt a warm stirring in his groin, before the white telephone on his desk rang.

Yanking out the earplugs, he answered the call from his secretary over on the administrative east wing. 'Yes, Omolara? What is it?'

'President Kuetey, I have Ambassador Agaja Dohou on the line. Are you available?'

Kuetey leaned back, the ambassador being an old acquaintance who had supported the coup that had brought him to power. 'Put him through.'

'Certainly, President Kuetey.'

Kuetey made another adjustment to the air-conditioning.

'Agaja! Family good?' he asked.

'Very well, thank you, Odion. Imani and the children?'

'Yes, yes, we're all well, thank you. One of the grandchildren is to marry this coming April. You will, of course, receive an invitation. All quiet with Niger?'

The ambassador coughed a little, and after the pause: 'The Foreign Minister called me to his office. He wants us to stop pushing the Dendi further back. It's increasing the population of the Songhai on the border and causing concern.'

'No, no, no!' Kuetey reached for another tissue and patted his forehead. 'I will not have these Dendi people coming into Séroulé. They belong to northern Benin. We already have some in Douinesse. I have been tolerant enough with them, Agaja. I will personally call the Foreign Minister later today and tell him to take a hike.'

'I hope he listens, Odion.'

'He most certainly will listen.' The green telephone on his desk started ringing. 'Agaja, I have to go. I will call you this evening.' Kuetey ran the tissue back over his brow and switched handsets. 'Yes?'

'Odion, it's Ousmane—'

'Ousmane, I'm very busy. Why are you bothering me?'

'You have not seen my email and its attachment?'

Kuetey sighed and shook his head. 'Ousmane, what have I just explained to you? I said I've been busy. Please listen. Many times I've had to repeat this to you.'

'Yes, Odion. My apologies.'

'I'll look now.' Kuetey threw the tissue onto the mosaic floor and moved the mouse with his stout fingers to open the email in question. The body of the email simply read, and rather impertinently, he thought: *View attachment.*

Over recent months he had started to regard his brother-in-law as being a little stupid, and regretted listening to his wife's pleas by appointing him Director General of the State Security Service. This defacing business needed to be stamped out, and as yet it seemed Ousmane Sekibo had little interest in thwarting such an abhorrent crime, glibly remarking it was a matter for the state police.

Kuetey opened the attachment. A portrait of a mixed-race girl, head and shoulders only. 'A half caste. So what, Ousmane?'

'Name: Shani Bălcescu,' said Sekibo readily. 'Presently applying for a fifteen-day visa from the Séroulèse Embassy in London. Country of residence: Czech Republic. Recently won a four year scholarship to study at St Thomas Aquinas College, Oxford. Her passport states that last week she was in Timişoara, Romania. Mother's name: Zinsa Bălcescu, formerly Zinsa Dangbo.'

Kuetey lightly touched his eye patch and felt a tremor in his chest. 'The blood of Zinsa,' he murmured.

'What was that? I didn't hear you properly, Odion.'

Kuetey glanced at the handset and Ousmane Sekibo's babbling voice. 'You say she is at the embassy, now?'

'I will send you CCTV footage the minute she leaves.'

'There must be no hold up with the visa. Make sure, Ousmane. And keep a check on her. When she arrives in Porto Sansudou, let's see if she goes to Kabérou.'

'And we will deal with her there?'

'You will bring her back to Porto Sansudou. To me, and only me. Understood?'

'Every word.'

'And keep it within your department. There's no need for the generals to know about this.'

'Yes, Odion.'

'Be about your business, then.' Kuetey put down the phone and gazed into the expanse of green foliage and cream leather sofas beyond his desk. So, the blood of Zinsa Dangbo had finally surfaced. He looked back at the screen. 'Pretty girl,' he decided aloud, before smirking. *But for how much longer?*

Remembering the new console, he spun his chair back towards it. The prisoner was lying in a heap in the corner of the cage. Kuetey turned down the dial, having forgotten to do so before taking the first phone call. Picking up the handset on the yellow telephone, he waited for Ikemba to answer. Thirty seconds passed, then nearly a minute, before:

'President Kuetey?'

'Answer the phone more quickly in future, Ikemba. I have little time to waste.'

'I apologise for the delay, President—'

'He's not moving. The one you brought in from the state prison.'

'One moment, President Kuetey. I will go and check.'

Kuetey tutted and shook his head. Glancing at the poker-faced guard, he said: 'Have you noticed, we are always having to wait in this world. Wait for this, wait for that. It's all nonsense.' Kuetey lowered his eyes to Ikemba, shuffling about in front of the camera on the middle cage. He watched him pull a switch and unlock the gate. After turning the prisoner over, he left the cage, and finally the picture.

'President Kuetey?'

'Yes, yes, I'm still here, Ikemba.'

'I think too much electricity.'

'I was interrupted.'

'Shall I get you another one?'

'Get three. I want to check over the equipment. And find me headphones. I can't put up with these things in my ears.'

'Certainly, President Kuetey.'

Kuetey put down the handset, his gaze once again drawn towards the attachment his brother-in-law had sent over from State Security. 'The blood of Zinsa Dangbo,' he repeated, still feeling the raw shock of it all thumping away in his chest.

CHAPTER 7

Shani travelled from the Gare du Nord hotel she'd booked into over to Puteaux, west of Central Paris. As instructed, she left the Metro at Esplanade de La Défense, where she thought about taking a cab the rest of the way. But the winter sun had the feel of spring about it despite it being mid-February and, more to the point, she really needed to save every euro, the price of the flight to Séroulé and the cost of the visa itself leaving her savings virtually exhausted.

Shani made her way down a hectic Rue de la République, vehicles virtually bumper to bumper. Predictably enough, Andrei's funeral had proved to be an utterly dismal affair. Fifteen people, thereabouts, showed up, most of them from the bridge club. When she saw the coffin, the possibility Andrei had taken precious information with him briefly stemmed her sorrow. A preliminary search of the apartment had produced little of interest, though there was still time she felt to discover a detailed diary, or a handwritten account of her parent's life in Timișoara.

Seeing an opening in the traffic she crossed the road. The street she turned into had a steep incline, lined with deciduous trees that had something of a London plane look about them. Silencing her phone, she left it in her shoulder bag just as she came across a building matching the description she'd been given, the smooth red bricks creating symmetrical patterns against the grey ones. She pressed the bell alongside the name *Dubois*, and the door clicked open. She'd thought the street to be purely residential, but once inside the building she noticed names of companies on some of the doors.

'Mademoiselle Bălcescu?' called out a voice above her.

Shani turned towards the staircase, at the top of which stood a figure resembling the image she had found on her tablet in Timișoara, minus the designer stubble.

'*Oui*,' she answered, climbing the stairs. 'Monsieur Dubois?' she asked.

'*Oui*.'

After the handshake, Shani followed the journalist

across a parquet landing into a narrow corridor, which reminded her of the corridor that led to Harry Rothwell's study. She made a mental note to send him another email. Or perhaps this time she would call him. Keep him up to date with what was happening in her life. 'My French is rather hopeless,' she confessed, deciding to break the silence.

'Don't worry,' he said. 'I lived for a time in the Lake District when I was a child.'

At the end of the corridor they entered an office. Shani's eyes grew in size. She'd thought she was untidy, but this was something else. There was paper everywhere, from magazines and newspapers to handwritten and typed sheets of A4, some of it strewn along the windowsill, while heaps more lay on the mantelpiece, and even in the cast-iron fireplace itself.

'I'll take your coat. Nicolas is fine with me.'

'And Shani for me, too,' she said, watching him leave her jacket in a heap on top of a crumpled *Le Monde* broadsheet.

Nicolas manoeuvred a green tub chair closer to the desk. 'How long are you in Paris?' he asked, fiddling with a percolator on the floor over by the window. 'Coffee?'

'I will, thank you.' Shani sat and crossed her legs. 'I leave for West Africa tomorrow,' she said, while guessing Nicolas to be in his late twenties, or possibly early thirties.

'You have your visa already?' asked Nicolas, swinging round. 'You're departing from Orly, I take it?' He moved towards the door with a cup. 'I need to swill this in the washroom along the corridor.'

Shani watched him leave the office, mildly irritated over why he would ask a question, and before she had a chance to answer him he'd ask her another. She began to question her own judgement in coming to Paris, having expected a more professional set-up, rather than *being* set up because she suspected his intention all along was to photograph her and milk her for an article. Well, she wasn't going to play ball. She turned back to the mess. Filing clearly wasn't his forte. Must be annoying to live with, she imagined. In contrast, she had to admit his features seemed pleasantly proportioned, topped by slightly tousled blond hair.

The percolator on the floor gurgled briefly. Shani leaned around the side of the desk to take a look, and figured it was behaving normally. She sat back and studied the unframed print stuck to the wall opposite the window. There was something refreshing yet disturbing about the surreal landscape – possibly Mediterranean, she thought – and the highly stylised women in it. The painting's cryptic tone centred on the young woman in the foreground, separated from the others as though an outcast. Her isolation was emphasised further by a group of children part looking, part hiding under a rustic archway, its whitewashed walls luminous against the endless blue sky.

Nicolas reappeared and closed the door.

'I like that,' Shani said, pointing.

'Jean-Pierre Serrier. I keep meaning to have it framed, and long for the day I can get my hands on an original.' Nicolas poured their coffees and sat opposite her, the desk with its piled-high clutter a barrier between them. 'So, you have your visa already?'

'Without a hitch. I was quite surprised. You hear so many stories.'

'Yes.' Nicolas took a sip from a green mug covered in white dots, his greyish-blue eyes closely watching Shani. 'You say you are related to Tuma Dangbo. Correct?'

Shani folded her arms, interested to know whether her theory was on the mark, that Nicolas Dubois could supply her with little information – because, of course, he had none. 'My mother being Zinsa, the youngest of his nine children,' she said.

'I've only recently started to research Séroulé,'

mentioned Nicolas. 'Until now I've been working on Ghana and Togo, mainly. However, Tuma Dangbo has caught my attention – and not before time. But what proof do you have that you are related to him? To Zinsa?'

'My adoptive father, Andrei Bălcescu,' said Shani, 'one way or another managed to get Zinsa into Romania after the coup. He was an anthropologist, and presumably happened by chance to be working close to the village where the hunter, which you mentioned in your article, lived. Some sort of exchange must have taken place.'

Nicolas took another sip of coffee. 'But there's quite a leap here, don't you think?'

'Pardon?'

'Well, your claims... I'd just like to know how you arrived at this decision. Why is it that your adoptive father never mentioned any of this to you? Or did I happen to mishear you during the brief conversation we had over the phone?'

'No, you didn't. I can only assume Andrei wanted to protect me from General Kuetey.' Shani stiffened her gaze. 'And probably from journalists such as yourself.'

Nicolas gave her a wry smile. 'A predictable and possibly quite an accurate assumption—'

'But?' interrupted Shani, telling herself why she should care whether he believed her or not. A third rate journalist!

'Well...' Nicolas came forward and leant on the desk. 'I have to say there appears to be much presuming and assuming going on here. Again, recalling the phone call we had; some newspaper cuttings in a safe, a video relating to your birth, so you said. That aside, what you have told me so far can be found on the *Internet*, apart from the name Shema.'

Shani thought to tell him about her prosthesis, but if he didn't ask her himself it proved he was wasting her time. 'While Andrei lay dying, he asked for my forgiveness and mentioned Séroulé.'

Nicolas shrugged. 'Your word only.'

That was it! Shani stood up. 'Monsieur Dubois, you are questioning my integrity. Perhaps instead you should question your journalistic endeavours.' She snatched her jacket from the desk. 'Thank you for the coffee.' She turned to let herself out of the office, wanting the fresh air. In fact, she didn't want to be in bloody Paris, she wanted to be in Timișoara, to give herself a chance of recapturing that exquisite moment when Radu told her Zinsa had touched her before she died.

'I believe you, Shani,' interrupted Nicolas from

behind her.

She refused to face him. Was he out of his mind? He had tried to belittle her!

'I don't know much about what happened in Romania. Like I said, my main focus has been on Tuma Dangbo.'

All she could see was the desolate-looking wooden cross on the grave in the Cemetery of Heroes, and likely now to be covered in snow.

'Please, come and sit back down…'

Shani gathered herself, a growing sense that she had been speaking on behalf of her family, defending their dignity.

'…I'm sorry I had to be so fierce, so rude,' said Nicolas. 'And I understand how upsetting these past few days must have been for you, coping with the fact that Andrei never spoke of your connection with Séroulé – and, yes, his silence, I'm quite sure, was to protect you from General Kuetey.'

The last half dozen words made her whirl round. He was standing with his hands on the desk. He shrugged, which she interpreted as a peace-offering. 'You really believe that?' she asked.

'Yes. Yes, I do.'

'And perhaps to try and suppress that dreadful day in Timişoara?'

'Quite possibly. And your assumption that he wanted to avoid journalists getting to hear about you is, in my opinion, perfectly valid. Any information in the public domain regarding your existence and Kuetey would have found you.' Nicolas straightened. 'You know, since writing that article six months ago, I've had exactly that same number of people contact me claiming to be Zinsa's lost daughter. One of them being one-hundred per cent Caucasian, would you believe.'

'What changed your mind about me?'

'I can see Zinsa in you, in your features. Quite distinctly, actually.'

Shani sat down on the tub chair, her pulse racing a little. 'You can? As in what? My chin? My eyes?'

'Your high cheekbones, perhaps. And yes, well, your face generally.'

Shani met his eyes, and found what she took to be sudden solace in their blueness. Their quietness gave her reason to try and trust this man, this journalist who, after all, contrary to the majority of articles she'd seen, painted her grandfather as a staunch defender of civil liberties. Having built up her hopes, perhaps she'd expected too much from him.

She leaned forward and put her jacket back on the desk. 'You say you know more about what happened in Séroulé than in Romania, so are you able to give me an account of that day thirty-eight years ago in Kabérou? The day of the coup.'

'I believe I can.' Nicolas finished his coffee, and without taking his eyes off Shani set his mug down. 'The speed of the coup took everyone by surprise, of that there's no question, and it's been proved since that it was backed by the West. I'll come to that later. First-hand reports state that General Odion Kuetey personally went to your grandfather's retreat with his cohorts and slaughtered everyone – except Zinsa. The hunter who found her has since died, but I have spoken to a man from the same village as the hunter who remembers the day Zinsa arrived. According to his account, she didn't speak a word for a whole month, so deeply had she been traumatised. Kuetey had people search for her, so they had to hide her from sight. You've seen pictures of Kuetey?'

'Yes,' breathed Shani, absorbed by what Nicolas was now telling her.

'He has an eye patch. Well, there's a rumour that Zinsa, as she attempted to escape from him, literally poked his eye out with a stick.'

'Do you believe that?'

'Perfectly plausible, since he never wore an eye patch before the coup.'

Shani gestured with her hand for Nicolas to continue. 'Please,' she said.

'It's my belief that Andrei Bălcescu arrived on the scene within a couple of months. As you have deduced yourself, there actually was a group of anthropologists working nearby, this according to the old man in the village who claims he helped to hide Zinsa. He remembers one of these anthropologists, a white man, giving money to the village chief before taking Zinsa away. How your adopted father – or *grand*father, perhaps I should say – brought Zinsa into Romania we can only speculate, but I feel sure it was done almost legitimately, though not before switching her native country to that of Rwanda. And it's there where my research basically ends on Zinsa.'

'It strikes me that had it not been for the protest in Timișoara,' remarked Shani, 'I doubt if anyone could have tracked her down to Romania.'

'It appears Andrei did quite a decent job,' agreed Nicolas. 'But panic set in, I suspect, when Zinsa died. It was world news, meaning the Séroulèse State Security Service would have picked up the information, and known about you. To this day, Kuetey is consumed with wiping out anyone related to Tuma Dangbo. Andrei would have known this.' Nicolas picked up a pen from his desk and toyed with it for a moment, before looking directly at her. 'I have to say, I'm concerned about you going to Séroulé alone. And you're not exactly black, so you will stand out.'

'You're unnerving me,' said Shani, and meaning it.

'Just be careful. Don't be naïve.'

Shani met his gaze, mildly offended. 'Naïve?'

'Impulsive, then.'

Shani could relate to that, *being* impulsive. But perhaps there was an element of naïveté about her, too. Nicolas was likely to be much worldlier than herself. That said... 'I have to go, Nicolas. It's like a calling. A duty, even. Besides, I'll never be able to concentrate on my studies with this hanging over me.'

'Where are you aiming for?' asked Nicolas. 'Kabérou, no doubt. Correct?'

'I thought about spending my first night in Porto Sansudou,' Shani said. 'And taking the train up to Douinesse. I want to try and find my grandfather's retreat, to see if it's still standing.'

'I can tell you it isn't,' answered Nicolas. 'I've been. At a guess, Kuetey demolished it within days of the coup. All that's there is rubble and weeds.'

'I would still like to go.'

'Of course. I understand.'

'And I would like to speak to the old man in the village. Could you show me on a map where it is?'

Nicolas stood and sifted through some of the clutter on the desk. 'I'm in the middle of moving,' he said. 'I now have a studio off Rue de la République, although I'm not sure how I'm going to fit all this in there.' He plucked out from the tangle of papers a map with a yellow cover. Unfolding half of it, he pointed. 'The ruins are right here, a couple of kilometres from the town of Kabérou, and about fifteen from Douinesse, which is the capital city in the Tisounga region. Séroulé is made up of sixteen *départements*, or counties, you might say in England.'

Shani came around the desk and reached for Nicolas's pen. 'Where your finger is, by that river?'

'The River Tégine, yes.'

'Could I borrow this? It looks to be quite detailed.'

'Yes, of course.'

She was about to mark the point on the map when Nicolas stopped her, putting a hand on her arm.

Shani froze, the unexpected contact sending a shock through her – the sensation too brief to analyse beyond knowing it had not been unpleasant in the least. 'Sorry,' she managed to say, lowering her arm. 'I…I don't want to forget the location.'

'It isn't that. You can keep the map. It's just that if you were searched, it might appear suspicious. The thing to do is this…' Nicolas rummaged through a colourful bowl that looked as if it had been woven from the inner core of a telephone wire. '...Make a pinhole. So, this one here is the village before Kabérou, and this one here – approximately, is the retreat, bordering the forest where Zinsa made her escape. The rest is open woodland.'

Shani folded the map. 'Thank you.' She returned to her seat. 'You have something of a story here, Nicolas, don't you?'

'Yes.' Nicolas sat back down. 'Quite a scoop, in fact.'

'And I can't stop you, can I?'

'I'm not going to do anything.'

'Forgive me,' said Shani, forcing a smile, 'but there's a "but" here, isn't there?'

'I would like the exclusive, for sure. If and when...' Nicolas put his mug down on the desk. 'Contrary to what many believe, not all journalists are heartless. If the news leaked out while you were in Séroulé, it might well put you in danger. I think it's important that you do go. Food for your soul, as it were. But my advice is don't mention your grandfather to anyone, even if you believe it safe to do so. Kuetey has spies everywhere.'

Shani leaned back in the chair, relieved. A decent guy, this Nicolas Dubois, she told herself. He'd witnessed life's underbelly, she could see that. And she liked his practicality. 'General Kuetey,' she prompted, folding her arms. 'Not a particularly pleasant individual by the sounds of it.'

'A raging psychopath,' said Nicolas. 'When it comes to dictators paranoia usually kicks in at some point, insulating them from reality. Erase Kuetey's odious crimes against humanity and you are left with a quirky, somewhat cartoonish figure. In fact, with Kuetey the generals have now basically taken over. They run the show, the regime, and simply feed him with whatever he wants to hear.'

'And the West turns a blind eye to this vile regime?'

'Absolutely.'

'You said the coup was backed by the West?' mentioned Shani.

Nicolas refilled her cup. 'Kuetey exploited the fact that your grandfather hadn't increased the military's budget for three years, while he struggled to deal with the monumental debt left by his predecessor.'

'But why did the West support Kuetey?' asked Shani.

Nicolas lowered his eyes and pursed his lips. 'The superpowers and their multinationals are doing incredible damage to Africa,' he said, looking back at Shani. 'The plundering of minerals and oil, in return for a few clinics, schools, and the odd tarmacadam road here and there. But what's really at stake is the soul of a continent and its people. Your grandfather decided to make a stand. He wanted Africa, and all that lies beneath its soil and seas, for the people of Africa. So they got rid of him, and defiled his character.'

'The more you talk to me about him,' said Shani, 'the more I wish I could have met him. Had a conversation with him.'

'Well, you say that,' responded Nicolas, 'I can tell you there's a movement in Séroulé which champions precisely what your grandfather hoped to achieve. This movement also exists in Togo, Benin, and Ghana. It's largely underground, so it's hard to get details regarding its supporters. Which politicians, for example, might be involved – albeit covertly. But I know Khamadi Soglo would be very keen to meet you.'

'Who is this person? What does he do?'

'He's the main freedom-fighter.'

'Is he in Séroulé?' asked Shani. 'I could visit him while I'm there.'

Nicolas shook his head. 'It doesn't work that way, Shani. Khamadi would have a hard time evading informers if he was in Séroulé.'

'Where is he, then?'

'He operates between Paris and London. Besides, you can't fix a meeting like *that*.' Nicolas clicked his fingers. 'Certain protocols have to be observed. But with your permission, I will try and set one up. Though it could take weeks.'

'Okay.' Shani reached for her jacket. 'I hope something can be done, people made to understand. Your work is invaluable, and you've given me much to think about. I mustn't detain you any further, Nicolas.' She stood, and arrived at a decision. She wanted to hear *his* story, *his* background. How he got into journalism. 'Can I invite you to dinner when I get back? To say thanks.'

'At St Aquinas?'

Shani smiled. 'You've done your research. But no, not St Aquinas. It's too academic. I mean here, in Paris.'

'I guess we have a date,' said Nicolas. 'Look forward to it.' He put out his hand. 'But for me, right now, something positively mundane in comparison. A check-up at the dentist.'

Shani shook his hand, liking the firmness of his grip. Something gracious and respectful about it that made her reluctant to leave him. 'Good luck with that,' she said supportively, zipping her jacket.

* * *

Nicolas had ten minutes to spare before heading off for his appointment, and decided to make use of it.

Shani had obviously made her presence known in Timișoara, in particular at the hospital where her mother had been taken to. It only needed a bright spark, in his opinion, to cash-in on her visit. He went to *images* on his laptop, and typed in *Balcescu, Zinsa, Timisoara, hospital.* Nothing, apart from a few unrelated pictures of Zinsa, which he'd seen before. He reversed *Balcescu, Zinsa.* Still nothing. In the search bar he deleted *hospital* and added the name of the cemetery she'd mentioned she had visited during the phone call they'd had. Again, nothing. He opened up an image of the cemetery and eventually found the translation for *Cemetery of Heroes*, the search bar now reading *Zinsa Balcescu, Cimitirul Eroilor, Timisoara.*

He smiled, because his hunch had proved to be correct. The image he was interested in formed part of a newspaper article under the banner *ȘTIRI DIN TIMIȘOARA.* The article itself was headlined *MISTERUL LUI ZINSA.* He took a guess that *misterul* translated as 'mystery'.

He scrolled through *contacts* on his mobile phone and made a call.

'Françoise, can you spare a moment?'

'Hi, Nicolas,' came a cheerful response. 'Sure. Go ahead,'

'You can speak Romanian, if I remember.'

'I'm no expert.'

'Are you in front of your PC?'

'What is it you want?'

'Go to images. Type in *Zinsa Bălcescu, Cimitirul Eroilor, Timişoara*.'

'One moment… Zinsa Bălcescu, Heroes Cemetery, right?'

'You need to use the Romanian translation, otherwise you won't find it. Three in from the left…'

'I have it. Bit blurry. Looks like it was raining, right? You want me to read you the article?'

'Can you mail the translation to me? I need to dash.'

'It'll take half an hour.'

'You're a saviour. Time we hooked up.'

'Have to be next month, Nicolas. I'm leaving tomorrow to cover the election in Paraguay, of all places. A favour for someone. You know how it is.'

'Catch you when you get back, then. *Ciao*.'

Nicolas left his desk, slammed the door shut to his office and raced down the stairs to keep his appointment.

No question about it, he was going to have to explain to Shani it would be too dangerous for her to leave Paris for Séroulé, his worst fears now realised.

CHAPTER 8

Shani climbed the stone stairs to the first floor and let herself into her room with its dark brown utility furniture. She had to admit the hotel itself was a bit seedy, with cracked leather chairs in the poky reception area and grazed walls up the staircase. But more importantly, it was cheap.

The street below was bustling and she wondered how much sleep she was going to get. Perhaps by then it would have quietened down. She left the window and sat on the bed. It was already three-thirty. She called Christina in New Haven, Connecticut.

'Shani, where are you?' fizzed Christina. 'You've had your phone switched off.'

'Cheapy hotel in Gare du Nord. I've got my visa. How's Yale?'

'All work, no play. Have you met the journalist

guy?'

Shani played with a loose stitch on her jeans. 'It turned out okay, after a bumpy start. Talk about untidy.'

'Well, you have something in common by the sounds of it.'

'I'm not that bad!' Shani leaned into the pillows. 'Christina, do you think I'm naïve? Be honest.'

'Of course not. You know what I think. Impulsive, on occasion.'

'Impulsive? I know I can be.'

'Why are you asking?'

'Just something Nicolas said. He wasn't being impolite.'

'Are you going to see him again?'

'When I'm back from Séroulé. I've asked him out for dinner. A gesture to say thanks.'

'Perfect.'

'Christina, it's not like that!' Shani heard Christina giggle softly and found herself joining in. 'Behave, will you,' she said.

'Must go. Seminar in fifteen minutes. Heaps of kisses. Don't forget to call me.'

'The moment I land.'

Shani ended the call as it dawned on her in twenty-four hours' time she would have arrived in West

Africa – a journey of a lifetime, in more ways than one.

* * *

Her phone chimed as she left the shower. Shani put her towel down and reached across the bed for it, noticing a number rather than a name on the display.

'Hello?'

'Shani? It's…it's Nicolas.'

'Hi,' she said, pleasantly surprised, though stopped short of telling him so. The dinner date was as far as she wanted to take it for now. 'I must put you in my contacts.' She began to dry herself, balancing the phone on her shoulder. 'How was the dentist?'

'Oh, fine… Look, Shani, I…I don't think you should go to Séroulé. It's too dangerous.'

Shani sat on the bed, disappointed that this was what the call was really about. As it so happened, maybe she wouldn't have minded a quiet drink with him. 'Nicolas, I've spent a thousand pounds on a visa and flights,' she argued. 'I have to go. I *need* to go. Food for my soul, remember?'

'Shani, there's been a development. Where are you staying?'

'Maison Rouge. Gare du Nord. What development?'

'Maison Rouge? You're sure?'

'I'm certain. Why? I mean, I know it's cheap—'

'Look, I'll be there in about fifteen minutes.'

Her phone went dead. Shani looked at it, annoyed. No matter what he was going to come out with, she was going to Séroulé. She had no intention of shouting from the rooftops that her grandfather happened to be Tuma Dangbo. All there was to it! And why did he sound surprised about the hotel she was staying in? So it was cheap, so what?

She dressed, and as she did so felt the white pebble she'd taken from the grave in the pocket of her jeans. She leaned back on the bed and kissed it. 'You'll keep me safe,' she whispered. 'I just want my life to be peaceful, dear Mama, dear Papa.' She'd reverted to her original idea and named her brother Tuma, certain now her grandfather had behaved honourably throughout his presidency, as short-lived as it tragically proved to be.

Shani left the bed to floss and brush her teeth for something to do while she waited. She would listen to what Nicolas had to say. It seemed he had her interests at heart, although to heed his advice might prove challenging. She wiped her lips with a tissue and went and opened the door to wait for him.

A girl around her own age wearing a blue negligee drifted towards her in the corridor, an easy smile on her lips.

'*Bonjour*,' she said.

'*Bonjour*,' returned Shani, smiling, while thinking it to be slightly odd that she should be wearing just a negligee. The girl walked past and Nicolas came into view behind her. 'Hi,' she said to him.

Nicolas shoved her back into the room and yanked the door shut behind himself.

'What are you doing here?' he asked her in a taut whisper.

Shani flinched away from him. He seemed a different person, the roughness of his manner and the tension on his face unnerving her. 'I'm staying the night.'

'This is a whorehouse.'

Shani found herself backed up against a wall. '*What?*'

'A house of ill-repute. Call it what you will. The girl in the corridor happens to be a *fille de joie*. I'm telling you.'

Weak-kneed, Shani sat on the bed. 'Are you sure that's what the hotel is?'

'Surer than the saints above us.'

She shook her head. 'My mind's on overload. I'm so distracted at the moment.' She looked up and noticed his cheeks to be slightly puffed out. 'This place is cheap. I'll keep the door locked and put a wedge under it. I'm having to watch my expenses.'

Nicolas unexpectedly chuckled drily. 'Yeah, well, join the club.'

'You mentioned something about a development.'

'Did you bring a laptop or tablet, or whatever?'

'Yes. I wish I hadn't, actually. Perhaps I could leave it with—'

'Open it.'

'What, now?'

'Yes. Open it.'

Shani stopped short of her backpack, annoyed with him again. 'Look, Nicolas, I have to say this, you can be quite abrasive at times. It borders on rudeness. There's enough going on around me as it is, and I really don't need you ordering me about.'

Nicolas took off his jacket and tossed it onto the bed. 'Laptop, please. Better?' He made a point of meeting her eyes. 'I don't want you going to Séroulé. I have to make that clear to you.'

Shani extracted the tablet from her backpack, thinking how peculiar the moment was: they'd barely known each other a few hours, and already they were having what felt like a 'domestic'.

Nicolas sat on the bed, balanced the tablet on his knees and started to type. He glanced at her as she went over to the chair by the dresser with its chipped mirror. 'I apologise. Hardly an adequate excuse, I know, but I've got several deadlines ahead of me.'

'You're stressed?' Shani asked at length.

Nicolas looked up from the screen. 'It's just that all this has thrown me. I mean, *you've* thrown me.'

Shani sat up in the chair. He wasn't making sense. '*I've* thrown you?'

'Tuma Dangbo's grandchild, for God's sake. What do you expect?' He typed a few more words and turned the tablet towards her. 'So, what do you see?'

The image on the screen caught her breath. 'Oh, no... That's me at the grave in Timişoara.'

'Quite.'

Drawn by disbelief, she sat on the bed beside him to take a closer look at the image. 'How did you find this?'

'By putting Cemetery of Heroes into the search bar, basically. It's from a national paper. Do you know who might have taken it?'

There could only be one possibility. 'Yes, I think so. Radu, who witnessed my birth, and who showed me the grave, took me to the records building.'

Nicolas opened the article. 'Go on...'

'There was a clerk in there, working on his own. Thinking back, I might have given him the idea because I asked him if I could photograph the record relating to the grave. As I was leaving the cemetery, he was watching me.'

'I had someone translate this article.'

Shani noticed for the first time a faint scar parallel with his jawbone. 'What does it say?'

'Nothing you don't already know,' said Nicolas. 'Basically, it poses the question of whether or not you are Zinsa's daughter. But the point, Shani, that I want to impress upon you is this: if I found it, I'm quite sure the State Security Service in Séroulé with all its tendrils and surveillance apparatus would have found it, too.' His phone started ringing. He stood up and took the call, his back to her. '*Oui?*'

Shani gazed at the exposé on her tablet, Nicolas talking so fast in French that she could only translate the occasional word.

He clicked his fingers to catch her attention. 'Okay for me to look at your passport?' he asked.

Shani took it from a side-pocket inside her bag and handed it to him.

Nicolas flicked through the pages. '*Entrée Timișoara... Oui.*' He covered his phone and looked at Shani. 'The person I'm speaking to is called Osakwe, first name. He's close to Khamadi Soglo, the freedom-fighter I mentioned back at the office. He wants to say a few words to you. Okay?'

Shani nodded and stood up. Freedom-fighters.

What next? she wondered. Events in her life felt akin to an intriguing landscape rushing by while on her Kawasaki. She took the phone from him.

'*Bonjour*, Osakwe,' she said.

'*Bonjour*, Shani. You want me to speak to you in English?'

'If you wouldn't mind.' Shani pressed the phone to her ear, a background hiss making it difficult to catch every word. 'Thank you.'

'Well, we are all very excited to know that you actually exist. We want to set up a meeting between you and Khamadi. We will speak to Nicolas about this. In the meantime, we understand your desire to go to Séroulé, but it will be very dangerous for you. I understand you received your visa within hours?'

'Yes, I did,' confirmed Shani, sitting back down on the bed. 'You believe it to be suspicious?'

'In your case, I think it could be. Embassies around the world have certain names of people, towns and cities, et cetera, programmed into their systems. Séroulèse Embassies, though less sophisticated, are no exception. And when they checked your passport they would have seen that you entered Timişoara last week. Do you understand the point I'm making?'

'Yes, I believe so. My cover, if you like, is blown.'

'Shani, I strongly advise you not to leave tomorrow.' The voice with its mellifluous French accent paused. 'You are disappointed. Yes?'

Shani tried to hold back her tears. An hour ago she was so close to leaving for Séroulé. Why did it have to be *this* complicated? 'Yes, I am,' she said. 'But I thank you and Nicolas for pointing out this danger to me.'

'Shani,' said Osakwe, 'we will get you to Séroulé, to Kabérou, within the next six months. Sooner than that, maybe. Okay?'

'Thank you.'

'I will speak to Nicolas, now. Au revoir, Shani.'

'Au revoir, Osakwe.' Shani handed the phone back to Nicolas. 'He wants to talk to you.' She took sip from a bottle of mineral water while Nicolas babbled away in French. Ending the call, he looked across at her.

'There's no doubt about it now,' he said, 'you're definitely going to meet Khamadi Soglo. Something of a consolation, you have to agree.'

Shani put her face in her hands. 'Nicolas, I've just blown a thousand pounds – the cost of my flight and visa.'

'Better to do that, than lose your life. Anyway, these guys will get you in for nothing. As for the money, I'll give you more than that for the exclusive, if and when. It would take me a couple of months to pay you... Although, to be honest, you could make a fortune elsewhere, if you chose to do so.'

Shani took her hands from her face. When it came to her situation, he was all she had. And, he might *even* have saved her life. 'Nicolas, you can have the exclusive for free. I wouldn't charge you. Why should I want to do that?'

'Thanks.' Nicolas moved over to the window, glancing back at her a couple of times, but saying nothing. Like he had a dilemma on his mind.

'I do have one stipulation, though,' added Shani.

'Tell me...'

'That anything you write about me will help to blow wide open the West's dealings with Kuetey.'

Nicolas grinned. 'I like it, already. When will you return to Oxford?' he asked.

Shani shrugged. 'Tomorrow, I guess. I'm getting behind with my DPhil.'

'Oxford terminology for doctorate, I presume.'

'Yes.'

Putting his hands in his trouser pockets, Nicolas looked further around the depressing room with its noisy street outside. 'Okay,' he said finally, 'pack your things. You can stay the night at my studio. The bedroom's yours. I'm going to be working through much of the night itself. Deadlines, remember?'

Shani gazed at the threadbare carpet, not knowing what to think, apart from what was immediately inside her head. She couldn't get any closer to Zinsa. Her remains lay in Romania, of that there was no doubt, but she desperately wanted to start from the beginning – and that meant Séroulé.

She looked up, and had to wait a moment before Nicolas turned to her because she wanted to make eye contact with him. The tension seemed to have left his face, his cheeks less swollen. 'I owe you a sincere apology, Nicolas. And if I can stay the night at your studio instead of this weird hovel, then of course I'm very grateful.'

Nicolas offered her a weak smile. 'I'm just relieved that I got through to you before it was too late. Okay?'

'You're not the first person to have that problem.' Shani started to pack. How could she not have seen it was a brothel masquerading as a hotel? A hotel that happened to be called *Maison Rouge*! Christina would laugh her head off, providing she dared to tell her.

CHAPTER 9

With dusk falling, Shani caught sight of the Town Hall on Rue de la République, before following Nicolas into a smaller street on their right, where various commercial buildings and shops mingled with apartment blocks.

'I really liked Rue de Brazza, where you have your office,' she said. 'Lots of trees. I like trees. I used to climb them in the park when I was a child.'

Nicolas steadied her backpack on his shoulder. 'You're funny.'

'Because I like trees? Or because I used to climb them?'

'Because you're you.'

'Me?' Shani saw the smile she'd liked when seeing the picture of him on her tablet in Timișoara. 'I'm not so sure about me,' she said. 'Somewhat flawed. What an idiot for not suspecting it might be a brothel. I must be naïve.'

Nicolas laughed. 'Am I expected to say something, here?'

'Maybe. Your choice.'

'Like you said, you've been preoccupied. Don't beat yourself up over it. When we're distracted, our minds don't compute so well. That's what happened to you at Maison Rouge.'

They mounted a row of steps to reach a six-story apartment block. In the fading light, Shani noticed plants spilling out of window boxes onto the pale stonework, and thought it to be a nice place to live. She followed Nicolas across a carpeted lobby and into the available elevator.

'Did you say earlier you'd just bought your studio?' she asked.

'A couple of months ago.'

The elevator slowed, before coming to a cushioned stop. Nicolas handed her the backpack outside a door with *56* in green numerals.

'Wait here a moment,' he said. 'I need to get the key.' Further down the corridor, he reached up to a ledge above an archway leading to a stairwell. 'I left my keys at the office. I'm always doing it. Absent minded, you see?'

'Not quite the same as naïve,' said Shani.

'I regret saying that.' Nicolas turned the key in the lock. 'An unfair assessment, okay?'

'Not entirely. A possible by-product of being impetuous, let's say.'

Nicolas grinned over his shoulder and changed his accent to 'posh English'. 'Gosh, aren't we being frightfully pleasant. Don't you rather agree?'

Shani giggled and suppressed a playful urge to push him into the studio. She waited for him to switch on the light. And when he did: '*Oh là là*,' she breathed, taking in the white walls, maple furniture, and sandy-coloured bricks. 'I have to say this is *really* lovely.' Her hand on her chest, she followed him deeper into the living area, a vibrant abstract painting on her right, while set against the far wall a kitchenette complete with all the necessary appliances. 'It's so cute, Nicolas. And not at all untidy. I'm shocked.'

'I need to check on the guy below me,' said Nicolas. 'He's not in good shape.'

'And I ought to phone Dusana,' said Shani. 'Andrei's housekeeper. Tell her I'm heading back to Oxford tomorrow.' She went and sat on a stool beside the worktop that annexed the kitchenette to make the call.

Dusana listened as Shani filled her in.

'Darling, you must take their advice. But "rebels",

what is this?'

Shani winced. Why had she mentioned that word? Silly of her to think she could get it past Dusana. 'People…people who oppose the current regime. They are experts in this sort of thing, Dusana. Some of them are academics,' she added, and found herself holding her breath.

'I see—'

Shani jumped in to change the subject. 'Were the Bohemians playing at home today, Dusana? I'm sure they were.'

'They won.'

'Bravo.' Shani drifted over to the dormer window, watching cars in the distance speeding along an illuminated Rue de la République.

'When they scored,' mentioned Dusana, 'I heard the roar from my apartment.'

'Excellent… Dusana, I'm returning to Oxford tomorrow. I'll call you when I arrive. How are the cats?'

'Sleeping. We're all peaceful here.'

'I'll go now. Love you.'

'Love you too, darling. Always. And be careful.'

Shani put the phone back in her bag and took a closer look at the studio. An en suite shower cubicle on her right, and the partitioned-off double bed itself with yellow pillowcases and a sky-blue duvet. What caught her eye most of all, though, were the photographs that lay on top of the built-in dresser. She knew she shouldn't – but, hey, she needed to check out the guy she was staying over with. Safety first, obviously. She glanced through them. Many featured a pretty, athletic brunette larking about with Nicolas on a boat. Perhaps on the Seine, Shani wondered. She felt her mood take a nose-dive. She'd been kidding herself. Of course, there was always going to be someone in his life! She wanted to run from the apartment. And what did that tell her? That she needed to peg down her emotions, and refocus on Séroulé. That was, after all, the primary reason for her being here in Paris. She put the photographs back and returned to the living area.

On a coffee table sat a dog-eared book with a transparent sheath protecting its cover of a beautiful Indian-looking girl, and the title *Madeleine*. Shani picked it up to see if there were pictures inside to get an impression of what the book was about.

Nicolas breezed into the studio, setting a paper bag on the worktop. Shani smelt freshly baked bread.

'It's getting quite chilly,' Nicolas said. 'I'll put the heating on.'

'How's your neighbour?' asked Shani.

'He's OK. He used to be in the Foreign Legion, and took a few knocks which are beginning to catch up with him.' Nicolas shut the air vent above the dormer window. 'He's virtually wheelchair-bound now. And a little crazy with it, I have to say.'

'Crazy?' echoed Shani.

'He keeps a Walther and an Uzi, would you believe. They bring back memories of the good old days, apparently. I get his drift. Totally illegal, of course. He'd never get a licence for them.'

'I don't understand. They're guns, aren't they?'

'Yes. A handgun and a submachine gun, the Uzi being the submachine gun.'

Shani's eyes widened. She couldn't believe what he was telling her. 'Here? Below us? A submachine gun? Is the guy totally nuts?… Has anyone reported it?'

'I'm probably the only one who knows.' Nicolas went over to the kitchenette. 'He was eighty-two last week. I took him out to the countryside, so he could use his guns. Made his day. He's still talking about it even now.'

'Nicolas, you're as cracked as him.'

'I doubt if anyone could be quite as cracked, as you put it, as Jacques. Hungry?' he asked.

'I am, actually,' said Shani, recovering. She hoped she hadn't offended him by suggesting he was 'cracked'. She rather liked the fact that he might be. Well, a little off-center anyway.

'What do you fancy?'

'Do I smell freshly-baked bread?' she asked, directing her gaze at the bag he'd left on the worktop.

'*Oui*. From the street below.'

'Then you know what this adorable studio suggests to me?'

'The suspense is killing me.'

'Warm bread rolls, cheese, and red wine. There.'

'And that's it?'

Shani pursed her lips 'Mmm…any Nina Simone?'

'*Here Comes the Sun*, for starters?'

'Perfect.'

'You're easy to please.' Nicolas found the CD in a stack at the side of the player. Turning down the volume, he went back to the kitchenette and washed his hands.

Shani flicked through the book she had found. 'Nicolas, who is this girl?'

He turned from the sink. 'Noor Inayat Khan.' He began slicing the baguettes into quarters. 'She was a spy in the Second World War with the SOE – Special Operations Executive. A very brave one, at that. *Madeleine* was her codename.'

'Did she get through the war safely?'

'She was betrayed here in Paris, and detained at the Gestapo Headquarters on Avenue Foch, where she made a daring attempt to escape with a couple of other prisoners. If it hadn't been for an air-raid alert when they climbed out onto the roof of the building, they might have got away with it. She met her end in Dachau.' Nicolas opened a bottle of wine. 'Come and sit,' he said.

Shani left the book where she had found it. 'I hope I can get to Séroulé,' she mentioned.

'Of course you will.'

'It's occupying my mind.'

'Certain to.' Nicolas poured the wine. 'But Séroulé's a nasty place at the moment. I wish I could say otherwise.'

Séroulé aside, the photographs on the dresser were on Shani's mind, too. They were not in frames, or even standing upright. Maybe they'd broken-up? Or perhaps the girl could have even been his sister, or a cousin. She hadn't thought of that.

'What's your thesis about?' asked Nicolas, laying a slice of *Saint-Nectaire* on a chunk of bread.

Shani took a sip of wine, liking its full-bodied character. 'It's about the birth of modern-day internationalism, and its effects on civilisation. Or perhaps I should say, *side*-effects on civilisation.'

'I take it your opinion isn't overly favourable?'

'Globalisation governing fiscal policy? I hate it.'

Nicolas laughed. 'With a passion, by the sounds of it. Incidentally, I do too.'

'About a year ago, I started reading Edward Abbey. Have you heard of him?'

'*The Journey Home*, right?'

'Amongst others. But actually there's a telling quote in that book, simply: *Growth for the sake of growth is the ideology of the cancer cell.*'

'It's what got me to read the book. Do you have a supervisor at St Aquinas?'

'Yes. He's off-the-wall, somewhat. You'd probably get on with him,' Shani added, smiling. 'Going back to Séroulé for a moment, do you think Andrei was really out to protect me? Could there be another reason?'

'I can't see what it could be. Can you? I mean, what would you have done had he told you? You would have gone to Séroulé. Before that, probably Romania, staying longer than you did on this occasion, leaving yourself vulnerable to the media. I think you were lucky you got out when you did.'

'I'm starting to realise that, too.' Shani looked around herself, everything as delightful as when she first set eyes on the studio. 'What made you choose to live here?'

Nicolas refilled their glasses. 'I split with my partner. We sold the property we shared in Neuilly, a couple of kilometres away on the other side of the river.'

Shani flicked a wisp of hair away from her eyes. 'I'm sorry to hear that.' She felt awkward and fiddled with the stem on her glass, perfectly aware she wasn't being entirely truthful.

'We're still friends. It was very amicable. Basically, she wanted a family. She was five years older than me, and decided time was running out for her. I'm not quite ready for it myself.' Nicolas put his plate to one side. 'And you?'

'I recently split, too. He wasn't the man that I thought he was.' Shani didn't want to spoil the evening by mentioning she'd found pornographic images of amputees on his laptop. 'It happens,' she said simply.

Nicolas gave her his half smile. 'You know what I like about you?'

Shani lifted her head, preoccupied all of a sudden by the 'foot issue'. How was she going to put it to him, if one day it came to it? 'What might that be?' she asked. His gaze seemed so intense she lowered her head again to avoid it, wishing her life didn't feel so bloody…'disarranged'!

'Your sense of decency,' said Nicolas. 'You even managed to thank me for the cup of coffee after our contretemps.' He stood and began to clear the table. 'Unfortunately, I need to make a start on dealing with these deadlines.'

Shani happily took her plate over to the draining board and finished her wine, relieved by Nicolas's decision to essentially end the evening – and liking him all the more for giving them both the space to reflect on their friendship, if that had been his actual intention. 'Do you mind if I take a shower?' she asked. 'I really feel like I need it after Maison Rouge.'

'There's a clean towel on the chair in the bedroom,' said Nicolas from the sink. 'As for the bed itself, the bottom sheet's a couple of days old. Can you put up with that?'

'I'm just grateful. I don't care if it's a week old. But if you're working, I might catch an early night. Can I take *Madeleine* with me?'

'Of course.' Nicolas dried his hands and went over to a bookshelf. 'But take this one, too. It's more up to date. And these, *Twenty Jātaka Tales* from the original publisher that I managed to get my hands on. Noor rewrote the tales before leaving Paris at the beginning of the war.'

* * *

Focus on Séroulé. That's what she had to do. That's *all* she wanted to do! But still Nicolas and the foot issue continued to torment her because, of course, she'd started to like him. He had principles that appealed to her, his character well-rounded. She could learn from him, and understand *precisely* what was happening to Africa.

Shani left the towel on the back of the chair and put on clean underwear for the third time that day, and a powder-blue T-shirt with BOHEMIA stamped diagonally across the front of it. She wished she had some eye make-up for the morning.

The foot issue. Shani looked at the photographs of his ex on the dresser. How could she possibly be half as attractive as this? Her stomach wobbled, which invariably meant the start of an episode. She immediately put the photographs back. She was leaving tomorrow. He had his deadlines. She had her damned thesis… There was only one thing for it. She needed to give him a signal – confirmation – that she was 'interested'.

She sat on the chair and tried to marshal her thoughts. But it was hopeless. Fact was she was getting herself into a state. She could *feel* it happening, her anxiety levels rocketing, spiralling up through the epicentre of her being and taking control of her. Full-blown neurosis!

She went over to the door, and hesitated. This was the prelude to an impulsive act. But she couldn't stop herself, because she was desperate for a conclusion. She'd never sleep without it. And the palpitations in her chest had now reached such a crescendo that they began to frighten her, so she whipped open the door.

Nicolas's head shot up from his laptop.

'This is how I look.' It came out entirely wrong. In fact, she hadn't intended to say anything, just assess his reaction when he saw her prosthesis.

Nicolas left the laptop on the couch. 'Shani…'

She watched him stand, his mouth open – a picture of bewilderment. But then:

'I know how you look, Shani,' he said. 'Although…' He came over to her. 'Although, dressed like that…well, you look really lovely. The T-shirt suits you.'

Did he have to be so *agreeable* all the time? 'Nicolas, I'm trying to be brave here,' she sniffled. She put her foot out towards him. 'And this? This hideous thing?'

'I know about that, Shani.'

'You do?'

'It was mentioned in the article I showed you earlier.' Nicolas reached out and rubbed her shoulder. 'Relax. You're burning up inside.'

'The opposite. I'm drowning, Nicolas.' Shani looked down at the floor, unable to meet his eyes. 'Did the article mention that I had a twin brother?'

'I came across that some time ago. But it did jog my memory.'

'I punish myself, you see,' she said barely above a whisper, 'because I can't accept my disability. So I know what's going to happen. You've no idea of the mileage I'll get from this. Guilt, for example, that I survived and he didn't. And that I should be making better use of my life, although I don't know quite how.'

Nicolas guided her back into the bedroom. 'You need to calm yourself. We'll talk it through, if you want. Sit down.'

'You have your deadlines.' Shani sat on the bed. 'I've made a fool of myself. I just wanted you to know about my foot.' She looked up at him, his kind face made golden by the sepia hue from the Anglepoise reading lamp. 'You know what happened with the guy I was with? I found pornographic images of amputees on his computer. I couldn't believe it. It was horrible.'

'Then he was a jerk. A one off. A miserable intervention. It's not going to happen again.' Nicolas touched her cheek. 'I'll make you something to relax you, to help you to sleep. Hot milk, brandy, and honey. Okay?'

Shani nodded. 'Yes. Thank you.'

He left her and she put her face in her hands. She felt exhausted. Why had she done it? Shocked him like that? She almost laughed at herself for asking the question. What made a person reckless…? Shyness? Defective nervous system? She sniffed and searched for a tissue, her phone giving a short buzz. A text from Christina, checking up on her. She texted back to tell her that she was perfectly fine – which, she had to admit, couldn't have been further from the way she felt.

Nicolas came back in with a mug. 'I'm so sorry,' she said. 'I've made such an idiot of myself.'

'I want that to be the last time you apologise,' Nicolas told her. He left the drink beside the lamp. 'Okay?'

'Yes. Sorry. I mean… You know what I mean.'

'Because there's nothing to apologise for, is there?'

'I've disrupted your work, all afternoon and now this evening, too.'

Nicolas gestured towards the pillows and sat on the bed. 'Lean back. Put your legs on my knees. I want to take a look at this clever foot of yours.'

She stared at him, taken aback. Why did he have to go and say *that*? Particularly after having told him about her previous boyfriend and his 'interest'. 'I…I can't.'

'Why not?'

'Because it's… I mean, what do you want to look at it for? It's not a nice thing to look at. I don't like to look at it myself.'

'It's a prosthesis, for God's sake. I'm curious about the mechanics.'

'The mechanics?'

'I've seen quite a few in my time, but yours has more detail.' Nicolas cleared his throat. 'Shani, I understand that it upsets you, and that's the last thing I want to happen – for me to upset you. But I really would like to take a look at it. My father was an engineer, so I grew up in that environment.'

'That's where you get your practicality from?' asked Shani, feeling a surge of relief.

'I suppose I do. He was a gearbox designer in the motor racing industry, and something of an inventor on the side.' Nicolas smiled. 'Drove my mother up the wall with all the bits and pieces he kept leaving around the house.'

Shani noted that Nicolas talked of his father in the past tense. 'Your mother lives in Paris?'

'No. A little village outside Limoges. More or less central France.'

Shani looked at her foot. Had to be the weirdest day of her life, she thought. But she wasn't going to have Nicolas believing her to be a pathetic, self-pitying creature. She was Zinsa's daughter! 'In the interests of engineering,' she said, and swung her legs round onto his. 'To examine it properly you're going to have to take it off. You know how to do that?'

'This button on the side?'

'You press it in to disengage it from the sock.' Shani watched him, studying his hands. Sculptured, and strong. She leaned into the pillows, taking an image of his hands with her.

'I was right,' he said, turning the prosthesis over. 'A work of art. How it moves. What's inside it? Carbon fibre spring, I'm guessing.'

'Yes. I keep a separate prosthesis for when I play squash. Has a stronger spring for the high impact forces.' Shani decided not to hold back. If he was put off by the sight of her, it was better she found out now. 'You can take off the sock.'

'I've seen one like it before,' mentioned Nicolas. 'The same silicone look to it.'

Shani waited for him to fold down the sock, until finally her stump was laid bare. She wanted to throw something over it, but his attention had reverted to the prosthesis itself, again turning it over in his hands. 'Put it on the chair with the sock and cover them over,' she said. 'You can use my jeans.'

Nicolas straightened, bewilderment creasing his brow. 'Cover them both up?' he asked. 'Why?'

'It helps to stop the nightmares. Dusana, Andrei's housekeeper – I think I told you – came up with the idea.'

'Nightmares? What happens in them?' Nicolas paused, colouring slightly. 'I'm just curious, but if you don't want to tell me—'

'I don't mind.' Shani settled herself into the pillows. She watched his face, looking for clues to his inner thoughts. 'I can't quite believe I said that.'

'A day of surprises, for us both.' Nicolas carefully moved her legs aside and sat on the chair. 'I mean, Tuma Dangbo's granddaughter, right in front of me. That's my surprise of the day.' The half-smile showed itself. 'She's kind of a nice person, too – who happens to like Nina Simone.'

'I do.'

'So what happens in these horrible dreams?'

'It's been a while since I've had one. A bad one. But I suppose the most frequent one is when I slash myself. My stomach and chest, sometimes my face. I pull the knife across very fast, in a kind of frenzy. But there's never any blood, until just before I wake up when I turn to a mirror and find myself covered in it.'

'And how do you translate – or interpret – this

dream?'

'It's easy. Self-loathing.'

'Because you can't accept your disability?'

'Yes. But then I have daydreams, too. My favourite, if I can call it that, is running down a corridor with shards of glass blasting towards me, stripping off my flesh and shattering my bones into dust, an ocean breeze blowing away my existence. Then I'm free. It's like nirvana.' Shani added another pillow so she could see him properly now that he had moved to the chair. He was sitting quietly, his gaze reflective, directed at the floor. 'Say something. The last half hour hasn't been easy—'

Nicolas held up a hand. 'I want to put something to you. A different daydream, if you like.'

'Okay,' said Shani, intrigued. 'Try me. I promise I won't be difficult.'

Nicolas rubbed his fingers against his chin, taking his time – like a military strategist making certain nothing had been overlooked. 'You know, you have so much going for you,' he said. 'If only someone could get you to see it. Your intellect. Your decency. What happened to you is unfortunate, no question. I'm not trying to trivialise your suffering. I know it's there. I get that. But you can help others, you can give hope to people because of your unique experience.

You're a giver, Shani, already I sense this in you. Once you recognise this and act on it, my bet is any self-loathing you still harbour will fade away.'

It had been said to her before, although perhaps not so succinctly – and certainly not by any counsellor. All they'd ever really done was to take Andrei's money. But she wanted to be honest with him. 'I don't have the confidence to put it into practice, Nicolas.'

'But isn't that the key word? Practice. It's what gets us through life.' Nicolas stood from the chair and covered her prosthesis with her jeans, as requested. 'I'm doing this now against my better judgment. The only reason why I *am* doing it is because I've given you a hard time. But if you stay again, and I hope you do, no way will I let you off.'

'Your final word?' Shani asked, realising he had work to do. She didn't want him to leave. The room would feel desolate.

'My final word.'

'Then good luck with your deadlines.'

'Drink your milk,' he said over his shoulder. 'It'll be nearly cold by now.'

The moment he closed the door, Shani wondered whether to return to Oxford in the morning. St Aquinas felt mind-numbing against what was going on right here in Paris. She drank the milk, the brandy in it reminding her of Dusana and the night Andrei died. So much had happened since then. So many discoveries. And now, Nicolas. She supposed she would return to Oxford. She – maybe even *they* – needed time to reflect. For things to settle, to make way for whatever might happen next.

Shani reached for *Madeleine*, just as Nina Simone's rendition of *Mr Bojangles* drifted in from the living room. It was one of her favourites. How *did* he know? She looked at her jeans covering her prosthesis on the chair. Without a second thought she left the bed and swept them away.

'He wants me to like you,' she whispered. 'To see you as clever, for heaven's sake. I'll think it over. That's all I'm saying.'

CHAPTER 10

General Odion Kuetey stood sweating in the heat beside the swimming pool in the Manhattan Garden. Quite why he'd named it thus had long since faded from his memory, but he imagined it might have had something to do with a charitable ambassador from Washington who'd happened to be in town when the palace was under construction. Adjusting his eye patch, Kuetey gave up trying to remember and patted his bald head with a tissue while watching his grandchildren splash in the pool. He had eighteen in total, and half were present – the youngest ones.

'Odion, dearest…'

Kuetey turned, and smiled at his wife, his fifth in as many decades, although this one was the youngest at thirty-two years. 'Sweetness,' he responded, as Imani Kuetey drifted towards him in her voluminous green gown, a retinue of staff in tow carrying cocktails and fashion periodicals. Her braided hair sparkled as much as her hands with gold and pearls. He didn't mind such extravagance, because it extended to their bedroom, where she *did* things the others had either stopped doing or refused to do. When that happened, he would give them a one-way ticket and an apartment in the former capital city of Thekari.

'Odion, you promised me.'

'My dear?'

Imani folded her carmine talons around the Dubonnet cocktails, taking them from a boy servant. 'You promised me you wouldn't wear your uniform whenever we are taking it easy in the Manhattan.' She presented him with a glass.

Kuetey kissed his wife's cheek. 'My dear, as I believe I mentioned yesterday evening, I have a meeting with representatives from the Dendi people. They will be told in no uncertain terms that if they continue to cross the border live ammunition will be used. They don't belong to us, they belong to Benin.'

Imani flicked her hand for the servants to distance themselves. 'Can't you get rid of them?'

'I intend to.'

'I mean immediately, permanently. Send the army up there, or something.'

'And have the international community on my

back?' Imani's ignorance irritated him at times. 'It's not like it was thirty years ago. We didn't have this social media nonsense for interfering fools to latch onto.'

Imani sipped her cocktail. 'Odion, I've been thinking…perhaps a little trip to Milano would be nice. My wardrobe is so dull these days. It upsets me. And we have the US Secretary of State passing through next month.'

Kuetey fabricated an expression of shock and spread his arms theatrically. 'For the First Lady to be embarrassed by her wardrobe is a horror that must be dealt with at once. Of course you should go to Milano.'

'Without my Odion?'

'Unfortunately so, my dear,' said Kuetey. 'Much work.' But all he really wanted to say was: *Shut up, you stupid whore!* He was relieved to find his private secretary coming towards them. 'Yes, Omolara?'

'A call, President Kuetey, from the Director General.'

'I will take it in my office.' Kuetey gave his wife another shrug. 'For the President of Séroulé, there is little time for pleasure.'

'Odion, I worry.' Imani Kuetey gestured for a servant to bring her a cigarette. 'As handsome as you will forever be, you are older now. You must delegate more, take time out. Promise me.'

Kuetey started to leave the poolside. 'My dear, Imani, we will discuss the valuable point you have raised after I have met the Dendi, but now I must speak to your brother.'

* * *

Kuetey seized the green telephone on his desk. 'What is it now, Ousmane?' he snapped.

'Odion, er…well, there's been—'

'Yes, yes? Has she arrived? Is she here, in Sansudou?'

'There's been a problem, Odion.' Ousmane Sekibo's voice was no longer self-assured, as it had been when notifying the President that Shani Bălcescu had applied for a visa.

'A problem?' Kuetey reached for a tissue. 'What problem?'

'She…she never boarded the plane.'

'*What?*' Kuetey threw the tissue onto the floor. 'Are you saying the blood of Zinsa Dangbo is still in Paris?'

'Yes…well, no longer Paris, Odion. She left this morning from Gare du Nord. She has returned to England, almost certainly Oxford.'

Kuetey's bulk sank further into the swivel chair. 'But why has this happened, Ousmane? What caused her not to catch the plane? Have you frightened her off?'

'We think she's hooked up with a French journalist called Nicolas Dubois,' explained Sekibo. 'For the last two years he has been writing lies about us.'

'And you haven't dealt with him?' Kuetey clenched his hand. *Why* had he given into his wife's request for her brother to be put in command of the State Security Service? This was a foolish act, on *his* part. He was losing his grip! 'How have you allowed this to happen, Ousmane?'

'We've been concentrating on Khamadi Soglo—'

'That heap of shit. It's time you put an end to him, Ousmane, once and for all. You have the resources.'

'We have someone inside his circle. The agent in question has been with us for over two years—'

'Yes, yes, good to know. But what about Bălcescu? I am disappointed she's not on her way. *Very* disappointed, Ousmane.'

'We are in the process of assembling a plan, a wide-ranging strategy. When completed, it will be the end of these rebels, these provocateurs and their vile propaganda, once and for all.'

Kuetey patted his brow with a fresh tissue and leaned into the swivel chair. 'And Bălcescu?'

'A key factor. She will reduce the time of the operation by half – and likely to make it twice as successful.'

Kuetey gazed across the suite towards the National Guardsman, at attention alongside the soundproof door. He rubbed his brow with his left hand. This was not the news he had expected, the guarantee now up in the air with the risk of complications arising. 'Ousmane, I don't want Bălcescu to get damaged before I get to see her.'

'This will not happen, Odion,' assured Sekibo. 'You have my word. I will bring Bălcescu to you personally. She will be protected in silk.'

Kuetey felt a headache coming on. 'Ousmane, I want to examine this plan *before* you make the slightest move. Do I make myself perfectly clear?'

'Yes, Odion. I should be ready to present the outline to you by tomorrow afternoon.'

'Then make sure you do.' Kuetey cradled the handset. From a drawer beside him, he took out a blister strip and popped open six aspirins, swallowing them two at a time. As he put the glass of water back down, the left-hand screen on the console caught his attention. Ikemba was shuffling about inside the cage with a mop and bucket. Kuetey shook his head and snatched the yellow telephone.

He watched Ikemba leave the cage.

'Yes, President Kuetey?'

'Ikemba, what exactly are you doing?'

'Cleaning the cage, President Kuetey. The last one made a mess—'

'Listen, Ikemba, I told you to get me the one who was caught selling wristbands bearing anti-government slogans. This was over two hours ago.'

'There was a mix-up with the paperwork at the prison, President Kuetey. The right one is on his way now, the one you requested. Another ten minutes.'

'Then I will speak to the senior administrator at the state prison,' said Kuetey. 'But, Ikemba, don't waste time cleaning the cages. They are animals. Remember that.'

Kuetey slammed the handset down and lowered the room temperature with the remote control. Ousmane… Ousmane worried him. What if some careless idiot went too far and badly injured the blood of Zinsa Dangbo – or worse? It didn't bear thinking about. He glanced at the cages. He wasn't going to put Bălcescu into one of them. He wanted her to suffer and scream with such intensity that even the ghost of Zinsa would hear her – for thirty-eight years, the precise length of time he had suffered with pain on the left side of his skull.

He lightly touched his head at the point of the dull ache. A physician had once suggested to him that the ache was possibly *psychosomatique*. The next day, after he'd looked the word up in a dictionary, he asked the physician to visit him and personally chopped off three of his fingers. While the man screamed and gasped, he put it to him that the pain he was feeling was most likely to be *psychosomatique*, and not to worry himself too much about it.

Kuetey glanced back at the console and waited for Ikemba to appear with the prisoner, absently patting his brow with a tissue as he did so.

CHAPTER 11

The Underground at Marble Arch was crowded and overly humid. Shani unzipped her jacket and looked at her phone. Midday. She was cutting it fine. A glance at the map and she headed for the Central Line. With all the seismic shifts going on inside her head – aside from Nicolas – she'd hardly worked on her DPhil. Increasingly, she found herself identifying the global economic system, with all its convoluted mechanisms, as destructive; its dire effects pasted over, garnished, and upheld by economists she'd once respected, but now regarded as pawns preparing the ground for a supranational currency, and thus a monopoly of power, for what logic dictated as being a faceless cartel. So her thesis, if she wasn't careful, was going to resemble a caustic assault on internationalism from a fiscal perspective, and little else. The way ahead, she figured, would be to affiliate herself with those economists, by and large at the turn of the twentieth century, who saw the value in co-operation between nations, but without the detriment of a system that in effect amounted to 'legalised' usury.

Shani left the tube at St Pancras and joined a busy concourse in time to hear a Eurostar train thundering up to a platform above her. Anyway, she reflected, sipping from a bottle of water, all she really wanted to think about was Nicolas. She wondered whether they might cut a similar pose to the gargantuan statue by the main entrance, titled *The Meeting Place*. Not so much nose to nose, they were hardly that intimate with each other, but the embrace itself.

She told herself to relax, before catching sight of him by 'arrivals'. Putting the bottle in her jhola shoulder bag, she gave a tentative wave, not wanting the gesture to appear in any way dramatic. He flashed his full smile. She laughed, relieved, uncertain as to how he might greet her. They made up the distance between themselves.

'Hi, Shani.' Nicolas put his arm around her just above her waist and brought her to his chest, kissing her cheek, followed by another that came close to her lips.

Shani let the embrace linger, the decisiveness of his clinch exhilarating, and not the slightest tremor of nervousness in her bones. She saw that as a concern, because it left her vulnerable to her impulsive nature. A contradiction, in so many ways, low self-esteem combined with spontaneity. Even the string of shrinks she was subjected to in her teens could barely fathom her out.

She searched for something to say, sensing an awkward silence. 'Good journey?'

'Some snow in Calais,' said Nicolas, 'but it didn't slow us down.'

'So I see.' Shani brushed her hand against his as they made their way towards the Underground, wanting them to hold hands. How would it feel? she wondered. Celebratory? No question – absolutely! 'Can you still manage this weekend?' she asked, absorbed by the moment, fellow commuters little more than a vague blur. 'I've booked a guest room for you at St Aquinas.'

'I'd be crazy to miss out on such an invite.' Nicolas rubbed her back. 'One deadline to go, and an interview tomorrow morning.'

'Who are you interviewing?' asked Shani, loving it when he put his hand on her back, like he was tempted to draw her closer to himself.

'A representative from the Dendi. They're part of the Songhai people, who lie across several borders.

Kuetey's been hounding them for the past decade, trying to push them further back into northern Benin and Niger.' Nicolas shot her a glance, before clasping her hand. 'You're sure about this, Shani?'

Shani nodded and pressed her fingertips into his palm. 'Positive,' she said, managing to keep her voice perfectly calm against a sudden onrush of relief. We've done it! *And this is the moment I must remember. The gratifying shock. The suggestion of intimacy.* She looked across at him. Usual 'philosophical' half smile – and she liked that, too. A full smile and she might have associated it with vanity.

'I'm not sure how they're going to get us to wherever it is we have to go,' said Nicolas, 'but the chances are we'll be kept in the dark, literally. It's vital for these freedom-fighters to keep their safe houses secret, even from the likes of us. So don't worry about their methods.'

'I'm okay with it.' Shani leaned closer, until they briefly rubbed shoulders. 'This is completely new territory for me, so forgive me if I ask the occasional crass question.'

Nicolas nodded. 'Which means you're entitled to ask whatever. Don't hold back. We need to make our way over to Fulham.'

Shani left her hand in his. 'Then let's go meet

Khamadi Soglo.'

* * *

Shani raised the zip another couple of inches on her Barbour to fend off the biting wind as she leant against garden railings somewhere off the Fulham Road. It seemed that this was their reference point for whatever was going to happen next.

Nicolas casually glanced down the side street, before his eyes settled on Shani. 'I...I haven't mentioned how lovely you look.'

Shani laughed, and wished she hadn't for it must have seemed facetious. A silly, nervous reaction, she realised, triggered by the unexpected. She held on to the railing. 'Thank you, Nicolas,' she said. 'Kind of you to say so.'

Nicolas pursed his lips, as if unsure of himself. 'Was it so funny?' he asked.

'No, not at all.' The chemistry was definitely there, Shani thought, but the timing was awful. In a matter of an hour or so she would be introduced to the man who was determined to bring down Kuetey, murderer of her grandparents, aunts and uncles. 'Just took me by surprise,' she said. 'Feels a while since someone's made such a remark.'

Nicolas chuckled softly, and took his hands from his pockets. 'Undoubtedly you're being modest.' He pointed at a red van turning into the road. 'Could be for us.' And when it drew up alongside them, he said: 'I warned you it could be something like this.'

The black girl in the passenger seat, Shani noticed, had a vibrant red ribbon in her hair. But there was no friendly smile on her lips to accompany it. She simply directed them to the back of the van with her thumb and looked away.

Nicolas waited for Shani to climb aboard. 'Sit on the wheel arch,' he suggested. He found the light switch before closing the door, then banged with his fist on the bulkhead. The van started to pull away, and Nicolas perched opposite her.

Shani flicked her hair from her eyes as they gazed in turn at one another, swaying sometimes side-to-side whenever the van swung to the right or left, or came to a sudden standstill. *I haven't mentioned how lovely you look.* Seemingly a superficial observation, but with hopefully a lot more going on inside his head. How, though, might they regard each other by the end of the day? Nicolas's opinion on Khamadi Soglo was apparent enough, so she wasn't going to discuss the limited amount of research she had done on the 'freedom-fighter' with him. She wanted to form her own opinion. And whether or not the rebels themselves were benevolent, or ruthless? Perhaps both, she imagined. But did they recognise and abide by the Geneva Conventions? If they didn't, then regardless of General Kuetey's abominable conduct, she would probably walk away, disappointed – particularly with Nicolas.

The van turned sharply and they both nearly ended up on the floor, Shani managing to catch hold of a metal strut. Any other occasion and she imagined they might have laughed. The driver put the van into reverse.

'I think we must be here,' Nicolas said, righting himself.

They came to a standstill and the engine was switched off. In the background, Shani could hear a whirring sound that lasted for several seconds – like that of an automated garage door closing. She took a sip from the bottle of water and offered it to Nicolas, who shook his head.

'Where do you think we are?' she asked.

'Been about ten minutes,' said Nicolas. 'Can't be that far from Fulham.'

The door swung open, and the girl with the red ribbon in her hair silently waited for them to leave the van. If only she smiled, thought Shani, she might actually look quite pretty, rather than constantly sullen. There again, it came to her that these people were likely to be receiving horrific news on a daily basis of capture and torture of people they knew, whether intimately or otherwise. So why should the girl have to smile for her benefit?

Shani stepped from the garage into the kitchen, a fabric blind over the window so that presumably the outside world stayed outside. Already she was getting an impression how these 'freedom-fighters' lived their lives. Entirely focussed, any luxury purely incidental and fundamentally irrelevant. The driver closed the side door to the garage and patted down Nicolas. She, in turn, was dealt with by the girl, whose expression remained impassive, even when drawing her hands over her prosthesis. So these people *knew* about her disability, which made her feel all the more insecure – the sensation akin to her soul having been ensnared and laid bare for all to see.

The girl straightened, and Shani noticed a faint scar on her left cheek. She wondered if it was tribal in origin. Their phones were taken and deposited in her jhola bag on the worktop. She hadn't expected that to happen, but realised it to be a precautionary measure and so let it go. She cast a glance around herself, the room like any other suburban kitchen with its white goods and utensils. Here and there, brightly coloured packaging stood out, bearing the brand name *Mama's*

Choice.

The driver went back out into the garage, leaving the girl to lead them into the hallway. Adjacent to the staircase were two rooms, both doors wide open. In the back-room Shani could see people sitting at laptops, another speaking into a mobile phone. In the front room, a couple – male and female – were discussing something in French. They broke off when they noticed her and Nicolas.

'*Un miracle*,' said the man, spreading his hands in an exuberant display of hospitality. '*Un miracle absolu.*'

They both came forward into the hallway, flashing smiles and white teeth, hands extended. 'Nicolas,' said the woman. 'Shani. How honoured we are to meet you, to have you with us.'

Shani shook her hand. She looked older than herself, though not by much – gentle lines on her face. But Shani got a shock when the smile collapsed. In its place, a haunted look of desperation that gave the impression her eyes had sunk into her skull.

'Please help us to liberate Séroulé,' said the woman.

Their escort, the girl with the red ribbon in her hair, was on the bottom step of the stairs, tapping her fingertips on the bannister rail as if anxious to hurry along the proceedings. Shani shook their hands. She wanted to embrace the woman, to say that she was united in their struggle. But she knew little about it, about *them*. She was running blind. She did, however, kiss the woman's hand in a gesture of humility. '*Merci*,' she said, and smiled.

Shani climbed the stairs with Nicolas, and was directed by the girl along a landing towards a man of mixed-race hovering by the door at the far end. He was quite short, but the hulking muscles across his shoulders gave the impression he worked-out. The girl left them, and Shani was patted down again, but on this occasion her prosthesis prompted a hesitation. The man looked up at her.

'I have a disability,' Shani said. 'My ankle and foot.'

The man turned to Nicolas, and Shani realised from what she'd seen so far that Khamadi Soglo's bodyguards were not permitted to speak. That by itself appeared worryingly dictatorial.

With Nicolas frisked, the guard left them standing in the corridor while he entered the room.

Shani heard a soft murmur on the other side of the door and looked at Nicolas. 'Did you see that women's face when she turned off the smile?' she whispered. 'I'll never forget her eyes for as long as I live. She was pleading with me. And the girl…she seems very odd, the one with the ribbon in her hair. I can't work her out.'

'It's the way it goes sometimes,' said Nicolas. 'Characteristics of these particular rebels. A mystery to us, maybe – but it's their way. Their method. They have their reasons. At a guess we are merely satellite components within the plot.'

'*The* plot?' questioned Shani.

'It's obvious.'

'Not to me.'

Nicolas lowered his voice further. 'Khamadi hasn't brought you here just to say "Hi". He knows that you can play a role in whatever he has in mind. And in my opinion, they are going to launch a coup against the Kuetey regime. I've thought this for the past six months.'

'I'm expected to participate in a coup?' clarified Shani. 'In what capacity, for God's sake?'

'No idea, but it has to be on the cards.'

Shani shook her head, feeling bewildered. 'Now I *am* out of my depth,' she whispered, just as the door opened and the guard reappeared to usher them into the dimly lit room.

Shani waited for her eyes to adjust to the scant glow coming from the lamp on the white desk. Why couldn't the ceiling light be switched on? The lack of light annoyed her. Had the bulb blown, or what? The man sitting behind the desk stood, and her breath caught for he seemed so tall, with closely cropped hair and chiselled features. She didn't need anyone to tell her that she just happened to be staring at a warrior in his prime.

'Shani,' said Khamadi Soglo. 'A moment that will be with me for decades to come.'

Shani shook his hand, and though he was surely being gentle with her she sensed – unreasonably or otherwise – that she was touching someone as unpredictable as a defective hand grenade.

'Khamadi. May I call you by this name?' she politely enquired.

The grave atmosphere was eased slightly by a cordial chuckle from the freedom-fighter. 'Of course,' he said. 'I feel privileged that you should want to do so, you the granddaughter of Tuma Dangbo.'

'I'm told that you have a high opinion of my grandfather,' said Shani, 'and the aspirations he had in mind for the Séroulèse people.'

'The hopes that you speak of will be achieved within the not so distant future. This has been promised to the people themselves.' Khamadi turned to Nicolas and clasped his hand. 'My dear friend, your recent articles give me succour. We breathe the same air, that of liberation. Kindred spirits.' He returned to the desk and gestured for them to sit.

Shani sat on the bare wooden chair beside her and crossed her legs, resting her hands on her knee. *A warrior*, she reminded herself. When Khamadi made a steeple with his long fingers, she imagined those hands fighting, killing. The thought of what they could do began to unnerve her, until his mellow and utterly charming voice quashed her unease.

'I'm sure you've both worked this out for yourselves,' he said, 'but we intend to rid ourselves of General Odion Kuetey and his vile regime. I cannot say when, because I don't know. It's down to a combination of factors falling into place. Unforeseen unknowns will invariably arise. But I'm hoping for the coup to happen within the next six months.' Khamadi's eyes settled directly on Shani. 'To cut to the chase, I want you, Shani, to speak to the people the moment we neutralise the State Television complex. Once they know you are Zinsa's offspring, the battle cry will surely go out, nostalgia being the potent force that is.'

Shani shifted her weight on the chair, which was uncomfortable. No cushioning. But that was the least of her concerns. How genuine was this 'warrior' in front of her? Did he really have the people's interest at heart – or just his own and that of his cohorts?

Khamadi sat back in the chair. 'So, Shani, will you do this for us? For Séroulé?'

Shani glanced at Nicolas, and got nothing from his expression. Not that she could see much in the dim light. She turned to Khamadi, and chose her words carefully. 'I do not wish to offend you, Khamadi. And I am flattered. But where is the guarantee that if this coup is successful the vanquished regime will not be replaced by another? An even more sickening regime, perhaps. Give me that guarantee. For example, paint me a picture of Séroulé the day after the coup.'

Khamadi nodded quietly, and gave her a wry smile. 'A fundamental question, and it comforts me that you should ask it so directly. Your grandfather would approve.' The rebel leader leaned forward and steepled his hands again. 'The day Kuetey is gone, Shani, is the day we will not tolerate corruption invading our borders. Séroulé will be a peaceful nation, protective of its people, seeking to heal what is damaged – the orphans who are vulnerable to hard labour, prostitution, and voodoo practices, to give one example. The Séroulèse people are suffering at the hands of this monster the West created so that they could have our oil and minerals for next to nothing. We are exhausted. When you leave here, if nothing else, think of the countless children whose parents Kuetey has either tortured or let die through disease and starvation.'

Shani took a deep breath, and asked herself whether this was propaganda. The rhetoric of revolution. She chewed her lip, thinking hard. She liked what he'd said, obviously. But… 'Khamadi, I still don't see the guarantee. I want this coup, God's sake I do. But I must not allow myself to be governed by sentiment. Correct?'

'Absolutely.' Khamadi massaged his brow with his fingertips. 'I'm trying to think of the best way to do this.' His hands began to glide over the tablet on the desk. 'Have you come across the name Jacques Baudin?'

'I can't say I have,' said Shani. 'I'm beginning to feel I should have, though.'

Khamadi pushed a hand towards Nicolas. 'Would you like to explain while I search for something?'

Nicolas turned to Shani, leaning an arm on the back of his chair. 'Jacques Baudin was the minister for education in your grandfather's government. He was a much-respected influence, despite his young age. He is now in his seventies. At the time of the coup, your grandfather was about to make him his deputy.'

'I have the article now,' said Khamadi. He turned the tablet towards Shani. 'The page on the screen forms part of an interview from last October.'

Shani reached for the tablet and began to read.

What I am saying to you is this: with the Industrial Revolution behind us, and the Technological Revolution being the icing on the cake – as they say in this part of the world, we should in fact be in the midst of a spiritual and creative revolution, and in so doing preserving Earth's resources. But, of course, because of the global debt and the methodology and clearcut motive behind its fabrication we are being kept far from that, far from our natural spiritual habitat. Consequently, we find ourselves confronted more than ever by what Tuma Dangbo called "obsolete barbarism". A distraction, if you like, while a conquest unchallenged through the back door of civilization – for want of a better description, proceeds to build a totalitarian state, enslaving the people of the world in the process.

Shani tried not to betray her surprise, because she liked the passage. It came across as logical, and she loved politics and reasoning at its most 'logical'. Cut the crap and get to the core, was her motto. She handed back the tablet, and noticed Khamadi watching her intensely, without blinking. He could probably read her like a book, but she didn't intend to make it easy for him. 'Where does Baudin live?' she asked.

'Tehran.'

'Tehran?'

'He's something of a philosopher these days.

Iranians like that sort of stuff, you know. Past masters at it, really, if you go back to Cyrus and the Persian Empire.'

'Do you communicate with Baudin yourself?' asked Shani.

'Regularly. He will head the incoming government. Obviously, its members haven't been elected by the people. A year to eighteen months before that can happen.'

'Who elected these people?'

'Baudin, and what's left of Tuma Dangbo's inner circle.'

'Yourself?'

'I made suggestions, and that was about it.' Khamadi leaned back, his gaze not leaving Shani. 'People have fixed ideas about coups. They automatically assume the leader becomes head of state. I have no interest in such a position. So why am I doing this? I've lost much of my family, thanks to Kuetey. I've watched Séroulé disintegrate into a hell-on-earth, terror-ridden state. I could show you pictures and footage that will make you physically sick and that will haunt you for the remainder of your life. Am I out to use you? That is the question that is probably troubling you more than any other. Of course I am. Will you be in danger? Yes, you will – but we will do our utmost to protect you, both before and after the broadcast.'

Shani shifted and flexed her legs, finding the meeting more intense than she'd imagined. It felt very slick, like he was selling her a product – which, she supposed, in a way he was. 'I wish I could get inside your mind.' The remark flew straight from her subconscious. No filtering.

'Isn't it the same for me, when it comes to you?'

'Not really. So far as you're concerned, I'm an open book. An innocent. You already know that I'm going to help you, don't you?'

'Because, like the majority of people in this world, you have humanitarian virtues. And there's nothing you can do about it. Unfortunately, what we are faced with is a united evil spawning schism beneath the very fabric of civilisation, and the propaganda of nationhood in the modern world being the maker of war and economic uncertainty. The fact of the matter is countries have little in way of power these days. The multinationals are in bed with the moneylenders, period.'

The weight of his words caught Shani by surprise, perfectly aware he was describing the march towards 'globalisation' via duplicitous rather than by purely organic means. She turned to Nicolas, wanting his input. It was an appalling thought, but had there been any collusion in way of strategy to get her on board between them? Nicolas, after all, had some idea of her stance when it came to political theory. 'I'd like you to ask Khamadi a question.'

'I think you've missed a point, or an issue, that should be of interest to you,' responded Nicolas directly. At Khamadi, he said: 'The immediate debt concerns me, as it does others.'

'Of course. As we speak twenty-three billion dollars' worth of debt.'

'And you can reduce this amount without a program of severe austerity?' asked Nicolas.

'Yes. We can do that. It's not a problem. Unfortunately, I'm not at liberty to comment further, other than to say the essence of our fiscal agenda will be unveiled on the day of the coup itself.'

Khamadi's response set off alarm bells with Shani. Had Nicolas discovered a flaw? Or worse, that Khamadi was selling them a nightmare dressed up as a golden dream? She made a point of meeting his eyes, with all their intrigue. Eyes that she knew, as with the elegant hands, could become as deadly as a tumultuous bolt of lightning. 'I'm not sure if that's a good enough answer,' she said. 'In fact, it falls way short.'

'I know, but there's little I can do about it,' stated

Khamadi, 'because when it comes to this issue my instructions are perfectly clear. If news got out it could – *would* – jeopardise the coup. However, you might have better luck with Jacques Baudin, though I doubt it.'

Shani looked at Nicolas to get his reaction.

Nicolas shrugged. 'I can only refer you to what you said yourself in Paris: present-day internationalism, and its effects on civilisation. Or side-effects, I think you said.'

'What are you suggesting?' Shani asked Nicolas. 'Financial disengagement from the international community?'

'Perhaps, to some degree.'

Khamadi stepped in. 'What do you want, Shani? The horror to continue?'

'Of course I don't!'

'Then a coup is the only viable option. And that includes fundamental adjustments to the fiscal program.'

'I'm putting my name to this, Khamadi. I'm at a prestigious college in Oxford. As self-centred as it may sound, I need to be certain what I'm getting myself into here because if I make a wrong move, that's it. I'm finished.'

'I think you're being melodramatic,' said Khamadi,

'but I take your point.'

Shani again glanced at Nicolas, who gave her his half smile. He knew. Without a moment's further thought, she stood and held out her hand to Khamadi. 'I'm in. But don't go and ruin my decision by patronising me.'

Khamadi got to his feet to shake her hand, raising an eyebrow. 'After this interrogation?'

Shani settled herself down again on the uncomfortable chair and watched Khamadi peer at his wristwatch. The watch looked inexpensive from what she could see of it in the dim light. Leather, as opposed to a metal strap.

'For now, moving along,' said Khamadi, 'I would like one of you to give me a word. This word will appear as a text on your mobile phones. I'll explain in a moment – but for now, a word.'

Shani turned to Nicolas for a suggestion, when a word arrived out of the blue that had a special meaning – for both of them. Speaking to Khamadi, she said: 'Prosper.'

Khamadi blinked and came forward. 'Rather appropriate. How did you come by it?'

'It was the informal name given to a network in Paris in the Second World War, otherwise called Physician. I've been reading about an agent who was attached to it. To the SOE, that is.'

'I see...' Khamadi leaned back. 'At some point, you will receive a text with the word "Prosper". The moment you do so, both of you need to make your way to Tamale, in northern Ghana, where you will receive further instructions. Speed is of the essence. Nicolas, I know you are currently in possession of a multi entry visa for Ghana. Shani...' Khamadi opened a drawer beside him and produced a brown envelope, which he pushed across the desk towards her. '...This is your visa for Ghana.'

He stood. 'I believe that's everything. Nicolas, I hear you are interviewing a good friend of mine tomorrow, Aahil Bangura, who will speak to you on behalf of the Dendi and the difficulties they are facing with Kuetey.'

Nicolas rose with Shani. 'Yes. From what I've heard, he has started using live ammunition on them. They have always lived in comparative peace, but Kuetey is having none of it.'

'His days are numbered. Tell Aahil that he and his people are in my thoughts, and when all is done I will visit him.' Khamadi came around the desk. 'I apologise for this soft light,' he said, 'but I suffer from headaches from time to time. Ironic, really, so does Kuetey – or claims he does.'

Shani picked up the envelope from the desk. 'What will you do when it's over?' she asked. 'You say, or infer, that you want little to do with governance, providing of course the coup is successful.'

'I am a farmer from the very north of Séroulé, in the hills,' explained Khamadi. 'The farm is presently uninhabited, my wife and three children in exile in Cotonou, Benin.'

'Perhaps I will meet your wife one day?' Shani asked.

'There is no perhaps, Shani,' said Khamadi, shaking her hand. 'We eat from the same table, we breathe the same air. You will meet Jasira within a matter of months, of this there is no doubt whatsoever.'

CHAPTER 12

They broke their journey to St Pancras at Russell Square at Nicolas's insistence.

'This is very mysterious,' said Shani.

'But relevant,' Nicolas told her as they left the Underground.

After a short walk they came to Gordon Square. The kiosk selling tea, coffee, and basic snacks, appealed to Shani. She thought it so cute, like a children's playhouse.

'You need to close your eyes,' said Nicolas.

'Why?' Shani looked around herself. The leaves had yet to sprout from winter on the pollarded trees. 'I can't see anything of significant interest.'

'Trust me.'

She quietly reached for Nicolas's hand. 'If you insist.'

Shani trailed behind him, and wondered what

passers-by might make of their larking about. They left the grass and came onto a path, that much she knew, and before long was sure they had walked the length of the garden.

'Wait a moment,' came Nicolas's voice.

She sensed him move behind her, and then hold her waist. She was tempted at that moment to lean back into him, so that he might put his arms around her.

'Open your eyes.'

Shani did, and came face to face with the bust of young girl. Unable to quite believe her eyes: 'It's Noor!' she cried, before reading what was inscribed on the plinth.

NOOR INAYAT KHAN
1914-1944
G.C. M.B.E.
Croix de Guerre

There were more words inscribed on the right-hand side. 'Noor Inayat Khan,' Shani read aloud, 'was an SOE agent infiltrated into occupied France. She was executed at Dachau Concentration Camp. Her last word was *"LIBERTE".*' Shani looked up at the bronze bust. 'It captures her beautifully. So inspiring.'

'And if you look this side of the plinth,' said

Nicolas, 'it reads: Noor lived nearby and spent some quiet time in this garden.'

'I can picture her being here,' said Shani. 'Reading poetry, perhaps. Or even composing a poem of her own.' She noticed a bench. 'Do we have time to sit?'

'I've half an hour to spare. Warm enough?' Nicolas asked her.

Shani nodded as they headed over to the bench. 'So much seems to have happened today. I'm not sure where to begin.' Reaching the bench, Shani snuggled up to him rather than continue to hold his hand. Something different, she thought. 'How did you get that scar on your jaw?' she asked.

Nicolas laughed and put his arm around her. 'Talk about random.'

'I'm curious. I noticed it at Maison Rouge.'

'I see. It was a consequence of me being a little wet behind the ears. I took some clandestine photographs of a corrupt politician in Sénégal. Trouble was I wasn't being clandestine enough. I managed to escape, but a bodyguard took a flick-knife to me first.'

Shani winced and by reflex leaned further into him. 'That's horrible. He could have done some real damage to you, Nicolas.' She looked at Noor. 'It seems you're like Khamadi, in a way. Perhaps Noor, too. Without the danger, life becomes tedious. Am I right?'

'It's the fight for justice, Shani. A wholesome pursuit, don't you agree?'

'It's dangerous, Nicolas. I'd just like to see you championing justice from the side-lines, rather than on the pitch itself.' Shani met his eyes, and received a non-committal gaze in return. She wondered what he truly thought of her. 'I'm concerned, that's all.' She straightened her back, regretting the last couple of minutes. What right had she to tell him how to live his life? She wanted to apologise, but the moment had passed. Instead, she asked the question that had progressively begun to haunt her. 'Talking of Khamadi, do you trust him?'

'Khamadi? In what way?'

Shani shrugged. 'I don't really know. I mean…well, if the coup's successful might he and his followers dispense with those who shared my grandfather's vision?'

'You remember me mentioning to you that the underground movement in Séroulé also operates in Ghana, Benin, and Togo?'

'Yes.'

'I've heard there are a number of politicians in those countries sympathetic to the idea of leaving the international community and going it alone.'

'So it's true, a disengagement – of sorts?'

'Listen to what I have to say,' said Nicolas. 'Unlike Séroulé, neighbouring countries, such as Benin, are not faced with dictators courted by the West. When it comes to the actual coup, victory needs to be secured within hours, not days. Otherwise, the country will be awash with weapons and become another collection point for the brainwashed. Remember Iraq, and Libya? A huge amount of weaponry sent to Libya ended up in Mali, and via a separate route altogether into northern Nigeria, with predictable enough consequences.'

'And these politicians want to leave the international community because…?'

'They basically agree with Khamadi's assessment. I interviewed him a year ago. When it came to the international community he talked of a "dereliction of duty". Séroulé is deliberately being destabilized and ultimately robbed. If it continues, then migration is likely to occur on a colossal scale. So when you ask can we trust Khamadi, you might not agree with some of his methods, and the fact that he held back on some issues, but believe me against Kuetey he is a saint.'

'What if it ends in a bloodbath? That's my concern right now.'

'Séroulé's not far off that, with the regime doing the bloodletting.'

Shani took out of her bag the brown envelope Khamadi had given her and examined the visa, a background of mottled yellow-green with a broad vertical band of orange. 'It's valid from next week,' she said, 'and expires in three months. I don't know how they got my passport number.'

'Put it this way,' Nicolas said, 'I'd be worried if they hadn't managed to obtain it. We'd better go.'

Shani looked across the park at Noor, her heart heavy and drifting into a state of melancholy. She wished they could sit in this restful, evocative space for eternity. 'I'm sorry,' she said. 'I rather ruined things for a moment.'

'You did?'

'I look at Noor, and I see someone brave, formidable, and yet sensitive and glamorous. And then her life ended in Dachau, because like you she wanted justice.'

'Don't you?'

'Of course, but I'm not brave. And you are. I don't want to wake up one day and find there is no Nicolas for me to call or text.' Shani stood from the bench. 'I don't want to go to St Pancras with you. I can't stand goodbyes on platforms. I'll end up doing something mushy like crying. I'll probably cry anyway, but at least I'll be on the coach going back to Oxford.'

Nicolas started to laugh, just softly.

'What?' asked Shani.

'I was right about you,' he said, leaving the bench.

'Oh...?'

'You're funny. Delightfully so, I should add.'

Shani studied him with mock severity. 'Are you saying I'm cranky, Dubois?'

'That's the thing, I'm not sure what you are!' Nicolas took her hand. 'Come on, or I'll miss my train.'

They left the park, Shani glancing over her shoulder to take one last look at the bust, when her phone buzzed. She looked at the screen. A text from Christina. She would read it later. She was about to put her phone back in her pocket when she realised something they hadn't done. It wasn't too late. 'Nicolas!'

Nicolas jerked his head. 'What is it?'

'Why haven't I taken any photos? Come on, quickly. You and Noor. Us together. You on your own. We need to do this. There are people here, they can take one of us together. A couple of minutes.'

It took ten before Shani was satisfied, which resulted in them having to keep a steady pace back to Russell Square. The station was bustling, but they managed to squeeze themselves into the lift before the doors closed. Shani turned away the best she could from the other commuters. 'I want to come to Paris with you,' she whispered in Nicolas's ear. 'Am I being funny? Quirky?'

'Addictively, so.'

'Paris? Seriously.'

'Tempting, but we'll hardly have time together. I'm interviewing, remember?'

Three days until the weekend wasn't so bad, felt Shani. Be gone before she knew it. 'Khamadi's fired me up somewhat,' she said. 'I suppose I ought to make use of the energy, direct it at my thesis.'

The doors slid open, a train arriving at the platform over on their right.

'That's me,' said Nicolas. He held her face in his hands. 'Okay, the weekend.'

Shani readily put her hands on his shoulders. And then he did it. The kiss. No messing about, straight on the lips – and it was delicious. Vibrant with intimacy, and just the right amount of pressure to activate a range of senses, from the sensual to the jubilant. She chose to break away at that point, to keep it a perfect memory.

But it was hard, because all she wanted to do was to keep him from boarding the train. Instead, seeing that he was waiting for a response, she said: 'We're good. You know we are.'

'Like hell was I going to go for anything less, from the day you left my office.' Nicolas laid a hand on her cheek. 'Don't do anything foolish, like change or cut your hair. The long tresses…the perfect frame.' He shook his head slightly, as if in wonder. 'You're so beautiful, in so many ways. No more nightmares.'

She watched him slip away, an ache at the back of her throat.

Nicolas took his hand from his lips to throw her a kiss, before ducking into the crowd. And that was it, he was gone.

From the opposite platform, Shani heard the drone as Nicolas's train left the station. The sense of desolation she felt made her want to get out of London to the more familiar surroundings of Oxford. Her train came soon enough, and as she quietly brushed a tear from her cheek she decided once off the tube she would give Christina a call.

* * *

You're a giver, Shani, already I sense this in you.

She looked out of the window and watched as a couple of people got on the coach. The door hissed shut and they started to leave Hillingdon.

Nicolas was sitting on a chair, holding her prosthesis – the image crystal clear. And now

Khamadi Soglo's words to her:

...Like the majority of people in this world, you have humanitarian virtues. And there's nothing you can do about it.

Academia. The fact that she had gained a scholarship at St Thomas Aquinas gave her virtual carte blanche, even without a thesis to her name. But now, a crucial dilemma. All her life she had envied those who had an instinctive feel for practicality. To make a table, or a chair. Or to position seeds in the earth to grow and harvest food. Again, Khamadi Soglo:

Séroulé will be a peaceful nation, protective of its people, seeking to heal what is damaged – the orphans who are vulnerable to hard labour, prostitution, and voodoo practices, to give one example.

What was she? An orphan. And what was this? An Epiphany moment?

Nicolas, still sitting and holding her prosthesis:

You can help others, you can give hope to people because of your unique experience.

She didn't know the first thing about kids. But she knew what it was like to be an orphan. Of course she did. The heartache that went with it, that sense that you were on the outside looking in, and there wasn't a damn thing you could do to change it. The birthday parties, when parents delivered and collected. The isolation that cut so deep. A constant open wound. But what was she saying to herself? Make the switch from academia to engaging herself with Séroulé's orphans? Could this be her true vocation?

Like waking from a dream, the driver's voice gave her a jolt as it came through the speaker above her. She looked out of the window, dusk having fallen. They were just rolling up to the Queen's Lane stop. She gathered her belongings, left the coach, and walked back along The High towards the traffic lights.

By chance, she happened to catch sight of her supervisor about to leave St Aquinas from a separate wicket gate to that of the main entrance. Perfect timing, she thought, taking advantage of a gap in the traffic on Longwall Street.

'Harry,' she called.

Harry Rothwell paused in the act of getting on his bike, and for a split second looked confused, unsure where the call had come from before he spotted her.

'Shani.' He switched off the flashing light on his handlebars. 'You had a good day?'

'Interesting, I have to say.' Shani stepped onto the kerb. She couldn't help but notice the plaster over the bridge of his nose, and wondered what had happened to him. 'Could we get together when you have a moment? I've some ideas I need to run past you.'

'Of course,' said Harry. 'Have to be next week. I'll come back to you with a date and time.'

'Thanks, Harry… By the way, what happened to your nose, if you don't mind me asking?'

'My nose?'

'You've a plaster on it.'

'Oh, that.' Harry sighed and rolled his eyes. 'Back door fell on top of me, would you believe.'

'A door?'

'We bought the house with a cat flap. Always a draught. Sabine wanted the door off so she could fix and repaint it. I was wrestling with the top hinge when everything came away unexpectedly.'

'Harry, please be careful.'

Harry shrugged in a kind of *c'est la vie* way. 'Oil and water.'

'What is?'

'Do-it-yourself and me.' He turned his bike light back on. 'I ought to dash. Joining Sabine. A talk on ancient Roman gardens, or something to that effect, at the Ashmolean. I'll look at my diary and be in touch. Okay?'

'Thanks, Harry. Enjoy your evening.' Shani continued towards the main entrance. She wondered whether to call Nicolas about her 'moment'. Get his opinion. But he was probably as tired as she felt.

She'd send him a text instead, something nice. She smiled to herself while passing the lodge, and wondered when they would share a bed together. Looking at it from a practical viewpoint, once they did it hopefully it would lessen the anxiety she was starting to feel. Afterwards, or in the morning, pillow-talk, which sometimes she found to be the best part, and she reckoned Nicolas would measure up to that just fine, and that he was going to be as much a part of her future as Séroulé – which, she realised while unlocking the door to her study, more or less left St Aquinas out of the frame.

CHAPTER 13

Nicolas drifted down the corridor towards his studio, absorbed by Shani's text.

Thank you for the beautiful moment in the park xx

He switched the phone for his studio keys. There was so much about Shani Bălcescu that made him want to be with her. Such soulful intrigue – and he supposed by that he meant she had terrific depth to her character. Bravery, too, tortured by her disability and of never having known her parents, or the recently discovered twin brother. And it was here where he needed to be careful. A relationship built on pity would likely flounder. But he didn't think he did pity her enough for it to be problematic. Take away her disability and tragic parental background, he was left with an intelligent girl who shared his humanitarian concerns. And given the confidence, he sensed she could be terrific fun, leaving bystanders dazzled by her dishy smile and wholesome charm.

Nicolas opened the door and dropped his keys onto the maple worktop – and smelt aftershave. The hairs across the nape of his neck tingled. Shit. He could almost hear the intruder breathing, and felt sure he was standing in a semi-blind corner beside the settee. To make a run for it wasn't going to work. He was too far from the door. *Cheap* aftershave. A mindless thug. That wasn't good news. Double shit, in fact. There was a saucepan within reach. A jar of honey, too – nearly full, for extra propulsion.

Shani. The Séroulèse State Security Service's intention was too obvious for words. They were going to make a mess of him. He reached for his phone. Act casual. There was just a chance. His trembling screwed up the letters.

Gt asfee. Takrn

A sound behind him. He managed to get the phone into his jacket pocket before snatching up the keys with his left hand, his right simultaneously making a lightning arc, seizing the jar of honey.

The solitary black figure ducked, the jar missing him by a fraction. Nicolas grabbed the saucepan, crashing it against the intruder's skull. Fists flew, Nicolas using his keys in the onslaught, cutting first his assailant's face, and then his neck. A glancing blow came off the side of his face, before a wallop at the base of his spine threw him back into his assailant. *Two* of them!

They were edging him into the bedroom. Blows rained down on him, blood getting into his eyes, impairing his vision. He seized the miniature Anglepoise lamp from the bedside cabinet, his skin burning with cuts and adrenalin. Swiping the lamp around, he sliced the intruder's bloodied cheek, but nothing was going to stop this maniac! Backed up between the bed and the wall, he used his feet kick-boxer style, and caught sight of the black accomplice in the doorway, arms folded and looking bored. His legs were giving up on him, his attacker closing, grinning through a split lip and bloodied teeth. He put everything he had left into another kick, when an uppercut knocked his teeth together, sending stars across what was left of his vision until a fist slammed into his face with the velocity of a cannon ball.

He fell into shadows, and the sound of laughter. He could feel little in way of pain. He tried to find it. Where was it, for Christ's sake? Was he dying? He sensed he was being dragged along by his feet. Or could it be he was passing over from the life he knew and into the next? Hauled across a kind of no-man's land…perhaps by his father, who'd come to collect him. So it was *actually* true!

Then he started to choke on whatever it was trickling down his throat. Had he been knocked off his bike? He never rode it with particular care. Hands brought him to his feet, and he realised he could only open his left eye. He saw a reflection of himself in the walls of an elevator, two men alongside him – one dabbing his cheek with his sleeve. He remembered now. *Double shit.* He could still smell aftershave.

The doors parted, and the men hustled him out of the building towards a green car, his feet dragging behind him. As the car purred away, someone fiddled with his jacket sleeve. There was laughter again, before an unexpected pinprick near his elbow made him flinch. A warm, all-enveloping pathway sucked him down into a serene pool of dusk, with little more than flickers of light passing him by as they headed on through the streets of Paris and over the River Seine.

* * *

'Well, Nicolas, you know how it goes from here…'

The voice ebbed and flowed.

'…You've seen the movies, where the actor who plays my part says, "There's an easy way, and there's a hard way".'

His left eye saw himself sitting on a chair. He strove to look up. His face felt as if it didn't belong to him. Bloated and misshapen, he imagined. It was over for him. He knew that. Resigned to it. If not today, tomorrow, or the day after. At what stage would he beg them to take his life away from him?

No way out…

His interrogator was sitting behind a table. That much he knew. No bright lights shining into his face, no cigarette smoke. *You've seen the movies…* And this was just a short, puny, bespectacled man with shiny black skin and a neat, spiv-like moustache.

Nicolas closed his one eye and lowered his head, his wrists tied behind the back of the chair.

Fears are nothing more than a state of mind.

Where had he heard that before? Like hell it made sense to him.

'…We need answers, Nicolas,' said the man. 'Answers to questions that I will be putting to you. But let us start with your mobile phone. We've been back to your apartment. Perhaps you would care to enlighten us as to its whereabouts?'

Nicolas heard shuffling feet behind him, before someone coughed and spat. It told him his assailants were likely to be in the room. A possible basement chamber, bare of furnishings from what he could see of it apart from the table and chairs.

Exhaustion, he realised. Pray for exhaustion. For

unconsciousness. An ideal, of course. His trousers felt damp. He – or they – had done something.

Fears are nothing more than—

'Nicolas,' droned the voice, 'I'm asking you to answer a question, here. I have little patience for heroics.'

There. Here. No-man's land. What did he want to do? Cry to himself, or laugh at them? At the absurdity of it all. Of life... Shani. Oh, Christ. Poor, dear Shani. The game was up for her, too. *Dear God...*

The blood in his throat tasted tangy, like he'd swallowed horse manure. He wanted to smile through his broken face at the impromptu analogy, because he knew how he'd arrived by it...

...For he was with his late father, tending to seedlings in the greenhouse alongside the quaint potting shed. So peaceful. And now his mother, coming down the garden with their afternoon mugs of tea—

A hood was rammed over his head. He struggled instinctively, the fear back with him, quivering his insides. He'd been kidding himself, relying on theory to get him through it, before the 'passing over'. So end it now. You *have* to end it now!

It came from behind him, something rock-hard crashing against his shoulders with such force that it propelled him with the chair into the desk. Jagged bolts of pain ricocheted through his torso. No way out!

'Mobile phone, Nicolas.'

Hands came and straightened him and the chair, clumsily wrestling with them both until they were upright and once again sitting in unison.

'Take the hood off him. And check the car again.'

Nicolas caught his breath, just panicky gasps to begin with. That was the worst thing, not being able to breath, like he was in a confined space, because that had happened to him, when he was six years old, locked inside a cupboard by his sister.

He found himself staring at the desk again, at its scratched, indented surface. A pity, he thought, since it looked to be antique.

'You fool,' said the little man with the moustache. 'You cannot escape. We are going to take you apart, mentally and physically. But you do have a chance to save yourself here. We want to know about Khamadi Soglo. We know the two of you have been in contact...'

His father was smiling down at him, both of them drinking their tea, his mother's elegant figure swaying a little as she strolled back up the garden towards the house. His father put down his mug and sat him on the stool in the shed, and together they started to pot-up the seedlings.

A clatter of something striking the table and he

looked up. A length of cable; on the one end a plug, at the other two bare wires. And a cordless drill with a very fine drill-bit, no more than a millimetre. The size of the drill-bit told him they were going to drill into his bones, starting with his shins so he could see what they were doing to him.

A door opened and closed from somewhere inside the room.

The interrogator smiled as one of the men handed over his phone. Straightening his spectacles, he said: 'Been watching too many movies, Nicolas. Between the seats. The oldest trick in the book.'

Nicolas lowered his head. He couldn't remember if he'd sent the text...

...So he made a start on potting-up the sunflower seedlings. They were his favourite, and his father had given him a patch of ground in the corner of the garden for him to plant them out when the frosts were safely over. He could see it was going to take him hours, if not days, to get them all done.

CHAPTER 14

She'd done so much analysing since waking that she'd managed to give herself a thumping headache. It started with Nicolas. He'd responded to her text but she couldn't make sense of it.

Gt asfee. Takrn

What the hell did it mean? Was it a joke, or what? If only he would answer his damn phone. She so wanted it to work between them, and was determined not to become judgemental or possessive. The relationship was newly-born, though, so there was bound to be an intensity, which seemed to be one-sided. It was a concern.

Shani sat back in the chair and gazed across the Priory Quadrangle at the 16th century sundial above the Cecil Brampton Library. And now a greater concern had slowly but surely surfaced. It dawned on her that she might have done something very stupid.

She'd found Jacques Baudin's email address and had sent him a one-worded question. *Kosher?* Obviously, she couldn't mention the proposed coup, and up until she'd tapped the send key thought it a rather slick way to find out whether he was entirely on-board with Khamadi Soglo – that everyone was indeed in full agreement. Then the doubt started. She had visions of the Iranian secret police taking him away for immediate interrogation. Basically, had she endangered his life? Or was she overreacting?

She straightened herself in the chair and checked her email again. Nothing. The weather was foul, which depressed her even more. Constant, wintry rain. She'd put herself down for her first lunch at St Aquinas, partly in the hope of bumping into Harry Rothwell to find out whether he had fixed a time for her to discuss Séroulé and her possible role with its orphans. But then she remembered on Thursdays in term time Harry gave an eleven o'clock lecture to undergraduates at Lady Margaret Hall on the other side of town, so the chances were he'd be invited to lunch.

She sighed out of frustration and made a fist with her left hand, her right moving the cursor back to her email inbox. *God's sake, Jacques Baudin, answer my bloody question, will you!*

* * *

Lunch was in the Buttery with its intricately carved domed ceiling. Shani hadn't anticipated such a barrage of people coming up to her to congratulate her on her Fellowship. She strove to make an effort, still distracted by what might be happening to Jacques Baudin in Tehran. Asked by the Home Bursar about her lineage, she tried out the newly discovered fact that her mother was born in Séroulé. If anything, the conversation felt interrogatory, with quick-fire questions followed by wholly unrelated matters ranging from the rising cost of electricity to the proposed refurbishment of the Common Room pantry. She politely mentioned that she wasn't particularly clued-up when it came to carpentry and shelving, and from that point the Bursar seemed to lose interest in her. Shani took the opportunity to rush through her fruit salad.

Deciding against coffee in the Common Room, she made her way back across the West Quadrangle towards Staircase VII. While climbing the stairs, her phone chirped up an email.

Kosher. Merci. Merci beaucoup.

She trembled with relief, and for a moment couldn't get the key in the door. All was well! And Baudin was thanking her for agreeing to participate in the coup. She wanted to dance around her study. She closed the door, and decided not to respond. There was no need. One day they would meet, and she would hear first-hand stories about her grandfather, and possibly Zinsa. It felt weird, to have actually made contact with the man who was set to become Tuma Dangbo's deputy – and now, thirty-eight years later, was destined to head the interim government.

She fired-up her PC to continue researching Séroulé from a geographical aspect when her phone sounded its newly acquired ringtone, Youssou N'Dour's *Birima*. She looked at the display. Nicolas. Finally. Joy upon joy!

'Hi, Nicolas. I've been worried. I know I'm being silly—'

'Shani? It is you Shani, yes?'

Shani looked down at her phone. Nicolas's number, but not his voice.

'Who is this?' she asked. 'The phone you are using belongs to Nicolas Dubois.'

'That is quite correct,' responded the syrupy French accent.

'Then why are you using his phone?' Sudden panic clawed her throat and made it difficult for her to breathe. 'Has…has something happened to him?' It would explain so much.

'In a way, Shani, yes. But you can fix that by

coming to Paris—'

'No, Shani,' cried Nicolas, quite distinctly. '*Don't come to Paris. It's a trick*—'

A sudden scream that froze her heart.

Oh, my God... 'What the hell's going on?' she shouted back. 'Let me speak to him. Let me speak to Nicolas!'

'Calm down,' said the voice. 'Nicolas is fine, and he will stay that way so long as you arrive in Paris—'

'But you're hurting him! *Why?*'

'I find disobedience unacceptable, Shani...'

Shani detected a more chilling, altogether harsher tone in the French accent. But what the hell was this? Could it even be some kind of perverted test devised by Khamadi Soglo?

'...The moment you arrive in Paris,' instructed the kidnapper, 'you will call us on Nicolas's phone. And don't do anything stupid, like contacting the *gendarmerie*, because if you do we will execute Nicolas, and then we'll come after you. And we *will* find you. Understood?'

Shani put her left hand on her brow, as if to hold her mind together. 'I'll do anything you say,' she said. 'But stop *hurting* him...' She looked at her phone, and realised the caller had rung off. She called back, but there was no answer.

She put her phone down on the desk, horrified and numbed. It was a kidnapping. She could see it now. See what they wanted to do with her. Her pulse rocketed with indignation at Khamadi's promise to protect them. *Why* hadn't he or anyone else seen it coming?

Her phone rang. She snatched it off the desk and pressed it to her ear. 'Yes?'

'Hi, Shani. It's me… Are you okay?'

Christina. What a time for her to call. 'I'm…I'm fine.'

'Sure?'

'I was locked into my thesis—'

'Have you heard the news?'

'What news?'

'Jenny hasn't been in touch?'

'No.'

'Adrian's come out…'

Shani found she could barely concentrate on the call. If she were to mention that Nicolas had been abducted, Christina would likely to become hysterical. She had to focus, form a plan.

'…Jenny's totally freaked,' continued Christina. 'She's gone down to Cambridge to be with her sister. Apparently, Adrian's been having an affair with a college steward for the past three months—'

'Christina, I've got to go. I'm expecting Harry Rothwell, and I think he's at the door.'

'Call me straight back.'

'As soon as I can.' Shani ended the call and breathed out, hating the lie but finding she had no other choice. Jenny, Adrian, gay…but Nicolas had been taken from her, and they were hurting him. Badly. She found the text he'd sent her. *Gt asfee. Takrn* That was it: *Takrn* was *Taken*. Then the rest of it fell into place. *Get safe. Taken.*

At that horrific moment, when he realised he was about to be abducted, Nicolas had thought of her. Tried to protect her. But to help him, if that was at all possible, then she needed to act fast before the shock set in and muddled her mind. She started to gather essential items. Phone charger, passport, Ghanaian visa, just in case, trying desperately to be positive. What else? Tablet? No. She wanted to travel as light as possible. Adaptor for her phone charger. Where was it?... Still in her backpack. *Concentrate!*

She put everything into her shoulder bag and sat at her desk, oblivious to the Senior Dean with her bouffant hairdo walking diagonally across the Priory Quadrangle. Nicolas had been kidnapped. Who should she be relaying this information to? The police, here in the UK and in France? If she did, what would happen to him? The kidnapper claimed to have covered that angle. Her supervisor? Harry would tell her to go to the police. In fact, he might even contact the police himself, and she would be powerless to intervene.

It was a quarter to two. There was a chance Harry could be on his way back to college from a late lunch after his lecture at Lady Margaret Hall. He was now the last person she wanted to see, because he would want to pass the time of day with her. And what if she collapsed in front of him? No, better to leave through the back gate by the library – the Brampton Gate, or whatever the thing was called. She could then follow the path to Magdalen and emerge lower down into Longwall, taking a left at the lights and catching the coach to London in St Clements. The danger point would be a combination of her walking over Magdalen Bridge and Harry deciding to cycle home earlier than usual. On the other hand, if she left it a couple of hours, dusk would be falling...

Shani clenched her hands. Why all the detail? She took her phone from her bag and called Nicolas's number. No answer.

Forget about dusk, she told herself. She was leaving this minute, and she was going to wait for the coach in The High. Once in Paris, she could focus on trying to release Nicolas from these vile people – people who were clearly under instructions to lure her across the Channel.

So far, she had to admit while locking her study door, their strategy was proving to be utterly effective. And there was no one she could trust. Least of all, Khamadi Soglo.

CHAPTER 15

A distant sound of classical music. She moved along the corridor, and established its source adjacent to studio number 56. Shani put her shoulder bag down on the floor. On the journey over she'd come up with a strategy. She wanted to flush out the kidnapper, or his accomplice – if he had an accomplice. *And WE will find you.* It seemed he did have one. The strategy was dangerous, she didn't need to be told that. Completely reckless, in fact. But it had an element of logic, and could just work. She'd primed her phone with the message:

*KIDNAPPED BY THIS PERSON FOR
GENERAL KUETEY*

All she needed was a photograph, and it would be sent to more than thirty contacts, including St Aldates police station in Oxford and *The Guardian* newspaper. She'd never bothered to participate in 'social media', so *Twitter* and alike were of no use. An alternative strategy might be to approach Jacques Baudin in Tehran, via email. He could then contact Khamadi Soglo on her behalf. But the truth was she still couldn't bring herself to trust the rebel leader. He made her nervous, and might even make the situation worse with a careless, gung-ho ambush or whatever.

Gaining access to the lobby below had been straightforward enough. The moment she'd arrived someone was leaving. She'd flashed a smile, said *Bonjour*, and before she knew it had reached the elevator. It gave her a smidgen of confidence. In fact, it surprised her that she hadn't broken down, that she was behaving rationally – or *believed* she was behaving rationally.

Standing on tiptoe on her right foot, Shani blindly ran her fingertips over the ledge above the archway. A wave of relief, the sensation practically sensual, as if her mind had detached itself from her body and the latter was now misinterpreting her predicament. But he *had* returned the key from the evening when he rescued her from Maison Rouge. She wondered, as she had done throughout the excruciating journey to Gare du Nord, where the kidnapper had seized Nicolas. At his office, perhaps. Or simply off the street.

The music continued to drift from 55. She felt she should be able to put a name to the composer. Could it be...? Yes, Bedřich Smetana, she realized – and, coincidentally, Czech. Except she wasn't Czech, was she? No. Half Romanian, half Séroulèse. And now the perfect nightmare to accompany her true identity. She prepared her phone, her heart beating in her throat as she carefully unlocked the door. Holding her breath, she found herself counting to 'three' before flinging it open and pressing herself against the corridor wall.

What Shani saw through the phone's lens caused her to gasp. The sheer disarray: the aftermath of a violent clash that must have ensued the moment Nicolas had unlocked the door. She forgot about her phone, her hand clutching her chest, crunching up her jacket as she stepped forward into the studio. The maple floorboards were smeared with blood.

What had they done to him?!

Her hand moved to her mouth, eyes wide with horror. Above the sofa, a sticky residue clung to the wall that looked like...honey? The sofa itself was dotted with shards of glass, and the abstract painting she so admired skewed. She picked her way over the upturned saucepan on the floor to take a look at the bedroom. Blood spattered the duvet, and even the walls. She recalled the moment he kissed her at the station. The blood she was looking at had come from this man. From dearest Nicolas.

Shani sat on the bed, feeling faint. She looked around again, trying to make sense of what had happened. He must have put up a terrific fight. She wondered how many had attacked him. More than one, she guessed…

Oh, Nicolas, she screamed inside her head, *perhaps you are only a short distance from me and I can't HELP you!*

Madeleine was lying on the floor. She picked up the book and sat back down on the bed, and started to cry, her tears spilling onto the plastic sheath covering the jacket and Noor Inayat Khan.

'Help me,' she said aloud, before she seized the book with all her strength. 'Please, please, oh please, *help* me.'

Shani wrapped the duvet around her body, feeling his quiet masculinity – feeling Nicolas. She laid her head on the yellow pillowcase. Perhaps the most sensible thing would be to go to the *gendarmerie*, and quickly. Or should she email Jacques Baudin? But if the kidnappers found out she'd contacted people other than themselves and executed Nicolas, what then? She hugged the pillow, but it gave her little in way of comfort. How could it? At this moment, she could only be comforted by knowing Nicolas was safe. And he was far from that.

She had craved from way back in her childhood for peace to come to her one day in some form or another. And now she could confirm that it would be in death. The President of Séroulé would likely have someone torture her before that moment came, but she no longer cared – in fact, she welcomed the exchange for it was obvious they expected her to trade herself for Nicolas's freedom. And she would do just that. He was the better person, more useful to society than she could ever be. And when the end came for her, perhaps she would find her dear Mother and Father waiting to greet her. How joyous that would be. And her baby brother, Tuma. Only this time it would be for eternity.

…*Her dear Mother.*

Zinsa. She had omitted Zinsa from her thoughts. What was she thinking? *Omitted* her courage. How would Zinsa react to this situation? What would be her approach? Her strategy? It was doubtful she would be lying down on a bed, defeated by negativity! So what would Zinsa actually be *doing*? Fight, or flight. Answer: fight. Absolutely. How? In order to fight you needed to protect yourself. Logic. Remember: *Cut the crap and get to the core.* But what was his name?... The same as Baudin? It didn't really matter. She knew where he lived.

Shani left the bed and took a carving knife from a drawer under the worktop. Then primed her phone, and realised she hadn't even bothered to close the door, let alone lock it. She was hopeless. But that was going to *have* to change. Survival. She lodged the knife in an inside pocket on her Barbour and pulled up the zip. The corridor was deserted, just Bedřich Smetana building to a crescendo in 55. She turned the key in the door, and felt her resolve firm-up the muscles on her tear-stained face. At last, a positive step forward.

Shani took to the stairwell rather than the elevator, intending to go no further than the floor immediately below. Apartment *42*, she decided, was the one directly beneath the studio. But when she knocked on the door a pregnant woman answered it, a young child with a thumb in its mouth at her side.

'*Bonjour, Madame,*' Shani said. '*Je m'excuse.* I am looking for Jacques.'

'*Jacques? Oui.*' The woman pointed to her left. '*Quarante-trois, Mademoiselle.*'

'*Merci beaucoup.*'

Shani moved down the corridor to *43*, hearing laughter and clapping from a TV, she presumed, the volume giving her little choice but to bang on the door with her fist. The sound was turned right down, so she knocked again to make sure.

'*Oui. Oui. J'arrive!*'

She heard someone shuffling behind the door, and fiddle with the lock itself. When the door finally opened, she was greeted by an elderly man wearing red and white pinstriped pyjamas and sitting in a wheelchair. The more she looked at him the older he seemed to become, or was it the riled look on his weathered face that exaggerated his age?

'*Oui?*' he snapped.

'I am a friend of Nicolas—'

'Ah,' exclaimed Jacques. He waved a finger. 'You are the girl.'

'The girl?'

'Come in, come in. I can speak English to you.'

'Thank you,' said Shani, relieved. 'I'm sorry I speak so little French.'

'It's good for me to speak English.' Jacques manoeuvred his wheelchair to make room for her. 'Keeps the grey cells active. You understand?'

Shani came into the rather cluttered room in way of furniture and ornaments, the television tuned to a game show. She watched Jacques close the front door with a practised jab from a walking stick.

'Yes, the girl,' he said, turning the wheelchair to

face her. 'What is your name?'

'Shani.'

'Ah, yes. I remember.'

'Nicolas has talked about me?' asked Shani, surprised.

'Talked about you? I couldn't shut him up. But now I can see why.'

Shani took that to be a compliment. 'Thank you, Jacques…' Before she knew it, she had covered her face with her hands and was in tears. 'I'm sorry,' she mumbled. If only she could black out and wake up in a different world!

Jacques quietly leaned the walking stick against a side table, his watery-blue eyes narrowing. 'Shani, what's going on? Where's Nicolas?'

'They've taken him. They've taken Nicolas.' She took her hands away. 'He told me that you were once in the Foreign Legion.'

'Centuries ago. Who has taken Nicolas? Please, sit down.'

Shani sat on the arm of the settee and wiped away her tears with her wrist. 'I need you to give me a gun.'

'A gun?'

'Yes. Nicolas told me he took you to the countryside on your birthday so you could use your guns. Please, let me have one of them. I'll give you money, anything. I just need a gun. I promise, I will not mention your name to anyone.'

Jacques rolled his wheelchair closer to her, his tone still curious. 'But you say Nicolas has been taken. Who has taken him? When?'

'Yesterday evening, when he returned from London,' said Shani. She tried not to sniffle, her tissues in her shoulder bag in the studio. She checked the pockets on her Barbour, her fingertips brushing against the carving knife. As distraught as she was, she couldn't threaten Jacques to get a gun off him. That would be a step too far. Or would it, given the crisis? 'Or in the early hours of this morning.'

Jacques nodded. 'That explains it. The girl next door said it sounded like Nicolas had an elephant crashing around inside his studio. But who are these people? What do they want with him?'

'It's not Nicolas they want,' said Shani, disgusted with herself for even considering to threaten Jacques. Nicolas would be horrified. The kidnapper was making a monster out of her! She explained her story to Jacques, quietly and fluently, hoping for him to agree to give her a gun.

When she finished, Jacques peered across at her from his wheelchair. 'You would use the gun on yourself, if it came to it?' he asked her directly. 'What

I am saying to you, Shani, is this: imagine a scenario whereby you mistakenly believed all to be lost. You panic and take your own life, using a gun that I had given you. Then Nicolas is suddenly freed, or he escapes. What will he say to me? It's not worth thinking about, is it?'

'Jacques, to prevent myself from falling into the hands of Kuetey,' said Shani steadily, maintaining eye contact with him, 'I have to say I would probably take my own life whether I had a gun in my possession or not. Obviously, my objective is to free Nicolas. The kidnappers will not expect me to be carrying a gun. It will be a shock to them.'

Jacques nodded, but that was all. No words.

Shani interpreted his muted reaction that further persuasion was needed. It crossed her mind that perhaps she should show him the state of Nicolas's studio. She stood, and just briefly felt slightly giddy. A consequence of emotional rather than physical exhaustion, she assumed. It was also very warm in the room, so she partially unzipped her Barbour, careful to keep the knife concealed. 'Jacques, I really need to prepare myself before I contact them. I was told to call Nicolas's number the moment I arrived in Paris. I've already been here over two hours. Besides, if Nicolas could speak I'm guessing he would want you to arm me.'

A tender smile began to show itself on Jacques weathered face beneath the few remaining wisps of hair. 'I can see now why Nicolas is so taken by you,' he said. 'You're a good person, Shani. Resourceful, intelligent—'

'Jacques, tell me what to do!' cried Shani, feeling her judgement, her sanity, steadily disintegrating. 'I'm sick with worry. They have already warned me about contacting the *gendarmerie*, but should I contact them? I have my doubts whether they will take me seriously enough to begin with, by then it might be too late. It's very risky.'

Jacques held up a quietening hand. 'It's true. It's likely the authorities will make the situation worse for Nicolas. They can be clumsy, their success rate criticised in some quarters of late.' Jacques manoeuvred his wheelchair over to a chest of drawers. 'I'll give you the Walther PPK, like the one James Bond uses. How about that?'

Shani couldn't believe her ears. She'd won him over. 'Oh, thank you!' She slumped back down on the arm of the settee, drained now, as if she'd triumphed in a debate against the fiercest of opponents. 'Thank you so much, Jacques.'

'It has six bullets in the magazine, and another

ready to go in the chamber.' Jacques put the gun in his lap and wheeled the chair towards her. 'The safety catch is here. Okay?'

'Yes.'

'Take it. Feel it. Turn it in your hands.'

Shani took the gun from him. 'It's heavier than I thought.'

'Lighter than many, though.'

'I feel more protected.'

'Good. As for freeing Nicolas? I no longer have any contacts that could help you. Twenty years ago, yes. But not now. All I can do is to give you words of support.'

Shani weighed the gun in her hands. It felt like a piece of sculpture – a *brutal* piece of sculpture. 'Jacques, I'll get him back, and when I do I'm going to make the best picnic ever and get Nicolas to take us out to the countryside.'

Jacques stared back at her, his right hand stationary in mid-air. 'Are you sure, Shani?' he asked, a little excitement in his tone, his eyes with a childlike glint as they gazed up at her. 'To the countryside?'

Shani tucked the gun into the waistband on her jeans, pulled her woollen jumper over it and straightened her jacket. Because of the knife, and now the gun, she very carefully leaned forward. 'Without question,' she said, and kissed Jacques on his furrowed brow.

* * *

By the time Shani returned to the studio and found herself sitting on the bed the sheer exhilaration over receiving the handgun had left her. She glanced at the Walther, lying amongst the spattered droplets of blood on the duvet. 'Oh, Nicolas...' she cried, clenching her hands.

Her phone gave a quick buzz. She scooped it out from her pocket. The text simply read: *Mailbox*. Number withheld. She checked her email. Nothing. Mailbox? What did they mean? God's sake, why couldn't they speak to her? She read the text again. *Mailbox*. Why text her?

She stood up and paced around the living area, picking up the saucepan. Anything to delay speaking to *that* voice. Sitting on the stool next to the worktop, she re-examined the text. *Mailbox*. She put her face in her hands. Against her better judgement, she was going to have to contact the rebels – via Jacques Baudin. What other choice was there? Unless she went to the *gendarmerie*. Either way, she would be sidelined, and if Nicolas died...

Mailbox.

She took her face out of her hands and stared at

the front door, the door that led out into the corridor. No letterbox. Somewhere, then, there had to be individual mailboxes. Could that be what they meant?

Shani slid the gun back into her waistband, locked the door to the studio and entered the elevator. She scrolled through *contacts* on her phone for Nicolas's number – before hesitating. If they'd put something for her in Nicolas's mailbox, then they knew she was here in Rue Chante Coq. So why hadn't they come and taken her away?

Or had they put—? She couldn't bear to think about it, about something having been sliced off Nicolas – an ear, a finger – and put inside an envelope to show her they were serious. As if she had any doubts about *that*. The elevator doors opened, revealing a couple waiting to enter giggling affectionately at one another. Shani turned her head; she couldn't watch.

The mailboxes were positioned around the back of the elevator, two rows for each floor – apart from the top floor where the studios had a single row to share. All of them appeared to be locked, but when she reached up to *56* the cover was slightly ajar. She was confronted by a yellow carrier bag. Tucked inside it, a white woollen hat with a pink bobble, a mobile phone and charger, and a brown envelope with a slight bulge. They *couldn't* have...?

She pressed the button for the fifth floor in the elevator, and tentatively touched the envelope. There was no blood, and it was hard, not soft. What could it all mean? They already had her mobile number, so why give her another phone? And what was with the hat?

Inside the studio, she laid out the various items on the worktop. She felt sick with anxiety. These were professional kidnappers. So she hadn't a hope of understanding their methodology. She opened the envelope, which contained several more items. A piece of folded-up black wire with a bead-like object on the one end and a miniature USB connector for the mobile phone, she assumed, on the other. She tried it. It seemed to fit. The second item was an earpiece that resembled a very small hearing aid, and which more or less matched the dusky tone of her skin. Finally, a couple of green safety pins. She leaned back from the worktop and cast her eyes over the items. Meticulous, was the word that came to her. *Chillingly* meticulous.

The Nokia abruptly produced a discordant ringtone, jangling her nerves. She put a hand to her mouth, wishing it would stop, reluctant to answer the call. She picked it up – *number withheld* on the screen. She put the phone to her ear.

'Hello?'

'Shani?'

'Let me speak to Nicolas!' she shouted at once, slamming a hand on the worktop. 'I want to know—'

'Shani, Shani, this is not the people who took Nicolas. This is Khamadi.'

Shani straightened – a sudden reflexive jerk, like she'd been struck by electricity. Khamadi? What the hell was going on? She became suspicious. 'Prove it,' she said.

'You were with me yesterday, with Nicolas—'

'The code, dammit. Say the code.'

'Prosper. A network in Paris, Second World War. You've been reading about an agent who joined it. You didn't name the agent.'

She couldn't speak. A lifeline? But... 'Do you know what's happened?'

'Yes. Osakwe... You remember Osakwe, don't you? You've had a conversation with him, I believe—'

'I remember.'

'He will answer your questions on the phone you are holding. He is heading the operation in Paris.'

'Why are you calling me, then?'

'Because I need to apologise to you, Shani.'

'And so you bloody should!' She felt relief – of course she did. But anger, too. Such a barrage of emotions, clashing, spinning, pulling – *disorienting*. 'I might never see Nicolas again,' she said, and sat on the settee. She wanted to throw up; it felt that awful saying it out aloud, admitting to herself that it could actually happen. 'You don't know what it's doing to me. Where the hell was the protection? You should have started it *before* we came to see you.'

'We have been – *I* have been – distracted. There have been difficulties—'

'Distracted?'

'Three days ago, we lost the best part of a sleeper cell in northern Séroulé. My younger brother being one of the fatalities. Yes, we should have protected you the moment we got to hear you'd applied for a visa, and likewise protected Nicolas. We failed you, and I apologise unreservedly for that.'

Shani stood and swept a hand through her hair. As hard as it was for her, she had to take Khamadi for his word and suppress her anger. This was about Nicolas. 'Okay,' she said, 'let's move forward. When will Osakwe call me?'

'The second we end this call.'

'I'm sorry about your brother. Despite everything, I mean that, Khamadi.'

'I know you do. It's in your character. Now we focus. Okay?'

'Yes.'

'I will leave you with Osakwe. He's not to blame for what's happened.'

'I understand… And, Khamadi, thank you.'

Shani checked the charge on the phone. Almost full. Had they a plan? It seemed odd they should dump the stuff in Nicolas's mailbox without making physical contact with her. It made it harder for her to shake off the suspicion they were keeping her in the dark somewhat. Or even 'controlling' her. The coup was paramount in their minds, Nicolas and herself secondary threads. Useful, but not vital.

She was about to get herself a glass of water when Osakwe's call came through.

'Khamadi has spoken to you, Shani?'

'Yes. I have a number of questions.'

'Of course,' agreed Osakwe. 'You want to know how we found out that Nicolas had been abducted, presumably.'

'Yes.' Osakwe's accent was so smooth, more so than she remembered it to be at Maison Rouge. 'Have the kidnappers been in touch with you?' she asked.

'Not at all. When you visited Khamadi, both your phones were cloned. A basic precaution.'

'Cloned?' It took her a second to fathom what he meant. 'Underhand, more like. Khamadi should have explained.'

'Perhaps. I'm afraid we function in different worlds. But, Shani, I would like to ask you a question.'

'Such as?'

'What made you go to Nicolas's apartment?'

'I thought I might be followed by one of the kidnappers. I planned to photograph him and make it viral. As it happens, your people clearly followed me from either St Pancras or Gare du Nord.'

There was a pause. 'Should I regard you as foolish, or brave?' asked Osakwe.

'Impulsive.' She wondered whether Osakwe had any respect for her. Probably not. More foolish than brave, then. 'Was it Gare du Nord?'

'Yes. It was doubtful you would fly. We're avoiding eye to eye contact. There's little point, and by not doing so removes elements of risk. But I can tell you that the building is under surveillance.'

'*Properly* under surveillance?'

'Three men. Front and rear. As it happens, you being there could be useful, should one of them pay a visit. Is there any evidence they took Nicolas from the apartment?'

'Definitely. Plenty of mess.'

'Okay. Shani, we must halt our questions for the moment, because I need you to contact the kidnappers. The call is overdue. Yes?'

'Yes.' Shani sat herself back down on the stool beside the worktop. What if they made Nicolas scream? 'Osakwe, do I have to? He's such a horrible person. He must be to do what he's done.'

'Shani, we need information. I want you to tell them that you're at a hotel in Gare du Nord, and that you are exhausted. Say you will call them at ten o'clock tomorrow morning for instructions. Obviously, you don't give them the name of a hotel – just the district, Gare du Nord. Understood?'

'Yes.'

Osakwe cleared his throat. 'Now, Shani, if you refuse to play ball with them they might try…try to upset you. Do you know what I mean by this?'

'They will hurt Nicolas. This is what you are telling me?'

'If it's too much for you, tell them you will re-establish contact at ten o'clock tomorrow and cut the call. Okay?'

'Yes.'

'Call them now. I will ring back in roughly ten minutes. Silence the ringtone on the phone I have given you.'

Shani did as she was told and put down the Nokia. Picking up her own phone, she scrolled for Nicolas's number, her hands shaking so much that she accidently thumbed Jenny's number. She cancelled it and continued down, and wondered if Osakwe was nearby. So, they'd actually followed her from Gare du Nord.

'You are in Paris, Shani?'

'Yes,' she told the syrupy voice that had spoken to her in Oxford. 'I want to talk to Nicolas.' ...*You vile bastard!*

'Where in Paris?'

'A hotel near Gare du Nord.'

'What hotel? The name of it?'

'That's my business. I want to speak to Nicolas.'

'Don't try my patience—'

'I *want* to speak to Nicolas.'

'He's at another location. What hotel, Shani? Maison Rouge?'

Shani was shocked. Khamadi's hunch was correct, they'd shadowed her from the day she entered the Séroulèse Embassy in London. 'You followed me there?' she asked. Osakwe needed information.

'Of course. We'll come and collect you. We'll take you to Nicolas—'

'I'm not at Maison Rouge.' *Why wasn't Nicolas with him?*

'What hotel, then?'

Had they hurt him more than they'd intended to do? She was struggling to focus. 'If you followed me to Maison Rouge, then you have likely followed me here. You should know where—'

'We have Nicolas. And you want to see him, don't you, Shani?'

Tears pricked her eyes. 'You haven't…hurt him, have you? Not since we last spoke.'

'He's asking for you, that's all.'

'Where is he?'

'Perfectly safe. Don't worry. He's very good at playing cards. I didn't know that. Did you?'

'No.'

'What hotel, Shani?'

'I'm exhausted. I'm…I'm mentally disturbed.' Shani pulled herself together, realising by chance she'd found a convincing angle. She'd *lived* with it virtually her entire life. 'I'm tortured from above, and now you're throwing me over the edge. I can't…I really can't take any more of this.'

She heard the kidnapper mutter *Jeeesus Christ*.

'You're damaging my mind,' she cried. 'Breaking it up…I don't know what I'm doing, what I'm thinking. You make me want to *kill* myself—'

'Shani, calm down,' said the kidnapper.

She'd hooked him, she could tell by his tone. It

was after all presumably imperative she was delivered unharmed to Kuetey.

'Just give me the name of the hotel. We don't want to hurt or upset you. Nicolas is asking for you. We'll even bring him to the hotel.'

She was tempted, and perhaps between them they could overpower the kidnappers, or raise the alarm. But how badly injured was Nicolas? 'I need to rest,' she said. 'I'm on medication, for God's sake. Don't you know anything about me? You've put me under terrible pressure. I'm falling. It's happened before. It's not my fault. I'm trying to do the best I can.'

'Okay, okay, Shani. Okay. We'll let you rest. Calm down. Nine o'clock tomorrow. But any monkey business, and it's bye-bye Nicolas. You got that?'

'Yes. Thank you. I must…' Shani realised the kidnapper had already ended the call.

She tossed her mobile onto the worktop and went over to the sink to grab a glass of water, her throat burning. Thank God they hadn't made Nicolas cry out to her, that he was at another location – apparently. But how harshly were they treating him? Surely the phone call would have carried greater persuasion if they'd got him to speak to her. So why hadn't they? Was he lying unconscious somewhere?

The Nokia started to vibrate. Shani quickly poured

a second glass of water and answered the call. 'It's going to be nine o'clock tomorrow, Osakwe. That's when I'll get my instructions.'

'How are you feeling, Shani?' asked Osakwe. 'Tell me.'

'A total wreck.' *Ten hours of rollercoaster emotion*, she verged on shouting, *so what do you bloody well expect?*

'London tells me the call was successful, so congratulate yourself.'

'I didn't get to speak to Nicolas. The kidnapper told me he was at another location. They followed me to Maison Rouge, for God's sake.' She gulped down some water. 'Osakwe, can I meet you, like now? Are you in Paris?'

'I'm south of the river, Shani. About ten kilometres from you. I have work to do here.'

'To help Nicolas?'

'Every waking moment. I want to talk you through what we've given you. Okay?'

'Yes.' Shani turned on the stool and saw the gun on the duvet. Something inside her told her to hold back from mentioning it to Osakwe, still convinced they were keeping information from her. 'I've opened the envelope,' she said. 'I take it the wire is a microphone, and the wireless earpiece is compatible with the Nokia?'

'Correct. Simply attach the wire with the pins to the inner lining of your jacket. More about this tomorrow—'

'How many of them are there?' interrupted Shani. 'Do you know?'

'We think three. It's quite a small cell, sometimes conducting operations for financial gain without the knowledge of the State Security Service. They are thugs, little else. In the last half hour, we have successfully hacked into the main kidnapper's phone, the one who spoke to you. Our aim is to intercept during their reporting back to Porto Sansudou, and falsify the location where the Security Service wants the exchange to take place.'

Shani nodded. Osakwe seemed to know what he was talking about. Thank God. 'Why the woollen hat?'

'To help disguise you from CCTV, should it be necessary.'

'You will call me tomorrow morning, Osakwe?'

'Yes. Seven o'clock. It'll be tight. If you need to call me, there's a number on the Nokia you can use. Obviously, this phone is only for communicating with me. Understood?'

'Yes, of course.'

'Should something happen to the phone I've given you, use a public phone to contact me. Write my number down and keep it safe. Okay?'

'Yes.'

'I want you to try and get some sleep, Shani. Try not to worry too much. We will get Nicolas back.'

'Thank you. He means everything to me, Osakwe. I have no family.'

Shani wiped a tear off her cheek and left the phone on the worktop. This time tomorrow, where would she be? In Nicolas's arms? Or on her way to Séroulé and into Kuetey's murderous hands?... Probably better not to speculate. She already had enough fear churning up her insides! She scribbled the Nokia's number onto her Eurostar ticket and put it in her bag, noticing as she did so the Ghanaian visa. For safe-keeping, she tucked it away on a bookshelf and then found herself standing over the gun in the bedroom. She hadn't wanted Osakwe to know about it. Why? What would a clever strategist do? Keep something back? Prepare a parallel strategy, one that was completely secret? It made sense. First question: What skills could she put to good use? There were few to choose from, apart from one which stood out above all others.

Shani sat on the stool beside the worktop and opened up *Maps* on her phone. She found Rue Chante Coq, and even the bedroom's skylight. She took a left onto Rue de la République, before changing her mind. It would be too busy, certainly at eight o'clock in the morning. She went back, and minutes later found exactly what she had hoped to find. She made a mental note of the street: Lucien Voilin. The strategy would give her flexibility, and she was tempted to call Osakwe, but if he told her it was too risky and not to proceed it would leave her without an option – unless they, of course, had prepared one themselves.

Sleep. That was the most important issue as of this moment. For Nicolas's sake she needed to be alert in the morning. She double-checked that she'd turned the key in the lock, and then struggled to heft the settee over to the door. She found that by using all the chairs in a line, and with the table from the kitchenette pushed up against the worktop, entry to the studio became virtually impossible – noiselessly so, at least. She had the gun. And Osakwe's number. And people were apparently watching the premises – 'protecting' her.

A shower. She had no clean underwear, but she could rinse what she was wearing. Good thinking. She slipped off her clothes and prosthesis and hopped over to the shower cubicle.

We failed you, and I apologise unreservedly for that.

She liked the shower gel. Quite minty.

Three days ago, we lost the best part of a sleeper cell. My younger brother being one of the fatalities.

How could her senses appreciate the shower gel at a time like this?! Her mind felt jumbled up, like an electrical circuit on the blink – misfiring here and there as memories ricocheted off fear and the fact that she'd never actually experienced hatred before. It was like being devoured by acid as it stripped away the life she was accustomed to living, leaving in its wake outrage and solitude.

She dried and dressed herself in one of Nicolas's T-shirts – massively oversized, but it would have to do.

London tells me the call was successful, so congratulate yourself.

She brushed her teeth, took off the stained duvet and changed it for a fresh one, stuffing the dirty linen into the washing machine so she didn't have to look at it.

I like trees.
You're funny.
Because I like trees?
Because you're you.

The lamp had a dimmer, so she turned it down until there was enough light for her to see what she was doing. She slipped under the duvet and centred herself on the mattress. To the left of her, she had *Madeleine*, and on her right, the gun. The same model James Bond used, Jacques had told her.

Don't do anything foolish, like change or cut your hair.

Her head felt heavy, her body numb. She was exhausted.

Nicolas has talked about me?

Talked about you? I couldn't shut him up.

Nicolas, cried a distant voice. *Dearest Nicolas…*

CHAPTER 16

The diffused glow radiating from a raffia lightshade bewildered her, before she remembered. Straightaway, part of her wished she hadn't – or couldn't. She was of course in Paris, Nicolas's studio. But Nicolas had been taken from her. Struck by the thought that she might have overslept, Shani quickly checked her mobile phone for messages. Nothing. The Nokia, likewise. She breathed, relieved, and collected herself. It was close to six-thirty. She'd slept for six hours. Something of an achievement given the crisis. She dragged herself up to sit on the edge of the bed and reached for her prosthesis. She hadn't covered it over since the night Nicolas asked her to renounce the habit. There had been no nightmares – apart from what reality had now flung in her face.

Shani recalled the parallel strategy from the previous evening, and in a matter of seconds rejected it. It wasn't just risky, it was downright insane. To visit a side-street and wait for a motorcycle to appear, threaten the rider with the gun and seize the bike. Then park it in close proximity to where the exchange was expected to happen. A miscalculation on her part, and the consequences for Nicolas could prove disastrous. A more constructive approach would be to trust Osakwe, and that meant telling him about the gun.

An image of Nicolas sitting on the chair over to her left swept aside Osakwe. How were they treating him? It felt like her life, let alone his, had hit a wall at the speed of sound and now lay broken, fragmented. Suspended, even, in some unalterable way. The kidnappers had the edge. Every detail covered.

In the kitchenette, she searched for and found a jar of instant coffee. While waiting for the water to boil, she opened the small awning window. Dawn light was creeping into the skyline. She drew the frosty air into her lungs to clear her head before moving the table back to its rightful position, likewise the chairs and settee. Finally, she straightened the painting. Her underwear had dried on the radiator. She quickly dressed, her stomach beginning to knot and tighten at what lay ahead. She sat on the stool beside the worktop and tried to distract herself by looking at the pictures of both herself and Nicolas on her phone.

Smiles and occasional laughter, despite their concerns over Séroulé. Two young lovers in Gordon Square – with the woman who had become her heroine, Noor Inayat Khan, gazing quietly at them both in the background.

The harsh ringtone on her newly acquired Nokia made her jump. Osakwe. Unless the kidnappers had already acquired the new number.

'Hello?' she said, her throat dry despite the coffee she'd been sipping.

'Morning, Shani,' chirped Osakwe. 'Did you sleep?'

'I've been awake about twenty minutes. I'm having a coffee.' Shani went and picked up the gun from off the bed. She still had reservations, because she wanted to keep it. Survival.

'Shani?'

'There's…there's something I need to tell you.'

'Such as?'

'I have a gun.'

A pause. She heard Osakwe quietly breathing, like he was deliberating. Then:

'What sort of a gun?'

'I've forgotten the name, but James Bond uses the same type – or model.'

'Walther PPK?'

'That's it.'

'Fully loaded?'

'I don't know. Six bullets, I think, and one ready to go in the chamber.'

'Where did you get it? Nicolas's apartment?'

'I can't say. I promised. I want to keep it.'

Another pause. 'Well, full marks for initiative.'

'I can take it with me?'

'Absolutely. We planned to issue you with one, but if you're happy with the Walther that's fine by me. You know about the safety?'

'Safety?'

'Safety catch.'

'Yes. It's on the left side of the gun. What happens now?'

'I want you to head out to Rue André Suares, in the 18th Arrondissement.'

'Arrondissement?' asked Shani. 'That means district?'

'Yes. There's a great deal of building work going on around there at the moment. The kidnappers have used this area before. Our interceptor in Porto Sansudou has instructed them to make use of the location again.'

Shani made notes. 'What station? Esplanade de la Défense to where?'

'Porte de Clichy. Get a bus down to Défense. If I

remember, you need lines one, and two. Yellow, dark blue. Take you about an hour from where you are now.'

'Will someone be following me?'

'Distantly, on occasion. I'll explain when you reach Clichy.'

Distantly, on occasion. The remark sounded somewhat blasé to Shani. Secondary threads, she reminded herself, the build-up of tension in her stomach relentless. It actually hurt, not just a flutter but a dull ache. 'Osakwe, this is going to be quite a challenge for me,' she said. 'I'm an academic, for God's sake. I know nothing about this way of life, only what I've seen in films.'

'It won't be a problem for you. You didn't get into St Aquinas without being brave, or competent. As we speak, the finer details are coming together nicely.'

Shani wished Osakwe's confidence would rub off onto her. 'I'm leaving now,' she said, and cut the call. She finished her coffee and glanced again at the picture of Nicolas before she closed her phone, replacing it with the gun. The metal was cold – and confusing, in more ways than one. An inert and seemingly harmless object. And yet, positively lethal. There was now a chance she was going to have to use it, so a couple of practise shots would have been useful.

* * *

Shani made it to Porte de Clichy within the projected one hour frame, and bought a scarf to assist her disguise from a charity shop that was opening-up for the day. Wearing the woollen bobble hat and with her hair tucked in her Barbour, she decided to pass the entrance to the street where the exchange was due to take place. It felt both important and logical to familiarize herself with the immediate area. The app on her phone told her to cross the main highway, Avenue de la Porte de Clichy, but she didn't. She put the phone in her pocket and turned up the collar on her Barbour. Minutes later, and by using only her peripheral vision, she saw the entrance to Rue André Suares. Just as Osakwe had mentioned, it looked to be part of a building project, the odd crane here and there.

Shani carried on, and took a right into a quiet street, both in way of traffic and pedestrians. She slowed her pace. Why use a building site for the exchange? She couldn't see the sense in doing so. It wasn't the weekend. Unless it was going to happen after dark. How the hell was she going to keep herself together for that length of time? She looked over her shoulder to see if she was being followed, hopefully by one of Osakwe's men. She appeared to be alone. A car drove past – before her phone rang. Nicolas's number! Surely the kidnappers hadn't already identified her? Or had they followed her the moment she left the studio? Perhaps waiting outside on the street for her to emerge?

She found she needed to sit down. There was a children's play area opposite, the swings and slide without a soul. She sat on a bench, and the moment the call ended spoke to Osakwe on the Nokia.

'They've called me. It's only eight-thirty. I said I would call them at nine.'

'What did they say?' asked Osakwe.

'I haven't spoken to them.'

'All right,' said Osakwe. 'Listen to me. When it comes to the exchange, you mustn't argue, no matter how startling my instructions may sound. Understood?'

'Yes.'

'Where are you exactly? At the station?'

'I wanted to take a look at the street, André Suares. A very distant look,' she quickly added.

'I'm not too happy about that, Shani,' complained Osakwe. A definite pause, possibly for effect, thought Shani. On reflection, she realised he had a point. 'From this moment on,' continued Osakwe, 'we have to be absolutely straight with each other. Nothing outside the box, okay?'

'Yes. I'm sorry. But haven't you anyone following me?'

'There's no need at this stage, providing you do exactly what I tell you. We're going to use a car to rescue you both. It will be silver in colour. A silver Citroën. The interceptor in contact with the cell has told us they've accepted the location. This is where you're going to need all your courage.'

'Tell me.'

'For this to work, you demand that Nicolas walks towards you, for a final embrace, if you like. Do not bend from this. Nicolas needs to get behind you. You are going to be his shield. This will work because they are forbidden to harm you. The order has come directly from General Kuetey. How do you feel about this, Shani?'

'Scared,' Shani said at once. It sounded ludicrous! 'Petrified, in fact. You're sure this instruction has come from Kuetey?'

'Positive. You have to trust me on this.'

'I don't like it.'

'Shani, look at the timescale. Less than twenty hours. We are working like crazy on this, trying to predict and cover various scenarios. It's risky, I don't deny that—'

'All right, all right, Osakwe, I follow you.' The more he talked, the more nervous he made her feel – as if that was at all possible. Then a thought, or potential hazard. 'What if one of the kidnappers is positioned behind me?' she asked. 'He will get a clear shot at Nicolas.'

'At the one end of the building site there are a few derelict sheds and railway sidings, and that's about it. We have a couple of snipers monitoring the area. They checked out the sheds earlier this morning. The kidnappers will, we believe, release Nicolas from the east, from one of two rundown apartment blocks.'

Her phone rang. Nicolas's number. Shit! 'Osakwe, they're calling me.'

'Take the call. Final point, don't worry if they ask you to go to another location first.'

'Why should they?' Shani asked. She had a bad feeling.

'To make certain you are quite alone. Call me straight back. Good luck.'

The call ended, abrupt abandonment in its place. She switched mobiles, the 'bad feeling' not shifting. There were too many unknowns for her liking. And was there a back-up plan? She'd forgotten to ask. Sometimes when Osakwe spoke to her it felt like he was giving a pep talk to a salesperson. But without him, where would she be now? Locked into some hare-brained idea of her own, no doubt. She took the call.

'You are still at Gare du Nord?'

'Yes.' She recognised the accent as being the same man. 'I want to speak to Nicolas. Now!'

'Why are you shout—?'

'Let me speak to him.'

'In a moment, Shani. Just calm down. Don't make me say that to you again. You hear me?'

'I...I'm sorry.' It was like something – *his* voice – was pulling her apart, with nothing to hold on to. No hope whatsoever. Osakwe sounded amateurish in comparison. She found herself crying. How was she expected to cope? 'You can take me,' she said, meaning every word. Her hand came into contact with the gun in her pocket. A simple squeeze on the trigger if it came to it. 'Nicolas doesn't deserve what you are doing to him.'

'You are a good girl...'

And now physical fear. Her skin crawled at the thought of this man touching her. *Come to me, Zinsa!*

'...This is what I want you to do. You head out to Rue Fragonard. In this particular street you will find a docking station for bicycles, all of them identical, for the public to pay and use. The Metro will take you there. The station you require is Porte de Clichy.'

'I want to speak to—'

'Yes, yes. We'll let him speak to you.'

She could hear something going on in the background, muffled voices. 'Nicolas?' she called.

'Shani, you must listen to me—'

'Oh, Nicolas,' she cried out, putting a hand on her brow. She hadn't the strength to stand and fell to her knees on the dew-laden grass. 'What have they done to you? Tell me. Your voice is frail—'

'Shani…Shani, you mustn't come here—'

She heard a crash, and a dull moan that faded away.

'What the hell are you doing to him?' she screamed.

'I've told you already,' shouted the kidnapper, 'I don't take kindly to disobedience—'

'Stop hurting him, you monster!'

'*Get* yourself to Rue Fragonard. You have one hour, otherwise we'll slit his throat.'

Shani fought to stand and more or less collapsed onto the bench, tears streaming down her cheeks. She looked up at the slate sky, then across at the slide. The play area seemed like it was moving; the ground in front of her juddering. Was this it? Her mind finally caving in, imploding over the sheer weight of dread she was carrying.

...Otherwise we'll slit his throat.

She couldn't believe how much his voice had changed. And *still* he was trying to protect her. She felt the gun again, this time not through her jacket but the cold metal itself. She wanted to kill them – all of them. Obliterate their vile minds. It shocked her, such violence coming from within her, but it was *they* who had crossed the line. She transferred the gun to her shoulder bag, wanting to detach herself from it as much as possible.

How far was she from Rue Fragonard? She took the Nokia from her pocket and made the call.

The moment Osakwe answered she gave him her concerns.

'Did you speak to Nicolas?' asked Osakwe.

'Yes. Just for a moment. He sounded very weak. I don't think I can help him except by handing myself over. I don't care anymore. Maybe I'll get a chance to use the gun on them. But really they have it covered. I can see they have. You've got to believe me.'

'Shani, we need to look at the positives—'

'My nerve's gone. I'm in a terrible mess!'

'Shani—'

'I'm feeling strange, sort of giddy, like I'm emotionally exhausted.'

'Shani, the positives – please. For Nicolas. We know he's alive. The groundwork has been achieved. The snipers are in position. The driver is ready. But I need information from you. What are your instructions?'

She blew her nose. Osakwe. He knew how to play her, and was her only hope, literally. Between them they had Nicolas's life in their hands. So she had to trust this man she'd never even met, trust him when he said they were 'working like crazy' behind the scenes. 'I've got an hour to reach Rue Fragonard. I told him I was at Gare du Nord. I need to search my app for Rue Fragonard?'

'I'll look for it. Give me a moment…'

Shani opened up her phone, and focused on a picture of Nicolas on his own. He looked so beautiful, his tousled blond hair, his composed features – luminous with kindness. How dare they touch him!

'…Shani? Where are you, exactly?'

Shani went to find the name of the road. 'I'll have to ask someone. There are factories here, tennis courts…' She turned to her right, a bearded man in green overalls strolling towards her. *Rue Saint-Just*, she was told, and relayed the information to Osakwe.

'Okay, I know where you are. Go back the way

you came and take a left down Avenue de la Porte de Clichy, keeping well away from Rue André Suares. Go over Boulevard Berthier, and Rue Fragonard is on your left. It's quite hectic around there, with boulevards crossing one another. You're less than ten minutes from Fragonard, so you need to lose time. Find somewhere for a coffee. It might be an idea to ask for a shot of something. Brandy, or whisky. Whichever you prefer. When did you last eat?'

'Oxford, before they called me.'

'You need to get some food inside you. You said you were feeling faint.'

'I'll try.'

'You have the mobile charger?'

'Yes.'

'Ask them in the café to give the phone a charge. Set up the mobile with the microphone under your collar and call me when you're ready to leave. Put the gun in your waistband, rather than in your shoulder bag if that's what you are doing. It's a quicker and easier draw. Okay?'

'Yes.' So, Osakwe knew she was carrying her jhola bag. Perhaps the snipers had already seen her and reported back to him. A comforting thought, at least. 'I'm worried I'm going to let you and Nicolas down,' she said.

'I didn't quite hear that, Shani. Now get your coffee with a shot, and have something to eat, and we'll talk again.'

Shani put the phone back in her bag. Her imagination couldn't have conjured such terror, she told herself – because she couldn't see how it was going to work. Did Osakwe really believe the kidnappers would allow Nicolas to walk towards her? That was going to be the tricky part. She was bloody useless at lying!

CHAPTER 17

She found a small café with a red awning on Avenue de la Porte de Clichy. The woman bustling about behind the counter gave her a friendly smile, and was happy to charge the Nokia. While the woman sorted her out with a cheese-salad baguette, Shani checked the bars on her own phone. Not too bad, even so she wished she'd topped it up before leaving the studio.

She asked for a shot of brandy in the coffee and took the tray over to a window that looked out onto the street. The café was becoming busier by the minute. Ordinary people starting their day, some with domestic or business concerns, perhaps – but not one of them carrying a Walther PPK handgun with six bullets and 'one ready to go in the chamber'. She sat on the only available stool and looked at the time. Thirty-eight minutes left before she showed up in Rue Fragonard. She struggled with the baguette, her appetite still non-existent. In the watery reflection of herself in the window, she noticed that the white hat with its pink bobble made her look slightly comical, like she'd landed a part in a film production where her role was that of a dysfunctional nonentity – 'dysfunctional' being the operative word, she supposed.

Shani, we need to look at the positives... Osakwe. This was not a great time to beat herself up!

She finished the baguette and made a start on the coffee, trying not to grimace. The brandy began to take the chill out of her, but did little to lessen her mounting trepidation. The challenge ahead felt like a chunk of fiction she couldn't relate to. She simply couldn't get over how Nicolas's voice had changed. She assumed he hadn't slept, and that would have had some effect. But what else? What insane torture had they applied to get information about the rebels out of him? She rechecked the time on her phone. Eighteen minutes to go. Her hands were shaking so much that her cup clattered when she set it back down on its saucer.

The most convenient place for her to keep the Nokia was in the right-hand pocket of her Barbour. Using the knife from her baguette, she quietly drew the lining up onto her thigh and made an incision in the pocket so that the wire would remain hidden. To avoid drawing attention to herself, she followed the sign to the washroom – to find it engaged. Worried about the time, she pinned the microphone below her collar while walking back along the corridor. Finally, she inserted the earpiece, pulled down the bobble hat another inch, and called Osakwe.

'I'm wired up,' she told him, barely above a whisper.

'You've eaten?' Osakwe asked, pitch-perfect in her ear.

'Yes. And a coffee with a shot. I'm leaving the café.'

'How do you feel? Tell me.'

'Scared,' repeated Shani. She wove back through the crowded tables and stepped out onto the bustling pavement. 'Scared like I've never ever been before.'

'Of course... So, let's get ourselves a result. I've sent one of the snipers over to Fragonard, but you won't see any sign of him. Okay?'

'Yes.' Virtually next to the café was a motorbike park-up area. She couldn't help but notice in amongst the bikes an MV Agusta – her dream bike. A moment's distraction. But that was it now. She pretended to rub an itch off her nose, just to be on the safe side should the kidnappers have spotted her. 'What if they decide to change the location?' she asked.

'There's been no indication to suggest they will,' responded Osakwe.

'I'm on Avenue de Clichy. There's lots of traffic.'

'Fragonard is on your left.'

'I can see it. I'll go.' Shani cut the call before Osakwe. She hated it when he did it first, not only a feeling of abandonment but a reminder of the colossal responsibility she was carrying. And if she screwed-up? For sure she would be a tortured soul for the rest of her days. Her shaky disposition made that a certainty.

The bicycle docking station mentioned by the kidnapper was halfway down on the right. She stood next to it, her mouth dry. She chewed the side of her tongue to produce some saliva. Perhaps she ought to have contacted the *gendarmerie*—

Her phone sounded. Nicolas's number.

'Yes?' she answered, her voice breathy.

'Come further down,' ordered the kidnapper. 'I'll tell you when to stop.'

Shani followed the instruction and wondered where he might actually be. In an apartment above her, presumably. Or a parked car, watching her through binoculars. Horrible.

'The red Mercedes, beside you. Empty the contents of your bag onto its roof.'

Shani stood stock-still. She didn't need to be told that she'd made a dreadful mistake. 'Pardon?' she asked, stalling for time – or that by some miracle she had misheard him.

'The red car. Empty your bag on its roof.'

The handgun. She hadn't put it in her waistband, as Osakwe had told her to do. A simple task. And now what? Without the gun, they would have virtual control over her. She started to empty the bag, little by little.

'Shake it out!' snapped the kidnapper. 'Don't waste my time.'

Shani tried to leave the gun in the bottom of the bag by using sleight of hand, but he was on to her.

'I said shake the bag, keeping your fingers pinched together.'

The Walther fell with a clatter onto the roof. She felt physically sick, her stupidity having in effect placed a noose around Nicolas's neck.

'There we go, Shani,' came the kidnapper, his tone euphoric, resonating from her phone. 'What a silly thing for you to have tried. Where did you get it from?'

'A friend in Oxford,' she answered, having predicted the question. It crossed her mind to put the gun against her head and walk out into the street.

Make the kidnapper panic in some way. *This will work because they are forbidden to harm you.* Osakwe. 'He's…he's with a gun club. I'm not going to give you his name,' she added, hoping it made the lie more convincing.

'And you told him about this?'

'He doesn't know I've taken it. I knew where he kept it. He showed it me once. I have keys to his house—'

'Okay, okay, don't tire me. There are people coming on your right. Take the gun from the roof. When they've gone, put it under the car.'

Shani waited for the couple to pass her, a child with a Donald Duck baseball cap skipping along in front of them. She handled the gun. There was little point to put it against her head. The kidnapper might even laugh. And what if a stranger happened to be watching through a window? With the recent terrorist attacks in France the street would be sealed off in minutes and she would be arrested. She put the gun under the car.

'I want to get this over with,' said the kidnapper. 'Go out of this street the way you came in, turn right and cross over Boulevard Berthier. Walk down Avenue de la Porte de Clichy until you find Rue André Suares, over on your left. You got that?'

'Yes. Rue André Suares.'

'You've got fifteen minutes.'

Shani put her hairbrush, tissues, toothpaste, Osakwe's charger, and everything else back into her bag and walked away from the Mercedes, tempted to retrieve the gun. But she daren't. At least they hadn't switched the location. She turned right at the end of the street, and found a stall selling refreshments. She bought a bottle of Perrier and drank half of it. The gun. She'd let everyone down – already. She came across a tiny alleyway about a hundred metres from Fragonard, ducked into it and called Osakwe.

'I've got to be quick. I've messed up – big time.'

'What happened?'

'I forgot to hide the gun. I'm so sorry. He made me empty my bag onto the roof of a car.'

'Red Mercedes, right? Could be the car they're using.'

'Osakwe, I don't have the gun!'

'I understand. Fine. We can continue.'

'Why didn't they come out of the apartment, or wherever, and take me?'

'Because they're still uncertain whether you're alone. The last thing they need is a shootout. Kuetey would go ballistic. Their lives wouldn't be worth living. Did they tell you to head for André Suares?'

'Yes. I have about ten minutes.'

'They might have put a tail on you. Where are you?'

'In an alleyway.'

'Okay, get out of there. We're staying with each other from now on. So listen carefully: you cannot be seen talking into the wire. If it's absolutely necessary for you to talk to me, cover your mouth. Be subtle, don't overdo it.'

Shani left the alley. She had to get herself another weapon: it would have to be a knife. Several shops and cafés further on she came to a grocery store, went inside it and hastily scanned both sides of the single aisle. At the far end was a small display of paring knives. She chose the largest, which amounted to a blade ten centimetres long. She sealed the purchase and started to leave the shop.

'Shani, what are you doing?' came Osakwe's voice. 'I can't hear the traffic.'

She brushed the back of her hand against her nose. 'I've been in a shop. I've bought a knife. They're not going to take me alive.'

Osakwe paused. 'All right, all right, Shani. I understand.' His voice sounded strained, as if laced with hurt. 'But we're going to make sure it doesn't come to that. Okay?'

'I'm having to pick up my pace.'

She'd never seen so much traffic. She made it across Avenue de la Porte de Clichy and into the quieter side street of André Suares, where she rubbed a hand across her lips. 'Why is the building site deserted?'

'A legal dispute, I've been told,' said Osakwe.

Shani rounded a slight bend. She couldn't see any sign of the red Mercedes. She loitered at the curve, and wished she'd visited the washroom back at the cafe. She tried to ignore the need.

Her mobile sounded. Nicolas's number.

'Yes?' she answered.

'A simple exchange, Shani,' said the voice. 'That is, we will set Nicolas free if you come under our protection. You understand?'

She switched to the phone's speaker for Osakwe's benefit. 'Yes. You're not going to harm me?'

'Of course not. We just want to talk to you. No one's going to harm you. So, if you look ahead, some of the boarding and corrugated sheeting is missing opposite you. Go onto the actual waste ground…'

Shani cut across the street and entered a colossal building site, although from what she could see no actual construction had started. Just ten foot high piles of gravel across a network of muddy tyre tracks filled with rain water, and the cranes she'd seen earlier. The two apartment blocks Osakwe had mentioned were now directly in front of her. A glance over her shoulder and she saw what she took to be the railway sidings and wooden sheds – a derelict air about them.

'…Come further onto the site, Shani, so we get a clear view of you.'

'How far?' she asked, reminding herself she needed to keep Osakwe informed.

'Another fifty metres.'

'Walk another fifty metres?'

'Yes. Five, zero.'

Osakwe's voice came into her right ear. 'Walk less, Shani. Don't go the full fifty. Where you came in, will be your point of exit. Repeat what he says to you as *little* as possible. I can hear him—'

'Come further over, towards the apartments,' interrupted the kidnapper.

Shani stood firm. This was it now, the performance of her lifetime. Her knees quivered, and she found she could barely breathe – akin to stage fright, she imagined. She prayed they wouldn't hurt Nicolas.

'I'm not moving from here,' she said, 'until I get to see Nicolas. I have done everything—'

'Yes, yes. We will send him. It's not a problem. But first, I want to know why you went into that store on

Porte de Clichy.'

Shani hesitated. She couldn't think of anything to say but the truth, the question so unexpected. 'A knife.'

'You bought a knife?'

'Yes.'

'To replace the gun?'

'Maybe.'

'Don't get smart, Shani.'

'I want to see Nicolas—'

'Throw the knife down,' instructed the kidnapper. 'As far away from you as you can.'

'When I get to see Nicolas.'

'What did I just say to you?' reacted the kidnapper. 'Hey? I said don't act smart. Right? You throw the knife away, and we'll send you Nicolas.'

Shani relented. Anything to see him. The knife landed beside a mound of gravel over on her left. 'I've done it.'

No response from the kidnapper, just background hiss.

Shani kept her eyes focussed on the two apartment blocks, sixty or more metres in the distance. It was cold. She wanted to get her woollen gloves out of her bag, afraid by doing so she might unnerve the kidnapper. She waited. Time seemed to suspend itself, like it didn't exist. Like nothing existed – apart from the twisting in her stomach telling her it could only be the wretchedness of fate, her arch-nemesis!

She brought her phone to her lips, and was about to protest at the time it was taking them to honour the agreement when a figure emerged from the apartment block directly ahead of her. It moved slowly, weaving a little as if drunk, stumbling at least twice.

'You see,' came the kidnapper, 'Nicolas is in good health.'

But to Shani, Nicolas looked a different person. His face was dirty, his hair tangled, like he'd been sleeping rough for months on end. Then she stopped breathing, because to her horror she realised that the dirt on his face was dried blood. When he finally reached her, his eyes made her gasp. They seemed to stare through her, as if the life they'd once held had been drawn out of them. Bile or vomit smeared his blue jacket, and there was a burn mark on his neck. She tried to speak, but no words would come.

'...So walk towards us, Shani. Nicolas is free to go now. I'm sending someone down to greet you. We'll take good care of you.'

'Shani,' came Osakwe's voice, 'get Nicolas behind you and break contact.'

Shani found she couldn't take her eyes off Nicolas. She wanted to cry and hold him in her arms, to bathe and heal his wounds.

'Shani,' shouted Osakwe, 'get him behind you. *Now!*'

Osakwe's voice felt like a detonation inside her brain. And yes, Nicolas was actually with her. They were *together* again! Lifting her phone: 'Monster!' she yelled at the kidnapper.

'Shani, this is business, you understand—'

Shani cut the call. 'Get behind me, Nicolas.'

Nicolas shook his head. 'They have rifles trained on us. I told you not to come here—'

'You don't understand,' said Shani, seizing his jacket. She could feel her skin tingling with the sting of imagined bullets. He *had* to obey her before she passed out! 'I'm in contact with Osakwe. So get behind me, for God's sake.' He began to do as he was told. 'Try and shrink yourself. I'm your shield…' Her phone started ringing.

'Osakwe, they're trying to make contact.'

'Ignore it,' ordered Osakwe. 'The car's waiting for you. Move faster. We're almost there.'

'Nicolas, we have to go quicker—' The second her phone stopped ringing, a deafening report crackled like a roll of thunder around the building site.

'*Shani!*' yelled Osakwe, 'Scare tactics. Nothing more. Keep Nicolas with you. Twenty metres and you're out of there.'

'Osakwe,' cried Shani, 'they're trying to shoot us down.' Her legs briefly buckled and if it wasn't for Nicolas she would have fallen. 'I'm…I'm going faint.'

'Swallow hard,' countered Osakwe. 'Breathe deep. You can do this. You're so close. Remember, they're not allowed to harm you.'

A second shot rang out, kicking up earth barely a metre from them.

'Nicolas…help me.' He rubbed her stomach, and held her more firmly. She started to cry. God, how she *loved* this man. They were going to live or die together. Nothing else mattered.

A sudden movement, straight ahead of them. Shani wiped her eyes, and saw a figure sprinting towards the perimeter fence.

'Run now,' croaked Nicolas.

'Osakwe,' yelled Shani as another mighty shot echoed around the building site, 'a guy left the apartment block. He's heading for André Suares.'

'*Merde*,' groaned Osakwe. 'Get in the car.'

The silver Citroën was a couple of metres to their right, facing away from the apartment blocks for an immediate exit out of André Suares. The nearside rear door was open, waiting for them, the driver revving the engine.

A frightful scream from down the street.

Shani looked up, and saw a passer-by fleeing a gunman taking aim. With the rear of the car facing him the driver was oblivious to the danger, unless he happened to be looking in a mirror. But he wasn't, he was looking at them. She screamed at him just as the Citroën's rear and front windscreens exploded, throwing a wave of blood and shattered glass over the bonnet. The gunman swung the rifle to his right, and now had them in his sights, edging closer – barely fifty metres away. Bystanders darted behind him, dashing from the street, when a shot from somewhere jolted the gunman's head forward, his bulk collapsing to the ground.

'Shani, cross over and come down the street,' ordered Osakwe. 'No time to waste.'

Shani grabbed Nicolas's jacket and made for the opposite pavement. 'You need to move faster,' she told him. 'Come on!'

'It's my right leg...'

'See the open window above you, Shani?' hollered Osakwe in her right ear. 'Two floors up. Okay?'

She saw a gloved hand emerge from the window in question.

'Catch it.'

Shani fumbled the catch, the gun clattering softly onto the pavement.

'Get the hell out,' Osakwe told her. 'And keep your heads down. CCTV.'

Shani whipped the gun into her shoulder bag and detached herself from the earpiece as they passed the body in the street. She kept her hand on Nicolas's jacket, trying to get him to move faster. Worst case scenario unfolding! Where the hell was the back-up plan? Or was handing her the gun *it*? The apartment blocks were now directly on their left, two kidnappers remaining – supposedly. They turned the corner onto Avenue de la Port de Clichy. Shani saw a taxi in the traffic. She tried to flag it down, but the driver shook his head and pointed straight ahead.

Nicolas was struggling. She kept him close to the shop fronts before something caught her eye: a biker in red and white leathers waiting at a pedestrian crossing. The park-up area she'd seen earlier... *Parallel strategy!* A chance to flee the vicinity. She shouldered Nicolas into the entrance of a newsagent, the unexpected shove virtually sending him through the door.

He regained his balance. 'Christ, what are you doing?'

Shani looked at him as a cacophony of sirens drew

closer. She couldn't bear the sight of his bloodied face, twisted with pain, and fought against taking him in her arms. 'Keep your head down because of CCTV, and don't move from here.' She didn't wait for a response and as calmly as she could joined the pedestrians crossing the boulevard, keeping a short distance behind the biker. He appeared totally relaxed, almost sauntering, no rush – opposite to the tension in her body, every sinew as taught as an archer's bow. They arrived at the bikes together. The MV Agusta had gone. He made directly for a red Ducati, alongside a pale-green scooter. Shani stood next to the scooter and cradled the gun in her shoulder bag, in her left hand she had a biro and some paper for his phone number to show that her intention wasn't to thieve the bike off him. Psychology. Soften the blow, the outrage.

'Hi,' she said.

The biker turned to her, just as he was putting on his helmet. He gave her a casual smile. 'Hi, there.'

American, or Canadian. A good-looking guy, her subconscious was telling her. Dark hair, and in his thirties. Beautiful, tender blue eyes. 'Saw the helmet. Mine's so damned heavy.' Shani glanced at the box under the seat on the scooter, making him believe that's where it was. 'Do you mind if I quickly try on yours?' He lowered the helmet. 'I don't want to hold you up.' She stopped short of fluttering her eyelashes, partly because she wasn't any good at it.

Another smile. 'Not a problem, lady.' He handed over the helmet. 'It's a Bell. Carbon. Pricey, but it's gonna be lighter than what you've got, I'd imagine.'

Shani swiped off the bobble hat. 'Kind of you.' While putting on the helmet she watched the biker produce a key and insert it into the Ducati's ignition. That was all she required him to do.

The boulevard was hectic with traffic and pedestrians. No one else in the bike park-up, though. Without giving herself time to think, she shoved Osakwe's gun into his side, keeping it concealed in her bag.

The biker spun to face her.

'This is a gun.' Shani showed him just enough for him see she was telling the truth. 'I'm desperate.'

The biker took his hand from the key. 'Hey, lady, what are you trying to—?'

'I'm really desperate,' asserted Shani. The visor, goddammit, had started to mist over! 'I'm dealing with life and death. So move away.'

'Now, lady—'

Shani hardened her tone. This was the point where she either gave up and ran off or got what she wanted. 'I'm not going to warn you again.' She thrust her left hand out towards him. 'Write your number down. I'll call you this evening, telling you where I've left the bike.'

The biker's mouth opened, but not a sound came out.

'You want me to blow you away?' she hissed. 'Because I will. They're trying to kill my boyfriend. Then it's going to be me. So I *really* am desperate. Make no mistake.'

'Wait a minute—'

Shani showed him the gun again and dug it deeper into his side.

'Okay, okay.' The biker took the pen. 'Whatever you say…'

Then suddenly he took a lunge at her, but as he did so Shani accidentally squeezed the trigger on the gun, the ensuing report stunning both of them.

Shani was quick to recover. By some miracle she hadn't hit him.

The whites of the biker's eyes had grown to the size of golf balls. 'Jesus,' he muttered.

Had the noise of the traffic muffled the shot? She daren't look at the pavement behind her. 'Final warning,' she said, and realised she must have knocked the safety off when she tried to catch the gun. From her peripheral vision, she could see pedestrians moving along. There wasn't a crowd forming. Perhaps they'd thought the bike had backfired.

Shani quickly mounted the Ducati, turned the key and fired it up – the biker frantically scribbling down numbers. She was ready, first gear selected. He offered her the slip of paper. She snatched it, let out the clutch, and headed out of the park-up.

She merged into the traffic, and briefly disengaged the clutch to test the throttle's sensitivity. The Ducati responded with a feral howl as she drifted over to the left and made an illegal U-turn, taking advantage of a pedestrian crossing. An unexpected gap in the traffic gave her the opportunity to put down a screamer in first gear to familiarize herself with the bike's monster acceleration. The adrenalin charge kicked in, prickling her skin, but it didn't give her the usual high. Any other time on the same bike, without question.

She pulled up sharply alongside the newsagent, blipping the throttle, dreading a possible stall and being unable to restart the bike. She had to beckon Nicolas, detecting from his hesitant stance that he couldn't believe his eyes. She beckoned him again and this time he limped over. She felt him struggle behind her, and blindly gave him the bobble hat. CCTV. He got the message and took it from her. She lifted the visor on the 'pricey' Bell helmet to clear a corner of mist and put on her woollen gloves, her hands freezing. Nicolas put his arms around her. *Beautiful*, she thought. So natural, and akin to the sense of refuge she'd felt in her 'skeleton dream' in Timişoara as the wail of sirens continued to descend on Rue André Suares.

CHAPTER 18

They travelled out of Clichy for several minutes, before Shani swung into a side street. She'd noticed a *Bureau de Change*. Money, and she needed to discuss with Nicolas their next move. Should they abandon the bike? As for money, she only had a few euros left, apart from the two-hundred pounds she'd drawn out at St Pancras. It crossed her mind to use an ATM, but by doing so would reveal her identity and possibly link her to the shooting.

Shani dismounted the bike and lifted her visor. 'That guy, in the car,' she said.

'We can't do anything to change it,' Nicolas told her.

His face was still a sight, worse if anything with small blotches merging with the dried blood. Probably the cold weather, she imagined – or rather, hoped. She pulled down the bobble hat another inch for him. 'What have you got in way of money?'

'Nothing. They took everything, including my passport.' Nicolas shivered and tucked his hands into his pockets. 'I've got cash and a duplicate passport and ID card back at the studio, but it's too dangerous for us to go there. Osakwe, or one of his crew, will have to get it.'

'Duplicate passport?'

'Journalistic precaution.'

'Oh, I see. I've got two-hundred, sterling. There's a *Bureau de Change* at the end of this street. That'll keep us going.' Shani began to unstrap the helmet. 'You're freezing. Put this on.'

Nicolas shook his head. 'No. We should stay with the bike to get us out into the suburbs. The law will punish you more than it will me. You're the rider. I haven't the strength to argue.'

Shani tried to hold back her tears. He looked a shadow of how she remembered him in Gordon Square. And then he did the worst thing he could have done to her. He lowered his eyes and reached for her hand.

'Shani, dear Shani,' he said, 'where do I begin—'

'No, Nicolas.' The Nokia in the right-hand pocket of her Barbour was ringing. 'Don't you dare make me cry. If I start, I'm not going to stop. I'll fall apart!' She spoke to Osakwe.

'We're okay. We're parked-up several miles away.'

'Nicolas?'

'Don't ask. We need you to go to the studio. My Ghanaian visa is tucked away in the bookshelf.'

'Okay, and well done, Shani.'

'You don't know the half of it,' said Shani. 'I'll hand you over to Nicolas.' She gave Nicolas the phone. 'I'll get the euros,' she told him.

* * *

Shani stood in the queue at the *Bureau de Change* on Boulevard Haussmann. It dawned on her that she probably looked somewhat bizarre wearing the crash helmet. Possibly threatening, too. She raised the visor as a compromise. CCTV cameras seemed to be everywhere, on all four walls. She was worried about the bike – worried sick, in fact, her stomach verging on somersaults. The rider must have reported it by now, and given an accurate description of her. What a mess.

The queue shortened. Three away from the counter. She became conscious of a man wearing a suit casting 'casual' glances at her. Security guard? Or was she becoming paranoid? She fumbled for her purse in her jhola bag, her hand brushing against the gun. *Oh, my God...* She'd completely forgotten about the gun. And of all places to be carrying one, as well as wearing a crash helmet! She managed to get the notes out of her purse, making a slight show of doing so, her heartbeat thudding so hard that it was making her feel giddy. What if she fainted? Someone would go through her bag in the hope of finding her name. If only she could lean against the damn counter!

Two in front of her now. Just an enquiry, it seemed. The man nodding briskly, before moving away. One to go. She glanced at the exit. The 'security guard' was now standing alongside it, preparing himself to block her from leaving. How was she going to explain the gun? Perspiration felt to be streaming from her face. She turned away, looking for a waste bin to get rid of it. There didn't seem to be any. How ridiculous!

Shani looked straight ahead, and realised the woman behind the counter was speaking to her. She lurched forward and slapped the two-hundred pounds down on the counter, shoving it under the screen. '*Euros, merci,*' she said.

The middle-aged woman wore a stern expression beneath her extravagantly coiffured hair. She shuffled through the notes, twice, gave the total in French, and then went through the same robotic procedure with the euros before pushing the bundle of notes under the screen.

'*Suivant*,' said the woman impassively.

Her head down, Shani pretended to count the notes as she made for the exit. The man hadn't moved. She carried on 'counting', expecting a restraining hand on her forearm at any moment. Nothing happened, apart from the glass door swinging open automatically in front of her and being hit by a wave of fresh air. She breathed, deeply. Outright heaven, like she was floating through a blossomy orchard. She tucked the euros into her purse, and while waiting to cross the boulevard felt her phone vibrate in her pocket. Kisses from Nicolas, perhaps – a bit of fun. God, how she needed some light-hearted fun! She fished the phone out of her jeans, only to find on the screen a number she didn't immediately recognise.

'Hello?' she said, and because of the traffic she made use of the phone's speaker.

'Shani—'

'Osakwe…'

'They've taken Nicolas!'

'*What?!*' A gap in the traffic, and she started running. What the hell was Osakwe saying to her? 'That's impossible,' she yelled. 'We're miles away—'

'He was talking to me. They've got him. They must have slipped a transmitter into a pocket…'

Shani cut the call and sprinted into the side street. She could see the bike, but no Nicolas. Then further on, walking away from her, Nicolas being guided by a black man towards a red Mercedes. Nicolas was clearly trying to baulk him, pushing his shoulders back – until the man clouted him with his right hand, over which draped a raincoat that Shani suspected concealed a gun. Bastard!

She had seconds to act, but there was only one thing she *could* do. She pulled Osakwe's gun from her bag, came within ten feet of the abductor, aimed at the man's backside and pulled the trigger. The gun kicked back at her, the report deafening in the confined street, but she knew she'd hit him the moment he threw his head back and gave a guttural wail. From her peripheral vision she saw Nicolas shoving him to the ground, then she was past them.

People screamed as they bolted, giving her a clear path, her vision already locked onto the little man in the Mercedes' passenger seat. His neat moustache and tightly cropped hair intuitively told her that it was he who had spoken to her, and had likely tortured Nicolas: her hatred now complete. But she *mustn't* kill him. Too complicated. That much she knew as she watched him through the screen trying to unbuckle his seatbelt. He'd seen her, heard the shot probably.

She aimed the gun and shattered the side-window, and promptly smacked the barrel against his face, before firing at his legs. Someone was trying to pull her away. But she hadn't finished. *Like hell, she had!* Another three shots. Blood spurted as the man fell onto the driver's seat, his hands pushed outwards, pleading with her through a crunched-up face.

'Shani!' Nicolas snatched the gun from her and tossed it onto the back seat. 'We go.' He pulled the bobble hat down over his eyebrows.

They passed by the abductor, kneeling on the pavement, his trousers soaked in blood. Shani climbed onto the bike and fired the ignition. The needle on the rev counter flicked up into the red zone and she spun back the throttle. Nearly over, she told herself – body and mind saturated with adrenalin, making her feel like she didn't belong to herself, that she'd flipped into some kind of frenzied meltdown.

Nicolas tucked his hands into the pockets on her jacket. The feel of his arms around her helped to stabilize her, until a blue light flickered in the Ducati's mirrors from a separate side street too close for comfort. Shani straightaway released the clutch and ran the Ducati down towards the boulevard where she'd exchanged the notes. She had to dodge between curious onlookers as they hovered in front of her, evidently uncertain as to what it was they were supposed to be looking at.

The police car came within twenty metres before she was able to pile on the power, the Ducati suddenly howling down Boulevard Haussmann. She flicked up a gear when the lights in front of her switched to a perfect green. But now a red light, vehicles swerving out of the way in her mirrors, allowing the police car to rapidly shut down the distance.

She took a chance and wove across the junction, drivers to her right and left blasting horns as they braked and skidded around each other. Then she was past the lights, slamming the power back down and snatching gears as she threaded the bike through the traffic, before arriving at a roundabout. No time to decide. She shifted her weight to the right and cranked the Ducati. Nicolas leaned with her, seeming to put his trust in her and connect with the flow as they sped west out of the city.

* * *

Shani negotiated a series of narrow streets off Rue de Paris, trying to decide amidst an unwelcomed flood of tears where she might abandon the Ducati. Had they got away with it? She couldn't see how they could have done. The biker must have given the police a good description. He was still her prime concern. But what precisely had she done wrong? 'Borrowed' a bike. She had the owner's phone number, and intended any moment now to call him. She'd fired the gun in self-defence and to save Nicolas from being re-abducted. Nothing wrong with that, surely? Possession of an illegal weapon? Definitely. That was about it. Six months' prison sentence at the most. Even that, by her reckoning, would be unfair.

With her tears now on the verge of becoming a hazard, clouding her vision, she killed the engine in Rue Saint-Pierre and dismounted the bike without saying a word to Nicolas. She couldn't understand why she was crying. Was it relief? Why wasn't she celebrating with cartwheels down the pavement? On her left was a narrow pedestrianised street, completely deserted. She took off her gloves and helmet and put them down on the cobblestones. Leaning against a wall, she watched Nicolas turn into the street and limp towards her: dried blood still on his face, and whatever that streaky mess was on his jacket.

'Shani?'

She flew at him, beating a fist against his shoulder. 'You promised me,' she yelled. 'You promised me, Nicolas. You promised me no more nightmares.' She buried her face in his other shoulder, sobbing.

'It's okay now, Shani…'

'I love you. God's sake, I do.' She looked up at him, and saw the pain on his face. She took her hand from his shoulder. 'No one comes close to understanding me the way you do.' She leaned back into him. 'It's that simple.'

Nicolas put his arm around her. 'I smell terrible. I must do… But I didn't tell them anything, Shani. I didn't tell them about Prosper and the meeting with Khamadi—'

Shani put her fingers to his lips. 'It's all right. Don't upset yourself.' She began to gently clean his face with tea tree wipes from her shoulder bag. 'When I last spoke to Osakwe, he thinks they might have planted some kind of transmitter on you.'

Nicolas checked his pockets, finding nothing. He removed the jacket with a struggle, his right arm stiff and awkward. A small incision had been made in the lining at the back. He tore open the fabric, and a silver disc the size of a ten cent euro dropped onto the cobblestones with a tinny rattle. 'He was right.'

Shani picked up the helmet and kicked the transmitter away. 'I want to dump all this. Your coat, too.'

'I'm freezing, Shani. I haven't eaten anything.'

She gave him his jacket. 'When we turned into the

street, I noticed a charity clothes shop. We'll get something in there.' Shani looked at her phone. 'We'd better call Osakwe. Three missed calls from him.'

'I need trousers, too.' Nicolas met her eyes as he started to shiver against the icy breeze blowing down the street. 'I'm sorry, but I…' He looked away. 'I messed myself, Shani,' he mumbled. 'They put wires on me—'

'Don't.' Shani helped him ease his arms into his jacket. 'When we're more comfortable, and you want to talk to me about it all, then of course you must. But not now. I'm too fragile.' They walked back into Rue Saint-Pierre.

'We'll get a taxi out to Fourqueux, about five kilometres away,' Nicolas said. 'It's peaceful, a forest nearby we can take walks in to help calm us down. I have a friend there who runs a small hotel on behalf of his elderly parents.' He glanced across at her. 'You got the euros?'

Shani patted her shoulder bag. 'Yes.' She reached for his hand. Perhaps now there was a chance that things could get back to normal – whatever 'normal' might be. She felt they had earned it. *Two young lovers in Gordon Square.* That was the starting point. What had happened between then and now, nothing but a hideous intrusion.

CHAPTER 19

While Nicolas showered, Shani spoke quietly over the phone to Osakwe. 'I'm worried about him. I think they've done quite a bit of damage.'

'What have you noticed, apart from some bruising?'

'He struggles with his right arm and leg. Especially his arm.'

'Okay, I'm coming over. But I want to talk to you first, without Nicolas. There's...movement.'

Shani sat on the bed. 'Movement?'

'Yes.'

She wondered if Osakwe was referring to Séroulé. 'I see,' she said.

'It's going to be about half an hour before I reach Fourqueux. You should have Nicolas settled by then. Is there a bar, or lounge?'

'Yes. But I imagine locals use it, too. I might be

recognised.'

'No need to worry about that. I'll explain when I arrive. Okay?'

'Yes.' Shani put her phone back in her jeans, mildly curious over Osakwe's remark. She drew the curtains while hearing Nicolas in the en suite still under the shower. The room itself was apparently 17th century she was told by Nicolas's friend, Alain. She liked him straightaway. There was no fuss or drama as he listened to Nicolas, just the occasional sympathetic nod. She had a feeling that Alain's parents, the proprietors of the hotel, were fairly religious, a small wooden crucifix in a gilded recess in the reception area alongside brochures specifying nearby places of worship. She hoped they were out of town. Or better still, France itself.

Shani sat back down on the bed and looked at the second-hand tweed jacket they'd chosen in the charity shop. She rather liked the pale grey herringbone-pattern, and a snip at twenty euros. Despite Nicolas saying the police would find the Ducati within hours, she'd insisted on calling its owner from a kiosk to apologise for the grief she'd caused him. The biker immediately launched into a breathless rant: '...My bike's all over the news. You're crazy, lady!' At that point she'd mentioned she'd left the key under the back wheel and hung up.

Reminded they were likely to be headline news, they checked the windows of an electrical goods store in Rue de Paris, where every channel was showing mobile footage of her either on the Ducati with Nicolas, or in the side street firing the gun into the Mercedes. Then two screens started to show footage of the carnage in Rue Andrés Suares, a reporter talking live from the entrance to the cordoned off street. It was at that point when they left the store and headed straight to the charity shop, dumping her Barbour in a bin in the street – a brutal end to a cherished item of clothing.

Shani glanced at the en suite when she realised she hadn't heard the slightest sound for a while. She went over to the door. 'Nicolas, are you all right in there?'

'Drying myself.'

Reassured, Shani sat in the cord-upholstered armchair by the window, wondering what Osakwe might look like. Warrior-looking, like Khamadi Soglo? She recalled Osakwe's terrifying phone call after she'd visited the *Bureau de Change*. She could easily have killed both men in the street. Happily so, in fact. Her feelings hadn't changed. They were monsters. With any luck they would be thoroughly investigated, and past crimes exposed, then sentenced. But what if that didn't happen, and after treatment they were released from hospital? Revenge? Was she – *they* – going to have to look over their shoulders for the rest of their lives?

Nicolas emerged, a towel around his waist, and she got a proper look at him. It was hardly a sight she wanted to remember. Apart from his right eye, there were bruises to his thighs, stomach, and an almighty one across the back of his shoulders. Red marks that looked like cigarette burns peppered his neck and chest, but he had mentioned something about 'wires' – and that could only mean electricity.

Shani put her arms very gently around him, when an idea in way of precaution came to her. 'I think tomorrow we should take some photos. Confirmation of their cruelty.' She held him more firmly, luxuriating in the tranquil warmth of his body. 'I had my doubts this morning,' she said, 'that such a moment as this could ever happen.'

He gave her his half smile. 'You weren't alone thinking that.'

Shani focused on the swelling around his eye, a smudge of purple in the bruising. 'I don't want to keep fussing, but do you think you should see a doctor?' she asked. 'Get someone to check you over?'

'I just need to lie down.' He kissed her brow and gave her his damp towel.

Shani turned back the duvet. 'While you were showering, I asked Alain if he wouldn't mind sending up some orange juice and sandwiches.'

Nicolas eased himself onto the bed. 'Thanks. The wonder in my life, that's what you are.'

Shani kept her eyes above his waistline while she covered his nakedness with the duvet, finding the temptation borne out of arousal subdued by a greater desire to care for him. Kneeling beside the bed and stroking his hair: 'You smell nice…' She returned the kiss, just quickly on his brow as her phone chirped in her pocket. She stood and looked at the screen. 'It's Osakwe. He'll have the stuff from the studio, hopefully. I'll go down.' She poured him some juice and left the tray of sandwiches on the bed. 'Feel up to meeting him?' she asked.

'Osakwe?' Nicolas straightened the duvet with his left hand. 'Sure.'

'Can you remember Jacques' number?'

'Jacques? Why?'

'I borrowed one of his guns. He knows you were taken, so he's probably worried.'

'I know his number. I'll call him.'

'I don't have his gun. Long story.' Shani gave him her phone and went over to the door. 'Try and eat something.'

***

Osakwe proved himself to be the perfect gentleman, pulling out a chair from the table in the semi-alcove for her and seeing that she was comfortable before sitting opposite. He wasn't at all like Khamadi, his features rounder and softer, matching the tone of his voice.

'How is he?' Osakwe asked, between sips of coffee.

'I've got him settled. I'm praying the damage isn't in any way permanent.'

'They were thugs,' hissed Osakwe. He glanced at the practically empty bar. 'But one's dead, and the other two are in hospital. Well done for that.'

'The driver of the car,' asked Shani, 'who was he?'

'A friend. His name was Chieng. He followed you from Gare du Nord to Nicolas's apartment.'

'Who killed the gunman?'

'One of the snipers.'

Shani reached for her lemon tea. 'That was you who handed me the gun?'

'Yes. I was using an apartment without the owner's consent. It's common practice in this kind of environment.'

'I'm worried about the biker. He had a good look at me.' Shani cast a glance around the bar herself. They didn't seem to be attracting any attention. 'I don't think we should stay here. We needed a place to clean Nicolas up and for him to rest. It's more or less served its purpose—'

Osakwe lifted a hand. 'Don't worry.' He started to smile. 'They're looking for a thirty year old south-east Asian woman, the description given by the biker.'

'*Thirty?*' Shani managed to whisper against her dismay. She leaned forward. 'I'm only twenty-four. Do I look thirty, let alone Asian?'

Osakwe leaned back, quietly watching her. No decipherable expression.

'What?' asked Shani, his silence making her anxious.

He slid his coffee cup to one side. 'What you did today was top notch. We're all proud of you. Khamadi, everyone.'

Shani came forward, leaning her arms on the table. 'All in the line of duty. Isn't that what you say?'

'You went way beyond that line. Nicolas is a very lucky man. And if I'd known you could ride a bike I'd probably have made use of the fact.' Osakwe pushed a brown-papered package across the table. 'This is for Nicolas. There's a course of antibiotics in there, should he develop an infection – a chest infection, for example. It can happen after such trauma. Also, vitamins for him to take, and antimalarial tablets for you. As I mentioned to you earlier, there's movement.'

'Nicolas isn't going to be fit to travel for at least a week,' Shani said, 'if not a fortnight.' The way Osakwe was talking… A medic of some description?

'Don't worry. He should be fine by the time you get the code. Has he eaten?'

'Not by the time I left, but I've been urging him to. I got the owner to make sandwiches.' Shani finished her lemon tea. 'How is Khamadi, by the way?' she asked. 'He told me about his brother.'

'They were close. It's been tough for him, but I can honestly tell you that he is genuinely upset we didn't protect you sooner.'

Shani looked at the package, and asked the question she had asked herself. 'You seem to know about medicine, and such like?'

'My training got cut short. I was doing it in Cuba. Khamadi contacted me, and the rest is as you see it.'

'I'd like you to examine Nicolas,' said Shani. 'Particularly his right arm.'

'I'll take a look. I've brought everything you required from the apartment.'

'Thanks. We owe you.' Shani moved her chair back, anxious to check on Nicolas, finding it difficult to rein in her concern. 'Shall we go?'

* * *

Shani switched on the bedside lamp, rather than strike Nicolas with the harsher overhead light.

'Nicolas?' she called softly. When he opened his eyes, she said: 'I have Osakwe with me.'

Nicolas smiled up at them and brought his hand out from under the duvet.

'Left-handed now are we?' observed Osakwe, shaking hands. 'Seem to remember you as right-handed.'

'It's not broken,' said Nicolas.

'That might be so,' interrupted Shani, 'but you *do* have a problem with it.'

'Ah, I smell a conspiracy,' said Nicolas.

'Osakwe trained as a doctor. An opportunity I'm not prepared to dismiss, that's all.' Shani made way for Osakwe and went and sat in the chair, listening to them talk in French for several minutes before Osakwe turned back the duvet to run his hands over Nicolas's body, flexing his knees and arms. She tried not to look, dreading to think where else they might have put the wires he'd mentioned.

Osakwe straightened, and she realised they were already saying their goodbyes. He turned to her. 'I'm leaving.'

Shani followed him into the corridor. Closing the door slightly behind her, she whispered: 'What do you think?'

'It'll take a week. A tendon in his right arm has been badly knocked. The pain he's feeling would be similar to that of tennis elbow. There's some heavy bruising, but other than that the physical damage is superficial. Mentally?' Osakwe shrugged a shade ominously. 'It could take longer. Keep him warm, feed him – be there for him. When he's able, go for walks. Talk about the future. Bring sunshine to his thoughts, basically. Okay?'

Shani nodded. 'Of course. What happens now?'

'I'm leaving Paris tomorrow. Not until after the coup will we see each other again.'

Shani put a hand on his arm, and Osakwe drew her into a hug. 'Thank you,' she said. 'Without you…' She shook her head against his broad shoulder. 'I don't want to think about what might have happened. And I'm so sorry for the friend you lost today.'

Osakwe sighed and let his arms fall to his sides. 'That's where I'm off to now, to inform his wife.'

Shani kissed Osakwe's cheek. 'I can only offer you my heartfelt sympathy.'

Osakwe nodded, and without another word made his way towards the stairs.

Shani closed the door to the bedroom, content in the knowledge she expected to see him once the coup had been realized – with any luck, in their favour. She looked at Nicolas, who seemed to be sleeping. She started to undress, the silky glow from the bedside lamp like a caress against her skin.

'Has Osakwe left?' asked Nicolas, keeping his eyes closed.

'Yes.' Shani sat on the bed to remove her prosthesis. She had the strangest feeling, because here they were about to share a bed together despite the fact they'd barely kissed, let alone had sex – as if they were doing everything in reverse.

'Shani?'

She turned on the bed to face him. 'What is it?'

'I want our children to grow sunflowers. Lots of sunflowers.'

Our children...? She smiled and took off her woollen jumper, surprised that she wasn't shocked. Perhaps it was because she could quite easily picture him being inspirational when it came to fatherhood: adventurous, educational and considerate.

'It's a nice thought, Nicolas,' she said. 'I mean it.' Looking back at him: 'Why sunflowers?'

'My father always allowed me a patch in the garden to grow sunflowers. That's what I focussed on when they... It's what I thought about, that's all.'

Shani leaned over to kiss his brow. 'You're like a

tree, my favourite tree, with endless branches I can climb onto and wrap my arms around.' She traced his lips with her fingers, her pulse rising, excited by the prospect of them sharing a bed together. 'I'll be a moment. I'm going to shower.'

She took off her underwear in the en suite and rinsed it. Her skin felt dry, and to put on a little eye make-up in the morning would be luxurious, but she hadn't any with her. An image of the biker unexpectedly popped up. *Thirty?* Stupid man. She shouldn't have bothered to have called him. Just abandoned his bike and left it at that.

While under the shower, she decided it was important for them to have sex as quickly as possible, to complete and make perfect their bond. Besides, it would help to distract Nicolas from dwelling too deeply on the nightmare he'd been put through. Equally so for her, come to that. *Talk about the future. Bring sunshine to his thoughts.* She wasn't expecting much in way of gratification, considering the state he was in. But that didn't matter.

She dried herself off and opened a cellophane envelope with its T-shirt inside advertising the charity shop. It was completely bland, white with *Domino* written in black across the front. At least it fitted. At the washbasin she realised her toothbrush, paste and dental tape had been moved from the right of it to the left. That was good. Nicolas had definitely used them, and in doing so had revealed the extent of his rituals when it came to personal hygiene. She rinsed her mouth, turned off the en suite light and sat on the bed in the glow of the lamp. Other than her skin feeling dry, her body felt surprisingly nice and trim, like she'd just played a hard game of squash. She didn't mind if he saw her naked.

In fact, nothing mattered right now. Hygiene, or anything else. They were alive, and together. Nicolas could have been killed. She could be so finicky at the oddest of times! And that was enough of that, too. Self-bloody-analysis. She had a chance to turn the page here. *No more nightmares.*

'Nicolas?' she asked, massaging her stump which was throbbing dully.

'I'm listening.'

'Did you speak to Jacques?'

'He said he's looking forward to the picnic.'

'He doesn't have one of his guns now.'

'He gave it away for a good cause. His words.'

She leaned back and drew the duvet up to her chin. 'How are you feeling?'

'Aching.'

'I mean mentally.'

'I'm okay.'

Shani took him for his word, that he was being honest. *Okay* was perhaps the best they could hope for.

'You saved my life, Shani. Had they got hold of you, they would likely have taken me out at some point. That's probably why they planted a transmitter on me. Or used us both to try and draw in Khamadi.'

Shani flicked her hair away from her eyes. 'Seems to have worked both ways. I was miserable, making no headway with my disability. But not now.' She felt Nicolas turn onto his side.

'Where did you learn to ride a bike like that?' he asked her. 'I look at your physique, and the way you move, the way you walk, is so graceful. Like a ballerina. I don't know where you get the strength.'

Shani smiled as she gazed up at the ceiling with its irregular, roughly-hewn oak beams. *The way you walk…* She liked that. 'Strength doesn't come into it as much as you think,' she said. 'It's more to do with balance and flow. It's like poetry.'

'So where did you learn to ride like that?' repeated Nicolas. 'Czech Republic?'

'Yes. Riding bikes gave me an escape from my disability. Gave me a whole new freedom, in fact. I have a Kawasaki Ninja and some biker friends back in Oxford.' She lifted a hand to brush a wisp of hair from his brow. 'We had a good bike today. A triple nine Ducati.'

Nicolas turned onto his back. 'Sorry, just a bit too uncomfortable on my side.'

Shani wanted to stay with his gaze and so leaned on her forearms. 'It's amazing,' she said, deciding to make vocal her thoughts.

'What is?' asked Nicolas.

'Guess.'

'Us?'

'In one.'

'It wasn't difficult.' He reached up and ran his hand through her hair. 'I'm aching so much it's almost hurting.'

Shani refrained from giggling when she realised what he was actually referring to. It didn't feel appropriate to giggle after the day they'd had. But her happiness made her keep her smile. 'As if you're not hurting in enough places,' she said, and kissed lips, taking her time. She wanted to hold onto every thought, every movement, so the images would forever be fresh in the day-to-day corridors of her mind. She moved her lips to his brow, to the tip of his nose, his neck, and then again to his lips, her body tingling with expectation.

Nicolas traced her cheekbones with his fingertips.

'It's true, I'm lying next to an amazing girl.' He stroked her hair. 'I've got to be the luckiest guy going.'

His remark touched the pulse of her being, drawing her ever closer to unchartered rapture. She reached over him to turn off the lamp, using it as an excuse to shift herself smoothly onto his body.

'You will be gentle?' he said, a streetlight filtering through the curtains revealing a grin on his bruised face.

'Now that's a risk you're going to have to take,' said Shani, failing to keep the smile from her own lips. 'You're impossible!'

'And you...' Nicolas ran the back of his hand down her arm. '...You are magnificent, *ma chérie*.'

She started to peel off her T-shirt. 'It's a position I'm not particularly fond of for future reference,' she said, feeling her heartbeat soar for *all* the right reasons. 'But given the circumstances, Monsieur Dubois, it'll do quite nicely, I have to say.'

CHAPTER 20

A knock on the door, and the guard glanced enquiringly at General Kuetey – who in response silently held up a hand. Kuetey clamped his eyelids together and focused on his breathing as he wrestled to calm himself. For the sake of maximum effect when it came to instilling fear, he needed to suppress the outrage tearing up his insides. Nothing as catastrophic as this had happened to him before. He would be the laughingstock of the military if they got to hear of it, his power-base weakened as a result – the potential for others to take advantage only too graphic. Twenty-four years. And in the palm of his hand! He took a final breath and opened his eyes, then gave the guard a brisk nod. He was ready. And when the door opened:

'Ousmane,' greeted Kuetey amiably while with a deliberate flourish he flicked several switches on the console, leaving the skeletal prisoner in the middle cage fighting for his life. He'd debated whether to exhibit the prisoner's torment, but that would be too much of a distraction and far from subtle. Kuetey waved a hand at the door for the guard to leave the presidential suite. 'Take a seat, Ousmane.'

The Director General of the State Security Service dutifully did so at the desk which, with its sweeping curve, resembled a fixture more suited to a hotel lobby than a palace. Ousmane Sekibo's long face and blunt features conjured a bemused look as though life at some juncture had played a merciless joke on him, and as a consequence he'd decided to mistrust it.

Sekibo leaned stiffly into the cream leather armchair, and as if trying to portray himself at ease, crossed his legs. 'You are well, Odion?' he asked the President at length.

'Yes, yes, but rather troubled.' Kuetey reached for a tissue and wiped his perspiring brow. How could the idiot lean back like that, he was asking himself, knowing what he'd done – or *hadn't* done?

'Troubled?' queried Sekibo. 'I have to agree, we are living in troubled—'

'Ousmane, let me be frank,' interrupted Kuetey. Throwing the tissue onto the floor: 'You had a ten per cent increase in your budget last year. Correct?'

'Yes, Odion.'

'I have heard news from Paris, and I know that you have, too.'

Sekibo shifted in the chair, and brushed an imaginary fleck of dust from his trousers. 'The cell became corrupt, Odion. We were told there were five operatives, but there were only three. Two were killed last month due to the cell acting outside its remit. The cell was, if you recall, set up by my predecessor.'

'Predecessor?' snapped Kuetey, annoyed with himself for not taking matters into his own hands *before* the kidnapping of Dubois. 'But this cannot be used as an excuse, Ousmane. You have been at your post – the post I generously gave you – for over a year.' Kuetey opened the file in front of him. 'One year, two months, eleven days, to be precise.' Closing the file: 'Three problems persist. The girl Bălcescu, the liar Dubois, and the provocateur Soglo. Let us start with the last, the most dangerous to state security – and thus to your safety and wellbeing, Ousmane, if you get my drift. Where precisely, might I ask, is Khamadi Soglo as we speak?'

Sekibo quietly cleared his throat. 'Soglo is currently in London. As I've mentioned before, Odion, we have an agent in position right inside his network—'

Kuetey slammed a fist onto the desk. 'So you keep

telling me.' He paused to try and stem his searing fury, and doubted whether the 'subtle approach' was worth it. 'What results is this agent getting for you?' he demanded.

'I can confirm that Osakwe Babangida is very much alive,' said Sekibo, showing little sign of having been ruffled by the brief outburst. 'Before I left my office the agent made contact and informed me that it was Babangida who directed Bălcescu in Paris. The agent in question cannot communicate with us on a daily basis, being physically too close to Soglo.'

'I will come to the blood of Zinsa Dangbo in a moment,' said Kuetey. He reached for the keypad and adjusted the room temperature. Turning to Sekibo, he saw the embodiment of incompetence staring back at him, amplified further by Sekibo's bland features. A decision was needed, he told himself – and he was already halfway to making it! 'Let me concentrate your mind for a moment, Ousmane. Khamadi Soglo wants to spread a wicked kind of education amongst the people – *my* people.' Kuetey straightened his back, as if suddenly he was launching into a national broadcast. 'He will deceive them with his rhetoric about liberty. Undermine the solidarity, our courage and hopes, and all that holds us together as a country. Such brainwashing is very dangerous, more so than a nuclear bomb, would you believe.' Kuetey patted his brow with a fresh tissue. 'My people are in peril of this man, this…this deceiver. First and foremost, I have a duty towards my people. You understand this, Ousmane?'

'Yes,' answered Sekibo. A hefty pause hung in the air. 'Every word, Odion,' he added.

'So, when do you expect to close the net on him? To finish him?'

'We expect him to relocate to Paris before the end of the month,' said Sekibo keenly, as if relieved the discussion had now taken on a more practical perspective. 'Within six days we will have a cell fully operational in that city, consisting of three snipers, an operations manager, and a counter-surveillance specialist, aside from the usual scouts. Before then, I want to give our double agent an opportunity to obtain more information regarding Soglo's sub-networks. We are convinced there are sleeper cells in both Nigeria and Benin. It is better we extract this kind of information in the field, rather than through torture, otherwise the networks will hear of his seizure and melt away, only to reappear at a later date.'

Kuetey grunted broodingly, mildly surprised by Sekibo's lucidity. But that said… 'Let us return to what happened earlier this afternoon in Paris. I understand Bălcescu shielded Dubois when the exchange was supposed to take place. What do you draw from this?'

'That Osakwe Babangida had information that she was not to be harmed.'

'Yes!' Kuetey shifted his bulk in the swivel chair and leaned back. 'Exactly that. And what does this tell us?'

'That it is likely we have a failed operative within our midst... An interceptor.'

'And that Khamadi Soglo is running rings around the State Security Service.'

Sekibo's brow had begun to shimmer with perspiration, as if it had finally dawned on him that he could be demoted – or worse. Far worse. 'Odion, I assure you that Soglo will be either caught or terminated. Babangida and many others as well. When they come to Paris, it will be the end of them. I just need a few more days to find out the current locations of the sleeper cells.'

'If you terminate Soglo in Paris,' said Kuetey, 'I want his head brought to me – literally. Understood?'

Sekibo's thyroid cartilage bobbed as he swallowed.

'Use the diplomatic baggage system. It works very well for that sort of thing.' Kuetey picked up the Montblanc pen that had been presented to him at a state banquet at Hôtel Matignon and started pointing it at Sekibo. 'Now, what of this one who writes lies about us, this Nicolas Dubois?'

'He is presently in the west of Paris. We have information—'

'Coming in from French national news programs,' interrupted Kuetey, a note of triumph pervading his treacherous tone. Time to turn the screw, he thought, so that Sekibo left the presidential suite without the slightest doubt over his future, let alone his existence on the planet. Putting the pen back down: 'You have no more information about this than the French do themselves, other than his name, and all they have is the fact that this bitch Bălcescu, this filth of the seed of Tuma Dangbo, was last seen heading out of the city with Dubois as a passenger on a bike she herself had stolen. The bike has since been recovered. Did you know this?'

'It is rumoured she called the owner—'

'It is not a rumour, Ousmane, but most definitely a fact. What if the police get to know it is Bălcescu, and take her into custody? How will I reach her then? Have you thought about this?'

Sekibo straightened himself in the chair. 'I promise you—'

'I don't want your promises. I want *action*. I want

results.' This time both of Kuetey's fists came crashing down onto the desk, his mouth frothing at the corners. 'Let me tell you what I want. I want the blood of Zinsa Dangbo, unmarked, the liar Dubois, and the provocateur Soglo, either in person or his severed head, presented to me in this room within ten days. Do you understand?'

'Yes, Odion.'

Kuetey plucked another tissue from the green box beside him. 'Then be about your business.'

The mild sense of satisfaction that Kuetey experienced when Ousmane Sekibo departed the office with his head down, like a man heading for the gallows, left him disappointed. Where was the intensity of old? He was tired, of course. And not one son out of nine half capable of running a market stall let alone the country. Was this what it had come to? Surrounded by fools and their incompetence? He needed to make a few examples to eradicate such complacency, and quickly. Bălcescu had distracted him, taken his eye off the ball. He just needed to get his hands on her!

Grunting his way out of the swivel chair, Kuetey lumbered over to the picture window and waited for Sekibo to walk across the freshly clipped lawn in the Manhattan Garden. These were dangerous times, he reminded himself. He had watched the nonsense of the Arab Spring unfold, seen Mubarak and the rest of them go, and as they went he had seen how fickle the West had proved itself to be: one minute shaking Muammar al-Gaddafi's hand – a British prime minister even going as far as to embrace the man – the next, sending in warplanes. As easily as that, the West could decide to back Khamadi Soglo.

Perhaps he should be looking towards the East, to Russia. Or even China. The French would be the first to protest, of course. But at the end of the day, oil hadn't saved Gaddafi's neck. Quite the opposite. And Séroulé had more than just oil. In the Randara mountain range, the 'spine' of Séroulé, there were significant deposits of kaolin. And now rutile had been discovered in the north of the country.

Ousmane Sekibo. Kuetey shook his head in disgust as he watched the Director General trudge towards the Security Service's compound. Imani was set to leave for Milan in the next few days with a view to augmenting her already outrageously extensive wardrobe. Perhaps he would send his brother-in-law to the Séroulèse Embassy in Germany at the same time to manage a routine check-up. Once in Berlin, an appalling and newsworthy incident of some description would occur, resulting in the tragic termination of Ousmane Sekibo's life. He, Kuetey, would personally conduct the operation.

He nodded to himself and left the window to open the door, beckoning the Guardsman back inside.

CHAPTER 21

They became the most blissful days of her life – ever. Twelve, in total. As the days unfolded in Fourqueux, they went for gentle strolls together in the nearby Forêt Domaniale de Marly le Roi, where kings, and latterly presidents of the republic, had hunted in days gone by. They laughed, teased, made love, worked on the speech she was expected to deliver once the State Television building in Porto Sansudou had been taken – and, more than anything, they opened up their hearts to one another. She learned that Nicolas hadn't been immune from tragedy himself, his father having died in a power boating accident. His death had had a devastating impact on Nicolas's younger sister, who'd suffered with anorexia for ten years before her body finally gave up on her. She'd died in his arms, his mother too distressed to be present at the bedside.

Then, what she came to dread, because of her

idyllic sojourn with Nicolas, actually happened. The one-worded text appeared after they'd showered and before taking breakfast.

Number Withheld
PROSPER

Her stomach did its usual wobble, and suddenly conversation between them became stilted. She remembered saying something to the effect they didn't have to go through with it. But then Nicolas posed the question: wouldn't it be on their conscience for the rest of their lives if they didn't? Of course, he was right.

* * *

Shani snapped out of her reverie. A flicker of fear crossed her gaping eyes, thrown by the sound of the twin-engined Cessna as it droned through the night sky, leaving behind the city of Tamale in northern Ghana.

She looked across the aisle at Nicolas, his eyes closed with his legs stretched as much as the seating arrangement would allow, seemingly oblivious. Silly, really, but she couldn't wait to show him off to Dusana. She would surely be thrilled, that Nicolas was further proof her tomboy teens had now become little more than a 'peculiar' memory.

She looked away. The plane could accommodate up to ten passengers. In front of them were eight men, four on the portside with her, and four in front of Nicolas. They made her nervous because they didn't want to engage in conversation, barely communicating even with each other. They wore jeans and T-shirts mostly. All of them were black, and carried rucksacks and kitbags of various sizes. So who were they? Some kind of a crack taskforce, hand-picked by Khamadi Soglo himself? She could only wonder.

The pilot reduced the throttle, and the plane began a partial descent before levelling back out. Shani caught sight of what might have been a small village beside a moonlit swamp, or lake – just a few lights showing. A fishing community, perhaps. She turned again to Nicolas, his eyes now wide open.

'We're about to land?' she whispered, not wanting to draw attention to herself.

Nicolas glanced at the starboard window next to him. 'Could be we're crossing the border into Séroulé,' he said, leaning towards her, 'and the pilot's trying to evade radar detection.'

Shani nodded. Perfectly feasible, she supposed – though she now half expected the plane to be targeted by a heat-seeking missile, or whatever. Mere seconds passed before the engine note dropped yet another octave, the plane now skimming treetops at what seemed a terrific rate of knots. Shani settled herself again. So she was coming home, or so it felt, for it was here where Zinsa had arrived into this world. She recalled Radu's words to her at Timișoara's County Hospital, translated by Horia.

Radu vividly remembers the moment you were born, and that she did not open her eyes to see you… But that she touched you before they cut the cord. And you made a lot of noise, so she would have heard you.

Shani wiped a tear from her cheek.

Coming home…

A thump jolted her spine as the plane struck terra firma. Looking out of the window, Shani realised they'd landed on a grass strip, the pilot taxiing sharply to the left. One of the men in front of her sprang from his seat, disengaged the locking arm on the door and threw it open. Before the plane had coasted to a standstill he was gone. Shani watched his comrades follow suit, the 'procedure' fluid and ostensibly reassuringly proficient.

Nicolas took her hand and led her down the aisle. The Caucasian co-pilot gave them a brisk salute, indicating 'farewell', his left hand on the door's locking arm. His manner suggested he and the pilot didn't intend to hang around – the engine revs already climbing.

Shani jumped to the ground with Nicolas, and the Cessna promptly buzzed away from them, gathering pace along the airstrip until it became airborne. There was no sign of the 'taskforce' as the plane melted into the inky night sky. But then Nicolas pointed at a flickering tail-light.

'I think they're in that truck, or whatever it is, over there,' he said.

As he spoke, Shani watched a pickup approaching them from the same direction, its headlights partially illuminating the makeshift airstrip. 'This must be for us,' she said, and shivered.

'So it seems.' Nicolas put his arm around her. 'Cold?'

'I expected it to be warmer.'

'The savannah heat can drop away fast on a clear night like this.'

The vehicle pulled up alongside – Shani dumbstruck to find the driver was none other than the girl from the safe house in London. Just as she had done back then with the red van, she thumbed them to climb aboard, the difference being she actually smiled.

Shani waited for Nicolas to lower the tailgate. 'Did you see the driver?' she whispered. 'It's her.'

'Who?'

'The girl from the safe-house.' Shani levered herself up onto the pickup and swung her legs round. 'It's definitely her. She might not be the greatest conversationalist going, but I feel better for seeing her. A familiar face, I suppose.'

Nicolas brought up the tailgate and slotted the locking pins into place. 'Wouldn't be surprised if she's part of Khamadi's inner circle,' he said.

Shani sat cross-legged, until she found the bumping too uncomfortable. She chose to squat instead. 'Those guys who hooked up with us for the flight looked serious.'

'Probably saboteurs. Rugged and focussed, you know?'

Shani leant against the bulkhead and breathed the air: the same air Zinsa would have breathed.

Coming home.

But it was now so much more than that, she told herself. The eradication of the monster Kuetey and his vile regime, followed by the re-claiming of Séroulé from the greed-ridden toxic multinationals – the latter being the dominant challenge, she imagined.

* * *

Guided by moonlight and the girl, Shani followed Nicolas across a gangplank over a stream to one of several wooden shacks grouped together, all of them on stilts and with thatched roofs. A peasant community, she presumed. She felt lightyears away from St Thomas Aquinas. There, it was safe, even cosy, her day to day existence as predictable as she chose it to be.

Shani entered a dimly lit shack, only to find Khamadi Soglo sitting by himself at a table that had nothing on it apart from a mobile phone. She was familiar with his good looks, but not against candlelight – the tawny glow enhancing the velvety tone of his ebony skin. He pushed back the chair and stood.

'Well done both of you,' he said, smiling. 'We're right on schedule.'

Shani shook his hand, but then Khamadi wanted to give her a hug. She all but smelt the testosterone, the physical power of the 'warrior' that she'd sensed back in London. She'd imagined he'd be wearing combat fatigues of greens and browns and a peaked cap. Instead, he wore a cotton shirt and trousers with a narrow belt, his appearance that of a cool handsome guy off a street in Paris or New York, or wherever.

'What spirit you have, Shani,' he said, grinning

hugely. 'Your courage was spectacular. I don't see how you can disagree.'

'Without Osakwe, it wouldn't have been possible,' said Shani.

Khamadi lifted his shoulders in a gesture of acknowledgement. 'Osakwe played his part, but you were the one at the sharp end, as they say.' Khamadi turned to Nicolas. 'You have healed from what those pigs did to you?'

Nicolas nodded. 'Ninety per cent. The odd ache.'

'Good. I need you to be fit.'

The girl moved away from them towards a separate table, where ceramic pots sat alongside kitchenware that included an oversized wooden pestle and mortar.

Khamadi lowered his voice. 'Monique speaks little. Do not be offended by this. As a child she witnessed her father tortured to death, her mother repeatedly…' Khamadi gave them a grim sigh. 'Let us say, she has seen more than her fair share of horror.'

Hearing Khamadi's words, Shani felt that what she was seeing and hearing now resembled accounts she'd only ever read about in say *The Guardian* over a coffee, surrounded by lavish comfort and without fear for her life. And as for Monique, herself, with her harrowing past, here was veritable courage. She hoped she could be friends with her. Perhaps somehow get her over to England, and have her stay in Oxford.

'This is *akpeteshie*,' explained Khamadi as Monique carried a tray over to them with four clay beakers and a plastic bottle, the liquid inside milky-looking. 'It's made from sugar cane juice. A little fiery, so be careful. Nicolas, I've no need to warn you.' Khamadi poured a small amount of *akpeteshie* into the palm of his hand, scattering the liquid across the dusty wooden floor. 'But first we must honour the Gods,' he said. 'In particular, the Supreme Goddess Mawu, creator of all things. Only Mawu can give *Sekpoli*, the breath of life.'

Shani was curious as to the extent of Khamadi's faith, whether in truth he regarded Mawu as pure fiction. 'The way you describe her, Khamadi, makes it an uplifting ritual,' she said, scattering *akpeteshie* with Nicolas and Monique.

Khamadi raised his glass. 'To the liberation of Séroulé.'

Shani repeated the toast with the others and downed the liquor. It wasn't until between her second and third breaths that it happened, what felt to be the claws of a tiger savaging her throat. 'I'm on fire,' she gasped, her eyes watering over. 'My God...what have you done to me?'

Nicolas laughed with Khamadi, but Monique merely smiled, and said:

'You did not believe, Shani. This is Mawu's lesson to you. I'm sorry.'

Not wanting to offend Monique, who she assumed 'believed', Shani met her eyes and thought they looked so beautiful, the depth of their brownness spawning intrigue as well as warmth. 'Monique, I'm not going to make that mistake again.'

When Khamadi put down his beaker, Shani found herself watching him closely. His jaw pulsated slightly, and she realised he was actually grinding his teeth. A habit of his, perhaps, when feeling tense. And how he must be feeling that. The responsibility, the preparation – years of it, no doubt. 'The point of no return?' she asked.

Khamadi nodded. 'We have to make this work. It can't be done again. Not for another decade, at least – by then, who knows.'

'Then we will *make* it work.' Shani glanced at them in turn. 'I've thought of Zinsa a great deal these past few weeks. No great surprise there. You can accuse me of deluding myself, but at times I felt she wasn't so far from me. I really believed it. I had to. And still do. If Zinsa is with us, then so is my grandfather, Tuma Dangbo.'

'And Goddess Mawu,' said Monique, smiling.

'And Goddess Mawu,' agreed Shani, turning to her. 'Indeed.'

'Nicolas,' said Khamadi, 'this is your preface, your prologue. Okay?'

Nicolas tapped his head. 'Word for word.'

Khamadi gave Shani an awkward glance, twisting the corner of his mouth as he did so. 'Shani, we want you to carry a firearm. Do you object to this?'

'Not at all.' But as she spoke, Shani could only wonder the extent of the danger she was going to be exposed to. A question, she decided, not worth asking. A coup d'état by nature was surely an unpredictable beast.

They were given Glock semi-automatic pistols – which Shani found heavier than the Walther PPK. She turned it over in her hands, noting the safety catch, then tucked the barrel into her waistband and covered it with her powder-blue *BOHEMIA* T-shirt.

'I want to leave my shoulder bag here,' she said. 'It's too restrictive.'

'Your passport and papers are inside?' asked Khamadi.

'And money, not that there's much of it.'

'Keep your passport and Ghanaian visa on you,' Khamadi said.

Shani did as she was told, and handed him the jhola bag. 'It's quite precious to me,' she mentioned. 'Given to me by my housemates, after I graduated.'

'It'll be safe here.' Khamadi roughly folded the bag, like it was a towel destined for rags, and tucked it behind the table. 'It's time for us to leave,' he said, extinguishing the candles with his fingers.

The Toyota pickup was switched for a silver Chrysler jeep. No explanation was given as to why. Shani sat with Nicolas in the back, Khamadi in the front passenger seat, while Monique drove.

They travelled on dusty tracks to begin with, the going rough in places – jarring and jolting. Then the relief of a tarmacadam road. It went in a straight line and held little in way of traffic. Shani watched Khamadi take frequent calls on his phone, and noted he appeared positive in his responses and relaxed in way of demeanour. The calls were in French, so she could only go by his mannerisms and the fact that Nicolas hadn't picked up on any issues. Comforted by this, Shani settled back into the seat and began to doze, leaning her head on Nicolas's shoulder.

* * *

When she came to, the jeep had stopped in a wooded area.

'It'll be the battery connection,' Monique was

telling Khamadi. 'It happened the other day.'

'Pull the catch for the bonnet,' Khamadi told her. 'I'll see if I can fix it.'

Khamadi got out just as Nicolas opened his eyes.

'What's happening?' he asked with half a yawn. 'Why have we stopped?'

'Monique thinks there's a loose connection on the battery,' said Shani.

Nicolas straightened up. 'I'll give him a hand.'

'It's okay,' Monique said, 'he knows what to do.'

Just as Monique spoke, Shani heard some rustling, and what sounded like a muffled grunt somewhere over on her left. She peered into the dense shadows beyond the tree trunks, the nape of her neck beginning to tingle. Khamadi still had the bonnet raised… Another groan, from the same direction. Her head snapped back round. An animal sound? Surely not that of a human out here?

'Did you hear that?' she asked.

'Hear what?' responded Monique.

'A sort of groan, or mumble.' Shani looked at Nicolas. 'Did you?'

'No. Probably Khamadi swearing.'

Monique sniggered.

'I'm being serious,' said Shani. She reached for the gun at her side and flicked the safety catch. 'I heard it, twice—'

At the blink of an eye a harsh light flooded the immediate area, blazing from lamps on metal poles that virtually encompassed the jeep. The bonnet was slammed down, not by Khamadi but a shorter figure wearing a black balaclava.

'Oh, shit,' muttered Nicolas.

'What is this?' reacted Shani, trepidation crushing her chest. She fought to breathe. 'Monique…Monique, tell us – quickly. What's happening?'

'Can't be an ambush,' said Nicolas. 'How could they have known we'd break down at this exact spot?'

'But where's Khamadi?' cried Shani. 'Monique? *Where* is he?'

'Get out,' said Monique.

'What?'

'I said, get out! Both of you.'

Two more masked figures emerged from the bush, one of them throwing Khamadi to the ground. He'd clearly been roughed up; blood streaked his left hand, his shirt torn across the shoulder.

Shani couldn't accept the site of Khamadi on the ground. How could *this* be happening? She looked at Monique. 'I don't understand. You can't be with Kuetey?'

'You're a fool, Bălcescu,' said Monique. 'And so is your idiot of a lover. Neither of you could see through Soglo. Now get out.'

Doors were yanked open, and a gun waved at Shani's face. She still had the Glock. She hadn't concealed it, yet the masked man didn't seem concerned by it. She left the jeep with Monique. As with the kidnapper, she found she couldn't kill her. But surely this time there had to be a mistake? A *mis*understanding? Desperate for an explanation, she aimed the gun at Monique's left shoulder. The masked man left her to it. *Why* wasn't he reacting to the threat?

'I'm going to fire this at you, Monique,' she said. 'You need to explain.'

'I don't have to explain—'

Shani squeezed the trigger. The gun responded with a hollow 'click'. Frantic, she fired again. The same devastating result.

Nicolas followed suit. Nothing. As if he knew the gun had been deactivated, he didn't bother with a second attempt and instead threw it to the ground.

Shani wheeled round on Khamadi as he was being dragged to his feet, blood at the corner of his mouth. 'How could this have happened?' she yelled. She felt herself drowning in her own hysteria, because she *knew* now that Monique had planned it all, assisted by the State Security Service. Khamadi was nothing but an amateur in comparison. 'All our efforts,' she told him, 'all your planning – for what?'

'Chigaro,' interrupted Monique, 'bind their hands with the plastic ties. Simba, Otieno, take down the lights. We're done here.'

When the men tore off their balaclavas, Shani saw that none of the faces matched those who had travelled with them from Tamale. So where had those eight men gone? She prayed they were nearby, that they'd been tipped off and were now waiting for the right moment. Maybe they needed time to set up the ambush. Yes, of course, there was that hope, the hope that Khamadi had been savvy enough to coordinate back-up of some description.

'I'm not moving,' she said. 'To hell with you, Monique. Or whatever your real name is. You can shoot me here. It doesn't bother me.'

'Shani,' said Nicolas, 'don't talk this way.'

'Why not?' she snapped. 'This woman intends to take us to Kuetey.' She glared at Monique. 'Correct?'

'Perfectly,' replied Monique.

'Have you any idea what he is going to do to me?' Shani told her. 'My mother took his eye out. I'm Tuma Dangbo's granddaughter.'

Monique shrugged. 'It's not my problem.' She walked around the jeep to face the three of them, and as if it was an extension of her index finger pointed her gun at Nicolas. 'For him, the one who writes lies about us—'

'Bullshit,' said Nicolas. 'Everything I've written about the regime has been the truth. Validated in just about every language.'

'For him,' said Monique steadily, 'I get two-hundred thousand dollars.' She moved along to Khamadi Soglo, battered and crestfallen, his eyes to the ground. 'For this one, the one who has deceived you, and his followers, I get another nine-hundred thousand dollars.'

Khamadi slowly looked up, as if his eyes were reluctant to meet Shani's. 'I've told you no lies—'

Monique slammed the gun into his face, splitting open his cheek. 'Shut up.' Her steely eyes flicked to Shani. 'He wants the coup so he can be President. It's laughable. He's a country boy. I bet he told you about the farm he has in the north. He has no farm. He doesn't have two francs to rub together.'

'I don't believe you,' said Shani. She had to stall for time. Those eight men… 'He doesn't want to be President—'

'Let me guess,' interjected Monique, 'he told you about the orphans in Séroulé? I'm sure he did. Go through the streets, you will find no orphans. Yes, like any country, we have some – but they are cared for. He speaks ill of the money system. Yes, we have a little debt, but we are doing fine, thank you very much. Under President Kuetey, we are not so badly off. But he…,' Monique pointed the gun at Khamadi, '…he is a nightmare. Did you even bother to research him thoroughly? He is wanted for assault, for rape – yes, rape, I tell you.'

'Shani, these are complete lies,' hit back Khamadi, clutching the wound on his hand.

Monique held the gun up to his face and tapped his cheek with the barrel. 'You continue to interrupt me, Soglo, and I swear I'll cut this side wide open twice as bad.'

Shani watched her move closer to her, a sadistic smile on her lips. No warmth in her brown eyes now, and they were far from intriguing, their gleam more indicative of extreme psychosis.

'But for you,' continued Monique, 'I get one million two-hundred thousand dollars.' Sweeping the handgun across the three of them: 'And all of you together, an extra four-hundred thousand.' She began to laugh, quietly at first, and then exuberantly, throwing her head back. 'You don't know the half of it. Kuetey will be so beside himself he will give me more, perhaps as much again. I'm telling you!'

'So you've sold out to evil,' Shani shouted. 'Because that's what Kuetey is. He killed my aunts and uncles, he killed my grandfather and grandmother – slaughtered the lot of them.'

'Tuma Dangbo starved the people,' cut in Monique, the residue of laughter wiped off her face in a split second.

'It's a lie,' said Shani. 'And you know it is. Made up by Western governments.'

'Then you are mistaken. You have listened too much to these two. You have been very foolish.' Monique glanced at the shortest of the three men. 'Chigaro, I told you to put the ties on them. And take their phones.'

Shani looked at Nicolas, the palpitations in her chest refusing to subside. She started to give up on those eight men. 'I know she's lying,' she said.

Monique spun on her heel to face her. 'You can think whatever you like. It doesn't bother me. When I look at you, I see one million two-hundred thousand dollars, and that's all.'

Shani relinquished her phone before her hands were drawn behind her back, the plastic tie wrapped and secured around her wrists. The man was hardly gentle, the plastic cutting into her. She didn't care what she said now. 'You dreadful person,' she told

Monique. 'And it is you who is the fool. An absolute fool, at that.'

'Get in the back of the jeep, the three of you,' snapped Monique. 'Simba, you're driving.'

It was a struggle, Shani unable to support herself with her hands. She followed Nicolas and eased herself across the seat, Khamadi obediently doing the same beside her. She hadn't any time for him. Not now. He'd failed her – twice. Blood was still seeping from the gash to his cheek. She heard Monique talking staccato French to the two men who were not coming with them, before sitting in the front passenger seat and slamming the door. Shani realised Osakwe's name hadn't been mentioned. So which side was he actually on? Had she been deceived by him as well?

Nicolas turned to her. 'I'm so sorry,' he said as the jeep jolted off down the track. 'How this could have happened…' He shook his head. 'God's sake, I've no idea.'

'I would probably have been taken at the airport over a fortnight ago if I hadn't have met you,' said Shani, knowing before the day was out she would likely be facing Kuetey in the flesh. It was hard to believe. Someone who delighted in torturing people. Even children, according to one site while conducting her research. 'At least we had those twelve days together,' she said. 'I'll take them with me to my last breath.' Shani glanced at Khamadi, whose cheek had started to swell up. 'Were any of those things she said about you true?'

Khamadi shook his head. 'No.'

'I saw you as a warrior—'

Monique began to laugh again as insects swooped around the headlights streaming out in front of them. 'A warrior,' she said, shaking her head. 'I've heard it all now.' She made a call on her mobile phone, speaking rapidly in French, the same name cropping up several times in the conversation.

'*Merde*,' muttered Nicolas under his breath.

'What is it?' Shani asked.

'She's asking to be patched through to the Director General of the State Security Service.'

Monique whirled round with the phone. 'Smile you guys, you're on camera.'

Shani leaned back into the seat, swallowing hard. Something as small as a penknife was all she needed. To just slide the blade into her wrist – maybe giving a little cough to conceal her action if there were guards nearby – before jerking it up between the tendons, puncturing or even severing if she was lucky enough an artery. She knew she had the grit to see it through. She'd thought about doing it before, in the past, when depression had overwhelmed her – though that seemed like a different life, now. She would make some excuse to have the plastic tie removed, enabling her to commit the act.

Shani lowered her head. Where the hell was Osakwe? And those eight men?

CHAPTER 22

General Kuetey straightened his eye patch before leaving the en suite, the green telephone with its direct line to the Director General of the State Security Service beckoning him. He glanced at the National Guardsman over by the door, poker-faced and at attention, as protocol dictated. Privately, Kuetey wondered how these people managed to stand stock-still for such a length of time without keeling over or, more puzzling, wetting themselves. He had to hand it to General Nzeogwu, he knew how to select the most disciplined.

The phone was still ringing. 'No time for the President,' growled Kuetey, before snatching the handset. 'Already you trouble me, Ousmane. It is eight forty, *not* eight forty-five.'

'You have not checked your email, Odion?'

Kuetey sighed, exasperated by his brother-in-law's

disregard when it came to the President's daily routine. 'Ousmane, I have just told you, the time is eight forty. When I say something, *listen*. It is not such a difficult request I am asking from you, is it?'

'No, Odion. But I have excellent news for you.'

Kuetey grunted as he made his bulk comfortable in the swivel chair. Turning to the mini refrigerator on his right, he took out a tin of Persian caviar and a plastic spoon inside a sealed polythene wrapper. A health practitioner had once mentioned to him that a daily dose of caviar would, without fail, keep his sperm count in perfect order. Kuetey took it upon himself to decide upon the correct dosage required, which proved to be a tin a day, half at 09:00 hours, and the remainder at 17:00 hours.

'Odion?' called Sekibo tentatively, drawing out the name. 'Are you…are you still there—?'

'What is this news?' grumbled Kuetey as his stubby fingers struggled with the seal on the tin. 'Surprise me. See if you can make my day, Ousmane—'

'Khamadi Soglo, Shani Bălcescu, and the liar Dubois,' announced Sekibo, 'are all inside the country and under arrest.'

Kuetey felt his pulse trip over itself and leaned towards the desk for support, perfectly shocked. He blindly put aside the tin of caviar and fumbled for a tissue. 'Is...is this true, Ousmane?'

'I can assure you it is, Odion. In your email you will find a link to footage taken after their arrest. It is the beginning of the end for these rebels, Odion. I am now seeking Osakwe Babangida. My informant tells me he is somewhere inside Quartier de Magenta, in Thekari.'

Kuetey found himself trembling so much that he became concerned for his health, the excitement possibly affecting his heart. That would be just his luck! He heard himself voice his incredulity. 'Ousmane, you have surprised me.'

'A question of time, Odion. Our patience has now been rewarded. Soglo entered the country yesterday, early morning. Bălcescu and the liar Dubois came in on a flight from Tamale at around midnight, the plane touching down on an airstrip near Sompére.'

'And now? Where are they now, Ousmane?'

'Agent Monique—'

'The agent you kept mentioning to me?'

'Yes, Odion.'

'So where *are* they?'

'She is bringing them into Porto Sansudou, as I speak. A matter of an hour before you will get to see them. I will come over at this point, to make certain all is in order and that you are satisfied with the result.

I can only stay briefly because of my visit to the Berlin Embassy you asked me to conduct.'

'Ousmane, forget about that,' said Kuetey. He saw no reason now for his brother-in-law to experience a 'newsworthy accident'. 'Send a subordinate. Tonight, we are celebrating. But for the moment, we will keep this to ourselves, to give us time to maximise propaganda when it comes to Soglo. Understood?'

'Yes, Odion.'

'And Bălcescu?' asked Kuetey, holding his breath. 'Bălcescu is in good health? No injuries?'

'She was captured unharmed.'

'You're positive?'

'Absolutely.'

Kuetey breathed. The most perfect moment of his life, he told himself, on the point of being presented to him. 'What do you think Soglo was doing inside the country?' he asked. 'A planned coup? Do you have information?'

'Difficult to say at this stage, Odion. We need to subject him to torture – and as quickly as possible, in my view.'

'Of course. I will personally attend the sessions,' added Kuetey, while sensing a tingle in his groin at the prospect of the provocateur leisurely being put to death under his guidance.

'We want to bring them in through the west tunnel, Odion. The quietest of routes. As agent Monique correctly identified, if Khamadi Soglo's supporters get to hear that he's inside the country and under arrest at the palace, it could cause bedlam on the streets.'

'She has a remote?'

'Yes, her controller issued her with one yesterday.'

'Very well. But for now, be about your business, Ousmane, and I will see you shortly. Well done.'

Putting down the handset, Kuetey looked at the guard. 'Twenty-four years,' he hollered, lightheaded with the exhilaration prancing through his veins, 'and at last I have the blood of Zinsa Dangbo. But not only this, I have Khamadi Soglo you will be delighted to hear!'

The elation stayed with him as he busily turned to the console and flicked several switches. There was just the one prisoner, in the middle cage. He looked to be asleep in the corner, doubtlessly exhausted from the previous day's ordeal. Kuetey turned the dial a couple of degrees until the man twitched, a muffled wail coming from the headphones. Spinning the dial anti-clockwise, he reached for the handset on the yellow telephone, and waited. And waited some more. Too long, *again*. This wouldn't happen at Buckingham

Palace! How could *he* be one of *them* with such indifference as this within his own palace?

'Good morning, President Kuetey.'

'Listen here, Ikemba,' retorted Kuetey, 'you are taking too long to answer the telephone. I am the President, and I have little time to loiter. Every minute of the day I am working to serve my people, and to ensure that all state affairs are in perfect order.'

'I apologise, President Kuetey. In future I will be sure to answer the telephone immediately, regardless of what I might—'

Kuetey rolled his one eye. 'Yes, all right, all right, don't burden me with this and that. I want you to feed and water the prisoner. Do not bring me any others. I'm expecting Khamadi Soglo.'

'*The* troublemaker, Khamadi Soglo?' asked Ikemba. 'He has been apprehended?'

'Indeed he has, Ikemba,' answered Kuetey a little haughtily, straightening himself in the chair. 'It has taken some planning on my part, but the correct result has now been achieved. You will have the pleasure to deal with him at some point.'

'To assist in ridding this man from the soil of the Democratic Republic of Séroulé, President Kuetey, must be the highest honour—'

'Yes, yes, all right, Ikemba,' cut in Kuetey.

Ikemba's curious talent was that he could weary him with flattery in a matter of seconds. 'Soglo will be brought in through the west tunnel with two others by State Security people. So be prepared. Now, remember what I have told you to do with the prisoner.'

Kuetey replaced the handset and opened the email from his brother-in-law. He studied the footage – which barely lasted a few seconds, as it happened. But there the three of them were, sitting in the back of some jeep, or whatever. He scrutinized the film, freezing it at various points. Soglo looked in bad shape, but the girl – as Ousmane had stated – appeared unmarked. He wondered how scared she was, and what she was thinking. The other one, the one who had told lies, he would be the first to be caged. And the blood of Zinsa Dangbo would be forced to witness his prolonged electrocution from the beginning through to the very end – every excruciating, mind-shattering second.

CHAPTER 23

From inside the Chrysler jeep, Shani watched Monique point a remote device at the metal roller-shutter in front of them. She didn't know their precise location, other than they were in the *de facto* capital city, Porto Sansudou. The time on the Chrysler's facia was 09:30, the city hectic with life. Yellow motor scooters were everywhere, the Krendor Taxi Company owned by the President's eldest grandson thriving since there was little in way of competition – that much she knew from the limited research she'd conducted on Kuetey's immediate family. A couple of sites had boldly claimed that the few entrepreneurs who had dared to cross swords with Mesego Kuetey had either ended up in the harbour with their throats slit, or had been found at the side of the road out of town with a gunshot to the head.

The jeep was driven into what appeared to be a

warehouse. Shani felt a fresh wave of fear, the shutter rattling back down behind them like the proverbial final nail in the coffin.

Monique ordered them out of the jeep. Taking her phone from a trouser pocket, she began to tap something into it until Khamadi unleashed a lightning move, kicking Monique's legs straight from underneath her. He raised his right leg and was about to stamp on her face, only to be halted from doing so by a pistol shot skimming his head from the driver known as 'Simba'.

Monique rolled away and leapt to her feet with the supple grace of a tigress. She staggered back as if in shock, before picking up her phone from off the floor and glaring viciously at Khamadi. 'I'll watch you die for that,' she hissed. 'I will be the last person you will see on this earth.' She resumed whatever it was she'd been doing with her phone.

'Ikemba?' she said at length. 'Not today, Ikemba. I have something much better than porn. Be ready… Yes, this minute. The President is going to be very pleased. What's that? He has already told you about Soglo? Okay… Yes, two others… Yes, you can do that. Wait for us, we'll call him together.' Monique returned the phone to her khaki jeans.

Khamadi started to speak. 'Let Shani and Nicolas

go free—'

Shani had barely turned her head when Monique slammed a high-flying kick into Khamadi's gut. She watched him double over, and then fall to his knees as he fought to get air into his lungs, a thread of saliva hanging from his mouth. Shani made a move towards him, to help him.

'Get back,' ordered Monique.

'You've hurt him—'

'Shut up, and do as I say.'

Shani hesitated, until Nicolas spoke.

'Do as she says, Shani. We know she's evil.'

Monique ignored the remark and stood over Khamadi, sneering down at him: the victor over the vanquished. 'Get up, you dumb peasant,' she said.

Khamadi struggled, still heaving. He wiped the saliva from his mouth.

'Listen to me,' appeased Nicolas to Monique, 'I regret what I said. I'm sure you're not evil, just misguided in some way. We can get rid of Kuetey. It is possible with Khamadi's help, with his contacts. He is not the bad person you take him to be. But Kuetey, there you have something genuinely evil. I assure you.'

Monique cocked her head and stared at him wide-eyed, as if his suggestion might be something to consider – before laughing. 'Why do you tell so many lies?' she asked. 'Why?'

'He doesn't,' shouted Shani, stalling for time, anything to delay whatever plans had been made for them. Perhaps Khamadi might recover enough to have another go, and succeed. Or maybe they actually could get Monique on board. 'I know him.'

'For how long?'

Shani hesitated, sensing Monique was out to ridicule her. 'Why don't you try reading his articles?'

'Because they're full of lies!'

'Why would he lie?'

'Because he's a journalist, and that's what they do. Exaggerate. Lie. Fake news. A known fact.'

'Not all—'

'Oh, shut up.' Monique waved her pistol across them. 'You're pathetic, the lot of you. I'm going to get my money. If I don't hand you over now, *I'll* be the one who suffers. You think I'm that stupid? When my other option is two million dollars for myself and a flight to California.' She turned to Simba. 'Ikemba is waiting for us. Pull up the cover.'

Simba gave Monique his gun. He walked past Khamadi, now standing but with an infirm stoop, and lifted a shiny aluminium cover a metre square.

Shani looked down into the hole. The concrete steps leading into darkness made her shiver.

'Now get the flashlight from the jeep,' ordered Monique.

***

Simba led the way with the flashlight. Behind him, Shani found herself sandwiched between Khamadi Soglo and Monique. The tunnel was claustrophobic and looked dangerous, the irregular walls damp and coated in places with yellow clumps of fibrous mould. She shivered again, and reduced the pace, trying to think. What if she simply fell to the ground and refused to move?

As if aware of such a tactic, Monique poked her with the handgun.

Shani whirled round and glared at her, resignation binding with trepidation.

'Keep moving,' snarled Monique. 'If you mess me around, I'll hit you.'

'You're utterly vile,' Shani told her. 'Insane, probably!'

'Blame your mother, not me. She's the one who took his eye out.'

'She was protecting herself. She was *six* years old, that's all—'

Another prod. 'Simba, move faster,' said Monique. 'This silly bitch is getting on my nerves.'

Shani splashed through a puddle. Crying quietly, she

thought of Dusana and her beloved cats – worlds away from the hellish nightmare she now found herself immersed in. Harry Rothwell and his Christmas crackers. What day was it? Had to be a Thursday. She imagined he would be on his way over to Lady Margaret Hall for his eleven o'clock lecture with undergraduates. Christina, beautiful Christina with her gorgeous, luminous-blonde hair, envied by all their friends. She would get her doctorate, marry, have her children, a second home somewhere in Provence – or was it Tuscany…?

They came to an abrupt halt in front of a metal door, and Shani watched Simba press a bell, which triggered an absurd jingle as if whoever installed it had decided to play a macabre joke on 'the victim'. And there must have been hundreds of victims, suspected Shani, who had been forced along this same tunnel, never to see the outside world again.

The door edged open, and a shaft of harsh light flooded the tunnel. A man with pinched features stood by the door as they emerged into what looked like a storeroom, with cardboard boxes stacked on top of one another. Shani rapidly became aware of an atrocious smell, like an invisible wall of stale sweat and faeces.

Monique blinked against the fluorescent lighting.

'Ikemba,' she said with her first smile of the day, 'you see, I have Khamadi Soglo. What do you think to that?'

'Incredible,' said Ikemba. 'You are the best, Monique. I have said this many times. The President sounded very happy. There will surely be celebrations in the palace tonight.' Ikemba edged closer to Shani, his oily eyes roving. 'This one is very pretty,' he said at length.

Monique shrugged. 'I've seen prettier, Ikemba.'

'No, no. Very pretty, I tell you,' insisted Ikemba. 'Nice skin.'

'Why don't you ask the President if you can have her?'

Ikemba's head spun towards Monique. 'You think, Monique? You think there's a chance?'

'You can only ask.'

Bile swam into Shani's throat. She hadn't understood every word, but the man's mannerisms betrayed his repulsive objective. Unable to make use of her hands, she did something she had never done before in her entire life, she spat in someone's face – Ikemba's face.

He grinned at her while he wiped his jaw. 'Monique,' he said, 'all these years and I've found the perfect one. But I will have to discipline her. I can tell you that for nothing.'

'If you say so,' said Monique. 'We need to get moving. I've a busy schedule. A debrief over at State Security.'

Ikemba led the way, shuffling out of the room into a broad corridor, where three cages sat side by side. 'Hey, Soglo,' he called over his skinny shoulder, 'the President has already told me I will be the one who will deal with you.' Pointing at the first cage, he said: 'This is where you will go. Your new home, Soglo. But how long will you last?'

Ikemba dipped his hand into a sack and threw what looked like a handful of seeds into the second cage. 'Animals,' he muttered contemptuously.

Shani drew closer to the cages, the feeling that she had entered a corridor of inconceivable horror as undeniable as the stench itself. But then... 'Oh, my God,' she breathed when seeing the motionless figure in the middle cage, skeletal and wearing just a loin cloth as he sat in semi-darkness on his haunches alongside a bowl of water. He stared back at them in silence, his feral eyes fear-ridden, like they were caught in the headlights of an oncoming truck.

The ground started to slip away from Shani. She made an attempt to lean against a wall. She wasn't sure, but she thought Nicolas was at her side, shouting something about getting her water.

But that was all she heard, her senses lost to oblivion as she flopped into the blackness below her.

* * *

General Kuetey put down the tissue he was holding to answer the yellow telephone.

'Yes, Ikemba?'

'We are ready to bring up the prisoners, President Kuetey.'

'They're here?' Surprised, Kuetey absently patted his brow. 'With you? Already?'

'With Monique. She is—'

'Yes, yes, I know this girl. How many people have you there, exactly?'

'The three prisoners, Monique, and another agent... One moment, President Kuetey. I'll ask his name.'

Kuetey turned to a screen on his far right and opened up an image showing the empty warehouse – one of several exits from the palace should an immediate 'unthinkable' evacuation be required. He reversed the footage to when the silver jeep entered the building. Fast-forwarding, he watched the dust-up between the girl agent and Khamadi Soglo. She was certainly lithe and feisty, he thought. Just his type, in fact. And with Imani away in Milan...

'Simba,' notified Ikemba. 'Agent Simba.'

Kuetey turned from the screen to face the console. 'Ikemba, order them all into the left-hand cage so I can see them.'

'All five of them?'

'That is what I said. *All* of them.' Kuetey scrutinized the console as the figures started to shuffle into the cage. Bălcescu. There she was, bewildered, if not scared-looking – and now, virtually within reach. The liar was leaning against her, like he was propping her up. Well, little did he know that this was going to be the last occasion he touched her! All of them had their hands bound. Kuetey straightened and spoke into the handset. 'Get the girl to bring them to me, but not with the one called Simba. There's no need for him to be here.'

'Yes, President Kuetey. You will unlock the lift?'

'Of course I will,' spat Kuetey. 'How else are they expected to come up?' He slammed the handset down and looked at the guard by the door. 'Bring the other two in from outside.' Taking a plastic key from a desk drawer, he levered his bulk out of the swivel chair and lumbered over to the en suite, where he inserted the key into a panel alongside the elevator. The lift's motor hummed quietly, and Kuetey anxiously tried to straighten his eye-patch. He looked at the lift's doors, where there was just enough reflection. He would have that Monique before the end of the day, but not if he looked like a clown with his patch skewed!

The red light on the panel switched to green, and his pulse duly responded, slamming away in his chest like he was forty years younger. He turned briefly to the three National Guardsmen. 'Come closer... That's enough.'

* * *

Shani cursed Monique under her breath when she prodded her with the gun as she goaded them into the lift, her left cheek grazed from hitting the wall when she fainted. The fact that it stung viciously was the least of her concerns. She'd noticed that Ikemba had eagerly followed her into the lift, pushing past Monique. Shani hoped he wouldn't stand next to her – but he did exactly that. She tried move away from him, edging closer to Nicolas.

'Ikemba, did the President want you to come too?' asked Monique. 'The maximum is four. It says so on the wall.'

'I'm very light,' said Ikemba. 'And so is the girl. We've had up to six in here, many times.'

Monique elbowed Khamadi out of the way so she could press the button.

The doors closed, and Shani became aware of

Ikemba's rancid body odour clawing at her nostrils, suffocating her as much as the lift itself. She watched him turn his back on the others, and slowly stick his tongue out at her before wiggling the tip of it.

Shani jolted her head back, repulsed. 'Get him away from me!' she screamed, before kicking him. 'Get him away from me!' Instinctively, she tried to release her hands, revulsion blocking the pain as the plastic tie gouged into her wrists. 'Get him *away* from me!'

Nicolas shouldered Ikemba into Khamadi. 'You piece of shit!'

'Ikemba, what are doing?' shouted Monique.

'Nothing,' said Ikemba, lurching from Khamadi. 'I wasn't doing anything. She's crazy.'

The lift slowed, then more so until it came to a cushioned stop. The doors parted, and as Shani stepped out with Nicolas she found herself facing the monster who had murdered much of her family, effectively forcing her mother into exile. According to the *Internet*, Kuetey was seventy-three, yet there were few wrinkles on his face, and his bald head seemed abnormally shiny. While his one eye pitilessly took her in before settling on Ikemba, she realised cosmetic surgery had undoubtedly played its part.

'What are *you* doing here?' Kuetey asked Ikemba.

'I thought I should escort them, President Kuetey,'

Ikemba said boldly. 'Because of their importance to you and the State—'

'Ikemba,' interrupted Kuetey, 'I've told you before, I don't want you thinking too much, assuming this and that all the time. It gives me a headache. Now, stand aside.' Kuetey waved his hand, beckoning Monique to step closer while smiling pleasantly. 'You are the hero of the hour, we can say…'

As Kuetey babbled away to Monique, Shani looked at Khamadi's bruised and vacant face. His eyes seemed to have sunk into his skull, and from that alone she realised he'd given up. He avoided her gaze, staring blankly at the exotic flora in front of them. To be taken in by a double agent… How could he have been so negligent?

'Thank you, President Kuetey,' responded Monique. 'It is an honour to serve you, and the People's Democratic Republic of Séroulé.'

Kuetey acknowledged Monique's submissive tone with a brief nod of his head, before turning to Nicolas. 'So, you are the one who has been writing lies about me. Yes?'

Nicolas pushed back his shoulders and faced Kuetey head-on. 'Let Shani go. She has done nothing to you. Nothing at all. I am the one who has to be punished for writing about you in the way that I have.'

Kuetey chuckled. 'Such hindsight.' He looked away, as if disinterested, before smashing the back of his hand against Nicolas's jaw. 'What a pity you appear to have no foresight.'

'Stop it!' cried Shani, putting herself between them to prevent Kuetey repeating the action – but his gaze was no longer on Nicolas.

'What is this mark?' he asked Monique, touching her scuffed cheek before Shani flinched away from him.

'She hit her face when she fainted at the sight of the criminal in the cage, President Kuetey,' said Monique. 'Please accept my apology.'

Kuetey threw up a hand. 'Don't worry, don't worry.' He started to laugh, a guttural roar that filled the presidential suite. 'I tell you, the weakness of Tuma Dangbo is present with us today in this one, his granddaughter,' he declared. He waved his hand in front of Shani. 'You see my hand?'

Shani refused to speak. *Zinsa, come to me!* That was all she wanted now. To see Zinsa, and for Zinsa to wrap her arms around her, to take her away from this demented tyrant.

Kuetey waved again. 'You see my hand?' he demanded.

'Yes,' shouted Shani. 'You murdered my family.'

Kuetey smiled. 'Well, enjoy your sight while you can. The recipient will, I'm quite sure, be delighted that an appropriate donor has at last been found. She happens to be a personal friend of my wife's.'

Her stomach turned over. So that was the plan. He was going to donate her corneas, leaving her blind. He had no intention of putting her to death. And Nicolas? Of course, before the operation, she would have to witness… No. *Absolutely not!*

Kuetey moved along to Khamadi Soglo. Lifting his one eye to take in the rebel leader's full height, he said: 'Your end has come, Soglo. I will show you what I have in store for you in a moment. You and the liar here, that is.'

Shani noticed Ikemba had stepped forward. The nightmare couldn't get any more obscene, surely?

'President Kuetey?' said Ikemba.

Kuetey turned from Khamadi. 'What is it?'

'I have a small question.'

Kuetey sighed irritably, puffing out his cheeks before shaking his head and rounding on Ikemba. 'I have just asked you, "What is it?" How can I answer you if you don't tell me what the question is?'

'I…I was wondering if I should watch over the girl while you are busy with Soglo and the one who tells lies about us?'

Kuetey's thunderous face gave Shani a fissure of hope.

'Are you taking me for a fool?' asked Kuetey.

Ikemba's jaw dropped. 'President Kuetey—'

'I've told you before,' said Kuetey, 'if you want that sort of thing you get it from the state prison. The head administrator's quite aware of your peculiar tendencies. Do you understand?'

'Yes, President Kuetey. Oh, yes, most certainly.' Ikemba couldn't speak fast enough. 'An error on my part—'

'Then get back to your business. Now!'

Ikemba retreated into the elevator and pressed a button on his left, his eyes fixed on the linoleum floor.

Shani watched Kuetey give Monique another broad smile as the elevator doors slid together. 'You will receive a medal for this, young woman.'

'Thank you, President Kuetey.' Monique glared at Khamadi. 'This one has tried to deceive the people with his falsehoods. He also viciously attacked me earlier. I humbly beseech you to deal with him in an appropriate manner.'

'And I will, Monique. But it is the blood of Zinsa Dangbo...' Kuetey went back to Shani '...who is the biggest prize for me. Kuetey, without any warning, whipped off the eye patch. 'This is what her mother did to me.'

'Zinsa was trying to defend herself,' retaliated Shani, and when he turned to her she saw a veined hole inside a bloated face. Then the horror of all horrors, that he might actually rape her! 'She was a child at the time. An innocent.'

'She was a nasty little rat, as I recall,' reacted Kuetey. 'Vermin, like the rest of them.'

'My grandfather only wanted to prevent the West from exploiting Séroulé—'

'It is now considered an archaic debate. Irrelevant—'

'How can corruption be irrelevant?' hit back Shani. 'How can greed, *your* greed, and that of your horrible cohorts, be dismissed?'

Kuetey waved a finger. 'Typical rhetoric from a misinformed student. Is that the kind of rubbish they teach you at university? That and cancerous socialism, or whatever nonsense happens to be in fashion?'

'Conceited and as vile as you are, you are nothing but a puppet!' persisted Shani. She knew her fate, and something inside her began to suppress her fear. Had Zinsa come to her? Of course. God bless you, Zinsa! 'Like all terrorists, you've done what was required of you, your crimes promoting the repugnant concept of introducing a global police state. In effect, a world government!'

Kuetey continued to wag his finger, his one eye deadly-looking. 'You are in enough trouble as it is. Do not talk to me in such a way.'

'Both Zinsa and I will talk to you how we wish. Yes, she is with me, in this room. You didn't know? I can feel her, hear her.' *Incredible*, her fear was gone! 'And you know what Zinsa's telling me? She's telling me you're a terrorist through and through, and what happened to Gaddafi will surely happen to you—'

'Shut up!' shouted Kuetey at the top of his voice.

'Only it will be the Séroulèse people, not the West, who will—'

'I said *shut up*.' Kuetey's face was apoplectic as more beads of sweat surfaced on his brow. 'Don't you *ever* mention that man's name to me again, or I'll have your tongue cut out.' Kuetey glared at her a moment longer, before beckoning Khamadi Soglo to follow him. 'Come, I want to show you something.' He went behind the desk and lowered his bulk into the swivel chair.

'I thought this console was a myth,' said Khamadi, his first words since leaving the warehouse.

'Well, you can see that it isn't,' said Kuetey.

Shani scanned the presidential suite. Kuetey was distracted, and Monique looked bored. She still needed that sharp implement. There were also the three guards to consider, one of them by the picture window. What if she charged at the window? He wasn't going to shoot her, was he? No, of course not. So if she charged at it her head might break the glass enough for her to sever her jugular, or perhaps her throat…

'Before the sun has set,' Kuetey was telling Khamadi, 'I will have extracted from you the information required to break your network, and all its sub-networks.' Putting back his eye patch, Kuetey pointed at the middle screen. 'This is where you're heading, Soglo. You see this cage, this wretch? Look what happens when I turn this dial.'

Shani had a side view of the screen, enough to see a figure spring into the air, and as it did so partially spin around before dropping to its knees: a twisted face with pinched features jerking involuntarily in front of the camera.

Shani noticed Kuetey blink and lean forward.

'Ikemba…?'

A split second later Kuetey had crashed to the floor as she, herself, went flying past Nicolas.

CHAPTER 24

Breathless with bewilderment, Shani picked herself up with Nicolas's support, Monique having rammed her to one side. The scene across the presidential suite was quite different. She remembered Monique slipping quietly behind her. And now she realised why, to attach a silencer to the pistol. She'd heard the muffled shots as she hit the floor, the outcome of those shots being three dead guards.

'What are you doing, Soglo?' demanded Kuetey, flapping about like a beetle on its back as he tried to right himself.

Khamadi pulled a gun from behind his shirt while keeping his foot on Kuetey's chest, and Shani realised that his wrists couldn't have been bound properly in the first place since he'd obviously yanked the swivel chair out from under Kuetey. She looked back at the guards, two of them having fallen on top of one another, blood still dripping from their foreheads as their vacant eyes stared out at her.

Khamadi spoke into his mobile phone. 'We have a green light. Proceed with *Cascade*.' He turned to Monique. 'Cut the ties on them.' After she'd done so with a short-bladed knife, he said: 'Nicolas, get the bodies away from the door and lock it. We'll take their rifles. Monique, your condition?'

'Flesh wound. The last one got a shot at me.'

Shani turned to her and saw Monique clutching her left arm below the shoulder, blood seeping between her fingers. Despite being unlucky with her injury, it was clear to Shani that Monique's marksmanship was made all the more remarkable by the pressure she must surely have been under.

'There's no key to lock the door,' Nicolas called over.

Khamadi glanced down at Kuetey. 'Where is it?'

'Soglo, get your foot off me,' growled Kuetey.

'*Key?*'

'The lock is broken. You can't use it. Now get off me!'

'Shani,' ordered Khamadi, lifting his gaze, 'go with Monique to the en suite and assist her. I want out of here.'

Shani numbly trailed behind Monique, her body

still stinging with adrenalin. This was crazy! She didn't know where to start to unpick it all. A total reversal. Or was it? Who the hell was she supposed to trust now?

Monique was talking to her.

'...Bandages.'

'What?'

'We need bandages. Come on. Wake up. Help me.'

The en suite was massive. That much Shani could take in. Tiled in ocean-green, a flat screen moulded into an enormous Jacuzzi. Looking at Monique, she said: 'I don't get this. Did you stage-manage everything?'

Monique started to unbutton her short-sleeved khaki shirt, blood dripping from her elbow. 'We thought it better you didn't know.'

'You thought *what*?' Shani felt a detonation of outrage sweep like wildfire through her, causing her to tremble. 'You could have told us, for God's sake. I've just been through hell. You put our lives at risk. And we're still in danger. There must be guards everywhere.'

'True.' Monique looked across at her. 'But had we told you, what would have happened if you or Nicolas went and lost it with your emotions and gave everything away? Or if Kuetey had inflicted pain on you, or Nicolas? We didn't know how he was going to receive us, how he might react. We could only guess. And now we are right inside. Apart from my arm, everything is perfect.'

'You actually cut Khamadi's cheek.'

Monique let the shirt fall to the floor, to reveal a black sports brassiere. 'All the more realistic,' she said, and shrugged.

'But you know that horrible man, Ikemba. If you're with Khamadi, how come you know *him*?'

'I had to gain knowledge of the basement. I used an obsolete tunnel without cameras. Ikemba was more than obliging. He was addicted to pornographic material, and I fed that addiction.' Monique lifted her injured arm. 'Now clean me up and find some bandages.'

Shani tried to calm herself. She was alive, and so was Nicolas, the immediate threat marginally downgraded. She had no choice but to accept their unorthodox methods and help these people. She took some toilet tissue from the holder and pressed it against Monique's wound. 'Where's Osakwe?' she asked.

'At a guess, in the capital – or what used to be the capital, Thekari. I haven't been told his whereabouts.'

'And he's second-in-command?'

'Yes. When you came onto the scene we radically

altered our strategy. Without you, I doubt we could have penetrated the palace. Hopefully, the coup will be a lot less bloody as a consequence, meaning your involvement will have saved countless lives.'

'I've never heard you talk so much,' said Shani. 'Is this the real Monique?'

'I guess.'

'Hold this against your arm while I fill the basin.' Shani turned an ornate gold-plated tap, the head of a swan as its spout. 'We're not safe here, are we?'

'No. But we now have assault rifles from the guards, and Kuetey as a hostage for the time being.'

'"For the time being"?' echoed Shani, probing.

'I don't know what Khamadi plans to do with him.'

Shani started to clean up Monique's arm, recalling Nicolas's conversation with her in London about the Dendi people and Kuetey's ruthless determination to see them banished from Séroulé. 'With this being a multi-faith country,' she asked, 'are Muslims fighting alongside Christians against the regime?'

'Yes. I'm Muslim. So there you have it.'

'From the Songhai?

'Zarma, to be specific.'

Shani hastily soaked more tissues, a small fold of flesh on Monique's arm plainly visible. 'I'm no expert, but I think you need stitches,' she said.

Monique glanced at the wound. 'Find some bandages. Look in the cabinets.'

Shani flicked open two mirrored doors. Various pots and tubes, but no bandages that she could see. 'Nothing.'

'Get Khamadi to ask Kuetey.'

Inside the office suite, Shani found Nicolas guarding the door with a rifle while filming with his phone. Kuetey himself was back in his chair, copying something off the computer onto a piece of paper.

'Quickly, quickly!' Khamadi was saying.

Kuetey glanced up from the screen. 'By pointing a gun at me you are violating all human rights, the Geneva Convention—'

Khamadi struck him with the pistol. 'Shut up and copy the numbers down. And keep your left hand on top of the desk where I can see it.'

'We need bandages,' said Shani. 'Does he have any?'

'Bandages?' demanded Khamadi at Kuetey.

Kuetey waved the pen. 'Under the hand basin. And take that gun away from my head, Soglo. It is Ousmane Sekibo you should be dealing with. I have warned him many times about his methods…'

Shani went back to Monique. 'Right in front of us,'

she said, and squatted to open a drawer. Empty. She tried the one below. 'Everything's here—'

'Then fix my arm. You have to move faster, Shani. We need to get out. What's Khamadi doing?'

Shani tore the wrap off an adhesive dressing. 'He's making Kuetey write something down.' She pressed the dressing to the wound.

Monique nodded. 'Contact numbers for the generals. A known fact, Kuetey doesn't trust mobile phones. What an idiot. Doubtful, but he might even have saved himself had he one.'

Shani put a bandage over the dressing and deftly threaded a safety pin through it. Picking Monique's shirt up off the floor, she asked: 'Are you married?'

'You ask me that at a time like this?'

'I'm out of sorts,' said Shani. 'Hardly surprising.'

'I'm not married.' Monique buttoned the shirt herself. 'I have a lover. Coming up to three years. He's with Osakwe, so probably in Thekari.'

'Who were those people who flew in with us from Tamale?' Shani quickly washed her hands. 'Eight men.'

'Demolition experts. There are two bridges over the river Tégine. If it comes to it, we might have to blow them up to restrict the army.' Monique rubbed her right arm. 'Feels good. We're ready to go.

Thanks.' Monique put her hand in her pocket. 'Before I forget, here's your phone.'

Shani took it, and realised something. 'Nicolas has his phone.'

'I gave it to him when I cut the tie.'

'Oh…' And then a doubt which she wanted to dismiss, but couldn't. 'Did you ever discuss anything with Nicolas—?'

Monique shook her head. 'Don't worry, he was in the dark as much as you. We need to move.'

Shani followed Monique out of the en suite.

'All of you, in the lift,' instructed Khamadi. 'Kuetey, get out of the chair.'

'What are you going to do, Soglo?' demanded Kuetey, his eyepatch askew as beads of perspiration skated randomly down his face. 'You cannot treat the President of Séroulé with such dishonour!'

'Kneel,' ordered Khamadi. 'Shani, might be wise to close your eyes.'

Inside the elevator, Shani covered her face with her hands. So, this was to be Kuetey's fate. The dictator was still remonstrating when she heard a muffled shot. She took her hands away, only did so too early. Khamadi fired a second shot, the bullet violently jolting the tyrant's head over to the left.

Shani watched in a daze the rivulet of blood trickle

across the mosaic floor as Kuetey lay curled up in a near perfect foetal position – on his way to finding himself in Hell, perhaps. She didn't feel elated, perhaps because it had happened so unexpectedly. But as Khamadi photographed the corpse from various angles with his phone, his shirt spattered with the dictator's blood, questions needed to be asked. Surely, International Law had been breached? Was this a window into the future for Séroulé? The law of the jungle, and little else? Jacques Baudin would never allow that to happen, surely? When Khamadi finished, he came and joined them in the elevator.

'Shouldn't he have gone on trial?' asked Shani.

'His crimes have been well documented.' Khamadi pushed a button and the doors closed. 'Remember, this coup is far from over. Just the beginning, in fact. Take a moment to think about yourself.'

'What do you mean?'

'What was he going to do to you? Blind you, to start with. God knows what else he had in mind. If I hadn't got rid of him, and this coup backfires... You get the picture?'

'Yes.' Shani didn't think twice. 'Thank you.'

'Séroulè's lived with enough horror thanks to that monster.' Khamadi's fingers glided over the phone, flicking through the pictures he'd taken. 'All that's required now is to post his elimination on social networking sites the world over.'

Monique's phone shrilled. 'Number withheld,' she said. 'Might be Sekibo.'

Khamadi took the phone and listened without speaking, then cut the call and gave it back to her. 'Definitely Sekibo, trying to make contact with you.' He left the elevator. 'Okay, we're getting behind,' he said. 'At a guess, we're minutes away from all hell breaking loose.'

Simba was waiting for them, supporting the prisoner they'd seen in the cage. 'I've put Ikemba's clothes on him, but he's not in good shape.'

Khamadi went up to the man, whose constant shivering suggested he'd caught a virus or was verging on starvation. 'You know who I am?' he asked.

'Soglo?' said the man, his frail eyes anxious. 'Is it you, Soglo?'

'Yes, *mon ami*. Give me your name.'

'Chidi.'

'What was your crime, Chidi?'

'I sold cigarettes in the street without a licence.'

Khamadi gently held the man. 'Do not be afraid, we are here to help you,' he said, and covered Chidi's ears in the embrace while looking at Simba. 'He's too weak for the tunnel,' he whispered. 'His muscles are gone.'

'If we leave him,' said Simba, 'anyone coming down here will kill him.'

'We have to take him,' said Shani, fearful of what Khamadi might have in mind. 'If we leave him, we are no better than Kuetey. I'm telling you!'

'I will carry him,' Khamadi said. He took his hands away. 'Chidi, I'm giving you a piggyback along the tunnel. Have you the strength to hold onto me?'

Chidi nodded, but then held out his hands. 'Tie my arms around you.'

'Someone, anyone,' ordered Khamadi, 'find string, or whatever.'

Shani joined the others in the search. Khamadi *still* worried her. Would he have abandoned Chidi? She had so many doubts about him. An enigma, no question. He had knowledgeable people assisting him, though. Osakwe. Baudin. Monique – presumably!

The cages came into view. She looked over her shoulder, Nicolas not far behind her in the corridor. In the middle cage was the horrible man called 'Ikemba', virtually naked, his gaping eyes still swollen with terror. If this place wasn't Hell itself, she thought, then it had to be just as hideous.

Turning from the cage, she spotted a reading lamp nearby with its flex trailing on the floor.

CHAPTER 25

Ousmane Sekibo sat at his desk. Something wasn't right... Not right at all. The gold carriage clock alongside his conventional family portrait now showed the time to be almost eleven-thirty. He picked up the handset and spoke to agent Monique's controller again.

'Are you certain that this is the number she is currently using?'

'Yes, Director General. I have triple checked. I can only assume there's a lack of reception at her present location.'

Sekibo lowered the handset and ran the operation through his mind – as he had done virtually every hour over the past two days. He knew each and every detail intimately, and still he could not see a single flaw. It was perfect. A work of genius on his part, in actual fact. The three of them captured within twelve hours. As for Osakwe Babangida, his arrest was surely imminent, troops having now sealed off Quartier de Magenta in Thekari.

There was Omolara, of course, Kuetey's personal assistant over on the palace's administrative east-wing, but he wasn't at all sure whether his brother-in-law had told even her of Khamadi Soglo's arrest. He didn't want to put his foot in it. He tried for the umpteenth time to contact Ikemba Dougbé, who for eight years had rarely left the basement. As before, his call went unanswered.

Sekibo stood and wiped a handkerchief over his blunt features. Christ, he thought, I'm getting like Kuetey. Next I'll have boxes of goddamned tissues all over the desk! He put the damp handkerchief back in his suit pocket and cast a glance out of the window at the palace. He couldn't quite put his finger on it, but it looked different. Silent. No one to be seen. Like it belonged to a different era. And in a way, he supposed it did. The President had become too self-indulgent. Too inward looking. This obsessive nonsense when it came to the girl. He'd been half-tempted to put a bullet in her head simply to get rid of her. He wiped his face again and left his office, abandoning his habitual 11 o'clock coffee and croissant. The worry had crushed his appetite.

Sekibo followed the path from the State Security compound that wound its way through the manicured Manhattan Garden, flashing his identity pass until he arrived at the palace's gleaming white marble staircase. Just about the only portion of the building, he'd thought on occasion, that was aesthetically agreeable. He raced up to the third floor... Sekibo swore. *Why* were there were no guards outside the presidential suite?

He listened at the door. Nothing. Then he remembered the door was insulated to prevent the slightest sound from within being heard. He reached down for the gold-plated knob, his pulse like that of a drumbeat careering towards a crescendo.

'Odion?' he called, his voice awkward. 'Odion...?'

The full horror hit him as he opened the door. He shut his eyes instinctively, and when he opened them nothing had changed. The President of Séroulé lay face down in the centre of the suite, his head resting in an astonishing amount of blood. Elsewhere, crimson smears directed his shaken gaze to the bloodied corpses of the guards themselves. Two head shots, and an upper chest shot – on the most senior of the guards. Professional. In every respect. He drifted deeper into the suite, which had taken on the appearance of an abattoir.

Let me give it to you precisely, Ousmane. Khamadi Soglo is running rings around the State Security Service.

Monique, he realised. The whore Monique… If he could get hold of her, he'd break every bone in her body twice over and tear her apart with his bare hands!

Sekibo took his phone from his pocket, his fingers trembling as panic set in. Catastrophic. That's what his day – his *life* – had now become. Unless…

'General Nzeogwu,' he said, 'you need to get your men into both the used and disused tunnels to the palace. Urgently.'

'What is this?' said the gruff voice at the other end.

'We have a full-blown crisis on our hands. President Odion Kuetey has been assassinated.'

'*What?* Have you lost your mind, Ousmane? Are you drunk?'

'It has all the hallmarks of Khamadi Soglo,' continued Sekibo, ignoring the general's fatuous remark. 'Seal the tunnels. And get your troops over to the State Television building, and all other government buildings. Make no mistake, General Nzeogwu, we are dealing with a coup d'état.'

He hung up and hurried from the suite. The President was gone, and he, Ousmane Sekibo, would be one of the first to be put into shackles, if not shipped off to The Hague itself. What choice did he have now? South Africa, or Saudi Arabia? He raced back down the staircase. Most probably South Africa, he decided, the Foreign Minister a personal friend. Besides, he had more money in the Jo'burg account should manoeuvring his wealth become an issue. Cosmetic surgery, a new wife and some kids, maybe. That was his future, unless Khamadi Soglo could be tricked into making a tactical error over the coming hours.

***

Shani jogged after Simba up the steps and into the warehouse, the danger seemingly more palpable by the minute. For the first hundred metres she had found herself bringing up the rear in the tunnel, before asking Nicolas to change places. It was just too scary – like in a dream, hands could have grabbed her and covered her mouth so she couldn't scream as she watched the others disappear ahead of her. Every few seconds she glanced over her shoulder to make certain such a fate hadn't actually befallen Nicolas. And now she dreaded to think what might be in wait for them beyond the roller-shutter because alarm bells – literally or otherwise – must surely have sounded; telephone calls to Kuetey worryingly left unanswered. And from there, the chain of command dismayed by the news of the assassination – the generals and their cosy, corrupted lifestyles under threat. And of course, that wouldn't do!

Shani watched Khamadi fire his handgun at the camera attached to a joist in the ceiling, shards of glass and plastic showering the concrete floor. He quickly removed the flex from Chidi's arms. 'Nicolas,' he said, 'there's an Olympus camera under the front seat in the jeep. Make use of it.' Khamadi opened the rear hatch. 'Chidi, you can lie across this area.'

Chidi winced as he folded his crippled body into the narrow space. 'I'm so cold, Soglo,' he said.

Khamadi's phone started ringing. 'We'll find you something as soon as we can,' he told Chidi. Taking the call, he spoke quietly into his phone between ominous gaps of silence. As if conscious everyone was watching him, he turned his back.

Shani suspected from his body language bad news. She looked at Monique, whose expression gave no clue as she too watched and waited. Blood had seeped through the dressing on her arm, and Shani wished she'd brought spare bandages with her.

Khamadi ended the call and came towards them. 'Okay, this is the situation,' he said, 'we have a couple of observers on the roof of a building nearby. Two armoured jeeps have rolled up and are in a V-formation outside, blocking our only exit. A fortnight ago a disused tunnel linked to this one was filled in with rubble and can no longer be accessed. These two jeeps were probably in the neighbourhood, so more will follow. Now they're here, we're going to have to deal with them.'

'How?' asked Nicolas.

'We have equipment concealed in the jeep: grenades, rifles and ammunition.'

'Then keep that stuff as a back-up,' said Shani. She felt they were overlooking the obvious. 'Use me.'

Khamadi looked at her. 'What are you talking about? Use you, like how?'

Shani turned to Monique. 'What ID do you have? Nothing from State Security?'

'My internal pass...' Monique tailed off, her puzzled expression lifting.

'Exactly,' said Shani. 'We're on the same wavelength.'

'Shani, what is it you have in mind?' demanded Nicolas. 'This is enough danger.'

Shani noticed Monique had drifted away from them, thinking hard about how to execute such a plan. 'She's a born actress,' she told Nicolas. 'We can testify to that. An armoured jeep for ourselves, and get rid of the other one. Right, Khamadi?'

Khamadi turned to Nicolas. 'It's a plan. No denying.'

'I don't like it,' said Nicolas. 'Christ, no! How many people in these things? What type are they?'

'J-Eight, armoured patrol vehicles. Up to six.'

'Shani,' called Monique from the roller-shutter. 'Khamadi, get the remote ready.'

Shani touched Nicolas's cheek. 'By asking Khamadi to bring out Chidi we've lost time—'

'Shani, I wasn't going to leave him,' interrupted Khamadi, heading for the Toyota.

Shani made a last attempt to pacify Nicolas. 'We'll have an armoured jeep for ourselves,' she repeated, and turned away, not giving him a chance to sway her decision.

She joined Monique, who quickly wiped her fingers over her wound.

'Not very nice for you. Sorry.' Monique smeared Shani's cheek and jaw with her blood.

'How are they going to back us up?'

Monique looked past her shoulder. 'Khamadi's getting Simba and Nicolas into position, out of view from the street. Like Khamadi said, we've got stuff concealed in the jeep. I don't think we'll need it. Just the rifles we've taken should do it.'

'I must be crazy,' said Shani, watching Monique

tuck her handgun into her waistband and cover it over with her shirt. 'Surely, we should have had back-up out on the street, in case this sort of thing happened?'

Monique twisted her mouth. 'I've got to confess, we didn't factor in possible prisoners. Without Chidi we would have been out of here.'

'And it's just our bad luck these jeeps were in the neighbourhood?'

'Quite. Times like this you give out as little information as possible, even to those you believe you can trust. You keep your guard up at all times.' Monique met Shani's eyes. 'I'm going to have to play it rough. When the shutter's up by about a metre that's when I'm dragging you out. Put up some resistance to begin with. Keep your hands behind you, as if they're bound. Okay?'

'Yes. Hell, I'm scared,' said Shani. This was it now, she told herself – never, *ever* again would she act or say anything without being methodical beforehand. She knew she'd upset Nicolas, and hated herself for it. She looked over her shoulder to find him, but could only see Khamadi holding the remote. 'You're positive you have your ID?' she asked Monique.

'Yes. Ready?'

'As I'll ever be.'

Monique signalled to Khamadi, and the shutter

fluttered, then hummed and rattled as it recoiled into itself. 'This will be over before you know it, I promise.'

Shani felt Monique grab a handful of her T-shirt below her nape, almost choking her. Bloody hell, she thought, she wasn't joking about playing it rough. More rattling, before she was yanked outside, catching the side of her face on the shutter in the process. Monique lifted her to her feet. Exactly as Khamadi had been told, Shani saw two armoured jeeps sitting in a V-formation. She didn't have to pretend to be terrified as she was frog-marched to the nearest one, Monique already yelling at the driver.

'Get after Soglo. He's escaped!' Monique slapped her ID against the window.

Shani wriggled, and Monique jerked her back.

'Get the window down, you idiot!' screamed Monique.

The driver frowned and started to do so. 'We were told to seal off a tunnel—'

'Listen to me, I've just *told* you, Khamadi Soglo's escaped. He's wounded and limping badly. He took off down there. We've got the others, and this bitch.'

'Who is she?' asked the driver.

'Tuma Dangbo's granddaughter. Soglo was going to use her to make a broadcast. You've got to get after him. We'll keep the other jeep here, for the President—'

'We heard he'd been assassin—'

'Misinformation given out by the rebels to cause anarchy. Now *get* after Soglo. You know the President himself is awarding two million dollars and automatic promotion for whoever captures him alive?'

The front passenger leaned forward. 'Two million dollars? That's what you said?'

'For starters—'

The driver was already reversing and Shani found herself hustled over to the second jeep. This was going to be dreadful, she imagined – but necessary, if they wanted the jeep for themselves. She could see people gathering at the end of the street.

Monique shouted out an order. When the driver refused to lower the window, she slapped her ID onto the windscreen. 'We're bringing the President up. How many have you in the back?'

The driver mouthed *three*.

Monique gesticulated for him to get the window down. 'The girl goes in the back. She needs to be under guard at all times – orders from the President himself.'

Who is she? mouthed the driver while looking at Shani, who gave another credible wriggle.

What? Monique mouthed back.

The driver lowered the window a couple of centimetres. 'Who's she?'

'Listen, we're bringing the President up.'

'The President? Kuetey?' The window slid another centimetre.

'Khamadi Soglo's escaped. I've ordered the other jeep to go after him. He's badly wounded. I need your men to protect the President when we bring him out. You say there's three. Correct?'

'Yes. I didn't realise…'

'I'm going to join the search for Soglo. The girl needs to be under guard. Get them to open the back up.'

Shani writhed as she was marched to the back of the jeep. Monique banged on the armour-plated door.

'Open up!' she screamed.

The door inched open. The three men inside wore expressions of bewilderment while gripping their rifles.

'Is the President still alive?' asked one of them.

He never got a reply as Shani witnessed all three leave this world, their heads jolting at different angles, the incessant percussion ringing out like a battery of firecrackers that carried on after Monique had finished, only at the front of the jeep. Monique released her grip on her and began to drag the bodies out, Khamadi and Simba doing the same with the driver and front passenger. Nicolas was propping up Chidi, the latter squinting against the explosion of sunlight. Shani ran to him.

'Don't hate me, Nicolas. Please!'

'What am I going to do with you?' he yelled at her.

'Don't hate me.'

'You idiot! You courageous, heavenly, bloody idiot!' He touched the side of her face. 'Never do anything like that to me again. Got it?'

'Yes. Of course. Never again. Promise.' Shani turned to the jeep. Monique, it seemed, was doing the driving, Khamadi climbing into the passenger seat. Shani took up her position with Simba, Nicolas and Chidi in the back. Her eyes adjusted to the dim light, the windows virtual slits. Monique handed over her gun to her. Shani kept her fingers well away from the trigger. Her hands touched wetness wherever she put them. She quickly wiped the blood onto her jeans. In a sense, her idea had killed five men. Husbands, perhaps, and fathers of young children. But there was no time to analyse, to reflect. *Us, or them*. That had now become her guiding principle. There could be no leeway. Little room for compassion.

'…Okay, Monique,' Khamadi was saying, 'go, go!'

Shani held Nicolas's hand, reassured by the gentle

squeeze he gave her. It was true, she would never disregard his feelings again. If she did, then really she didn't deserve him, reminded as they bobbed about in the jeep of their journey in the red van with Monique in Fulham. It had been somewhere around that moment when her affections for Nicolas had truly kicked in. When this was over, she wanted them to go away to a quiet corner of the world to recover. Turquoise. She desperately needed 'turquoise'. Turquoise sky, turquoise sea. She recalled her turquoise mug sitting on her desk in her study back at St Aquinas. How was she going to readjust...? Perhaps she didn't have to. Or was the truth of the matter she didn't *want* to? Séroulé's orphans. A practical, soul-nourishing challenge, surely?

She realised Nicolas had released her hand to familiarise himself with the Olympus camera. Khamadi was on his phone, this time using its speaker so presumably everyone could share the call.

'Osakwe, what news in Thekari?' Khamadi asked.

'There's been some shooting on the people,' hollered Osakwe. 'But there's mounting gridlock, which is working in our favour. The really good news is that defections from the military are steadily growing.'

'Keep your courage, Osakwe.' Khamadi cut the

call and made another. 'Kofi, what is your situation?'

'We have the power station behind State TV in our control,' crackled the reply. 'We've put a Redeye launcher on the rooftop should they bring in paratroopers.'

'Get back to me if the situation deteriorates.'

Quite suddenly, pieces of paper began to flutter down like tickertape from the sky, chased after by pedestrians.

'What's going on?' Shani asked.

'Flyers, informing people of the coup,' said Khamadi, 'and hopefully to get others onto the streets. With the head taken off the snake, this is now the most critical phase. Flyers have already come down in Thekari, and I imagine Douinesse.'

Shani kept a tight grip on the handgun Monique had given her, trying to be optimistic. Clever idea, but the odds had to be overwhelmingly against them. What chance did they have against a fully equipped, Western-backed army? She looked at the gun in her right hand, and in the gloom saw the name Steyr on it. Monique... Monique intrigued her. Intelligent – fluent in English. Confident. Her own person. Capable of being both fierce and gentle to the extreme. Physically attractive. Though not quite having the build of an Amazonian, a warrior all the same, and a perfect match for Khamadi

– who, Shani noticed, had in his hand a slip of paper. From it, he dialled a number into his phone, again activating the speaker to share the call.

'I take it this is you, Soglo?' came a gruff voice.

'Indeed,' said Khamadi. 'General Nzeogwu, there's an easy way, and a hard way.'

'The easy way being to get your men out of the country before we string them up.'

'That's not going to happen, General. Already there are defections in Thekari. No doubt you are aware of this—'

'This is nonsense, Soglo. You have been seriously misinformed—'

'I'm keen for this to be as bloodless as possible,' said Khamadi, 'but we will go all the way if need be. And you will be the first to be tried, unless the people themselves get hold of you. Who knows what may happen to you?'

From the window slit opposite her, Shani caught a glimpse of a group of young women throwing up their hands and dancing, while curious drivers took flyers from passers-by, then blasted their horns with approval.

'Liberty beckons, General,' continued Khamadi, turning from the group of girls. 'It was an abscess waiting to burst. You know it yourself. For five years there's been no wage increase for the military. As Kuetey became more paranoid, so he gave more to Ousmane Sekibo.'

'Soglo, I'm telling you—'

'So here's the deal,' stated Khamadi. 'Get your troops back into their barracks, and we'll protect you across the border so you can be united with the millions of francs you have amassed and taken out of Séroulé.'

'Very nice speech, Soglo,' chuckled the general. 'Wholly inaccurate, naturally. That aside, it doesn't get you anywhere. I don't do deals.'

Monique answered her phone as the traffic slowed into a bottleneck. She glanced at Khamadi. 'Defections in Douinesse. It's been confirmed.'

'General,' said Khamadi, 'I've been informed that soldiers are defecting in Douinesse. It's over for you. Make your choice, call me back.'

As Khamadi hung up, a flyer flipped onto the windscreen.

A COUP IS NOW UNDERWAY
BE STRONG AND COURAGEOUS
IN HEART AND IN SPIRIT
— ARMÉE SÉROULÈSE DE LIBÉRATION
NATIONALE —

Shani leaned up to the slit in the armoured bulkhead. 'What do you think?' she asked Khamadi.

'He'll go for the deal and leave quietly.' He glanced over his shoulder. 'The quicker we get more defections, the quicker he'll be swayed.'

'They'll come,' said Nicolas, capturing a couple of street children with the Olympus as they jumped in unison to catch a flyer. 'Like you told him, an abscess waiting to burst. They're old men and out of touch, been living in a bubble for the last ten years.'

A small van sat at an angle ahead of them, stationary between lanes. Monique hit the accelerator and gave it a glancing blow, the jeep effortlessly thrusting it aside. As they passed, Shani saw that they'd torn the van's nearside wing off, exposing the entire front wheel.

'What about the air force, Khamadi?' she asked.

'No news as yet. But they will be surprised to discover we have portable surface-to-air missile launchers positioned at each of the three airbases.' Khamadi turned his head. 'How's Chidi doing?'

Shani looked past Simba. Chidi had his eyes closed. His face seemed rounder, and perhaps brighter, she thought. 'He's okay. He's not shivering so much. Just resting.'

Khamadi took another call. 'Yes?'

'Nafari, reporting in,' came a charged response over the speaker, the caller virtually yelling. 'We have heavy fighting at State TV, but our snipers are managing to contain it. The building hasn't been penetrated. Have you heard about the palace, Khamadi?'

'What about it?'

'We can see it from here. It's on fire.'

Shani looked at Nicolas. 'Has to be good news,' she said.

'A decision by the generals to get rid of incriminating evidence,' surmised Nicolas. 'They must be panicking.'

'Understood, Nafari,' said Khamadi. 'Remember, this critical phase has hours to run, and that's if we're lucky, so keep your head. No celebrating.'

Monique parked up outside a general store. Further down, the army had blockaded the street with trucks. Two of them were on fire, pumping columns of black smoke into an otherwise passive skyline.

Khamadi pointed to their right. 'That's where we're heading, the store itself. Keep low, and bring your weapons.'

Shani left the jeep. 'What about Chidi?' she asked.

'He's safer there for the time being,' Khamadi said.

Shani followed him over to the store. Inside, a

woman with closely cropped hair and crooked teeth stood behind the counter. A handgun lay casually in front of her on top of a pile of magazines.

'The twins?' Khamadi asked.

The woman glared at Khamadi and pointed over her shoulder with her thumb. 'One day you'll get me hung, Soglo – God be with me.' She picked up the gun. 'I'm out of here.'

'Use the jeep,' Khamadi told her. 'There's a guy in the back. Take care of him.'

Monique steered Shani into a walled yard with padlocked wooden gates. Simba dragged aside a sheet of corrugated steel to reveal a ladder leading down into a muddy hole. Monique descended, followed by Nicolas and Simba.

Shani put her foot on the ladder's first rung, then the second and third, before she heard a menacing hollow beat drawing closer. A helicopter? Khamadi's eyes seemed to be searching for it. A split second later and it was as if her organs had leapt from her body as a fearsome *whoosh* erupted across the street. She looked up, a surface-to-air missile hunting down its target, leaving a frenzied streak of vapour in its wake. The impact sheared the helicopter's rotor blades clean away from the fuselage, causing the latter to spiral violently until it crash-landed onto a high-rise building. Ignited fuel spilled out over the rooftop just as a cataract of flame shot skyward.

Khamadi grinned. 'Nice work boys,' he said aloud.

Shani looked up at him from the ladder. She was shaking so much that she had to put both hands on the top rung to steady herself. Nothing mattered now: her prosthesis and all that she'd managed to upset herself with in her life instantly irrelevant. This was war. And God, yes, it was *trauma*tizing – only infantile morons could possibly glamourize it. The constant din, the magnification of death itself...

Khamadi was talking to her. 'Come on, Shani, we have to move.'

'This tunnel actually takes us to the State TV building?' she asked.

'Under a side street and petrol station, first.'

Shani peered into the hole, and once down the ladder had to consciously force herself to follow Simba. Petrol station? She shuddered, which had little to do with the dampness of the tunnel. Petrol stations had underground tanks, and they were now in what amounted to a war zone. But then that particular fear was swept aside for another. In the beam of Simba's flashlight, she could see a series of wooden slats and makeshift props, from broom handles to steel pipes and what looked to be cast iron guttering. Could any of this really prevent the ceiling from collapsing? And would they be rescued if it actually happened?

Beyond Simba, Shani became aware of another light, which introduced her to a mud-caked enclave, where they had to huddle, but at least they could stand upright. Nicolas and Monique shuffled to one side, revealing two identical shiny faces wearing red bandannas. She presumed these to be 'the twins' Khamadi had mentioned back at the store.

'Hey, Soglo,' grinned the one on the left, 'our co-workers want to know how many goats you're giving us for the tunnel?'

'I'm saying twenty,' bolstered the other twin. Before he froze, as if struck by lightning. 'No…wait, my stars are saying twenty-*five*, I tell you!'

'Same rotten humour as your Mama,' Khamadi said. 'Now make the hole, and be quick about it.'

Shani tried to find a comfortable position for her prosthesis, the floor of the tunnel uneven and slippery. And now a *distinct* waft of petrol vapour – she was convinced, and wished Khamadi hadn't mentioned the filling station! She wondered if a tank at some stage had accidently received a glancing blow with a sharp implement. Or had litres of the stuff been syphoned off over the past months? That, she supposed – *prayed* – was the more likely scenario.

One of the twins came and picked up an iron bar beside her feet.

'Stand back,' he warned, and thumped the ceiling with it. After several blows, a slab of cement and a number of bricks hit the mud. The twin set about widening the hole. 'Get the ladder.'

His brother took the ladder from Khamadi, who had brought it with him from the entrance. A couple of gentler pokes with the iron bar and they had an opening wide enough to climb through. The twin who had done the prodding went up the ladder first with the flashlight, followed by his brother, and between them gathered all the rifles.

Shani climbed the ladder and found herself in what appeared to be an empty room, barely larger than her study at St Aquinas. She took Monique's gun from her waistband, noticing as the flashlight passed over her that her jeans and top were coated in grime. How were they going to come across on State TV? They looked like a bunch of gun-toting bank robbers.

One of the twins waved the flashlight at a door, the other taking aim with his Kalashnikov.

'Hey!' interrupted Khamadi. 'Calm down you two.'

'We're ready to roll, Soglo,' said the one gripping the Kalashnikov. 'My stars say so. I'm telling you.'

'Just hold back, or you'll be seeing more than

stars.' Khamadi took his phone from his pocket.

Shani looked at Nicolas. On the other side of the door she could hear the distant sound of gunfire. Then someone shouted out what sounded like an instruction in French. She reached for his hand. 'What's being said out there?'

'Something about the roof,' said Nicolas. 'I didn't quite catch it.'

'Where do you think we are?' Shani asked.

'State TV basement, I imagine.'

Monique came up to them, and Shani noticed that she had a smear of mud across the opposite cheek to the one that had the 'tribal' scar. The two seemed to go together, she realised, and for a split second she envisaged Monique prowling down a catwalk, with stunned onlookers muttering comments such as 'wholly aboriginal'.

'We're waiting for a report,' said Monique. 'Should the building be in the hands of the military, we're going to have to wait for reinforcements to clear them out.'

Shani brought Nicolas's hand to her grazed cheek. He put his arm around her, kissed her hair and brought her to his chest. Her eyes began to ache, a dam of tears steadily building. *Think* turquoise, she told herself. A 'turquoise' holiday with Nicolas. She leaned further into him, hearing Khamadi on his phone over in the far corner of the room.

CHAPTER 26

Khamadi managed to catch a signal on his phone by standing alongside an air vent, away from the group. He called back the number on the screen.

'Rufaro, I've been out of range. Are you still with us?'

'Why shouldn't I be?' countered Rufaro Touré, Deputy Commissioner for Séroulé's State Police. 'Why would you ask such a question?'

'We cannot express enough our gratitude,' said Khamadi.

'The Commissioner's sitting in his office, but he doesn't look at all well. In fact, it looks like he's taken his own life. Nothing to do with me, you understand. There's a gun on the floor beside him, would you believe… I'm a patriot. You know that don't you, Soglo? I've never lined my own pockets.'

'I know you haven't, Rufaro.'

'And now we have this opportunity. Right?'

'Right.' Khamadi felt his heartbeat resonate, Rufaro being a crucial ally. 'What news, *mon ami*?'

'Heavy defections in Douinesse, in case you didn't already know. I've told the chief of police not to have his men fire live ammunition on the people. He's still choosing his side, but as the defections grow he'll come into line. Looting has started in Thekari, mainly government buildings, and it'll happen here in Porto Sansudou soon, too.'

'If it goes seriously residential,' said Khamadi, 'or shopkeepers find themselves and their property under attack, then you will have to resort to live ammunition. Those who have defected from the army can offer assistance, under your command, as previously discussed.'

'Make the broadcast. No time to waste, Khamadi.'

'About twenty minutes. Stay with your good judgement and courage.'

Khamadi made another call, keeping one eye on the feisty twins and their Kalashnikovs. 'Nafari, we're ready to go. What conditions can we expect?'

'It's all yours, Khamadi, we can keep it open for you. No problem with that. Osakwe wants you to know our boys have downed three Rafale fighters at Klenskou. No more take-offs from that airbase since then.'

'Tell Osakwe I'll call him before we go on air.' Khamadi slipped the phone into his pocket, but before joining the group turned his back to gather himself. This was it now, the final push. A boyhood dream shared with Osakwe. Years of planning, and of learning. There'd been mistakes on the way, but like many of those around him, he was not of military bearing, just a patriot like Rufaro, seeking liberation from a hideous regime. Every family had a story to tell of dire despair, torture, rape, and death. Despite protestations early on by governments in the 'free world', they soon shut up and turned a blind eye whenever humanitarian ethics endangered shareholders' profits. That, by itself, was about to change!

A hand suddenly clasped his arm. Khamadi swung round, expecting Monique but instead saw Shani. Huge brown eyes and high cheekbones, like her mother.

'You okay?' she asked.

'I'm fine,' he smiled. 'Are you?'

Shani shrugged. 'Weaving my way through bouts of neurosis.'

'Bouts of fear, I would say. And let me tell you, everyone in this room has experienced that today.'

'Including the twins?'

Khamadi winced for effect. 'You got me there. Just plain crazy.'

'They're getting twitchy.'

'Okay.' Khamadi reached for the rifle he'd leaned against the wall. 'Tell me one thing, Shani.'

'What's that?' she asked.

'Did you really feel Zinsa with you when you were inside the palace?'

'I like to think I did,' said Shani. 'I felt different. Stronger. Emboldened. Like I was harnessed to something. To an energy. I can't explain it beyond that.'

'You don't have to,' said Khamadi. 'Not to me. They're with us. All of them. Thank you.' Khamadi put his hand on Shani's shoulder and steered her towards the group. He, too, had felt inspired inside the presidential suite, and now that energy was back with him, but like Shani he couldn't define it beyond its ethereal allure.

'We need the third floor,' he explained, casting his eyes across the group. 'That's where we'll be transmitting from. The lifts are off-limits in case of a power failure, so we make for the stairs. Be prepared for teargas. We have masks inside the building on the first floor. If a canister comes in, throw it back out –

with caution. They can burn you.' His eyes came to rest on the twins. 'You two horrors, I want you supporting Nafari. But don't blow away any of his boys.'

'Now?' called one of them, his Kalashnikov aimed at the lock on the door. 'Tell me now, Soglo!'

'Keep the rifle at a steep angle,' ordered Khamadi. 'There might be people—'

A furore of percussion erupted around them, empty shell cases pinging onto the floor as the door steadily disintegrated. The other twin kicked the remnants away from the frame, before the pair of them disappeared up a row of concrete steps, their indecipherable high-pitched shrieks akin to battle cries.

Khamadi looked over his shoulder at the group. 'Have your wits about you,' he warned. Then, at Shani and Nicolas, as he led them out of the cellar: 'Both of you, keep close to me at all times.'

'You don't have to tell me!' said Shani.

They came up onto the ground floor. The austere reception desk was predictably deserted, the glass doors at the front of the building blown in by the torrent of gunfire raging in the street. They climbed the stairs and entered a lobby, meeting no personnel, only snipers at the shattered windows and a haze of cordite.

'Keep your heads down,' instructed Khamadi.

Second floor. Again, no personnel, and fewer snipers. Khamadi swore. He spoke to one of them, who shrugged. Had the technicians fled the building? There would be no broadcast without them! Nicolas might have some relevant knowledge, but could he set up live-streaming? Third floor... Not a soul. 'Look for them!' he shouted. 'Look for the personnel.'

Famas rifle poised, Khamadi ducked into an abandoned studio where banks of lights, screens, and a portable camera were directed at a couple of easy chairs, separated by a vase of orange dahlias on a bamboo side-table. In the far corner, to the left of the surreal display, another door. Khamadi glanced at Shani and Nicolas, Monique and Simba elsewhere – evidently checking other rooms.

Cover me, he mouthed.

Silently gripping the handle, Khamadi whipped open the door and poked the Famas inside. An abrupt scream, followed by whimpering. He put his head past the doorway, and discovered a group of men and women cowering on a set of metal steps leading up onto the roof.

'We're the good guys,' shouted Khamadi, his senses floating with relief to the point of inebriation. 'I'm telling you. Now get out into the studio so we can make the broadcast.'

At a nearby window, a civilian helicopter was chopping through the grey sky, until it began to hover above a white rectangular building. Khamadi watched it closely just as Nicolas moved Shani into the centre of the studio. 'Wise decision,' he said. 'Stay well away from all the windows.'

'What's that building?' Nicolas asked.

'The one on which the chopper's landing? State Security,' Khamadi answered. 'You can bet your life that egg-beater will be for Ousmane Sekibo. Despite being the idiot he is, he has much to answer for. I don't want him skipping the country.'

'Can you get me a pilot who can fly that?' asked Nicolas.

'Why?' Khamadi was looking around at the nervous personnel, still clustered together but now inside the studio. 'Come on, you lot. I want a proper table, two chairs and a mike.' He came back to Nicolas.

'After the broadcast,' Nicolas told him, 'I want Shani out of here. We've been pushing our luck all day.'

Khamadi studied him, then Shani. After he'd put her on air, she was no longer key material and he was happy to see her safely leave the city. Unlike Nicolas, whose journalistic reporting when it came to Séroulé was guaranteed to be both emotive and cultured. But he'd already guessed what was coming. 'Kabérou?' he asked.

'Yes,' said Nicolas. 'For sure, I'm wrestling with my instincts to stay. To be right on the inside like this.' He glanced at Shani. 'But after what she did for me in Paris, and the future I see for us…?' He shook his head. 'My conscience will burn for eternity if something happens to her.'

'Nicolas,' called Monique. 'We need your help. The lens seems to be jammed on the camera. We can't change it.'

'Go and help them,' said Khamadi. 'We're losing time.'

'I'm with Nicolas,' said Shani. 'Let us go after I've done my piece. I can't take much more. My nerves are stripped bare. I'm on empty.'

Khamadi watched Nicolas huddle with Monique and several others around the portable camera. There was likely to be a reporter, or someone willing to double-up as one, amongst them. 'Nicolas wants to get you up to Kabérou,' he said. 'You'll need that 'copter about to land on that building. Simba can fly those things. That's why he's with us, in case we needed his skills. You can take him with you. But you'll have to deal with it while I get things sorted over there.'

'"Deal with it"?' asked Shani.

'Go up onto the roof and get one of the snipers to take out the pilot.'

'You mean have…have him *kill* the pilot?' asked Shani, her hand moving onto her chest.

'Yes. Stay away from the edge. The surrounding buildings are not as tall, so any crossfire from them shouldn't be an issue so far as you're concerned. In fact, you're probably safer up there than down here.'

'But the pilot might be an innocent person, Khamadi.'

'Doubtful. Sure, it's a civilian craft. Sekibo's not going to use anything from the army. The pilot will likely be someone he knows. Someone just as corrupt.'

CHAPTER 27

Shani hesitated on the metal steps while hearing sporadic smacks from the snipers' rifles above her. By her reckoning, there was a chance that the civilian helicopter had been seized along with its pilot. So Khamadi shouldn't have asked her to deliver what amounted to a death sentence on an innocent human being. But what if she told the sniper to 'injure' the pilot?

With that option in mind, Shani opened the hatch and crawled out onto a flat roof. From her vantage point, she could see around a dozen snipers fanned out. The ballistic exchange between the ground and the rooftop stretched her nerve fibres to the point of nausea. Pockets of acrid smoke drifted past her, making her eyes sting while her hands burned from the heat on the roof itself. This really was a bad, bad idea. She should have refused outright.

The sniper she was edging towards suddenly looked over his shoulder as he lay on his chest. A bearded man, perhaps in his mid-forties, she thought. His frown betrayed his surprise that a woman had presumably come to join them. Shani held up a hand to hold his attention. Then when she reached him: 'You speak English?' she asked.

'English?' He shrugged. 'Hello. Yes. No. Goodbye.' His grin resembled a broken zip, the teeth that remained heavily stained and in need of being straightened.

Shani pointed. 'White building...*blanc* building. Helicopter. Khamadi Soglo wants it to stay. Injure pilot. *Tu as comprende?*'

'*Oui.*' The sniper thumped his shoulder. 'Boom!'

'Injure,' repeated Shani, having doubts over whether he had actually understood her. 'You injure him. *Oui?*'

'*Oui, oui.*'

'Don't hit the controls. *Comprende?*'

'"Control"?'

'Don't hit.'

The bad feeling returned as Shani watched the sniper squint ahead, taking in the distance – roughly that of a kilometre, she imagined. Then he turned to a rebel close by.

'Dawda,' he called. He made a rolling gesture with his hand and without a word spoken weapons were exchanged.

Shani noticed that the swapped weapon was longer and had the name "Barrett" on it.

The sniper gave her another zipless grin. 'Algiers,' he said.

'What?...' Shani found she had to shout. '*Quoi?*'

'Algiers.' He pointed. 'Boom! Algiers.'

'*Je non comprende.*' And to herself: *God's sake, what am I doing up here?*

The sniper shrugged and busied himself with the Barrett, setting down its spiked bipod. Lying on his chest, he crooked his right knee. 'Algiers,' he muttered. 'Boom!' Raising his head, he adjusted the front ring on the telescopic sight, then followed through with a series of finer corrections. Calmly taking his index finger away from the grip, he gave the trigger a tender squeeze, the resulting percussion smacking the ether as the shell casing spilled out onto the asphalt roof.

The sniper rolled onto his side, something of a glint in his eye. 'Bengo.'

'*Quoi?*' asked Shani, now with equal amounts of frustration and trepidation. She couldn't imagine what state the pilot was in, or whether he was even alive.

'Bengo. Er…binjo.'

'Bingo?'

'*Ahhh, oui.* Bingo!'

'*Merci beaucoup*,' said Shani, seeing Nicolas climb out of the hatch. '*Vive la Séroulé*,' she told the sniper and scrabbled away from him.

'Shani, Christ's sake what are you doing?' called Nicolas.

Shani reached him and stood up, blowing on her hands to try and cool them. 'Khamadi wanted the pilot taken out on the helicopter so we could use it,' she said, seeing the concern on his face – the scar on his jaw, she'd noticed, always seemed more profound when he was edgy. 'Simba's a pilot, apparently.'

'Khamadi shouldn't have sent you up here.'

'I asked the sniper to injure the pilot, but I'm not sure if he understood me. He kept going on about Algiers.'

Nicolas held open the hatch for her. 'Snipers' talk.'

'What?'

'Doesn't matter.'

'Yes it does,' insisted Shani. 'What did he mean?'

'At a guess, he was sending his brains to Algiers.'

'So the pilot's dead?'

'Probably. It's not your fault.' They started down the stairs. 'Wait 'till I see Khamadi—'

A ferocious detonation interrupted them and Shani seized the handrail as the blast vibrated through the building, from the foundations upwards, or so it felt to her. 'That must have been close!' she said before they emerged into the studio. It crossed her mind that out of desperation the military might be prepared to drop a bomb directly on the station.

Khamadi walked leisurely over to them, as if nothing had happened. 'We're almost ready. Did you speak to one of the snipers?' he asked Shani.

'Yes—'

'Khamadi,' interrupted Nicolas. 'Don't do that again. Shani stays with us at all times.'

'I didn't want Sekibo skipping the country. You were busy fixing the camera.' Khamadi patted Nicolas's shoulder as if to pacify him. 'Accepted. Don't worry.'

'Khamadi, you remember our meeting at the safe house in London?' asked Shani.

'Of course.' A furrow showed itself between Khamadi's eyebrows. 'What of it?'

'This is when you tell me.'

'Tell you what?'

'How you're going to reduce the debt. I want to know.'

Khamadi nodded. 'Very quickly, okay? We're

virtually ready… You still have mud and Monique's blood on you.' He looked over his shoulder. 'Monique,' he called, 'clean Shani's face. She can't be filmed like this.'

'Khamadi, tell me,' demanded Shani. 'I'm not going on air until you do.'

'It's quite simple, really,' said Khamadi. 'We're wiping the debt.'

'What do you mean?'

'We're not paying a cent.'

Shani felt blood rush from her face in disbelief, leaving her momentarily lightheaded. The man had completely lost it — shell-shocked, or whatever. 'You've got to pay it,' she told him. 'It amounts to a declaration of war. They'll annihilate this country.'

Khamadi lifted a finger. 'Listen to what you have just said. "A declaration of war. *They'll* annihilate this country." What are we looking at here? A world of chaos, but take a closer look. I would say *manufactured* chaos. Crystallised policy. Why? What comes out of such chaos? Answer me that?'

'Lawlessness, absolute,' said Shani. 'Nothing other than that.'

'Incorrect. Totalitarianism, because I used the adjective "manufactured". A new world order. And at the centre of a new world order? A world government, obviously. You said as much to Kuetey. But before a world government can openly be declared, what has to happen first? Think about it.'

'I can't think,' said Shani. The clamour outside seemed to be intensifying. 'I'm scared. Scared of what you're telling me, and scared of what's happening beyond that window!'

'The dilution and abolition of nationhood,' said Khamadi. 'Primarily through enforced migration and by stimulating social division. Ultimately, the human condition will choose enslavement in return for a moderated disengagement from fear and disorder. As for Séroulé's debt, that in itself is nothing but a consequence of pure chicanery. When it comes to theft and deception, Kuetey was an amateur in comparison.'

Shani let Monique wipe her face, the damp tissues mildly refreshing. She saw a thread of logic running through Khamadi's discourse – but it was dangerous. 'What about Séroulé's neighbours?'

'We have some on board. Three countries for sure. We aim to isolate and shield West Africa from the ensuing trauma. In effect, become self-reliant. Don't be fooled by the word "united". Depraved people use this word too. They will use it to sell you an immaculate dream. In reality? Wholesale misery and fear.'

'What do you think, Shani?' asked Monique. Then the same question to Nicolas.

'I had a rough idea something like this was going to happen,' said Nicolas.

'You did?' asked Shani, before she remembered him touching on it in Gordon Square. 'So you did.' She nodded slowly, taking it all in. 'I'm concerned for the people, to put it mildly.'

'I know,' agreed Khamadi. 'But the world is suffering badly, and somewhere, somehow, a cohesive stand has to be made. This is what your grandfather, Tuma Dangbo, taught us.' One of the technicians called for Khamadi to join them. He looked at Shani. 'You have a couple of minutes left to make your decision.'

Shani felt Khamadi's brown eyes drive into the depths of being. His stare was not in any way aggressive. Quite the opposite. Like the woman at the safe house, he was pleading with her. She spoke to Monique the moment he turned his back. 'How long have you known Khamadi?'

'Six years,' said Monique.

'Then I want the truth from you, Monique. Has he ever lied or tried to deceive you?'

Monique shook her head. 'No. Not that I'm aware of, truthfully.'

'And you, Nicolas?'

'Not at all.' Nicolas glanced at Monique. 'I need a moment with her.' He steered Shani into a corner. 'It's doubtful this can happen again,' he said, 'because the right people won't be in the right place. We have some of Tuma's people with us, people he trusted, handpicked by him. They have carried and refined his vision for over thirty years. It's going to go ahead, with or without you. But hey, Shani, you are going to kick yourself if you don't sit down in front of that camera. The people need to see you, hear you.'

Shani sensed her impulsive nature about to kick in, which she unquestionably didn't want to happen. The decision had to be arrived at logically, organically, but the frenzied environment was hardly conducive.

The world is suffering badly, and somewhere, somehow, a cohesive stand has to be made.

That was the sentence which did it for her. No matter from what angle she looked at it, it was undeniably true.

'If this misfires,' she said aloud, 'then I want to live in a quiet corner of the world where I don't get to read newspapers or listen to the news. How will that affect you?'

'Have you considered how many chickens we might start with?' replied Nicolas candidly.

Shani readily leaned up to him and kissed his jaw,

his unshaven face pricking her lips. 'Thank you,' she said. 'The perfect answer. Perhaps one day we might even choose such a lifestyle.'

* * *

Khamadi left Shani to go over her speech with Nicolas, imagining she wanted to make amendments after what he'd just explained to her.

While Monique cleaned his face, he called Osakwe. 'We're inside State TV. A couple of minutes from the broadcast. What news in Thekari?'

'Bedlam,' Osakwe shouted, his voice virtually obscured by the reverberating discharge of weaponry coupled to vociferous outbursts. 'But in a positive way. We can do this, Khamadi. So many defections that the army is in a state of flux. Looting is going to be our Achilles heel if we're not careful, at least in Thekari. Cardinal Zinsou has agreed to throw open the cathedral if refuge is needed. Likewise, Imam Jangana with the central mosque.'

'And the air force?' asked Khamadi. 'Nafari mentioned we've downed three Rafales.'

'Two more since then, at the Nandiro Airbase. That's all I've heard. No actual airstrikes on the infrastructure to my knowledge. Did you manage to contact General Nzeogwu?'

'About an hour ago. My guess is he'll go quietly

across the border. We'll deal with him another time.' Khamadi looked around himself. Shani was now sitting at the table, a microphone to the right of her. 'Need to go, Osakwe. We're ready to roll here.'

Shani pointed past him.

'Nicolas,' she said, 'can you ask the girl behind you if I can use her baseball cap? My hair's a total disaster.'

Khamadi sat down next to Shani and saw the State TV controller make a bee line towards them, like he was keen to get things moving.

'I'll count you down—'

'My apologies,' said Khamadi, 'your first name escapes me.'

'Pascal.'

'Okay. Pascal, have you looked at any of the social networking sites in the last hour?'

'No.'

'Then have someone from your team do so. You should find pictures of Kuetey. Gruesome, perhaps – but momentous.'

'*Mon Dieu*,' breathed the controller, pushing his spectacles up the bridge of his nose with his middle finger. 'You did it yourself?'

Khamadi responded with an instruction. 'You can bring the pictures of Kuetey up while I'm talking. But not when Shani talks. That's very important.'

Pascal nodded, started to walk away, before turning sharply on his heel. 'If this coup backfires,' he warned Khamadi, 'my colleagues and I will be strung up. That's the pleasantest outcome we can expect.'

'Don't worry—'

'There's no need for the majority of them to be here,' argued Pascal. 'We have an open channel. It'll be a straight live feed. You only require me, a sound technician, cameraman, and another technician to upload the pictures.'

'Where do you want the others to go?' asked Khamadi.

'Back on the steps, leading to the roof. At least they'll have some protection from the snipers should the military storm the building.'

Khamadi nodded. 'Okay. Now get that camera rolling.'

Shani adjusted the green baseball cap. 'How do I look?' she asked.

Khamadi glanced at Nicolas, standing nearby. 'What shall we tell her, Nicolas?' he asked, seeing a need for a dash of mirth. 'The truth?'

'I'm going for cute,' participated Nicolas. 'She's still armed.'

'A wise decision,' said Shani, straightening the

handwritten sheet of paper in front of her. 'I'm ready. Let's go for it.'

Khamadi quickly left his seat, and keeping himself at a slender angle peered down onto the street. The trucks were still burning, and despite the raging crescendo and the occasional figure breaking cover, he sensed his men were keeping the military at bay. But no sooner had he processed that observation than another hefty detonation caused a small window to explode across the studio. Everyone ducked, some even throwing themselves to the floor.

'Pascal, do you have another soundproof studio?' asked Khamadi.

'Not anymore,' said the controller, cautiously drawing himself up onto his knees. 'This was the last one.'

Khamadi returned to his chair, seeing the concern. The exception was Nicolas, briskly pointing the Olympus at Pascal – fiddling again with his spectacles.

Monique called over to Khamadi. 'Another two Rafales down,' she said. 'Seven planes in total.'

Khamadi nodded and glanced at Pascal. 'Let's do it.'

Pascal stood alongside the cameraman, put his spectacles back on and raised four fingers in front of Khamadi, folding them one by one before making a theatrical 'zero' with his thumb and index finger.

Khamadi brought the microphone closer, and focussed on the Ikegami camera, positioned on a tripod a couple of metres from the table. He took a slow, reflective breath to calm himself, seeing himself reunited with his wife, Jasira, exiled in Benin. It had been over eight months since they'd last set eyes on each other. And even longer when he'd last spoken to his children… He quietly exhaled.

'Khamadi Soglo,' he announced, '*Armée Séroulèse de Libération Nationale.*' Raising his voice further to carry it over the mêlée beyond the building's scarred walls: 'To the Associated Press in New York, *L'Agence France-Presse* in Paris, Reuters in London, and all relevant wires, we wish to inform you that a coup d'état is now underway in the People's Democratic Republic of Séroulé, West Africa. We would like to stress immediately that this is purely a matter of internal concern, and that we are not seeking outside assistance. We are presently putting into place a blanket no-fly zone over the country. We ask that all commercial flights be rerouted to a neighbouring country, forthwith. It should be noted by forces still loyal to the former regime that we have Redeye and Stinger missile launchers on rooftops in Porto Sansudou, Thekari, and Douinesse, in addition to other cities.

'I can now confirm to you that General Odion Kuetey received a fatal head injury approximately two hours ago. I can also confirm, contrary to what General Nzeogwu believes, that defections from the military have been growing steadily. Our message to the generals is clear-cut. If captured, you will be sent for trial, and dealt with according to International Law, which we as a country will respect and adhere to, apart from those elements that restrict the application of sound judgement.

'However, when it comes to the economic system, with all its brutal coercive energies, we have drawn the conclusion that it serves no purpose for our future. By this I mean that we will no longer engage in dialogue with those creditors whose artifice inflated Séroulé's external debt to its present figure of twenty-three billion dollars. This debt will be printed and used solely for environmental investment, that is to say the reparation of damage done by multinational companies, and the installation of crucial safeguards thereafter. From this we realise that we will need to staunchly protect our borders, for history alone informs us that when a country has a disagreement with internationalists of a certain kind, they will try all manner of means to undermine that country. In our particular case, apart from distortions appearing in the world's Press and the global community being guided towards imposing sanctions, the attempt at destabilisation will likely come from weapons being fed into the hands of those conditioned to dispense terror. The wellbeing of our citizens and the natural world is sacrosanct, and any ideology or system – financial or otherwise – that challenges this will be exposed as such and rigorously contested. Our banks will no longer create money out of thin air. They will merely receive finance from modest administrative charges, and nothing more than that.

'For the multinationals, we welcome your technical expertise, but we do not welcome the pollution and corruption that you bring with it. Any corporation seen to destabilize this country, or treat our citizens without the respect they deserve, will be told to leave our borders at once. On these matters, you may find similar statements issued over the coming days by neighbouring West African countries.

'For the Séroulèse people, who have suffered so appallingly as a consequence of a dereliction of duty by the international community, I have this to say: those intellectuals who were forced into exile after the assassination of Tuma Dangbo are set to return to Porto Sansudou. A caretaker government, headed by

Jacques Baudin, will be installed within twenty-four hours. In the meantime, it should be noted that looters will not be treated with compassion. We do not want to call for martial law, imposed by the state police, but if necessary to protect the majority then we will do so. I need also to inform you that all banks and ATM cash machines will close forthwith to avoid a run on the banks. They will reopen tomorrow, deposit holders limited to a maximum withdrawal of twenty thousand CFA francs, each day – over a period of six working days, when the situation will be reviewed.'

Khamadi reached for the microphone as the crackle of gunfire and occasional detonation persisted. 'On my left, here, I have a very special person, who many of you have heard rumours about over the years. Without further delay, I will let her introduce herself to you.' He moved the microphone across the table.

'A few words, if you will, Shani.'

* * *

Shani sat up straight. She couldn't help but wonder whether the transmission would be picked up by networks such as the BBC, and that it might even be seen by Fellows at St Thomas Aquinas College. Would they be taken aback? Probably. But then here, in Séroulé, where it ultimately mattered, wasn't she amongst friends? Amongst her people? The land where Zinsa was born?

She gazed down at her speech, and the photograph of her mother in the top left-hand corner. This was for her, more than anyone. That if dearest Zinsa were alive today, she could be proud of her daughter.

Shani drew the microphone closer, and started by apologising for her poor French.

'...But I promise you, I will attend lessons at the earliest opportunity,' she added. 'I will keep this as brief as possible, for there will be plenty of time for talking over the coming days. For now, I want to say only this: Little more than a month ago my adoptive grandfather died, the same man who raised my mother, Zinsa Dangbo, in Romania. I knew none of this, that is to say that Zinsa grew up in Romania. But as he lay dying, he mentioned Séroulé. From that moment, I set out on a journey to find my true identity. During my first meeting with Khamadi, in London, he said to me: *When you leave here, if nothing else, think of the countless orphans whose parents Kuetey has either tortured or let die through disease and starvation.*

'I'm ashamed to say, until that meeting I had little knowledge of your suffering. What I do know is that life is a gift, and that there are people in the highest of places who may appear caring and respectable on the outside, but who on the inside see it as their given right to abuse that gift for their own miserable ends. And as they do so, so they abuse the natural world which, not to put too fine a point on it, carries our life support system – surely, the most wondrous of all systems.

'So I put it to you, let this day be the most momentous of our lives, and for the future of this valiant nation, the People's Democratic Republic of Séroulé.'

Shani sat back, leaving Khamadi to take the microphone.

'State TV will bring you further updates, as and when,' he said, looking into the camera. 'For all our sakes, I ask you to consider the dawn ahead to be one whereby we can shake our neighbour's hand in reconciliation. Our enemy, though to all intents and purposes invisible since it operates for the most part behind a moral shield, is nevertheless a common foe, whatever our faith or intrinsic worth might be. In this, they are quite alone and separate from all of us.'

Shani watched Khamadi stand before turning to her. 'Nice words. Thank you.' To Pascal, he said: 'You can take over from here. Put that on a loop, interspersed with updates.'

Shani left her chair just as Nicolas lowered the Olympus camera and came over to the table.

'Khamadi, I want Shani out of here. No waiting around.'

'You'd better use the tunnel,' said Khamadi.

Shani held out her arms to Khamadi. 'A hug, for good luck.' She embraced him, the din outside just as menacing as a whitish swirl of smoke drifted through the shattered window at the back of the studio. '"With all its brutal coercive energies",' she said aloud. 'A splendid line for my thesis, if I ever get to complete it.'

'You must,' Khamadi told her. 'I fancy a provocative read.'

Shani smiled and let her arms fall to her sides. Turning to Monique, she said: 'I want to meet your lover, when all is done. *Insha'Allah.*'

'*Insha'Allah*,' echoed Monique, kissing both Shani's cheeks. 'I'll be thinking of you.'

'And I of you,' said Shani. She turned from them both, reaching for Nicolas's hand before following Simba out of the ruined studio.

CHAPTER 28

The State Security building already had several looters hard at work by the time they arrived. Shani wondered if this had been allowed to happen, since they'd witnessed no looting of shops on their way from the grocery store. Admittedly, the shops they'd passed had their shutters firmly closed. But if people had wanted to, she imagined they could have torn them down. The streets themselves were in virtual gridlock with vehicles strewn both on and off the pavements, which had obviously impeded the army. Aware she was uneducated in such matters, to Shani the strategy behind the coup nevertheless appeared rudimentary at times and perhaps, she speculated, this was the key to its apparent success – that the elementary aspect and the rebels' sheer audacity had out-foxed the generals.

She climbed a marble staircase behind Simba. A

bare-footed girl, barely the height of her waist, scampered past them clutching a gold carriage clock.

'Lucky find,' said Nicolas, as others struggled with office chairs and electrical equipment from oscillating fans to PC's and flat screens.

They came into a broad, deserted corridor, Simba looking keenly around himself. 'There has to be a door that will take us out onto the roof,' he said.

'Perhaps the one at the end,' suggested Shani.

The door in question had a mortise lock. Simba pulled a snub-nosed handgun from his pocket and fired it twice, the staccato shots ear-splitting in the confines of the corridor. He kicked the shattered door open to reveal a row of metal steps, not dissimilar to those that had led out onto the rooftop at the State TV building. Simba glanced over his shoulder. 'Keep your weapons drawn,' he warned, 'just in case.'

Her ears still stinging from the pistol shots, Shani sprinted after Nicolas up the steps. As she came onto the rooftop, she was astonished by all the hi-tech clutter, from telecommunication masts and satellite dishes to other weirdly-shaped installations that she guessed had something to do with the exchange and flow of information. She imagined it was one of these devices that had received her personal details when she handed over her passport at the London embassy while applying for her visa.

The helipad itself was over on their far left. Shani moved towards it, holding her breath when seeing the starred hole on the partially transparent cockpit. Simba opened the door and fiddled with the harness, blocking her view. Then when he did stand back, her worst fears were realised as the body slithered out onto the roof, part of its head blown completely away. It didn't seem possible that a single bullet could generate such a horrific sight, exposing shards of bone even and teeth stuck to hanging tissue. Shani took her hand from her chest, and noted the combat trousers. A flake of justification?

'Do you think he was with the military?' she asked.

Nicolas had his head down, gripping the blood-soaked shoulders as he heaved the body to one side with Simba. 'At a guess,' he panted. 'Not your fault,' he reiterated. He looked up, his face changing as his eyes grew wider.

Shani noticed. 'What—?'

A hand came from behind her and seized her throat, simultaneously yanking her backwards, away from them. In the same instant Monique's pistol discharged itself while being torn from her grasp, the strident report making her jump. Her instinct was to scream, but the grip on her windpipe was literally crushing the life out of her.

And then a terse command.

'Drop all weapons, or she gets taken out.'

Nicolas lurched forward.

'Drop it!' shouted the voice directly behind her.

Shani fought to get air into her lungs, a mere hint of it on each panicky draw. It hardly registered with her that Nicolas had let go of his gun, her fingers clawing at the plump hand on her throat. She saw her captor's gun swing towards Simba.

'And you, the same.'

'Give up, Sekibo,' Simba advised, dropping his weapon. 'It's over for you. Kuetey is long dead—'

'It's not over for me. There's enough fuel in that to get me to Niger. You the pilot?'

'Yes.'

'Get in and start it up.'

'We take off now,' said Simba, 'and there's every chance we'll be blown out of the sky. We have Redeye and Stinger launchers on rooftops around the city. We're in a no-fly zone. We have to wait for the all-clear.'

Shani sensed the man hesitate, to the point of relaxing his grip. She gulped air down into her lungs. Euphoria, that's what it felt like. Like the time when she left the *Bureau de Change* in Paris. She couldn't turn to look at the man. Was he short, or tall? He was strong, for sure. What if she slammed the heel of her shoe down his shinbone, giving them a chance to overpower him…? His breathing, she realised, had become shallow and anxious. But then:

'I'll take the risk. This is a commercial craft. Follow the river out of the city and maintain a high altitude.'

Nicolas withdrew and edged closer to Simba. Shani thought she detected his lips move a fraction. Did he have a plan? Three against one. They had to do *some*thing. But the awful truth was she couldn't visualize an option. Their abductor had a gun. Simba being the pilot had some value, for the time being. Kuetey was dead. She, like Nicolas, was of no importance to this man whatsoever. So how long was he going to keep them alive for?

* * *

The man known to Shani as Ousmane Sekibo, Director General of the State Security Service, sat up against the helicopter's tail boom, facing them. As a consequence of the seating arrangement, with their backs up against the partial bulkhead that separated the cockpit, eye contact with Simba was now impossible – which suggested that Sekibo was anything but careless.

The engine thrust increased towards a frightful howl, causing an unnerving vibration throughout the fuselage as the rotor blades began to whirl furiously. Shani gripped the padded seat and wondered when the thing had been built. With what seemed to be Herculean effort, the helicopter lifted itself up into the sky, and as it did so she caught sight of the State TV building over on their left, the army trucks parked-up nearby now blackened skeletons. Could Khamadi and Monique see them? Content in the knowledge, perhaps, they'd made it to the State Security building – unaware of the nightmare the three of them were now locked into. She turned away.

Double jeopardy, Shani realised. A desperate man with a gun, and a very real chance of being annihilated by a surface-to-air missile. A wave of nausea came and went, leaving her with the wobbliest of stomachs. The three of them should have predicted Sekibo would likely be hanging around on the rooftop. Her fault. Simba had mentioned to be on the alert. While they were dealing with the body, she should have been looking around herself, keeping watch.

Drawn by a sense of macabre curiosity, Shani found herself gazing at their abductor's hands – the right gripping the pistol. She wondered whether those hands had tortured people, leaving behind orphans.

Such awful, pointless damage. Self-defence aside, she could never set out to deliberately hurt another human being. Hurt herself absolutely, because of her self-loathing borne out of her inability to accept her prosthesis. Although, being with Nicolas that tendency to invent ever more destructive psychological fantasies to punish herself with seemed to have receded.

No more nightmares.

She wanted to cry. Cry in utter despair, for life seemed to have been one long nightmare since Nicolas said those words to her at whatever Underground station it was. Hadn't they just visited Gordon Square? Noor Inayat Khan… What would she do in a situation such as this? And after Noor, Monique. The woman she had reviled like no other, but who she now felt inspired by so intrepidly had she acted the part of a triple agent.

It wasn't quite true, of course, about it having been 'one long nightmare'. There had been those twelve blissful days in Fourqueux. She had been allowed to touch – to taste, utopia. But had it all been a tease compiled by fate, her apparent arch-nemesis, in preparation for the grand finale?

Fate determines many things, no matter how we struggle.

She could *so* believe it!

Fearful of alarming their abductor, she turned her head slowly towards Nicolas, wanting to read his expression. As she did so, the JetRanger dipped and lurched violently to one side. Nicolas's right foot flew out, throwing off Sekibo's aim.

Defying the danger, Shani leapt from the seat with Nicolas and seized the hand clutching the gun. She bit fiercely into Sekibo's wrist. A shot rang out, hitting the door, which flicked open – and then, a calamity. The gun fell from Sekibo's hand, only to escape her lunge as it slid along the seat and out of the flapping door.

Blind him! Shani realised. She came into the fray to try and jab Sekibo's eyes with her fingers. He swiped her away, his hand smacking the side of her head. She staggered back, seeing the ground swirl below through the opened door before seizing the bulkhead behind Simba. Instead of fear, outrage kicked in. How *dare* this man threaten her future with Nicolas?

She frantically scanned the immediate area for an implement she could use for a weapon. A fire extinguisher, anything. But nothing! She scrabbled over the seats to the opposite side of the fuselage and grabbed Nicolas's shirttail. Sekibo was deliberately edging him closer to the damaged door, raining blows down on him in quick succession. Shani dived between them to get at Sekibo's face, hitting, scratching and punching him but with little effect, his left hand repeatedly swatting her away.

Climbing back onto the seats, Shani kicked Sekibo hard, her target now being his crotch. With one hand gripping the bulkhead, she bashed his face with the other when he came in close, followed by another kick on his thigh until he grabbed her ankle – or what should have been her ankle, by chance pressing the button on the side of her prosthesis. Sekibo shot her a look of surprise when it detached itself from the locking pin, which gave Nicolas time to plant two massive blows on his bloodied face. With his arms flaying wildly as his hands feverishly searched for something to grasp, Sekibo toppled as if in slow motion through the damaged door, his diminishing shriek blending into the JetRanger's banshee whine as it smoothly righted itself.

Nicolas fell back, his lip bleeding.

'We have to go down,' Shani yelled above the racket. 'He's taken my foot with him!'

Simba frowned over his shoulder. 'Foot?' he asked, the intensity of his bewilderment combined with the request itself bordering comedy.

'Prosthesis,' explained Shani.

'*Prothèse de pied,*' translated Nicolas, wiping his lip.

Simba nodded and banked over to starboard.

Shani sat next to Nicolas and lifted his left arm around her shoulders. 'I'm sorry. My fault – I know it!'

'What are you talking about?'

'I should have been keeping watch.'

'Don't start that.'

'Start what?'

'Beating yourself up,' said Nicolas. 'Anyway, I was right about your foot being clever.'

That made her smile. Shani kissed him, and carefully dabbed his lip with a used tissue from her pocket. 'Do you think it saved us?'

'I think he was getting the better of me,' said Nicolas, taking the tissue from her. 'So yes, I suppose I do.'

'Amazing.' Shani snuggled up to him. 'I'll never curse my prosthesis again,' she said while Simba brought down the helicopter. 'I hope it's not damaged. If it is, I'm going to have to make myself a crutch. Not for the first time.'

Nicolas left the seat. 'Hopefully, I can find it.'

The JetRanger threw up a cloud of dust as the craft came to rest in a field covered in small mounds of earth.

'What are they?' asked Shani.

'Yams. A bit like sweet potatoes.' Nicolas leapt from the helicopter and set out across the field.

'Can you see the body?' Shani asked Simba.

Simba pointed over to his right. 'About twenty metres away.'

Through the blanket of dust settling around them, Shani could vaguely make out a heap of what looked like clothing. 'Yes, I see him,' she said.

'I'll give Nicolas a hand,' said Simba.

'Thanks.' Shani sat on the metal floor, her legs dangling from the fuselage. She watched as Simba veered towards the body and take a close look at it, presumably to make certain Sekibo actually was dead, though it seemed impossible that anyone could have survived a fall from such a height.

She turned her gaze to Nicolas. She'd never truly believed her maternal instincts would play a part in her life, but now – because of this man – she could actually picture herself planting sunflower seeds with her *own* children, as alluded to by Nicolas in Fourqueux.

Just as her eyes started to well up with emotion, Nicolas called over to her and held her foot aloft.

'Well done,' she said, relieved she wasn't going to have to rely on a crutch after all. Such a restriction would be a sheer bore. There was so much to see.

'Do you think it survived?' he asked, walking with

Simba towards her. He blew some dust off her prosthesis. 'Looks okay to me. See if it still works.'

Shani tried the locking mechanism, which did seem to work, and then stepped away from the helicopter. With her hand on Nicolas's arm, she leant her full weight onto the prosthesis. 'Feels good… I'm ready to go. How far are we from Kabérou?'

'About three-hundred kilometres,' answered Simba, building the JetRanger's thrust back up. 'In this, an hour and a half, easy.'

* * *

The helicopter chopped through the Tisounga region, northern Séroulé. Exhausted as she was, Shani couldn't sit back and close her eyes, for beneath her the magic of Africa was opening up. She wanted to embrace it all and draw it into her heart. She'd already witnessed a herd of gazelles throwing up a trail of dust as they crossed the savannah. And the sunset was still to come. She'd heard from a friend that African sunsets were the best in the world.

Nicolas pointed. 'We're coming to the ruins now. Way in the distance over there you can just make out the town of Kabérou.'

The helicopter's thrust dropped away, and Shani caught sight of the remains of her grandfather's retreat, covered in pale grass, like it had been scorched by the sun. She could imagine her mother running around as a child, having the time of her life, and perhaps playing tricks on her brothers and sisters – until the day Kuetey sprung his murderous spree and changed her life forever.

Simba landed the craft to the left of a sizable mound of earth. It seemed odd to Shani that there should be a mound there at all, the land being so flat. A consequence, she assumed, of soil excavated prior to the retreat's construction.

Simba squinted at his passengers through the bulkhead. 'We have about two-hundred kilometres left in the tank. I'll try and get an update from Monique on what's happening.'

Shani lowered herself from the fuselage and took Nicolas's hand. Together they walked up to the ruins.

There was little to see. Shani surveyed the blocks of concrete in amongst the grass, from which jutted the occasional vine-covered pillar, each leaning at a different angle from the other. The silent ghost of a shattered vessel, she thought, as Nicolas stood behind her and folded his arms around her shoulders; keen to hear her reaction, perhaps.

And what was her reaction to it all? Unequivocal sadness, obviously. 'I just don't get this power-thing, Nicolas,' she added. 'Why people go as far as torturing and killing for it. I suppose the really evil ones stand in the background and brainwash others to do it for them.'

Nicolas kissed her hair. 'Don't lose sight of what's going on here, in Séroulé. If all of West Africa is courageous enough to give notice to its godforsaken usury-driven creditors, other countries could follow.'

Shani nodded. 'You're right. I mustn't be gloomy.' Post-coup depression, she told herself. There was no denying Séroulé was taking a leap into the unknown, the rejection of the fiscal globalisation agenda without compromise. The penalties that were certain to arise would hopefully be vociferously objected to by decent folk across the planet – the majority by far.

'Behind that mound,' said Nicolas suddenly, turning Shani towards it, 'is the forest I told you about. It follows the route of the river Tégine to the right. That's where the hunter found Zinsa. By my reckoning, when Kuetey struck she must have been this side of the retreat. If she was anywhere other than in the immediate area of the mound, she couldn't have escaped into the forest because it's open savannah. She would have been caught before she reached it.'

'Let's go and see.' Shani picked her way over to the mound. 'This grass looks incredibly sharp,' she remarked.

Simba called out to them, beckoning them over.

'I'll go,' said Nicolas. 'Leave you with your thoughts for a moment.'

Shani carefully sat herself down on the mound, sensing a new way of life rapidly approaching her. Academia...? She felt she simply wanted to jettison the whole thing and get *really* practical. But then, she didn't want to disappoint her supervisor, Harry Rothwell. Perhaps in the coming weeks a compromise of sorts could be rustled up.

She lifted her head and saw Nicolas walking back towards her, before witnessing the oddest sight of all. Simba, for whatever reason, began to sing with gusto.

'Les étoiles sont belles, la lune est belle...'

Shani waited for Nicolas to join her. 'What *is* he doing?'

'Just as well we haven't any liquor with us,' said Nicolas. 'We'd be grounded for a week, or more.'

'What's happened? News from Monique?'

'General Nzeogwu's been arrested at the border along with a separate group of high-up officials from the government. The regime's basically no more. It's over. Finished. Just the mopping up, as they say.'

'You're kidding!' cried Shani. 'It's hard to believe. Various times over the past two days I've had my doubts.'

'I think it's fair to say we all have, including Khamadi.'

Together they climbed the mound, and Shani reached for Nicolas's hand. 'I want you to meet Dusana.'

'Look forward to it.' Nicolas glanced across at her. 'How are you feeling about Andrei these days?'

Shani gave a little sigh of resignation, her mind rewinding to when her adoptive father mentioned Séroulé on what became his deathbed. 'I'm okay with Andrei,' she said, because it was true. 'I can't imagine the depth of pain he and Rodica must have experienced on the day my parents were shot. And the loss of my twin must surely have compounded their agony. If they hadn't have got me out of Romania when they did then presumably I would have been targeted by Kuetey. Clearly, Andrei's primary concern was to protect me. So how can I ever begrudge him for that?'

She looked at Nicolas and waited a moment for him to meet her eyes. 'But what about us?' she asked. 'What are we going to do? Porto Sansudou, as a base? Can we afford to keep your adorable studio in Paris?'

'We can work something out. There's your story, remember.'

'I forgot. You won't mention Maison Rouge, will you?'

'It feels a long time ago.'

They reached the crest of the mound and turned to look back. The helicopter to the left of the ruins glinted in the late sun. 'I'm sure Zinsa must have come and played up here,' said Shani.

Nicolas put his arm around her. 'Listen to me,' he said, lifting the baseball cap she was still wearing to kiss her lips, and then her brow, 'despite the wonder of Séroulé, the people, the miracle of it all, if I'm looking for inspiration, for courage, I find all this in you.' He gave her his half smile. 'A shade sugary, maybe, but it's true.'

Shani leaned into him, perfectly aware that the heartbeat she was embracing had rescued her from an unhappy state of mind. 'We've found each other, Nicolas. Maybe it was inevitable, and all I had to do was to be patient. So perhaps I really should make my peace with fate.'

She lay her head on his shoulder and gazed subconsciously at a tree with a huge canopy in the near distance. In spite of the sun having seared the earth, a chill came into her spine. It was the silence, more than anything. Since they'd arrived she hadn't felt even the slightest breeze. Nor, come to think of it, had she seen or heard a bird of any description. It was as though nature itself had decided to abandon the ruins and the surrounding land.

'Nicolas,' she said quietly, taking her arms from around his neck.

'What is it?'

'I don't want to come here again. It's not a nice place for us to be. Perhaps when I'm very old, I might return. But only 'perhaps'.' She reached for his hand. 'Can we leave?'

Nicolas nodded. 'You don't have to explain.' He started to lead the way down the mound.

'Simba said we have two-hundred kilometres left in the tank,' said Shani, energized by an idea that happened to swoop in on her. A baptism of sorts, she supposed. 'Do you think we could fly half that distance, and camp out the night? I want to go to sleep to the sounds of Africa. Will it be safe?'

Nicolas grinned. 'Are you sure we're not going down that route of how many chickens we're going to start with?'

Shani laughed with him, feeling evermore the relief they had survived a hellish day. 'But seriously?' she asked.

'Catch ourselves some food from the Tégine on the way, and make a fire when we settle in for the night, we'll be fine,' said Nicolas.

'I've so much to learn,' said Shani. She smiled at the sight of Simba in the distance, still singing with supreme passion.

They left the mound, and Shani brought Nicolas's hand to her lips. It was obvious, of course. All these people ever wanted was their freedom to live the gift of life. And her wish, now? It could only be for wisdom and compassion to reign supreme in other lands; that, and watching sunflowers grow under Séroulé's gracious blue sky.

THE END

Printed in Great Britain
by Amazon